POWERS OF MIND AND SOUL

Laran is what sets them apart from their fellow Darkovans, their abilities to manipulate potent forces for good or ill, to mentally link with others of their kind, to communicate with all manner of birds and beasts, even to see into the future. These are their stories, tales of those who willingly use their *laran* to help Darkover and those who use it only for their own ends.

From a *laran*-less twin deprived of his brother's aid when invaders attack the land . . . to a demon unleashed by the workings of *laran* . . . to a child whose talents will lead her to a place beyond any Tower dweller's imagining . . . here are all-new adventures set on that most fascinating of worlds—Darkover.

A Reader's Guide to DARKOVER

THE FOUNDING:

A "lost ship" of Terran origin, in the pre-empire colonizing days, lands on a planet with a dim red star, later to be called Darkover.

DARKOVER LANDFALL

THE AGES OF CHAOS:

1,000 years after the original landfall settlement, society has returned to the feudal level. The Darkovans, their Terran technology renounced or forgotten, have turned instead to free-wheeling, out-of-control matrix technology, psi powers and terrible psi weapons. The populace lives under the domination of the Towers and a tyrannical breeding program to staff the Towers with unnaturally powerful, inbred gifts of *laran*.

STORMQUEEN!
HAWKMISTRESS!

THE HUNDRED KINGDOMS:

An age of war and strife retaining many of the decimating and disastrous effects of the Ages of Chaos. The lands which are later to become the Seven Domains are divided by continuous border conflicts into a multitude of small, belligerent kingdoms, named for convenience "The Hundred Kingdoms." The close of this era is heralded by the adoption of the Compact, instituted by Varzil the Good. A landmark and turning point in the history of Darkover, the Compact bans all distance weapons, making it a matter of honor that one who seeks to kill must himself face equal risk of death.

TWO TO CONQUER
THE HEIRS OF HAMMERFELL

THE RENUNCIATES:

During the Ages of Chaos and the time of the Hundred Kingdoms, there were two orders of women who set themselves apart from the patriarchal nature of Darkovan feudal society: the priestesses of Avarra, and the warriors of the Sisterhood of the Sword. Eventually these two independent groups merged to form the powerful and legally chartered Order of Renunciates or Free Amazons, a guild of women bound only by oath as a sisterhood of mutual responsibility. Their primary allegiance is to each other rather than to family, clan, caste or any man save a temporary employer. Alone among Darkovan women, they are exempt from the usual legal restrictions and protections. Their reason for existence is to provide the women of Darkover an alternative to their socially restrictive lives.

THE SHATTERED CHAIN
THENDARA HOUSE
CITY OF SORCERY

AGAINST THE TERRANS

—THE FIRST AGE (Recontact):

After the Hastur Wars, the Hundred Kingdoms are consolidated into the Seven Domains, and ruled by a hereditary aristocracy of seven families, called the Comyn, allegedly descended from the legendary Hastur, Lord of Light. It is during this era that the Terran Empire, really a form of confederacy, rediscovers Darkover, which they know as the fourth planet of the Cottman star system. It is not apparent that Darkover is a lost colony of the Empire, until linguistic and sociological studies reveal that Darkovans are of Terran extraction—a concept not easily or readily acknowledged by Darkovans and their Comyn overlords.

THE SPELL SWORD
THE FORBIDDEN TOWER

AGAINST THE TERRANS

—THE SECOND AGE (After the Comyn):

With the initial shock of recontact beginning to wear off, and the Terran spaceport a permanent establishment on the outskirts of the city of Thendara, the younger and less traditional elements of Darkovan society begin the first real exchange of knowledge with the Terrans—learning Terran science and technology and teaching Darkovan matrix technology in turn. Eventually Re[illegible] Hastur, the young Comyn lord most active in these exchanges, becomes Regent in a provisional government allied to the Terrans. Darkover is once again reunited with its founding Empire.

THE HERITAGE OF HASTUR
SHARRA'S EXILE

THE DARKOVER ANTHOLOGIES:

These volumes of stories written by Marion Zimmer Bradley herself, and various members of the society called The Friends of Darkover, strive to "fill in the blanks" of Darkovan history, and elaborate on the eras, tales and characters which have captured their imagination.

DOMAINS OF DARKOVER
FOUR MOONS OF DARKOVER
FREE AMAZONS OF DARKOVER
THE KEEPER'S PRICE
LERONI OF DARKOVER
THE OTHER SIDE OF THE MIRROR
RED SUN OF DARKOVER
RENUNCIATES OF DARKOVER
SWORD OF CHAOS

Other DAW titles
by Marion Zimmer Bradley:

Novels:
HUNTERS OF THE RED MOON
THE SURVIVORS (with Paul Edwin Zimmer)
WARRIOR WOMAN

Collections:
LYTHANDE (with Vonda N. McIntyre)
THE BEST OF MARION ZIMMER BRADLEY

Anthologies:
GREYHAVEN
SPELLS OF WONDER
SWORD AND SORCERESS I
SWORD AND SORCERESS II
SWORD AND SORCERESS III
SWORD AND SORCERESS IV
SWORD AND SORCERESS V
SWORD AND SORCERESS VI
SWORD AND SORCERESS VII
SWORD AND SORCERESS VIII

Marion Zimmer Bradley

Leroni Of Darkover

DAW BOOKS, INC.
DONALD A. WOLLHEIM, FOUNDER
375 Hudson Street, New York, NY 10014
ELIZABETH R. WOLLHEIM
SHEILA E. GILBERT
PUBLISHERS

Cover art and border design by Richard Hescox.

DAW Book Collectors No. 865.

First Printing, November 1991

1 2 3 4 5 6 7 8 9

DAW TRADEMARK REGISTERED

U.S. PAT. OFF AND FOREIGN COUNTRIES

—MARCA REGISTRADA,

HECO EN U.S.A.

PRINTED IN THE U.S.A.

Contents

Introduction

Every year, the subject keeps coming up; what to write for an introduction to this anthology. I could always take you on a short funny trip through my slush pile—it could hardly help being funny. A lot of strange things that go bump in *my* mailbox, for instance, all the letters I get from hopeful actresses who think I will have anything to say about casting MISTS OF AVALON . . . and who are positive they would be absolutely perfect for the part of Morgaine. Well, even if they would, it isn't up to me. They'd have to get in touch with Mr. Coburn. Then there are the feminists who can't believe that I have turned "this great feminist classic" (I swear I'm not making this up) over to—*gasp, shudder*—a *man*. Then there are the hordes of musicians who want to write the musical score; not to mention the feminist ditto who think themselves uniquely qualified for ditto. Not to mention the people who want to do one or the other because they either believe, say they believe, or want me to believe that they are a reincarnation of Morgaine le Fay. Well, jolly for them; but it's still not up to me. Now, if people were rational, I wouldn't get any more such letters. But that, as my first husband used to say, would be *sensible*. I can't expect *that*, can I?

It's a good thing I've made it clear Darkover is fiction. I still get questions at every conference asking—usually by some soulful overweight hyperthyroid—"Mrs. Bradley, how much of your work is *channeled?*" This question reduces me to hopeless rage. Why do they believe I'm not capable of making it all up? For some reason this reminds me of the people who still believe the late H. P. Lovecraft was a great occult adept, instead of the convinced humanist and rationalist he actually was. I wish I had a nickel for every fanzine article I have read purporting to prove that for some reason he was actually pretending this stance to protect his audience from the Devil or something, because he couldn't have made it all up now, could he?

People like this are not speaking in the literary manner—under which, as every writer knows, an imaginary country, planet, or world-view actually has its own reality, with which the writer tampers at his peril. There are some things I could not write about Darkover—not and keep any intellectual integrity, that is.

For instance, there was the time—after attending a masquerade which consisted largely of "Amazons" clad mostly like Frazetta covers—I wrote THE SHATTERED CHAIN, and said to the late, beloved Don Wollheim, quite in defiance of my usual habit (which is to leave all things having to do with covers, etc. up to the Art Department), "Don, if you put a naked Amazon on the cover, you can forget that you've ever known me. I'll never write you another book."

Of course, when I made that ultimatum, I had about thirty well-selling books under my belt. I wouldn't recommend it even now for the seller of a first novel, though writers are better off now than when I started writing.

Nowadays a writer can even advertise herself as a feminist and still get printed.

Which reminds me of the most astonishing thing in the history of MZB as a writer. A local author and I once shared a table at an autographing party and—just to make conversation—I inquired who was her publisher. She told me her work was self-published, and I guess I didn't look quite as impressed as I might have, for she informed me defiantly that "everybody *knows* a *woman* can't get published in science fiction." After I picked my jaw up off the floor I pointed out my thirty-plus s-f novels and asked how she thought I had gotten published, whereupon she stated (pityingly, I suppose), "Oh, Marion, everybody *knows* you sold out years ago to the male establishment."

I never was so shocked in my life. If I did, that's news to me. Granted, having kids to support, I committed the grievous (to a feminist) crime of believing that the editor, even if a man, knew what he wanted to print. But now that I'm an editor, I take the same privilege for myself.

Hence in these twenty-odd stories you won't find a single feminist tirade. Sorry, if that's what you're looking for. I have this nasty old-fashioned idea that if I wanted to make a political point, it might be more honest to hire a soapbox and hand out pamphlets at the local equivalent of Hyde Park Corner—where any looney can get up and make a speech advocating any craziness—including UFO Contacts, or even—horrors—Free Amazons in love with Dyan Ardais.

But you won't find them in here. Sorry.

Building

by Lynn Michals

One of the things I am always looking for can be summed up as something taking place "between the acts" of published Darkovan history. This story is about the forming of Comyn Council as Darkover began to emerge from the darkest of its darkest ages.

Lynn Michals is twenty-six years old and lives in Baltimore; she is working on a PhD in English Literature. She grew up in "the odd world of New Orleans' Catholic schools" and is now at Johns Hopkins—a student and a teacher at the same time.

She has helped excavate a Welsh castle, where she "dug up bits of medieval mutton bones someone had dumped behind the kitchens six centuries ago and found bits of cloudy glass in the drawbridge pit, which the castle's late-Tudor inhabitants had turned into a wine-cellar." She also spent a summer in the graveyards of New Orleans, working for a historical society that was trying to decipher names and dates on crumbling tombstones before they became completely illegible. She says that they did their best, but "I still doubt that the city has a very clear idea of who's buried where."

It's much easier to record the history of a purely imaginary society, as in this story.

Gregori Alton stood for a moment in the noisy street, staring at a rainbow and dreaming of peace. Then he shook his head clear of visions, followed his paxman into the smoky, crowded townhouse, and got on with the day's business.

"Zandru's frozen prick, where'd they all come from?" Donal asked him, looking in silent wonder at the mob of Alton kinsmen sprawled out on the cold floor.

"The Kilghard Hills, mainly," Gregori said wearily. "They're poor mountain lords with no place else to stay—a month in Thendara'd cost them a whole year of rents. But I wanted them to see what Lord Hastur's new Council is all about."

"Looks like they've got the idea—Hastur's giving them a little taste of life in the big city," Donal said, grinning at the heaps of drunken aristocrats. Most of them looked as though they'd spent the night being dragged backward through the gutters of Thendara before crawling home to collapse on the floor among their superbly bred hounds.

"Don't be so cynical," Gregori said. "This is only the second year we've tried to hold one of these Councils—they'll get the hang of it eventually. Come on, let's start waking them up."

Gregori and his paxman waded through the assembled lords of the Alton Domain, shouting, shaking, and dumping buckets of cold water on their heads. Gregori was red-haired, battle-scarred, and weary to his very bones; he had just spent a year and a half wreaking havoc in a blood feud against Ardais with one hand, and fighting off Aldaran raiders with the other. He had grown old before his time, bearing responsibility for an embattled Domain before he turned eighteen. Next to him Donal looked like a mere boy, slight and innocent, with wide gray eyes, a heart-shaped face, and no past to speak of—although before he met Gregori, Donal had been, among other things, a thief, a spy, a catamite, and a trained assassin.

The lords and their dogs growled and snarled, pissed in the fireplace, and demanded their breakfast. When they had been supplied with ale and cold meat and bread, Gregori pounded on the long table with the hilt of his knife and yelled for silence.

"Before we meet with the other Domains, the first thing we have to talk about is repairing the Great Road," he announced. "You all must've noticed that it's hardly more than a goat track from Syrtis to the Hellers—maintaining that stretch is our responsibility."

"What's wrong with a goat track?" old *Dom* Istven shouted. "It's been a goat track all my life, and it was a goat track all my blessed father's life before me. When're you going to marry, lad, anyway?"

"Aye, you gave Aillard a *nedestro* daughter, when d'we get a proper heir?" someone else bellowed, returning to the clan's favorite piece of Domain business. "A paxman's all very well to warm your bed on campaign, but he can't give us a son, now can he, for all his pretty face!"

"Shut up!" Gregori yelled, but by then the mountain lords were all shouting at once, at him and at each other.

"Shut up," Gregori repeated, using the Alton Gift of forced rapport. And there was dead silence.

"First, speak with courtesy of my sworn man, or I'll crack your fool heads open. Second, Lord Hastur is arranging a marriage for me with Ardais—it's all in the terms of our truce," Gregori said, for the hundredth time. "We went through all that yesterday."

A dogfight broke out in the corner, several lords began a crap game and drank themselves back under the table, and two others came to blows over the question of exactly who had failed to repair a tumbledown travel shelter midway between their lands—it was an ordinary Council morning in Thendara, in the sixth year of the reign of Marius Hastur, Lord of the Seven Domains. All over the city, the Comyn had dutifully gathered together to discuss their differences in an orderly fashion, as Marius had ordered. But none of them had any idea how to do it. There is nothing natural about sitting down in a large room and working out compromises—especially for a pack of petty dictators. *Merciful gods pity us tonight, when all seven Domains get together,* Donal thought, shielding Gregori from a flying tankard, watching an irritable burst of psi energy explode in a shower of sparks overhead. *There's better order in a thieves' den.*

At dusk Donal and Gregori slowly rode back to the Comyn Castle, behind four guards bellowing at beggars and peddlers and respectable townsfolk to make way for the Lord of Armida.

"You didn't have to jump down their throats like that this morning, about me and my pretty face," Donal said calmly. "I've been called a lot worse things than pretty, in my time."

"Don't be stupid, *bredu*. My drunken kinsmen'll

have to settle for cracking the usual bawdy jokes at my wedding; what's between the two of us is none of their business," Gregori answered—and slumped forward with the instinct of a good soldier, as a ragged, wiry man with a knife dropped from a balcony and landed behind his saddle. The blade grazed Gregori's shoulder instead of piercing his lungs, and Donal fell on the attacker, with his usual deadly grace.

It was over in a moment. An ugly gash ran through Donal's dark red hair and down his forehead, and the stranger's heart's blood soaked his shirt. Gregori crouched over the dying man, tearing open his mind, ruthless for the good of his Domain. Then he broke the contact, sobbing in pain—he had found all that he needed, and much more than he wanted to know. The Lord of Armida huddled in a gutter holding a dying shepherd from the Hellers in his arms, weeping for a burned cottage, a wife raped and murdered, and two sons dead in the feud between Ardais and Alton.

Donal felt what Gregori felt, and could do nothing to help him. So he cursed with cold, furious fluency at the greedy Thendara mob that had gathered to watch him bleed and Gregori cry—and the people scattered, horrified at hearing such language from a gentleman.

In the Hastur apartments in the Comyn Castle, the heads of six Domains had just begun to wonder where Gregori could be when he walked in on them, blood soaking the front of his jerkin, with an arm around his bloody paxman, and two guards carrying a corpse.

"I know nothing of this," Lord Ardais said coolly, as everyone's eyes turned to him. Julian Ardais was a middle-aged gentleman with dark hair and empty eyes: the eyes of a man who had spent too many winters in the Hellers, hearing the wind call his name. "Go ahead and search, if you like," he said, lowering his barriers. He held himself rigidly still while Marius Hastur rummaged through his mind. In the end, it was Marius who flinched and turned away—he was a decent man, and some of the memories lying around in *Dom* Julian's head didn't bear looking at.

"He did not know of this attack, Lord Alton. On my word," Marius said at last.

"Then this blood is washed away—the truce remains unstained and unbroken," Gregori replied formally, binding all his people to forget revenge and keep the peace. "Pardon me now, my paxman is injured. I'll return shortly to continue the marriage negotiations."

A *leronis* joined Gregori and Donal in the Alton apartments, and healed Donal's wound in a moment.

"So here we are, good as new," Gregori said bitterly, climbing into the fresh clothes his bodyservant brought. "And that poor old bastard is hanging on a gibbet in the marketplace, a warning to other desperate men whose lives've been wrecked by our wars."

"You're the only man I know, Greg, who feels guilty about surviving assassination attempts," Donal observed, lacing up the neck of his tunic. "The old man got what he deserved."

"The Comyn tortured and slaughtered his family, drove him mad, and finally killed him. Lord of Light! This Council idea *must* work—we're bleeding the life out of our people, feuding among ourselves," Gregori said. His eyes shone with a desperate hope. "We must find a new way."

Pigs'll fly, before the Comyn sit down together and sort out their little disagreements without murdering anybody, Donal thought. But he kept the thought to himself—if believing in a bright new age of peace made Gregori Alton happy, then Donal Hodge would do his cynical best to have faith in sweetness and light. In Gregori's incurably hopeful mind, Donal saw the brawling, bloodthirsty Comyn mob assembled in Thendara suddenly discover a concern for the common good, a rainbow of light bursting through the bloody darkness of their wars.

"I'd better get back to the others," Gregori said, turning aside from his dreams of peace. "Having that dead-eyed butcher for a father-in-law will be worth it, if it really ends the old feud. Get some rest, Donal, like the healer told you. Don't wait up—there's no telling how late I'll be."

"You're not going back out there without me, Greg," Donal said, buckling his sword belt. "Marry *Dom* Julian's daughter if you like, but I'll never trust you alone in a room with the man."

"I've got a dozen hulking guardsmen to look after me," Gregori protested. "Go lie down." But a paxman's first duty is to protect his lord, not to obey him. And Donal was an excellent paxman.

"Don't blame me if this consult lasts all night," Gregori snapped as they walked up to the Hastur apartments together. "They'll be drinking by now, and no one can shut up the Ridenow once they've got into the wine."

The meeting did last all night. A dozen high-ranking nobles from each Domain packed themselves into the audience chamber of the Hastur apartments, which had been crammed full of extra chairs for the occasion—some brought dogs and pipes, and all made good use of their host's wine cellar, as visiting noblemen were expected to. Gregori's kinsmen furiously tried to call challenge on Lord Ardais then and there, as soon as they heard of the latest attempt on Gregori's life; a minor border dispute erupted between Serrais and Valeron, and was settled by betting on a dogfight; and everybody drank themselves silly and shouted themselves hoarse, before agreeing to the proposed marriage between Ardais and Alton out of sheer exhaustion.

At dawn, Gregori stood with *Dom* Marius and Lady Arliss, the Aillard Domain Mother, numbly surveying the smoky wreckage of the audience chamber. A minor Di Asturien noble snored by the fireplace, his head pillowed on his shaggy hound.

"Blessed Cassilda help us, what a disaster," Marius said softly. "And I thought this Council was such a good idea."

"Oh, it wasn't really so bad, *Dom* Marius," Arliss said, with forced cheerfulness. "We did sort out a few questions. And nobody actually got killed."

"I'd thought of building a new room for us to meet in next winter, a bigger one where everyone would have a place to sit. But it hardly seems worth it if this chaos is the best we can do," Marius said.

"May I speak, my lord?" Donal asked, standing as always at Gregori's side, watchful and silent.

"Of course," Gregori said. "Shout your head off, Donal. Everyone else has."

"Lord Hastur, don't build a bigger room like this one, with a fireplace and cushioned chairs and tables for servants to leave the wine on," Donal said firmly. "You'll only have a bigger mess on your hands if you do. Build a room like nothing anyone's ever seen before—make it look like a holy place, light and bright like Hali. That'll spook your backcountry lords into behaving themselves, at least for a while. Then fill it with uncomfortable benches that can't be moved out of straight rows. And whatever you do, don't let anyone bring wine into it, or ale, or dogs, or dice. Then maybe you'll get some order, sir. At least it'll be a start."

"Thank you, Donal—I'll refer your suggestions to my *leronis*. It's a novel plan," *Dom* Marius said, looking at Gregori Alton's sweet-faced, cutthroat paxman in surprise, wondering how he had ever come up with such an idea.

Donal bowed silently. He had spoken on impulse, combining poor Gregori's impossible vision of sweetness and light with the ground rules of the annual conclave of Thendara's Guild of Thieves. But none of the Comyn suspected that their sacred meeting place had such dubious origins, when, a year later, they first stumbled into the brilliant hush of the Crystal Chamber to talk about peace in the heart of a rainbow.

The Ferment

by Janet Rhodes

One of the many other things I am always looking for in these anthologies is an unusual use of laran. *In* Marion Zimmer Bradley's Fantasy Magazine *I printed a story by Jacqueline Lichtenberg about a sorceress whose talents included enchanting bread to rise. "The Ferment" takes this* laran *seriously.*

Janet Rhodes began writing about three and a half years ago, and once she started she just somehow kept going. That's the story of all of us. She appeared in the last of these anthologies, RENUNCIATES OF DARKOVER, and she is still working for the Washington State Department of Ecology, as she has for the last 17 years. She says that "after writing the first story, I wondered how Kirsten discovered her ability to affect the ferments."

She is also working on a novel and says that "the transition to the novel-length story has been difficult and it is taking me a while . . . The story keeps pushing to get out, so I keep working on it . . . becoming more familiar with the characters . . . Not too surprisingly, I have become fond of the major characters . . . It is fun to learn more and more about them." This pretty well describes the creation of all the Darkover books . . . at least from my point of view.

Kirsten's fair skin burned red. The reaction to whispered words flamed across her face and disappeared under the collar of her shift. As she picked up her pace, hurrying down the long corridors of the manor house toward the kitchens, Kirsten heard giggles echoing off the stone and wood of the hall.

Sisters! she thought. *I wish they'd shut up before they wake the entire household.* Unbidden, their words rose up to hound her: "Where are you sneaking off to so early?" Millea had whispered as Kirsten passed her door, treading quietly in soft house slippers to avoid waking those still asleep at this early hour—long before the bloody eye of the Darkovan sun would blink open. Giggling, Anilda had added, "Are you going to make bread into lumps again? I'm sure that will impress your . . ." And she had used a word better suited to the stablehands, one that meant promised husband and implied more, far more than Kirsten wanted to think about, especially today.

For Kirsten knew she would never be a true Comyn wife to her promised husband, her lack of *laran* meaning the two would never come together in that oneness of mind and body experienced by the *laran*-gifted. Hurrying along, Kirsten wondered how he felt, being married off to one of the head-blind, to someone who possessed none of the psychic abilities that were the birthright of the noble families who ruled the Domains.

A few moments later, just as the fires of embarrassment were dying to spots upon her cheeks, Kirsten came to the entrance to the main hall—and stopped, her slippers sliding a little at the suddenness of it.

He stood just inside the great hall.

She had seen *Dom* Lennart before this, but she had never spoken to the Comyn lord her father had arranged for her to marry. The families, living many days' ride from each other, seldom attended the same gatherings. Anyway, in the four years since Kirsten had entered womanhood, it would not have been seemly for her to speak to a man who was not her brother or uncle or cousin.

Seeing him, the flush of her shame rose fresh, and she wondered what he could think of, marrying her, when the *leronis* of the Tower had found she lacked *laran*. Even though he was a younger son, he should be able to do better. . . .

Through the pulse sounding in her ears, Kirsten heard *Dom* Lennart call a greeting. Startled, she stuttered, fumbling for words, then stopped to stand silent, a hard knot gathering in her throat.

"*Damisela,*" said *Dom* Lennart in his quiet voice. "I am sorry to have startled you." Lennart removed his hat and held it before him with both hands. "I have been out with the horses," he said gesturing in the direction of the stables with one hand. "It's too dark to ride." He smiled. "But I was feeling a little—I woke up and—" Lennart shrugged. "I suppose you could not sleep either?"

Kirsten found her voice and spoke shyly as she stared at the floor in front of his boots, "No, *Dom,* I am up to start the breads for our meal."

The two stood awkwardly. Their meeting, even in such an open place as this, was ill-timed; they should not be alone together. But some force held them there, rooted to the floor. A wondering began to grow within Kirsten. Her cousins, Judyth and Cassandra, said there were rumors that *Dom* Lennart had little *laran* of his own. If that were true, perhaps he would be happy with her as wife, head-blind though she was. And Kirsten's father had told her that *Dom* Lennart had been promised a small holding in the hills. Rockraven, she had heard, was not a rich and fertile holding. But it would be their home, where they could make a life together.

Shyly, Kirsten lifted her head to this man who would be her husband and found her gaze drawn to his eyes. Suddenly, the room seemed to spin about her, forcing Kirsten to reach out and steady herself. A firm hand gripped her own. "Are you all right?" Lennart asked.

"Yes," she said hesitantly, because the floor still seemed to spin and rock beneath her feet. *What is happening to me?* she wondered. *And why today, of all days?* Abruptly, Kirsten pulled her hands out of Lennart's and willed the world to hold still. "I have to go now . . . to the kitchens," she muttered, then turned and walked slowly down the hall, her arms raised to provide balance.

Lennart watched after her, a frown furrowing his brow, until she disappeared down a side corridor.

Kirsten approached the kitchens with dread amplified by her accidental meeting with *Dom* Lennart. *Oh, why today?* she wailed inwardly, *why do I have to be the one to make bread? I should be in my rooms readying myself for the marriage ceremonies. Instead I am here trying to make bread into proper loaves instead of lumps as hard as rocks.* But Kirsten knew why. Her mother *Domna* Helene was of the opinion the future mistress of a house must be able to do the chores as well as any of her servants. When, under Kirsten's hands, bread dough seemed to have a life of its own—sometimes refusing to bubble, with the loaves sitting heavy on their wooden trays, other times growing overlarge and full of holes—the lady simply persisted in her baking lessons. Still, with all the practice, the ferments had continued arbitrary, and breads touched by Kirsten's hands were rarely eatable. All Kirsten had learned was that she could tell, as soon as her hands touched the mixture, whether the ferment would cooperate or not.

Entering the kitchen with heavy heart, Kirsten pulled on an overdress to protect her clothing as she worked. She scooped a double handful of the bubbly ferment into the pottery crock with a suddenly light heart. Realizing the ferment would not give stones for loaves today, Kirsten felt a thrill of anticipation course through her. With a rising sense of hope she covered the crock and placed it back on its shelf. *I may not have* laran, *but I can bake bread and take care of a household*, she thought.

To the leaven in the great bowl, Kirsten added flours, nut meats, sweet-tree sap, and spices, and began to knead the mess together. Cool and mushy at first beneath her hands, the dough soon became springy. Next, Kirsten turned it onto the stone platter where she could work more easily—pushing and pulling the dough in the relaxing, familiar kneading motions—until she had a smooth mushroom cap with tiny blisters on its surface. Letting the dough rest on the table, Kirsten cleaned and dried the bowl, then replaced the mushroom cap, rounded side up. Before leaving the kitchens to the servants arriving to prepare the morning meal, Kirsten carefully set the bowl in a warm corner near the fireplace.

After eating breakfast with her parents, brothers, and sisters, Kirsten returned to the kitchens. Cooks and serving-girls were already busy with the evening meal preparations, and Kirsten tried to look inconspicuous as she entered the room and crossed to the fireplace. She especially wanted to avoid the sharp eyes of Marisela, who ruled over the household servants. Kirsten had often wondered if Marisela sent withering looks at the bread dough the days it turned to stone under her hands.

Kirsten had no way of knowing what had ruined her loaves time after time. Not that Marisela or *Domna* Helene believed her. "If you would just be more careful, *damisela,*" Marisela had said more than once. "How will you watch over *Dom* Lennart's household when you cannot keep your mind on such a simple task as breadmaking?"

With hope clutching at her stomach, Kirsten came to herself and pulled the bread bowl down, set it on a side table, and lifted the cloth covering. The wonderful, warm aroma of active leaven assailed her nose, and Kirsten's stomach began to unknot.

Carefully, Kirsten checked the dough. Yes, it had risen enough, perhaps even more than to be expected in a few hours. Her confidence building, Kirsten found flour and set it to the side. Then she thrust a fist into the soft roundness filling the bowl and heard a satisfying woosh. Kirsten began to knead, adding small amounts of flour every little while. The dough smelled good; it had risen nicely in the bowl, and Kirsten felt reassured. For a moment, she dared to think ahead to a dinner with high, rounded loaves of warm bread on the trays. Of *Domna* Helene proudly—

Suddenly, Kirsten was jerked out of her reverie. To her horror, she felt a living thing in her hands. It heaved and stretched, overflowing the pottery bowl and sweeping over the uneven boards of the table. Feeling unaccountably dizzy and disoriented, Kirsten fell against the closed shelves behind her, sticky hands clutched to her breast, as the bulging mass fell to the floor and spread out. *Avarra's mercy, no!* she thought. *This cannot be happening! Mother and Marisela will . . .*

But Kirsten had no time to feel embarrassed. The room started swimming slowly before her eyes, then faster and faster until she sank into darkness.

Domna Helene, fetched by one of the serving women, ran into the kitchens to find Kirsten slumped on the floor and covered with flour and sticky dough. "What happened," she asked no one in particular. Then she gripped Kirsten's shoulders and shook her gently. "Kirsten, what happened? What in the name of Avarra were you thinking of?" When she got no response, fear clamped *Domna* Helene's throat, strangling her voice. "Kirsten, child, please hear me. And get up. Please? Right now! Kirsten, do you hear me? What's wrong?" She brushed a sticky strand of hair from across Kirsten's eyes and tucked it back into place, then stood up and rubbed at her eyes in frustration. A tension filled the room. Helene tried to shake it off, then focused on what to do, how to find the *leronis* Shoshanna, who had gone down into the village to help a sick child.

Kirsten did not hear her mother, for she was wandering alone in a gray world on a flat, featureless plain. She felt confused and disoriented. There were no landmarks. *Which way,* she wondered, *do I go to get home? Where am I . . . Oh!* And Kirsten cried out as her body stiffened, then crumpled.

In the kitchen, *Domna* Helene saw Kirsten's body arch once in a violent convulsion, then go slack. "Avarra help us!" she exclaimed and reached to check for the fever she feared must be consuming her daughter. No sooner had Helene placed her hand on Kirsten's forehead, then a commotion at the door startled her up and around; Marisela was determined to keep someone from entering.

"*Mestra,* what is happening. I heard the cry! How can I help?"

"Vai Dom." Helene hurried to the door and stood behind Marisela. "Now is not a good time. We, ah—"

The air about them crackled and spit. Lennart slammed down his barriers just in time to avoid most of the blast and fury of awakening *laran* out of control. He saw *Domna* Helene wince and look to the far side of the room with wide eyes. It was difficult to tell, but Lennart thought the source of the psychic energy lay behind a table on that far side of the room. He pushed past the two women, the terror of the cry that had called to him still reverberating in his mind. Behind him Lennart heard *Domna* Helene charge a servant to find a *leronis.* "And some *kirian,*" he shouted back over his shoulder.

"I'm on my way now," Helene called back.

Lennart grunted in reply as he stood by a pale mound covered with a snow of flours and dough. After a few moments, Lennart stepped backward in shock when he realized Kirsten lay under all the dough. Kneeling at her side, Lennart held his hands about two finger's width above her body and assessed her from head to toe, shook his head, then looked up. "*Domna,* where is the *kirian*?" he shouted and thought, *She is in crisis. Oh, Gods. This cannot be happening*!

In the overworld, Kirsten floated in a dream. It was monstrously cold. She felt dizzy and the colors of summer swirled and streamed and folded around her. Then, the summer turned to sticks and stones growing in a field of white flowers. Or was it paste? No, it was a sticky dough and Kirsten was growing there, too. Too? Yes, the sticks and stones were growing in the dough and if she touched one, it grew faster or slower, or even died. She turned it into a game, touching a group of stones and thinking "die" and they shriveled up. Then touching a stick and thinking "grow" and seeing it make another stick and the two made four and the four, eight. On and on the sticks and stones grew and there were so many of them, she thought she might be crushed. . . .

Meanwhile, in the manor kitchen, Lennart forced his worry to the far corners of his mind; it could only harm her. He noted the fever, the trembling limbs. He quieted his mind and reached out with *laran* to try to bring some peace to her body. Her mind was out of reach, tormented by her awakening *laran,* and her body shuddered with the pain.

The *kirian,* when *Domna* Helene brought it, proved to be of poor quality. "It's old," Helene said apologetically. "Only Darin needed it at all. None of the others seemed to have . . . the threshold sickness." Lennart gave her a worried look and pressed his lips into a line. Carefully, he poured a small amount of the drug into Kirsten's mouth, watched her swallow.

Kirsten felt a burning in her throat, then a searing fire. An army of scorpion ants stormed her. She fought to keep her jaws closed, to keep them out. But they kept coming and coming; there was no end to them. They stung her a hundred times and more, but she didn't die and she wished she would, it hurt so much.

Lennart was worried. The *kirian* had seemed to stop the muscle spasms and the crackling and spitting in the room. But now Kirsten's body lay limp, her mind far away. For all he knew she was lost in the overworld. He had heard of it happening: a person wandering there forever, while her body lived on, an empty shell slowly dying for want of food and water.

"All I want to know is, 'Can you monitor me?' " Lennart said. Marisela had returned to report that the *leronis* Shoshanna was nowhere to be found. Someone told her the *leronis* had gone to the far reaches of the estate to heal a sick child. "So," reported Marisela, her voice trembling, "I checked with the guests who have come for the marriage, and, of all things, there was a big cave-in over toward the Hellers, and the *leroni* from all around have been called in to search for survivors and to heal the injured." The woman had frowned, and added, "I tried. I don't know where else to look."

Lennart repeated, "Can you monitor me?"

Helene gulped. "Perhaps. If only Hebertt and I linked." She blushed. "Neither of us has very strong *laran*. So we weren't really surprised when Kirsten—"

Lennart knew immediately that the net of *laran* energies linking the three of them was very weak. The most that he could hope for, then, was that Hebertt or Helene would sense if he was in trouble and pull him out. *Remember,* he sent to them, *if nothing else works, touch my starstone. It should pull me back.* Either that, he thought in a locked corner of his mind, or it will kill me.

The overworld seemed empty, without landmarks to guide him. Far, far off in the distance, Lennart could see the spiderweb tracings that marked several circles of *leroni* working their psychic powers. But there was no time for him to think about them; he had to find Kirsten. With a rising urgency, Lennart reached out his mind and sensed . . . nothing. As far as he could tell, he was the only one in this area of the overworld. Kirsten must have traveled a very long way in the throes of the threshold sickness.

Carefully, Lennart searched through the grayness, calling Kirsten's name, listening for a response. He had no way of knowing how long he had been out of his body, traveling the astral planes, but it seemed like hours. Lennart felt a rising tide of desperation; soon he would no longer have the strength to continue the search. And Kirsten was still lost! In frustration and fear, Lennart cried out, forcing her name through a threat that felt raw from misuse. "Kirsten! Kirsten-nn-n!"

The suffocating weight of the gray world pressed in at her from all sides. Yet still she walked, as she had for what seemed days since the fire had died in her throat. There were no landmarks, nothing that told her where she had been before, where she was going.

Kirsten feared she was walking in circles, like the visitor from Thendara who got lost when he took refuge in the forest during a lightning storm. He had spent days walking in circles there in the forest, not a half a day's ride from the manor, before Kirsten's father found him. He had never known it, the trees and brush all looked the same to his city-bred eyes. Kirsten and her brothers had laughed at how silly he seemed. Everyone knew how to tell direction in the trees, there were so many ways: the flow of water in the streams, the southward reach of branches, blown by the winds from the Hellers, the location of the sun and the moons and the stars. It was so easy at home.

But here, in this strange place, Kirsten had no sense of direction, almost no sense of up and down. It was disorienting and disheartening. And she really wanted to be home— "Mother!" she called. "Father! Come find me. Please!" Kirsten walked and called, and her throat burned again nearly as much as it had when she was swallowing the scorpion ants. After a long time, she sat down. Her legs were cramped with weariness; her voice was gone from shouting for her mother and father. For the first time, Kirsten allowed herself to believe she might have died there in the kitchen, where she remembered baking bread. Something had gone wrong and all of a sudden she had been covered with sticky stuff and suffocating.

Abruptly, Kirsten sat up, then forced her complaining legs to stand. Someone had called her name! Kirsten was sure of it. She could hear him faintly through the enveloping mists, but could not tell what direction the sound was coming from. Kirsten turned on one foot, tilted her head, and turned again. At last she thought she had the right direction, but, when she started moving that way, the sound stopped. Confused, she fell to the gray ground, her legs refusing to hold her weight any longer. *It is no use,* she thought, *now I am imagining things. I cannot go on.*

Lennart knew that his strength ebbed rapidly, that he had to return to his body in *Domna* Helene's kitchen. In his heart, Lennart wanted to continue; in his mind, he knew he had to return. With what little strength he had left, Lennart used the power of his mind to mold the stuff of the overworld into a beacon—a brilliant light to reach out and guide his promised bride home, then he collapsed back into his body.

The first conscious thing he felt was chilling cold. Lennart had to force himself to chew the dried fruits someone placed in his mouth. Only the knowledge that the fruits would replenish the energy he had expended enabled Lennart to chew and swallow and keep the food down.

In the overworld, Kirsten raised herself from a stupor brought on by a paralyzing cold that seeped into her bones. For a moment, it seemed that a torch had been waved in her face, turning her closed eyelids red. But then it was withdrawn and Kirsten had to force her mind to wake up, her numbed legs to move. She was determined to follow the light, to find a way out of this place of chilling nothingness. Once standing, with her eyes forced open, Kirsten scanned the horizon where gray ground met gray sky.

At first she saw no break in the monotonous landscape and her heart sank. Then a blinking light, very faint, caught her eye. It took every bit of strength she could gather to move a step closer to the light. Then another step, and another. Slowly, the beacon grew brighter and its light cheered her. Someone else was out here in this place of nothingness. Someone was here who would know how she could get home. Kirsten was sure of it.

It took hours to reach the light. First, step by slow step; then, on her hands and knees—one hand, one knee, another hand, another knee, and on and on. Once she got there, Kirsten saw that the light stood alone. No one waited in its glow to show her the way home. No one.

Leaning up against the beacon, Kirsten cried. It was not fair. To have things go so wrong on the day of her marriage to *Dom* Lennart. She had tried so hard to find the way home. Kirsten found herself hoping that her parents would not be too upset with her, then wondering whatever she might have done that would make them upset. Abruptly Kirsten remembered the bread she had been making and how it was all ruined! Then something about the breadmaking forced its way into her groggy mind: she, Kirsten, had not done anything wrong, the ferment was wrong! The little sticks and clusters of balls were alive!

As exhausted as he was, Lennart refused to leave Kirsten's side. Marisela brought him sweets and dried fruit which Lennart devoured ravenously to replace the energy he had expended in the aborted trip to the overworld. Rarely did he take his eyes from Kirsten's unconscious form.

Domna Helene, coming back into the kitchen after checking again for Shoshanna's return, brought a chair and sat nervously washing her hands in the air. "Is there nothing else we can do?" Her voice trailed off uncertainly.

It was then, while he tried to think of a response, that Lennart felt a trembling in the psychic line attached to the beacon in the overworld. "She's there!" he shouted to the stunned faces around him. "She's found the beacon."

Before anyone could respond, Lennart gathered his fragmented energies and threw himself into the overworld, toward the place where his beacon lit the grayness. There, at the base of the beacon, Lennart found Kirsten, pale and barely conscious.

However, entering the overworld again had taxed his already depleted energies. Only with extreme concentration could he stumble closer to Kirsten, force his voice to call her name.

Kirsten lay dreaming, dimly aware of the beacon's blinking light. Then the ground shuddered and she sensed a presence. Her first thought was to ignore whoever was there. She felt too exhausted to move, to speak, to do anything. Then he called her name, and Kirsten found strength she did not know remained to her.

The form struggling out of the mists seemed familiar. As Kirsten searched her groggy memory, she pulled herself to her feet, using the beacon for support. The man's haggard face softened when he saw her stand. She saw his features clear and knew that Lennart had come for her.

For a moment, Lennart stopped as if to catch his breath. Then he wobbled, loosing his footing in the gray matter. "Kirsten," he cried, reaching out toward her.

"Lennart!" Kirsten pushed away from the security

of the beacon, stepped out unsteadily, and tottered toward Lennart.

She had covered about half the distance between them, when he started to tremble violently. He fell to the ground which seemed to fold up around him. "I cannot stay any longer," he called, ". . . must leave . . . follow me. . . ."

"No!" Kirsten tried to shout, but fear and disbelief closed her throat, making her voice a whisper. "No," she said again, louder, and dove wildly toward the place where Lennart's right arm and hand were disappearing into the misty ground of the overworld.

"But *laran,*" Kirsten exclaimed, disbelief making her voice shrill.

"From what I can piece together," said Lennart, "the problems you had baking bread were directly related to your awakening *laran.*"

"And I had no idea!" Kirsten laughed for the first time in days, startling Lennart. He smiled hesitantly and reached out a hand to clasp one of hers. A tendril of psychic energy wound around their hands and up their arms.

Don't you see? she sent to him via their telepathic link, *now we can be a real Comyn husband and wife!* The thought touched Lennart's mind lightly, shyly, and was gone like the morning mists in the midday sun.

Wings

by Diana Gill

This again tells something of a favorite character in HAWKMISTRESS. At least Orain is a favorite of mine, though I never got around to documenting his early life. I am glad to have it written by one of the young adults for whom HAWKMISTRESS was written. I found myself, at that time, in a sea of young redheaded girls, from my daughter, Moira, who was redheaded that year (by choice), to my niece Fiona and my foster daughter Jaida, who are redheads (by birth); all of them loved stories about horses. *The dedication of the book somehow got dropped, but at this late date it's a good thing to repeat it, especially as HAWKMISTRESS won some sort of prize for a young adult book that year.*

Diana Gill is sixteen as I write this and a senior in a suburban Philadelphia high school. She hopes to become a marine biologist, an ambition shared by one of my foster daughters who won a very prestigious scholarship from over 2000 applicants, which she gave up after a year, saying "I wanted to talk to dolphins, not dissect them"—an ambition we all share, I think.

"Or," Diana says, "an author; maybe both." Well, at least one of her ambitions has been achieved. The rest is up to her.

The day was clear, almost warm, a rarity for this time of year, even on the Plains of Armida. But Orain of Castamir did not notice the weather, could not care.

He stared blindly out over the valley stretched before him, seeing but not recognizing the lush green hills or the misty waves of the lake lapping around the base of a shining white Tower. Hali. The holy place of the gods, the *rhu fead*, the place which was the symbol of everything that was denied to him.

In his agony, the scene of the morning played over and over in his mind, like a street singer who only knew one song, or the chorus of a very long ballad. As if playing it over and over would make it go away or he would wake from a nightmare.

Like a *kyorebni*, the vision descended again, catching him in its foul claws.

Earlier that day he had been in the hall, grabbing some bread before going out to the stables. Looking around the room, he had noticed that the children of the Palace, royal or baseborn but Comyn all, were gathered in the hall. He spotted Ranald Ridenow and grinned. Waving, he kept looking, trying to find out what was happening. Farther on, his sister Jandria was sitting with Maura, Ranald's sister, whispering excitedly. He spotted his father to one side, talking quietly with the stranger who had arrived yesterday.

Tall, clad in the crimson/scarlet robes of a *tenerezu* or Keeper, the man moved with a fluid, almost boneless grace. Rings sparkled on his fingers and blue fire blazed from the jewel at his throat. Orain noticed and wondered at the silver-gilt hair, the pale yet dark eyes, the narrow, graceful hands. Perhaps the man had *chieri* blood? But why was he here?

Suddenly Orain remembered Carolin whispering to him at dinner the night before. "Do you see that man, over there? He's a *laranzu*, come from the Tower at Hali to test us for *laran*!" Carolin had said eagerly, eyes bright with excitement.

Orain looked around for Carolin's bright, blazing hair, only to recall that he and some of the other princes weren't quite finished with their lessons. They would be tested later, after the others.

Not that Carolin really needed to be tested, for no member of the Comyn with hair as bright as his, like Darkover's sun at sunset, could possibly be headblind.

Orain looked back over to where his father and the *laranzu* were, regretting Carolin's absence. They were friends and foster brothers, even though Carolin was kin to King Felix and Orain from one of the poorer families of the Comyn. Nodding to the stranger, his father beckoned to Lyondri who went with a smirk on his lips. Nervous, Orain put one hand on the comforting shape of his dagger and waited by a window.

About half a candlemark later, Lyondri came out, not needing even the small blue jewel clutched tightly in his palm to proclaim his admittance into the ranks of the telepaths. His smile was proof enough. Rakhal went next, returning with a small, self-satisfied grin.

Maura, nervous and pale, was called after that. Checking the sun, Orain noticed that she was gone for almost a candlemark before coming out. She went directly to Jandria, eyes brimming with happiness. His turn.

Orain took one step toward the small room which was set aside for the testing only to realize he was paralyzed with dread. Briefly it occurred to him that this test in many ways defined his future. To be head-blind would be to be kinless among kin, an exile in his own mind. Resolutely he thought of Carolin and walked slowly toward the room.

Inside, the man looked up. Perhaps sensing Orain's fears he smiled, pouring a few drops of a golden liquid into a cup. Orain took the cup, sniffing at the pale liquid.

"It's called *kirian*—it helps lower the mind's barriers." A pause, watching Orain swallow, staring intently at the boy as he fiddled with the blue jewel at his throat—what had Carolin called it? "How do you feel? Any nausea?"

Orain felt a little queasy but nothing more. Worried, he told the *tenerezu* so. Expressionless, the man handed a jewel like the one he was wearing only smaller, to Orain. Holding it, Orain remembered it was called a matrix.

"Look into the matrix. Do you see anything, feel anything? Concentrate on making the matrix glow."

Orain felt slightly disoriented, but try as he might, no pictures appeared, the jewel stayed dark. Gently, the man took the jewel from him. Looking with compassion at the boy—no more than twelve—Rafael hated himself for what he must say.

"You have *laran*, but only minimally. There is potential, but it is locked away, unusable. You will be able to pass it along to your sons, at least."

The boy, Orain, looked at him once, bitterly, and Rafael realized that the boy, like himself, was *ombredin.* Briefly, and with real pity, he said "I'm sorry."

Orain felt as if he had fallen into Zandru's ninth hell. He wanted to collapse, to scream out his rage and sorrow to the gods. Instead long hours of training took over; he bowed formally, murmuring *"Z'par servu, vai dom."* Then he was out the door and running, heading for the safety of the outdoors.

Orain clenched his hands. What could he do? The headblind were like cralmacs, barely human! And Carolin. . . . His throat tightened. Carolin was the core and soul of his being; he lived for the day when he would be Carolin's paxman. But now. . . .

Before today, before the disastrous news of the morning, their differences in station: Carolin, prince, Orain, minor noble, had been nothing—a tiny crack easily crossed. But the news of an hour ago had not only created a huge canyon between them, but had spawned thousands of smaller cracks and fissures. Not even the Heir to Hastur himself would cross them!

What should he do? How could he go back? By Aldones! Oh that he were a bird to fly away on the currents! A snuffling sound caught his attention and he turned around to see his horse, Stormchaser, grazing placidly on the sparse grass.

He couldn't fly, but he could run! He had supplies in his saddlebags, packed earlier when he had planned to go hunting with Carolin. And with all the excitement, no one would miss him, no one would care. Driven by misery, Orain mounted the sturdy gelding, and rode, heading into the hills, away from Hali.

Only a few hours later, the fair weather was gone. Ominous clouds scudded across the sky; the air was cold and damp. Thick, soft snowflakes floated lazily down, just grazing his cheek. Orain decided to halt as soon as he could find a resting place.

Luckily, only a few feet away was the opening of a cave. He examined the outside of the cave carefully, poking a torch at the opening—despite his anguish he had no wish to be eaten by a hungry predator!

Satisfied it was safe, he entered. The cave was large enough to hold horse and boy with space to spare. He brought Stormchaser inside and curried him, losing his anguish in the exhausting labor. After a small dinner of bread and cold rabbit-horn, Orain stared miserably into the fire, feeling again the pain and despair.

What was he to do? Where would he go? His thoughts slipped back to Hali. By now dinner would be ready and everyone at table, perhaps even King Felix if he was feeling well. He pictured the table, kin seated and talking merrily. For a moment, he wanted to turn back, go home. But then Lyondri's spiteful face appeared before him, laughing. Lyondri, who had *laran*, who was proudly, undeniably Comyn. Banishing the gloating face, Orain turned onto his side, huddled near the fire, trying to sleep, and hopefully, to forget.

He dreamed instead, nightmares, some of Zandru's finest come to haunt his night. He dreamed of his family renouncing him, of wandering through the Domains, accepted by none, despised by all. Of Carolin laughing. Carolin turned into a horrid amalgam of snake and monster, towering before him. Screaming, he woke.

So real was his dream that it seemed as if Carolin *really* was there before him, gray eyes gone steely with desperation. But it *was* Carolin! How? What?

Carolin pointed, moving only as much as he had to.

Orain looked and shuddered in horror. A stream of black, chitinous bodies spilled from a cleft in the wall that he had noticed but unfortunately dismissed. Scorpion-ants. One of the deadliest animals on Darkover.

He looked for his daggers, only to see they were only a few feet from the mass of roiling black. No hope there. He looked at Carolin, who looked at the fire where two brands still smoldered, stubbornly clinging to life.

Acting as one they moved, grabbing the makeshift torches and thrusting them at the nest. The scorpion-ants recoiled, but not before half their number had burnt. Carolin and Orain kept attacking, for they could not let even one escape to return later.

Only when every deadly insect was gone did Orain think to question Carolin's appearance. And when he did, he felt despair; Carolin had *laran,* how could he understand? Angry at Carolin for rubbing in his defect, hating him for the bit of blue which blazed out from among his clothes, Orain lashed out, unleashing his feelings.

"How did you get here? And why? Come to flaunt your position, your *laran*? Laugh at the poor head-blind fool who thought to pass himself off as Comyn?"

"No," Carolin said simply. "To be with the witless fool who ran away from his friends, leaving the people who care about him behind. To be with you."

Looking steadily at Orain, Carolin's voice broke and he stomped his foot as his temper flared. "Orain, you idiot! I don't care if you have *laran*, or if you were, were purple with green spots! You're my friend, I need you! Stop being a fool!"

Wanting to believe but finding it so hard, Orain

snarled. "That's easy for you to say—*you're* not the one who's head-blind!"

Carolin sighed. Pulling out his dagger, he held it, hilt first, out to Orain. "That's *not* true! You are my friend, and Comyn. Listen to me, please, *bredu*?" The last word was said shyly, hesitantly.

Orain looked into Carolin's eyes, and nodded all doubts gone. He took Carolin's dagger and held his own out to Carolin, hand trembling. *"Bredu?"*

Carolin took it, and they met in a fierce embrace. To his surprise, Orain found his arms sliding around Carolin, holding him. Standing there, he finally realized what Carolin had known all along, what Lyondri had known and hated him for. He loved Carolin, always had. He broke away, scared by the knowledge.

Carolin looked up at him and smiled, timidly. "It's all right, I know. Here, let me give you a gift, too." Taking one hand from Orain he cradled his matrix.

Orain's horizons expanded with a clap of thunder. Suddenly, he was flying, high above the ground, flying above a technicolor mist. Carolin was there, too, in a communion so deep and close he wanted to cry for joy. Nervously he voiced his thoughts, only to find that speaking was unnecessary, even unwanted in this meeting of minds and lives.

"Is this what it's like? To have *laran*?"

"Yes," Carolin thought plainly. In the glory of the sharing, in their newly found freedom, it was only natural for their bodies to come together. Arms locked, mouths met, legs intertwined. As each discovered the other's body, Carolin and Orain flew hand and hand into the mists. . . .

Stormchaser stamped, bringing Orain out of his daze. He looked at Carolin, riding before him. Carolin glanced over his shoulder and smiled, a smile as intense as a physical caress.

Although the moment of intense rapport had passed, he knew he would always have the memory to carry in his heart. And though the physical, too, would pass as the moment of rapport had, Orain knew he would always be with Carolin, as paxman and as friend.

Smiling, he spurred Stormchaser on, passing Carolin, racing through the forest toward home. Toward Hali.

The Rebels

by Deborah J. Mays

Again we have further adventures of a little-known character in Darkovan history: Varzil Ridenow, later surnamed "the Good," who appears briefly in FORBIDDEN TOWER and more at length in TWO TO CONQUER.

Ms. Mays lives in Tucson, Arizona, but she states in her biography that both she and her husband have "unrestrained Gypsy blood," and have lived, in nine years, in thirteen different places: from the bayous of Louisiana to Nome, Alaska. She adds that it is Alaska "that gave me my affinity for Darkover. Nome has got to be as cold as Zandru's seventh hell!"

She has a stepdaughter, Lori, who is now "on her own," and she lost a stepson to leukemia. She shares her house with three dogs and "four very spoiled parrots."

She says about Varzil, "I've always wondered how a man of the nobility, in a time when power struggles between kingdoms were the way of life, could have become such a rebel—a rebel who was at the same time a pacifist." It's this kind of speculation, of course, which makes a shared world anthology work.

Varzil sighed in exasperation at the blood-covered form kneeling unwillingly in front of him, and briefly contemplated having the man killed by the two guards who were already methodically beating him senseless. It was obvious the rebel leader was not going to cooperate with Varzil's plan to pass himself off as a fellow prisoner during the first few days of their forced march to his father's stronghold; and without the leader's endorsement, Varzil knew he would accomplish nothing.

Abruptly, the prince spun around and signaled to the guards to stop the beating. The rebel looked up at him in question, but there was no trace of hope in his eyes.

"Since you obviously don't care about your own pain, perhaps the pain of one of your men will move you to reconsider," Varzil spoke with deliberate coldness. He knew he was on the right track as he caught the unmistakable *No!* from the man's mind before the other locked his barriers tighter. That was no random touch; the man was *laran* gifted, Varzil thought to himself. What was a man with the shared telepathic gift of the nobility, doing fighting for the insurgents?

The prince's eyes narrowed thoughtfully as he realized that this discovery alone made the trip more than worthwhile. Possibly this was the very man who had been setting the suicide circuits into the rebel's minds, making the interrogation of captives virtually impossible.

As Varzil turned to give the orders for another prisoner to be brought in, he found himself unexpectedly flying through the air, impacting abruptly on a jagged stone wall. A few moments later he came to his senses with his head pounding and found his own dagger was being held tightly to his throat.

The prisoner spoke savagely, the knife drawing a thin line of blood—emphasizing his words.

"Understand well, Lord Varzil. I was already a condemned man, even before I laid hands on you. I have absolutely nothing to lose. Order your men out now, or prepare to join me in hell."

The knife let up slightly at the sound of the closing door behind the last guard. "Now, I have two things to ask you, my lord, in exchange for your life," the prisoner paused briefly. "The first is for your word that you will *not* use any of my men against me, or ever again use torture of one human being to force the obedience of another."

"I suppose I must say yes, since you're leaving me no choice," Varzil answered tightly as the pressure increased on his jugular.

"Now," the prisoner continued. "Why in the name of the gods are you out here? Did you really come all this way only to spy on us? We must have your father far more worried than I thought!" the man laughed bitterly at this last.

"Lord Serrais did not send me, and I am not a spy!" Varzil answered with as much dignity as one could when sprawled on the floor with the enemy sitting on your chest. "I came here, as I've already told you, to find out why you rebels continue to fight against what you *must* know are impossible odds!"

"*Not* to find out how many of us there are; where we are headquartered; how we are weaponed . . . ?" the rebel asked sarcastically.

"No."

"And you expect me to believe that?"

"I'm telling you the truth," Varzil answered dully, "but you know that I have no way to prove it."

After a long moment, Varzil could suddenly breathe again as the other rolled smoothly off his chest and wordlessly offered him the dagger.

Caught completely off guard, Varzil sheathed the blade without thinking—though normally he would have unhesitatingly cut down any man who had dared to draw steel in his presence. "Why?" he blurted out incredulously. "Why would you let me live?"

"All I wanted was your oath; the second question was just curiosity," the rebel answered with a brief bitter smile. "You give me hope, my lord. I never thought I'd see the day when one of the ruling family would care enough; would give a *damn* enough; to even *ask* why we are fighting. Killing you wouldn't aid the rebellion. But believe me, if I'd thought it would, I wouldn't have hesitated a second."

"Help me with my plan, then," Varzil said quietly. "Surely you don't fear me just talking with your men?"

The rebel snorted contemptuously at this. "You want to know why we fight, my lord?" he replied sarcastically. "You don't need this masquerade—I'll tell you. It's very simple—we're desperate. We would seek refuge elsewhere, but where? Where can we go where our villages won't be blasted, where our children won't die of strange illnesses, where our land and water won't be poisoned, where *clingfire* won't rain from the sky? We fight because there's no place on this world left to run!"

As Varzil called back in his guard, he grabbed the other by the forearm. "I'll see you tomorrow. I'll have dyed hair and common dress. I'm asking you to reconsider. . . ."

"Go to hell," the rebel answered with a growl, shaking off the hand.

It took direct orders and several threats before his men finally agreed to deliver him as a "captive" to the garrison commander, but a few short hours later, the young prince was enraged, scared, and bitterly regretting his victory.

Eventually, though, he was thrown roughly out of the command post and cursed and beaten to his feet, until he managed to stumble to the prison yard. Once there, he sank painfully to his knees.

"I told you that I wouldn't play your little game," the rebel leader was suddenly crouched beside him speaking in a low harsh tone. "You could have saved yourself some pain, *chiyu.* My men will all be warned of your identity; no matter what you do to me. I strongly suggest you get out of here now; this won't be a picnic in your father's hunting preserve; you wouldn't last three days!"

"I would get out, but I don't think I can," Varzil answered miserably. "All my men are on their way to Caer Donn. I knew you wouldn't accept me with safety nets—so no one here, not even the commander, knows who I am. . . ." He finished the sentence lamely, realizing how childish it sounded now.

"Caer Donn," the rebel repeated incredulously, shaking his head. "You can't be that much of a fool!"

At the prince's shocked look he continued coldly. "With their blasted starstones and sentry birds on guard, my men can't get within two days' ride of here—Caer Donn is just a rumor they've been passing around to try to throw them off the track. We won't be heading anywhere near it; you can be sure of that!"

"Then where will we be going?" Varzil asked around the sudden large lump in his throat.

"How should I know?!" the rebel answered impatiently. "Look, my little lord, you got yourself into this; you can get yourself out or not. Quite frankly, I don't care. I'll grant you one concession, and only one—I won't tell my men who you are for now, but only because there are several who would get a great deal of pleasure out of smashing in your skull as you sleep. If I hear you ask one military question, though, on that day I promise you, *chiyu*—you won't see another dawn!"

Things went from bad to miserable for Varzil as the next days passed in a nightmare of confusion. Following the lead of their commander, the other prisoners completely ignored him. He was almost always near the back of the line of march, and consequently received more than a fair share of the lash. He had been soundly thrashed for "arguing" with a guard, and by the middle of the third day he was so sore and exhausted he could barely move.

Struggling down a rubble-strewn slope, his foot turned suddenly on a loose rock on the trail, and he groaned loudly as his ankle twisted painfully under him. He lay where he fell, too drained to even try to rise again.

The rebel leader appeared at his side as if by magic and held out his hand. "Get up," he commanded coldly.

"I can't," Varzil answered with a shake of his head, fighting off the tears of pain and frustration.

"Damn you, get up, or they'll flog us both," the rebel repeated sharply.

"Just go on, leave me," Varzil mumbled, waving his hand.

The rebel grabbed him hard by the shoulder and shook him roughly.

"Contrary to the rest of us, you're here by your own choice! You wanted to play this little game. You wanted to understand desperation. Well, *chiyu,* you've only just begun. Now, damn you, get up!"

Varzil looked away from the rebel's blazing eyes, and tried once more to stand. With the other's supporting hand he found he could, and the hand stayed under his arm, steadying him for his first few stumbling steps.

"That's better," the rebel spoke softly now. "There'll be food tonight, you know. You can make it a few more hours with that thought, can't you?"

When Varzil turned to answer, the man had moved on again without taking leave.

They were indeed given a small bowl of boiled grain and journey bread that evening when they camped. Varzil immediately fell to tearing off hunks of bread with his teeth wolfishly. He stopped suddenly, looking around him curiously—the other men were carefully breaking up the bread and stowing it in their clothing. He followed their example regretfully, and the rebel leader sat down next to him, laughing harshly.

"Well, it seems that you can learn after all, *chiyu.* Maybe you *will* make it."

"I wish you'd quit calling me *chiyu,*" Varzil answered with an annoyed frown. "My name is . . ."

". . . best not spoken here!" the rebel interrupted hurriedly.

Varzil swallowed hard at this reminder, but he was so eager for any conversation after the days of being ignored that he quickly went on.

"How did you know we would get food tonight anyway?" He realized he still didn't know the man's name and finished hesitantly, ". . . Lord General," trying to translate the man's position with his men into a suitable rank.

"Lord General!" the man sputtered into his water mug. "Zandru's hells, where did you get that?! Rebels don't think much of titles, in case you haven't figured that out yet! You can call me Mikhail, and I think you'd better be Val for now—that can be short for a lot of things," he added in a low voice.

"And as to how I knew we would get food tonight?" he continued in a cynical tone. "Proclamation 416—The Directions for the Treatment of Prisoners in Transit, states we are to be fed every three days—whether we need it or not. Any more, and we might be strong enough to run; any less, and we can't seem to walk."

"Are you trying to tell me that my fath . . ." Varzil caught himself abruptly. "That Lord Serrais *knows* about this sort of mistreatment?"

"I'm trying to tell you that he *orders* it."

Varzil shook his head in denial. "He may be harsh and sometimes a little too quick to judge, but I've never known him to be deliberately cruel."

"That's what makes it even worse I guess," Mikhail spoke with a deep bitterness. "To him, it's not even being cruel—he actually believes we are less able to feel pain and hunger because we weren't born noble.

Well, my lord, we feel pain the same as you, and we love life and deserve to live just as much!"

"I know that. Don't forget that I came here to try to stop the killing!" Varzil replied haughtily.

The rebel snorted contemptuously at this. "You came here to play a game! Save your self-righteous lies for Zandru and your noble friends—I know better! You don't see us as people any more than Lord Serrais does—we're just your pawns."

"That's not true!" Varzil protested sharply.

"Val, do you deny that you thought of having me killed when I first opposed your plan?" Mikhail asked angrily. "Thought about it without any sort of remorse, because I wasn't really a person to you? Damn it, man! You ordered me beäten. You just stood there and let it go on and on. You never even saw the pain. Can you deny that's how it was, even to yourself?"

"No," Varzil answered in a choked voice, closing his eyes tightly at the picture in his memory. "Forgive me," he added quietly a moment later.

"You'd better get some sleep," Mikhail ordered abruptly, looking the prince up and down very curiously.

The next days brought even more hardships for the prisoners as the line of march turned from the long winding Rio Valley they had been following, to climb into the Hellers toward the first of the mountain passes. Each night's camp was higher in altitude and colder; as each day brought steeper and steeper trails. On the final day of climbing to the summit of the first pass, the men woke to a dark overcast sky and a bitter cutting wind. By midday, they were struggling through snow half a foot deep.

Trudging mindlessly forward, Varzil stopped briefly,

without thinking, to help up one of the younger boys at the bottom of an icy incline. The boy clung to him, and together they stumbled and slid on, bent almost double against the storm.

Over and over he hauled the unknown rebel to his feet, until the boy finally wrapped his hand in Varzil's pack strap and buried his face out of the biting wind, leaving Varzil to try and keep sight of their comrades through the blinding snow.

After what seemed like an eternity, the soldiers called a halt at the very edge of the treeline. They hastily erected a tent and piled into it, leaving their captives to fend for themselves, with only the storm for guard.

Mikhail moved quickly among his men, knowing they would just collapse where they were if left alone. He ordered them to move back into the shelter of the trees and to bed down in the lee of bushes or rocks, sharing blankets and body warmth.

As he struggled down the line checking on each man, he came to Varzil curled up alone. "Didn't you hear my orders, Val?" he spoke impatiently. Then abruptly he laid a surprisingly gentle hand on the prince's shoulder. "Never mind, I'll be back to bed down with you, then, when I'm done with the men."

"That won't be necessary; I'll be fine here," Varzil answered almost shrilly, shocked at the man's touch on his arm and the pity in his voice.

"Meaning, I suppose, that you'd rather freeze to death than stoop to sharing your blankets with a rebel," Mikhail responded coldly. "Suit yourself."

Varzil started to protest that that wasn't what he'd meant at all, but the rebel had already gone again. "Damn the man anyway," Varzil thought to himself.

No matter what he said the other always managed to twist it around!

A few hours later, the young prince knew he had made a grave, perhaps fatal, error. The wind had died down some, but the temperature was dropping lower with every passing minute. He was shivering uncontrollably and wished desperately that he could go to Mikhail and apologize, but he didn't know which of the snow-covered blànketed mounds around him contained the rebel leader, and he was still afraid of the other men. He was afraid of Mikhail, too, he realized dismally. That was why he had rejected his offer so abruptly.

He imagined he felt the rebel's hand on his arm and wondered briefly if he was beginning to hallucinate toward the end, but the hand moved up and took the blanket off of his face.

"I tried, damn you, Varzil. But I couldn't just lie there and let you freeze," Mikhail spoke in a gruff voice. "Do you want my help now, or no?"

Varzil was determined that this time the rebel would misunderstand nothing. "Yes, I'm begging you; please help me, Mikhail!" he cried through chattering teeth.

The prince more than half expected for the rebel to abandon him anyway with some sarcastic comment; but instead the other began digging into a snow drift, soon forming a small cave. Without a word, he half carried, half dragged Varzil inside and stripped off both their shirts, wrapping the blankets around them in a cocoon.

"Why did you come back?" Varzil murmured hesitantly when his shivering had subsided enough to speak.

"I don't really know," Mikhail sighed. "Maybe I'm

just sick of all the unnecessary deaths," he paused briefly. "Or maybe it's because I watched you help someone today. It seems you're no longer the man I first met in that prison cell."

"You'll never forgive me for that, will you?" the young prince asked quietly.

"There's nothing to forgive Val. That Varzil is dead," the rebel answered with a sudden laugh. "Do you honestly think I'd be in here sharing my blankets with *him*?" Then his tone grew more serious as he added softly: "When we get to where we're going, do what you can for my men. That's all I ask."

The dawn brought clear skies, though it was still bitter cold. A dozen men had frostbitten toes, fingers, or faces, but they struggled up and on under the relentless lash of their captors. Around midday, Varzil caught up with Mikhail as the other knelt at the side of a fallen comrade. The prince glanced briefly at the hurt man's face—he had blood freezing in little droplets down his chin from where he'd bitten almost through his lip.The man made no sound, but Varzil could see the clenched jaw and eyes closingly tightly every few minutes, betraying obvious agony. Finally the man took Mikhail's hand in entreaty.

"It's no use, Mikhail," he said softly. "Even if I make it through today, which is doubtful, what about tomorrow, and the day after that? The black rot is certain, and I don't want to die like that!"

After several moments, Mikhail pulled his hand free from the other man's and walked over to a large stone in the trail. He pried it up almost savagely and carried it back, kneeling again at the other's side.

The man looked at the rock in momentary horror, then twisted his head away blinking rapidly.

"You know they would never lend me a knife," Mikhail said quietly. "I think I can do it quickly, if it's still what you want."

The man nodded mutely, and Mikhail laid his hand briefly on the other's cheek. "Then turn your head away and close your eyes, my old friend. Val, take his hands," he added softly.

The man reached blindly toward Varzil, and as their hands met, the prince heard a quick: "Thank you, Mik," just before the stone crushed through the man's temple.

When the commander discovered the body a few minutes later, he had the men whipped furiously into formation.

"Which of you is responsible for this?!" he shouted, pointing to the corpse where the blood was already freezing into a thin puddle by the head.

"I am, sir," Mikhail answered calmly. "He couldn't go any further—both feet were frozen last night. He was one of my men. He asked me for the coup."

"He was *not* one of *your* men!" the commander responded enraged. "He belonged, as do you all, to Lord Serrais! Any further action based on such an excuse will *not* be tolerated! You sir," he pointed to Mikhail, "will be punished severely tonight for this outrage; and you would all do well to remember that you are *not* regarded as soldiers with the rights normally accorded to prisoners of war—but as oathbreakers, in rebellion against your rightful king. Do I make myself clear!"

* * *

Later that night, Mikhail was returned to the prisoner's lines from where he had been taken behind the main tent.

Varzil gasped involuntarily at the sight of Mikhail's battered face, but the rebel walked past him silently and lay down with a sigh on the blankets that Varzil had spread out. "Just let it go," he said tiredly.

"Mikhail, you're only one man. You've got to back off a little." Varzil answered softly, as he laid a hand on Mikhail's arm hesitantly—only to have it flung off violently.

"Get away from me, you bastard! Don't you understand anything yet? The day I walk by one of my men is the day they've won. The day they've defeated me! Nothing else they can do to me matters."

"Damn you, Mikhail!" Varzil exploded in return. "Will you *listen* for once! I understand more than you think. I know you too well to suggest that you abandon your men, but with forty-some odd people leaning on you, maybe it's time you learned to lean back just a little!"

"Do you think you could take it?" Mikhail asked harshly.

"Why don't you try me?" Varzil responded.

Abruptly, the rebel leader moved into a very surprised prince's arms. There was no sound, but Varzil could feel the deep heart-wrenching sobs vibrating through the other's body as the day's pent-up grief finally burst free. "I'd known him all my life!" Mikhail cried. "And I killed him. I killed him!"

Suddenly Varzil was sharing the rebel's pain fully undiluted, as Mikhail's barriers dissolved and they slipped into rapport. A Ridenow with the full empathic gift of his family, Varzil had no defenses, and he could only hold the other tightly in shared response.

"I'm sorry Val, I didn't mean to do that," Mikhail apologized quickly when he had regained control a few seconds later.

"I seem to recall asking for it," Varzil replied quietly.

Mikhail finally met his eyes at that. "Remind me not to call you *chiyu* again, my friend," he said gruffly.

The two were finally drifting off to sleep when they were startled awake by the sudden sound of steel meeting steel. The rebels quickly rallied to give the rescue party what aid they could, but soon saw their help wasn't necessary as their guards had been completely surprised by their comrades.

Varzil caught several of the new men glancing at him curiously as they went about their duties around the camp, but finally one approached him with a cup of warm stew. He handed it to Varzil without a word, then taking a quick look at his lacerated back, motioned him to the hospital tent.

Since that was where Mikhail had disappeared, Varzil went without protest.

As soon as he stepped into the entrance of the crowded shelter, a medical assistant sat him down and began peeling off what was left of his shirt and applying a soothing ointment to his wounds. Varzil thought to himself that nothing in his life had ever felt so good! He closed his eyes briefly in relief, but when he reopened them, he found the leader of the rescue party staring at him in open astonishment.

The man nodded curtly to the door, and Varzil obediently went out. He was relieved to note however, that Mikhail had followed him.

Once alone, the new rebel turned angrily to Mikhail. "You *do* know who he is, don't you?!" he asked accusingly.

"A friend," Mikhail replied.

"Damn it, Mikhail! We just lost thirteen good men to the likes of this bastard, and you're going to stand there and call him a friend?!"

"Enough!" Mikhail answered with his eyes blazing. He paused abruptly, taking a deep breath. "Look at him, *bredu,*" he said, with his voice now low and intense. "He marched with us, slept with us, bled with us, and died a little every day with us. You won't find one man here, including me, who gives a damn *what* his background is!"

The man looked at the ground rather than at Varzil and sighed heavily. "I've always trusted your judgment, my brother, although I can't say I've always understood your logic." He met Mikhail's eyes and smiled at shared memories. "But I guess that's why you're the commander. If you say he's earned the title of friend, so be it."

With that, he turned abruptly to Varzil. "Will you be riding with us, then, or on to Serrais?"

"I wasn't aware that I would have any choice in the matter," Varzil answered with a questioning glance at Mikhail.

"Val, my men follow me only of their own free will," the rebel answered softly. "You would be welcome, but the choice is yours. Think well though, my prince. If Lord Serrais chooses to view what you've done as treason, going there could very well mean your death. I've studied your father all of my life, I *know* what he'll do to you. He has other sons, Val. Sons who don't question."

When Varzil protested at this implication, Mikhail began speaking in a low voice—almost pleading. The other man slipped away quietly as the two argued, but returned later with a pack and riding beast.

The young prince took it as a bad omen when he arrived at Castle Serrais and was conducted unceremoniously to the king's audience chamber, without even being allowed to bathe or change first.

"My son," his father began almost gently, and Varzil breathed a sigh of momentary relief at this address—maybe things wouldn't be as bad as he'd feared. But the relief turned quickly to horror as he heard his father casually demand that he lower his barriers to the crowd of *laranzu* gathered silently in the corner of the hall.

At Varzil's shocked look, the voice of his father turned to a king's command.

"There are those that doubt your allegiance to myself and to Serrais. Do you hesitate at the only means of silencing them?" He gestured to the head *laranzu* to move forward as he continued with his orders.

"During the *laranzu's* probe, you are instructed to concentrate on remembering all you can of the rebels. Even small details you think unimportant may provide a means to their elimination."

"My lord, no! I beg you!" Varzil fell to his knees in entreaty. "I give you my word that I know nothing of military importance, and that I returned here out of loyalty to Serrais!"

"Will you make this easy or difficult?" the king replied, unmoved.

"Difficult, then, I should think," Varzil answered between clenched teeth as he returned to his feet defiantly.

Four guards moved in to hold him pinioned between them as the *laranzu* ran a hand lightly up and down in front of him, not quite touching his body.

"He carries a matrix; it will have to be removed," the man reported dispassionately, turning slightly to the king for permission.

The prince swallowed hard. The matrix, used to amplify his telepathic gift, had been keyed into him, body and brain, since he was ten years old. If it were removed by anyone without the training for it, he knew he could die.

As he looked into the cold eyes of his father's sorcerer, he knew the man didn't have that training, and didn't care that he didn't.

The *laranzu* ripped his dagger into Varzil's belt pocket without even attempting to match resonances with the matrix first. With total indifference, he spilled the stone into his bare hand and closed his fist tightly—knowing this would feel to the young man as if he were being crushed alive. When the prince's moans began to fade, he walked to a nearby brazier and held his hand with the stone over the flames, deliberately projecting his own pain through the matrix to the sensitive empath.

Varzil screamed incoherently over and over before he sank convulsing to the floor. There was a murmur around the court as the *laranzu* walked casually over to a telepathic damper and dropped the stone into its field. Then he approached the steps of the throne, barely glancing at the crumpled figure of the prince below.

"A few days without it, and he should be ready to interrogate," he reported without emotion.

Lord Serrais looked around the room in open challenge, and the murmurs died away abruptly. "Dungeon him," he ordered the guards curtly.

As Varzil was being chained, a man burst into the room yelling loudly.

"My Lord Serrais. We're under attack! The castle is completely surrounded!"

"By who, man? How many?"

"We're not sure my lord. They have no standards or recognizable colors. But they've a messenger at the gate."

"Conduct the man to me immediately," the king ordered sharply.

"Yes, my lord," the guard saluted briskly and left.

The king knelt at Varzil's side and began slapping him relentlessly to consciousness. When the prince groaned and opened his eyes, the older man demanded coldly.

"It seems your rebels are here. Did you know they would be marching on Serrais?!"

Varzil remained silent, sure it was some sort of trick, and slowly moved his hand up to wipe the blood from the corner of his mouth. As his head turned, he stared down the hall dumbfounded.

"Mikhail," he breathed silently in total disbelief.

Mikhail didn't kneel as he approached but bowed his head to Varzil in brief acknowledgment.

"Speak your message, rebel," the king ordered sharply, putting up his hand to stop the other's advance.

"As you wish," Mikhail replied. "Our terms are straightforward enough. Turn Prince Varzil over to us, or we attack. We have you surrounded and cut off. Even with your weapons, we would eventually prevail."

"That is open to debate," the king answered. "But what do you want with Varzil?"

"He is being tortured; we want it stopped."

"And that's all?"

"That's all."

Lord Serrais snorted in open contempt. "You actually expect me to believe that you'd risk the lives of all those men out there for the life of my son?!"

"I don't really care what you believe. The fact is, we're at your gates. What's your answer, my lord?"

"Tell me," the king asked sarcastically. "If the crown were to agree to a trade," he paused as if considering. "Say, Varzil for you—a prince for the leader of the rebellion. Would you agree to this?"

"Yes," Mikhail answered without hesitation.

"Just like that? No promises, no guarantees?" the king laughed.

"Just like that," Mikhail replied coldly.

At this, Lord Serrais stood abruptly, his smile fading, and gestured for the guards to take the rebel into custody.

Before he could continue his orders, however, he clutched his chest and turned startled eyes to where Varzil had crawled to retrieve his matrix.

No one dared interfere as the air began to crackle with electricity and the older man crumpled lifelessly to the floor.

Varzil struggled to his feet and looked around the room briefly—the men present were the king's personal guard. Taking a deep breath he asked quietly.

"You were my father's liegemen. Have I your loyalty as well?"

As if only just realizing they were standing in the presence of their new king, one and all, they dropped to their knees, murmuring their affirmation—such a change in power was, after all, a common enough occurrence.

Varzil smiled in gratitude. "Thank you, gentlemen. I take your actions as oaths sworn. You may stand." Then he turned abruptly to Mikhail and gestured for the guards to move away.

"You should have been days into the Hellers by now. . . ." His tone was partly accusation, partly question.

The rebel answered quietly. "Remember that time when you were so stubborn you almost froze to death, and I just couldn't make myself let you? Well . . ." he shrugged slightly.

"This wasn't a planned attack? You followed me?"

"Don't let anyone ever tell you that you'd make a scout, Varzil, we weren't more than two hours behind you the whole way."

As Varzil moved forward, Mikhail started to sink to his knees.

"Don't you dare!" the prince ordered sharply. "As you are so fond of reminding me, I have a tendency to get myself into a hell of a lot of trouble, but you got me into *this,* Mikhail! Now, damn you, you're going to help me!"

"As you wish, my lord," Mikhail answered obediently, his voice suddenly cold.

The new king stopped in shock at the other's tone. He knew he had just made another grave mistake with Mikhail. There was an excited murmur from the hall, increasing in volume, as he deliberately moved to within arm's reach of the rebel leader and pulled out a jeweled dagger from his belt. He held it out wordlessly to the other hilt first, his eyes pleading for him to take it.

"I'm remembering the last time we exchanged a knife," Mikhail said softly, his eyes meeting the prince's levelly.

"So am I," Varzil answered, his jaw clenching. "And wondering whether you've really forgiven me yet."

Mikhail broke eye contact as he silently sheathed the blade in answer. The acceptance of a knife stood as a pledge of brotherhood whether among commoners or kings, and the rebel wondered to himself why in the hell he was doing it.

"Thank you, *bredu,*" Varzil whispered quietly. Then he added: "I need your help Mikhail. Will you stay with me? Please?"

Noting the prince had *asked* him this time, rather than ordered, Mikhail commented dryly, "Well, it seems as if you *can* learn after all."

"I've had a relentless teacher," Varzil responded.

Mikhail could no longer control a grin at this answer, and Varzil unhesitantly threw himself into the rebel's arms at this rare opening.

"Touché, *bredu,*" Mikhail whispered softly as his hands moved up to embrace the other in return. Both were heedless of the shocked looks from the court—it was best they understood right now that their new king was Rebel!

A Dance for Darkover

by Diana Perry and Vera Nazarian

Vera Nazarian and Diana Perry went to Pomona College in Claremont, California, together. Diana is originally from Oakland, California, while Vera, I think, is from Southern California. Diana is also 24 years old and studied International Relations, says Vera, "while I studied Psychology and English and played with computers." This is Diana's first published story, while Vera has been selling to my anthologies since SWORD & SORCERESS II. She says this story is basically Diana's brainchild. Knowing Vera, I'm sure she's being modest.

I've often said that I can't imagine how I came to make dancing so important on Darkover; I can't dance at all, nor do I want to; in school they used to require that boy and girls dance in the gym at noon hour. That kind of dancing never interested me, even though my daughter is a really gifted dancer, dancing since age nine at the Renaissance Faire. In the eighties (my fifties! *Sorry, it's still hard to realize I'm that old. I ought to be, from the way I* feel, *about seventeen), I took a few ballet lessons. I asked Moira, "Would it surprise you to hear that for a woman of my age I'm pretty good at it?"*

She replied, "No. I must have gotten it from somewhere."

There was a heat wave in the Hellers. The air, scalding, obscene, beat upon the icy range until great chunks of primeval snow-capped rock shuddered under the onslaught, and then torrents of melting churning waters came down the slopes. They decimated everything in their path, took with them gravel, and uprooted the evergreens that had stood immovable at the base of the Hellers for centuries. . . .

Overhead, in the deep violet heaven, floated the trinity of jewel moons, Kyrrdis, Idriel, and Mormallor. But what of Liriel? Where was the peacock gem-moon?

Silence, in the deep purple velvet, while the heat continued beating in merciless dry waves all about, the heat. . . .

Alessandra came to herself with a start, feeling trickles of sweat on her neck. The temperature in the ship's cabin, and the low hum of the air vent indicated that she'd somehow, in her sleep, moved the personal temperature setting to "heat," which accounted for her nightmare. As she quickly readjusted the air flow to "cool," her gaze involuntarily came to rest on the incredible view out of the porthole. It made her stop all movement, as her heart gathered itself in a knot about to leap out of her chest. Old memory-feelings came surging back, and she experienced a sense of emotional vertigo unlike any she'd ever had while doing her wildest acrobatic dance-twists in zero g.

Below her, taking up almost all of the window view, was a dark violet planet. Even as her memory-thoughts flickered, the ship was plummeting down onto that primeval violet, until the blackness of space was forever obscured in the porthole, and the deep color of the planet came to engulf all sight.

She heard the intercom broadcast messages, but it came to her as though from a great distance of memories and time.

Cottman IV. Entering orbit in ten seconds. Five seconds. Now locked in orbit around Cottman IV.

The word "Cottman IV" had so little meaning to her. She knew a much better word for it, a more beautiful and expressive word for the violet icy place with heaven-high mountains and intensely proud people. Her people, and her home.

The word was Darkover.

His dark-haired head half-turned, Ruyven Di Asturien watched the great silver ship dock from a distance. An incredible lack of expression was on his deeply tanned face, while steel, barely held in check, glittered out of his cool grey eyes. Dan Lawton thought he knew exactly what was going through the guardsman's head, knew very well that only Comyn loyalty and bare civility held him there, second-in-command with the dispatch of men, to properly escort the "heiress" Aillard to Comyn Castle.

Alessandra Kyrielle Aillard had been summoned grudgingly by the Comyn Council to return to Darkover and be prepared to assume her duties as Heir-Designate to the Aillard Domain. Allesandra was the third daughter in an unfortunate line of Aillard women, all daughters of the late Aliciane Aillard, with the eldest, Daniella, married and childless, who had long since named the second sister, Briona, as her Heir. But now, Briona was dead. And Alessandra felt the weight of the unthinkable come tumbling upon her, the dead weight of unexpected responsibility and duty—a duty that moved in her blood and was not to be denied.

Lawton could sympathize with her, unlike this stern Di Asturien here who seemed older than his twenty-eight or so years, the face drawn into a mask of composure, his youth buried under layers of loyalty and tradition. He would be handsome if he'd let those lines smooth out; if he only eased the tightness of his Comyn mouth.

But he would never approve, thought Dan Lawton, just like all the rest of them, the Comyn, could never truly approve of this woman about to set foot on her home planet after an absence of seven years. A woman who had gone off world at the age of fifteen, taken by her "frivolous" father—*Was he truly frivolous or merely trying to handle his wife's untimely death*? thought Lawton—who had left as a child, only to become a woman, and somewhere among exotic glittering faraway worlds of the alien Empire, to establish a brilliant career for herself, as a world-class dancer.

And that was the main reason the Comyn could never approve. Alessandra Aillard was an intergalactic celebrity.

No self-respecting woman of the Comyn would allow that kind of public exposure to touch her, or engage in such a scandalous career. The Darkover-trained side of Lawton could see that in their eyes she was profaning the ageless native traditions of Darkovan dance, "perverting" and taking elements of the wild mountain *male* pride, and shamelessly incorporating them into her female wild but equally controlled modern dance sequences. That was his Darkovan side.

But the Terran half of Lawton marveled at her, at the fiery brilliant gymno-dancer, critically acclaimed in the highest intergalactic Performing Arts circles, and a recognized vanguard member of the Empire Dance Society. He'd seen holo-videos of her dance performances long before he had known that Regis Hastur would require this incredible woman's presence back on Darkover. He had seen her dance. . . . And yes, even now, Dan Lawton felt the seeds of politics grow and extend their clutches to envelop her. The Hastur was ever so subtle, and even this specific instance Lawton could see as a direct effect of the change, slow and sure, to which Regis was intuitively partial.

A clever move, this, to bestow a pro-Terran Heir upon the Aillard. And yet—what was she really like, this Alessandra? How much of her was molded by the Empire, and how much of true Darkover was left in her, to rule over the Domain?

These were the times of change, and only the future would tell all. In the meantime, he, Lawton, could only be there to observe.

And observe he did, as a petite woman clad in form-hugging Terran silver neared them, followed by an attendant. Her hair was flame, a torch in the sun, long to her waist and unrestrained. Together with the Terran suit it shone incandescent, metal on metal, and for a moment Lawton had to shake away an old superstition—she was like that fire-form demoness of the Forge Folk.

Next to him, the young Di Asturien stared despite himself. His icy lips then tightened even further.

Only—she must have been reading their minds. She

turned, and out of nowhere a proper Darkover cloak was handed to her, which she hurried to wrap about herself. Only flashes of silver now and then showed through the folds as she moved.

Before either of the men could open their mouths to speak, she paused a foot away, brisk and elegant. Green eyes raked them, warm, energetic. Her voice, too, was that of a Comynara proper, used to command, Lawton thought. And used to getting her way.

"Dan Lawton, I suppose?" she said. "I am Alessandra Aillard."

"My greatest pleasure, Ms. Aillard. Or, should I say *damisela,* Comynara?" Lawton was faultless in his smile.

The other man only nodded, looking intently, barely hiding his scorn. "Ruyven Di Asturien, *z'par servu.* We are to escort you to Comyn Castle—*damisela.*"

"No need for titles, please. 'Alessa' would do. Really, I always tend to forget about all that. But I suppose now is a different matter. Now that I am here. . . ."

Her words appeared to trail off as she spoke this, half to herself. And then, meeting their eyes, she burst out into a glorious somewhat childlike smile, ignoring the younger man's frozen scowl. "Yes, now that I'm here. . . . Then, by all means, lead on, Mr. Lawton, sir, and you too, *Dom*! Escort me, by gods, I do not care, suddenly I don't at all care *why* I'm here, only that I am here, home!"

Later that day, Regis Hastur was to witness yet another dour session of the Council, only this one's monotony was broken somewhat. They were arguing still, clutching at this last opportunity before the inevitable, those old timers did. The inevitable was the twist of events that had sent a woman, Terran in every sense of the word except blood, to be sworn in as the Heir-Designate of the Aillard Domain.

The chamber was restless. Regis, with his beautiful sad eyes and stark white hair, leaned his head with mild weariness. He listened for the hundredth time as some minor Comyn noble—old and spouting tradition—stood up to vent his opinion.

"We do not need this!" the old man was saying breathlessly. "What has Comyn become? What *are* we, what? What use is it to call ourselves Comyn when we no longer have enough pride even to sustain. . . ."

Regis' attention wandered, as he looked about him, at those people who were before him, Comyn. He noticed the many emptied benches, where only a half-decade ago, it seemed there was no room to sit, for all the energetic opinionated able-bodied men. . . . *How oddly, singularly sad . . . is change.*

And yet. I live and breathe it. Yes.

The speaker's voice continued in outrage as his mind winked in and out of reality.

". . . and the incredible shame of profaning one of our holiest traditions! See you what mockery she makes of it? Many of us have seen the Preserved Images—what call you them—*Videos,* damn *Terran* word—of her performances. How she twists and contorts! Like no normal human female, but the devil himself, from Zandru's Seventh Hell! And worst of all, she moves and you think: I've seen that before! Why, that's one of the fancy steps from the mountain Alton dance! Or else . . ."

Regis blinked. Video-images of a breathtaking limber body came to mind, fluid like quicksilver, faultless, as he thought of this woman Alessandra whom he had summoned to Darkover. She had danced with incredible intricacy, was a living torch, ultra-modern, spectacular in her acrobatic way of moving. He heard the faraway memory roar of applause, the alien monolithic theater dome. . . . And yet—in every movement of hers, every twist of her head, even the pliancy of the line that flowed from her hand along the poised curve of her arm and her torso—in this was *Darkover.* It spoke to him, it cried, it wept to him, the plaintive mountain soul. And in her, reflected somewhere deep, stood the violet skies. . . . And her hair, the torch, bled the same light as did the sun of Darkover. . . .

Yes, it would be good to finally see her in the flesh, to meet this woman who to Regis now symbolized what Darkover *could be,* a perfect blending of the old with the new, once the change he had conceived would be complete.

The familiar brash voice of a Ridenow brought Regis back to himself, and he involuntarily hid a smile. Lerrys had taken the floor.

"Enough, my fellow men," spoke Lerrys, throwing about him a look of friendly half-flippant scorn. "This has been foreseen by all of us as inevitable. I say, bravo to this *Domna* Alessandra! And not just bravo for what she does. I admire her, I say, for showing the best—yes, the best side of Darkover to the rest of the Empire! And that's more than any of you old chervines could ever aspire to!"

Lerrys darted a look at the Aillard box where the stoic tired form of Daniella could be seen, together with her brother Endreas. Endreas, fire-headed and beautiful, was the reason for his unusual zeal. Endreas was Alessandra's twin. His sister, meanwhile, the source of all this, was nowhere yet in sight.

Lerrys soon surrendered the floor to be followed by a few other tradition-minded Comyn who all sounded repetitiously the same. One noticeable exception was, in Regis' mind, the young Di Asturien second son, Ruyven. Unlike the ranting old men, he stood calm, poised, already well-respected by many, like a rock of inevitability, and spoke words of quiet irony that for some reason or another managed to touch the soul. "What say we, good sirs, to an estranged one among us? To one that had gone and come back *no longer* one of us? It seems simple to me. If it were my child coming back, I would say: 'Who are you, son or daughter of mine? If you can still *tell* me who you are, in a *language* that I can understand, in a language of my blood, then I will take you back in. Else begone, changeling, who is no seed of mine!' And this same thing must be said to this woman Alessandra who yearns to bear the name Aillard: 'Who are you, once-daughter of Comyn? Tell us now, so we can understand. Otherwise, you have no claim. Make yourself understood to the Comyn blood in us all.' And that is all that must be allowed her."

"Enough, Lord Regis! I demand an end to this." A strong female voice fell to interrupt, and there was silence. Everyone looked as Daniella, who had spoken nothing until now, rose to take the floor. Ruyven inclined his head respectfully, giving way before her, and smoothly controlled his anger.

Daniella, tired but proud Comynara, Lady Aillard, stood before them all. "My Lord Regis. My lords. I have been listening to all of you, for ages now, it seems. There is but one thing you all appear to miss, despite your fine words. I am Aillard. My sister is Aillard. In this final matter, only I have the last word. With all due respect, Lord Regis, not even Hastur himself can stop me now. Alessandra, sister of my blood, only makes me proud of her, and always will I stand behind her in this. And you, fellow lords, it would do you good to realize that more than anyone, Alessandra *lends us grace.*"

She paused. "I now name my Heir-Designate."

Rumbling went through the chamber, while Gabriel Lanart-Alton moved them all to silence. And then, as if on cue, Alessandra walked in.

And the Comyn stared at this faultless female form, clad as a proper lady of Noble House blood. She was so petite, so delicate, Regis suddenly realized, as he beheld her in actuality. Polite, full of impeccable decorum, she made her way to stand next to her sister. In a clear unexpectedly strong voice she repeated the words of the Oath, and her gaze never flinched as she met them all head-on. She stood haughty, and with her inborn grace it seemed for an instant that she was already the one in charge, already the Lady Aillard, despite the fact that her older sister was beside her.

What must be passing through her mind now. . . . Regis wondered. When the Oath was over and Gabriel closed the ceremony, Regis formally acknowledged the new Heiress of Aillard. He spoke polite words to her, but his mind raced ahead to what he really wanted to say to this one, to what he would informally say in the near future to her who was now a symbol of his, and privately stood for a new Darkover.

* * *

If it is true that all things change, then one thing that remains old and true on Darkover is Festival Night. Like a hundred fireflies, the lights burned from a distance in the many windows of Comyn Castle.

Ruyven Di Asturien's steel eyes changed expression for an instant only, as he saw Endreas Aillard, looking haggard, walk tiredly past him in the corridor of the Castle. He still found himself starting inwardly at the sight of the twin brother of the woman whom he had grown to *hate,* the one who'd been to the stars. How great was the resemblance. . . . He would see her in Endreas each time, all over again. As always, Ruyven was civil, impeccably polite to both but within him seethed murk and bitter anger. As always, the thought passed: *She has won them over to her side after all. They are all a part of it now, of the elemental* change *that the Hastur desires. They rush headlong, blind, into a future without a past. Without true Darkover.*

"I wish you good Festival, *Dom.*" said Endreas lightly in passing. His eyes looked drained today (*unlike his sister's whose were always bright*—again, that intrusive thought).

"And you also," replied Ruyven with a slight nod, and an ever-indifferent expression—the same that he used with *her.* "I look forward to seeing you dance tonight. The sword dance is an honor indeed."

With this exchange they parted. And Ruyven thought, *How ironic. Both of them are to dance tonight. Brother and sister. And yet, I only think of her. Of how again she will bewitch them all. . . . Blind fools.*

Earlier, Regis Hastur had personally requested that Alessandra Aillard dance the opening dance this Festival Night. It was to be her first public Darkover performance, and everyone knew that this was her real opportunity not only to redeem herself perfectly, but to gain true popularity where it mattered most—with the Comyn. In a way, this Festival was to be her showcase. What Ruyven didn't know was that against tradition, there were Terran correspondents to attend this Festival Night by exclusive permission, and her performance was to be recorded. Hastur wanted to make a statement indeed.

The great ballroom was filled to its limit. Everywhere, like a daze, it seemed, were familiar faces. Regis stood aside with a glass of wine and watched them, as always, life-weary.

Old Nicholas, father of Daniella and Alessandra, had returned to Darkover also, having taken the next shuttle flight after his daughter. Some thought him to be an old fool, but Regis rather saw a kind old child. Nicholas stood, honest and white-haired, speaking to a Comyn acquaintance of days past.

A few feet away, near the Ridenows—Lerrys' raucous laughter could be heard a mile away—were some of the Di Asturien women. *Domna* Mariel rested her heavy frame and sipped a fruit punch. Her children and grandchildren clustered all around: pretty budding Lorinda, thirteen; older Graciela with her own brood of three, as robust as their mother. Evan-Domenic, the *Dom*, stood some space away with his second son, Ruyven. The older son, Geremy, was not present, and the youngest, fifteen-year-old Keenan, did his first stint with the Cadets.

How time flies, thought Regis. And again, as more and more was his tendency nowadays, he began to see memory-images mix with the real. Instead of Evan-Domenic, he saw old Domenic Di Asturien himself, as he remembered him years ago, from the Cadets—tradition personified.

His heart skipped a beat as he thought he glimpsed his very own Danilo through the crowd, an innocent, younger Danilo, as he had been back then, not the wearied loyal paxman he knew at present. But no, Danilo was not at this Festival Night.

And then, was it those unforgettable piercing-sharp eagle eyes that met him? The swarthy handsome face framed by dark tight curls, the cruel curve of lips?—No! Why did he have to think of Dyan Ardais now, of all times? It was only the younger Di Asturien, Ruyven, with his ever-grim looks. Not Dyan, long-dead. . . .

Other shadows of the past flickered by. Regis was beginning to feel light-headed, and he put down his drink.

Soon, lights in the Hall were dimmed, the first dance about to begin. There were whispers of anticipation all around, a feeling of half-forbidden excitement. At last, they were all to see the woman and her living dance.

A spotlight fell upon a form of whiteness. They sucked in their breath as one—she was to do the Maiden dance, the most complex of the ancient women's dances, so steeped in tradition and antiquity that for years no one had attempted to do it.

Hidden musicians struck the first notes.

Alessandra lay prostrate on the floor, wrapped in a pale white robe of penitence, her hair streaming loose about her. She barely breathed. As the music developed, slowly, gently, like an opening blossom, she arose. The white fabric shimmered about her in many streaming folds, covering her torso but leaving her legs barely concealed under wispy strips of material. With movements combining unbelievable finesse and power, she began the ancient steps, gaining speed. Faster and faster her limbs flashed, without losing that grace for an instant, or missing the tiniest gesture.

The rhythm increased, and wailing pipes joined in, as the Maiden swayed and flew past them all, darting like a feather in the center of the Hall, calling and crying with all her body—without a single sound—for Aldones, her one and only Lord of Light, only to remain forever unfulfilled.

Odd, thought Regis, how such true anguish could be portrayed by gesture alone, by the flow of limbs, without single twitch of her impassive face.

In the final instants of the dance, Alessandra, the white blossom, became a blossom with a fire-core. For, as she spun, like lightning, her form blurred, and only the flaming hair defined her center to the unbelieving eye.

When she was done, she lowered herself on her knees, head bent forward, red hair spilling down her back. She did not hear the roar of their applause, was still the Maiden. As only the truest dancer could be. . . .

Ruyven stood in silence a few feet away. He did not applaud like the rest of them. An ice-core lay about his heart, especially now, for deep beneath it all his limbs trembled, and he knew that another instant, and he too would give in. . . .

But to do that would be to fall under the spell of death, to acknowledge the end of Darkover, which she personified. And that—*never*.

"Bravo!" cried Lerrys Ridenow. "The most perfect Darkovan dance I have ever seen in my life!" And this time he was unhesitatingly joined by countless others.

Alessandra meanwhile had gotten up, breathless, and now joined Hastur at the refreshment table. Her eyes sparkled and she was flushed with excitement, still.

"You have exceeded all my expectations, *damisela,*" said Regis, smiling. "To tell you the truth, I have seen recorded performances of you, but *this*—" he threw up his hands helplessly, laughing with pleasure. "I never knew a human body could *do* such things!"

Alessa laughed, a clear sparkling laugh, her cheeks still aglow. "Really, my lord! You must remember I was not the first one to do this dance."

"Not the first, but nevertheless, the *first.* No one has ever danced *that* dance before. It is yours, alone." The cutting voice of Ruyven Di Asturien sounded across her shoulder, and as she turned, the young man joined them.

"Begging pardon, Lord Hastur, I had to interrupt." His intense gray eyes openly met Regis', and the Hastur smiled lightly in turn, liking this man's directness, honesty, even if he was in the "other camp."

"I take that as a compliment, from you, of all people." said Alessa, looking up boldly to meet Di Asturien's gaze. Again he saw that *otherness* in her, the Terran polish that at moments was superimposed over her otherwise well-schooled Darkovan manner. Involuntarily, he darkened again.

It did not escape her sharp attention. There was what he thought to be clear insolence in her green eyes now, as she continued watching him—so polite, fragile, yet bursting with power. It had, from the first moment, been thus with them, a tension. They walked on sword-blades, it seemed, in each other's presence, and could sense it, ricocheting in each other's thoughts. Both had adequate *laran* to know it.

His polite compliment would rather be a stone thrown at me. Why? Why does he hate me so? thought Alessa. *Is it because of what I am? Then he is a blind fool.*

Regis's weaker telepathic sense also detected the tension, the conflict. Fortunately, another second and Lerrys joined them, together with a young Comyn, almost a boy, fresh out of the Cadets. The youngster gaped at Alessa as if she were the blessed Cassilda, and stuttered some awkward compliment. Lerrys proceeded to chatter, and for a moment Regis breathed a sigh of relief. If only Di Asturien would stop glowering at her so. . . .

Out of the crowd, another fine-framed flame-haired person emerged, Alessa's twin heading toward them. They were nearly the same height, brother and sister. Again, Ruyven noticed all similarities and differences.

". . . How did you ever manage to learn all the Darkover dance moves?" Lerrys was saying, "Now that is what I don't quite understand. You were how old when you left? And who ever taught you all this?"

Alessa was used to such typical questions. "Lerrys, believe me, the Terrans are not as ignorant of Darkover customs as all think. There was, in fact, considerable archived material on Darkover tradition that I studied in the Performing Arts Academy. Besides, one of the instructors was Darkovan, and fairly well-versed in the circle dances, and the—"

"Alessa, I need to speak to you— Begging your pardon, Lord Hastur."

She turned, seeing Endreas, pale as a sheet. He'd been staring silently for some moments, waiting to speak. She saw by his expression that it was urgent.

"Excuse me please, Lord Regis," she spoke, then stepped away before Regis could even open his mouth.

Brother and sister conversed in quiet voices, Alessa's face suddenly went dead, and then she came back to Regis' group.

"Is there anything wrong, *damisela*?" he inquired with concern, seeing something in her face. Ruyven also gave her a look of intensity.

"Nothing wrong, Lord, nothing at all," she hurried to reassure, her mutable face trying to adjust itself back, her emerald eyes a mask. "I must go help my brother change into his costume—with your permission. He will now dance the Sword Dance."

And saying that, she disappeared with Endreas in the crowd. Before Regis could protest, they were joined by Dan Lawton, the Terran Legate, and the conversation took another turn.

Alessandra followed her brother back to the Aillard apartments. She closed the door behind them. "Turn the telepathic dampers on," she said.

"Why, Alessa? That is so paranoid—" Endreas began.

"Just do it." Her voice was on edge, rising. "If anyone hears this, *anyone,* everything is finished. In fact, do you realize, when you spoke to me in the ballroom, anyone could have heard, picked it up. . . ."

"Oh, come now! What, that Endreas Aillard is too sick to dance the Sword Dance, and that his sister will do it in his stead? It would be sacrilege, of course, but not fatal. You could endure some public shame, Alessa, could you not?" He was pale, washed out, but like her, dripping sarcasm.

Alessa flared. "First of all, I have not yet said I will do it! How dare you assume—"

"You haven't said it yet, but you will."

"Don't you understand the shameless thing you're asking me to do? They say I am so—*Terran*—but yes, even I can see the wrongness in this. For a woman to do a man's dance in traditional Darkover! To show men's ancient *kihar*, to hurt these old-minded people, so proud, so easily wounded! Why, I pity them simply imagining how they would react to me, profaning what they treasure most, that pathetically idiotic—and yet, so dear to me—pride of theirs! For their sake, I cannot do this!"

"For their sake, you must! Oh, stop lying to yourself, Alessa! Man's pride indeed!" he mocked, "I know what you think of that! It is your *kihar*, your pride as well as any man's, and there is no one that can tell you otherwise. Your Terran ways—they alone should give you the confidence in yourself. The dance is a man's dance, they all think. But no, it is a *human being's* dance, a Darkover dance! You as well as any man are suited to it! Need I say more?"

And she regarded him in growing silence, he continued: "By gods, Alessa, you know I wouldn't ask you if I had another choice. I am so weak now, so weak. It was thus since morning. I couldn't even stand up before them all, even if I tried. And you know all the steps already. . . . Here, sister. Take the costume and put it on. We're still the same size, remember? Here . . . bind your hair. No one will ever know the difference between us. And the dance, it must be danced, is all I can say. Somehow, for the sake of all things."

"Yes . . ." she said then, beginning to tremble as she took the clothing from his outstretched hand. "At least this dance. I've always wanted to do this. Only this once, then. For Darkover. . . ."

Once more the ballroom lights in Comyn Castle were dimmed. Only this time they winked out into total darkness. Two torches appeared, flickering, as Guardsmen came to the center of the room carrying the ceremonial swords, placing them on the floor, crossed. They moved away. The man to come out was to be Endreas, one of the best dancers in Thendara. Indeed, like sister, like brother.

From a distance, a single drone-pipe wailed, and slowly awakening, was followed by the rhythm of drums. Some odd quality, quickening one's heart since the oldest time remembered, was inherent in this dance only.

The dancer, beating out the rhythm with his feet, came out in crimson and black, with a tight scarf headdress—a fierce barbaric garb of ages long gone. It never failed to move the audience, that rhythm, and that look of ancient mountain pride.

The Hall watched him in silence.

There was something wild, animalistic about the perfect sharp movements, a precision of the highest class. And yet, unlike the previous dancer, his sister, Regis thought, this one had a different quality about him—for grace and control were now augmented by greater strength and sharpness, and an odd hard-to-pinpoint sensual intensity that was masculine to the core. It captivated, drew one. . . .

The pulse-beat grew to a crescendo, as the dancer

spun, having snatched the swords like a fierce catman. Steel flashed, contorted, in an optical illusion of currents of bent lightning, as the swords were cleverly manipulated in elaborate gestures that emulated an ancient battle, fought to the death—for in this dance the opponent was always oneself.

He is like Dyan . . . like Dyan, all these years ago, who had danced the Sword Dance that once, and made the women swoon. . . .

And indeed, in Regis' blurring mind's eye, he again feverishly thought he saw the dark Lord Ardais, flashing past them all, full of leashed violence, in the wildness of the dance, as once he had been—proud, and beautiful and cruel, and oh-so-alive. . . . Was this night, then, to be filled only with memories of the past? Or was it that such memories were evoked by a far-too-quickly changing present?

At last, the drums and cymbals stilled with one final great crash, instilling barbaric terror. . . . The figure of crimson and black was, for the last instant, a spinning torch. And then, like a stone statue, unbelievably, it froze, swords poised overhead.

Only—the black head-scarf had come undone. Long flaming Sharra-hair spilled forth, down his/her shoulders, and with it spilled eternal shame.

Alessandra Aillard paused only a second, only long enough to *understand*, to feel the scarf slipping away, unraveling. She then crumpled away in a dead faint—its deathly quality only to be matched by the shocked absolute silence in the great Comyn Hall.

Ruyven was at her side when she came to herself, to the roar of scandalous babble all around her. He barely needed Regis to tell him to attend to her.

Alessa was pale as a sheet, the fact further emphasized by the redness of her hair, the culprit, scattered about her small frame. In the crowd, at some instant, she thought she saw her sister's equally pale tragic face. Not even Daniella could help *now.*

"I must leave," Alessa barely mouthed, raising her clear green eyes to him, and Ruyven wordlessly nodded, holding her up with his strong hands, helping her rise. The disturbed crowd made a wide berth around them. As they were quickly making their way out of the Hall, cries were heard: ". . . shameless hussy! She is no Aillard, never! Who allowed this outrage? I thought it was Endreas Aillard, truly, all along . . ." But mixed in with all these, other voices spoke: "But oh, what a brilliant dance that was! Never had a man danced so well as that woman, pretending to be a man! It still boils my blood. Why, she was better than that brother of hers, Endreas, ever was, and he's one of the best!"

They were out in the corridor when Ruyven let her walk on her own. But it was as if he weren't even there. Alessa walked, her eyes unseeing. She was stoic, ramrod-straight.

Ruyven involuntarily felt himself softening. His heart went out to her, because she was so proud, so steady, even when inside she was broken most.

"*Damisela . . .*" he said, his indifferent voice on the verge of breaking, "I will escort you back to the Aillard Quarters."

"I have never fainted before. I never knew what it was like: a moment of not wanting to be alive. . . ." Her words were measured, toneless. She never heard him.

"Come, you must change out of this unfortunate

costume, lady. Change and then rest. You'll need the rest, for difficult times might be now before you.

"Rest . . ." she echoed, her full lower lip trembling. Her face never moved a muscle, yet suddenly one after another, large tears started rolling down her cheeks.

I have wanted so hard to come back to this violet planet that is my home. All the time, even when I danced before millions, I only wanted to come back, and dance one single true dance, the kind that alone makes my blood quicken in my veins. . . .

She looked up to meet the steel eyes of this man who had, it seemed, read her mind. Only—they were steel no longer.

"You were insolent indeed, my lady. I would not have done what you have done out there. Ever."

She flared. "You, *Dom*? But you are not myself! And—you do not dance. . . ."

"And yet, dancing has nothing to do with it. You have come back to Darkover, so damn confident that your dual experience would be enough—old married to new, as they say—enough to modify everything here to your whim, and yet, remain apparently 'Darkovan.' Like our Hastur here, who thinks that appearances alone matter."

"Regis Hastur thinks nothing of the sort. He *knows*. He alone of all of you can truly see the reality, the fact that the only constant is change, and that the Comyn will eventually fall under its influence or else stagnate and rot, sacred tradition and all!"

"Yes," he said softly, "I see how sacred indeed it is to *you*."

"More than you think, son of a dying breed!" she exclaimed, for once her eyes truly wild, and then, unexpected to both of them, burst into loud racking sobs, her body doubled over, her gold-scarlet hair falling over her face, this time not to bring shame, but to hide the shame of tears.

He stiffened, also wanting to weep for some reason and, not knowing what to do, stood silent before her. Meanwhile, she sobbed in her own peculiar privacy, no longer caring, until her sobs quieted naturally into a dead peace.

They did not know it, did not read each other's souls, but both of them in those moments had lamented the inevitable dilemma of Darkover.

"Forgive me, Alessandra," Ruyven said gruffly. "I am upsetting you further, not that you need to be even reminded of what just happened, but—there is one thing I must know. *Why?* Truly, please tell me why did you do it? Why do this thing, knowingly? Is it because you wanted so much to show that even in this area, this long-held traditional matter, you can improve upon the old? For I admit, you *have.* But was it really worth all the needless hurt, for all of us, just to *prove* that?"

"Why do you . . . care?"

"I only want to understand—you . . ."

Her reddened eyes lifted to meet his. "Well, then, I'll tell you, *Dom* . . ." She paused. "I didn't want to dance the Sword Dance. Well, maybe theoretically I did, as would an artist desire to engage in her art. But in reality, I knew exactly what it would mean. It's just that something compelled me, oddly, something in my brother Endreas' words. He could not dance, out of illness—"

"And what of that? Some other Thendaran performer could have danced in his stead, someone other than yourself—as is proper, a man. Or, at worst, the whole thing could have been canceled—such things happened before."

"No!" she spoke hurriedly, interrupted. And then, "Don't you see, can't you understand what I'm trying to say now? Not that the dance itself mattered—rather, it is whether or not I *myself* could have *done what had to be done,* helped it along. I speak of that very tradition that you hold so dear. I wanted it to be *unbroken.* Others maybe, others would cancel the event. But I wanted so badly to do something Darkovan. To be, if only for an instant, more Darkovan than I could ever possibly be, in my position as a woman of Comyn. For I am, in the eyes of all, less than Darkovan, despite my blood. By doing that, by doing more than possible, more than is allowable for one such as myself, I would have shown to myself at last what I truly *am.* That I am truly complete—Comyn, Terran, human."

He watched her steadily, and for once his gray eyes were receptive. "I have spoken in Council, on the day you swore the Aillard Oath, something that now makes even better sense to me, having heard you out. I have said, *damisela,* that a prodigal son or daughter must still be able to speak the language of their parents, to be allowed back."

"And do you, Comyn man, do you understand the language that I speak?" she whispered, looking into his eyes. "I am the prodigal daughter, having come back to claim my birthright. . . . Not to rule Aillard, but rather, because I must, to *serve.* I have come back and brought with me a different new heritage, in addition to the old one. And with that new heritage, intermingled with the old, I speak to you. So, then, can you *understand?*"

Regis Hastur was surprised to see, after midnight had struck on Festival Night, that Alessandra Kyrielle Aillard, Heir Designate to the Domain, came back into the ballroom. Clad in a proper womanly dress, she was exquisite, in fact, her hair properly coiffed, her eyes shining like green metal, calm and haughty, as if nothing had happened. And yet, new things also appeared to be in her eyes.

And even more curious was the fact that the Comyn, when they saw her returned, did not immediately raise the racket of protest that Regis was getting so used to. Was there actually a new feeling in the air? And was it at all possible, that the Comyn knew, or were learning to forgive?

Of course, there were some who whispered and pointed at Alessa unbelievingly. They wondered at the extent of her insolence. And then there were others, who actually gave her glances of consideration.

Regis, inwardly fully sympathetic, had to put on at least a show of sternness. However, he approached her, and gently questioned her. Dan Lawton was not far behind. The Legate was bursting to know what exactly lay behind this whole "charade," as he thought. More politics?

There were several unobtrusive observers in the ballroom. Unobtrusive, if one can thus call a whole Terran reporting correspondent cadre, in the middle of a native Darkovan event. However, their video equipment was well-hidden indeed. They had recorded *both* the dances, and already the material was being processed to be broadcast intergalactically. . . .

Overall, the Comyn noticed Hastur's reaction to Alessandra, how he accepted her presence despite all things being as they were. But what surprised everyone truly was when the Di Asturien second son, known for his respect of old ways, approached this Aillard-Terran upstart and led her out for one of the couple dances.

To dance, so nonchalantly, after all *that!*

But Alessa was far from nonchalant. Indeed, as Ruyven's arm closed tight about her waist, and his dark-curled head leaned close above hers, Alessa felt herself reddening deeply, for she could read his thoughts. And what his thoughts clearly implied sent a warmth coursing through her limbs, because, for once, his intensity wore no mask.

For, Ruyven Di Asturien, when he finally heard the true *voice* of the prodigal daughter of Darkover, found that indeed they could still speak the same tongue, for it was the same tongue that lies deep in any Darkovan heart. Old or new did not matter. Neither did stagnation and change. It was only the fact that both coexisted and will continue to coexist on the paradox planet Darkover.

Simple, wasn't it now? *Or maybe not,* thought Regis. Seeing Alessa and Ruyven on the dance floor, light, young, so well-matched, it occurred to Regis Hastur that if the Di Asturien could accept her, then, eventually, so would Darkover. It would welcome Alessandra Aillard, for she had spoken out in the language of blood. . . .

Now, thought Regis, *if only Darkover would understand how relative things are indeed. . . . Then, Darkover itself might turn around and be accepted back into the arms of the Terran Empire whose prodigal child, some claimed, it was.*

But for now, at the rate things were going, the Hastur was prepared for anything. This, of course, included a heat wave in the Hellers, or—under those rare circumstances when memories and dreams overtake present reality—a missing moon from the sky of Darkover.

There is Always Someone

by Jacquie Groom

This story came from the Netherlands. I usually return stories which come to me from overseas because in all my years of editing I have very rarely (read almost never*) found a story from anyone not a native of America or England who can write well enough in English to make it worth the trouble of reading—even for me, let alone my readers! (If English is your native language be sure to tell me.) If this is chauvinism, you'll have to prove me wrong. (I'm speaking from experience.)*

Anyhow, I read this one and liked it; and couldn't resist the opportunity to share it with you. This is the first professional sale by Jacquie Groom who says she "practically hit the ceiling when your letter" of acceptance arrived. She is English—see?—but she has lived everywhere from the Falkland Islands to the Netherlands.

This story deals with a subject people are always writing about—usually badly; I'm glad to see it well done for once.

I've no friends on this planet anyway. And no living relatives anywhere."

Andrew Carr, The Forbidden Tower

"So you're really going to Cottman IV?"

Jenny, her face defiant, looked up at Phil. "I have to," she repeated. "I'm sorry I didn't tell you sooner but . . ."

Phil finished her sentence for her. "But when it comes down to it, this Andrew Carr means more to you than I do."

Tears in her eyes, Jenny shook her head. "It's not that. I love you. But I love Andy, too. We've been friends since I was six. And now he's in trouble. And if I don't do everything I can to help him, I'll never be able to live with myself." Jenny sat down, rummaging in her pockets for a handkerchief. Her search unsuccessful, she sniffed defiantly. "Please try to understand, Phil."

Phil looked unconvinced. He picked up the screen transcripts Jenny had left lying on the table. The first was a short message from Carr, dated some twelve months ago. *"Dear Jen,"* it read. *"Change of plans. Have decided to stay on Cottman IV. The strangest thing has happened. Will write later."*

Phil looked at her. "Did he write?"

Jenny shook her head. "I wrote, and got no answer. Well, things do go astray. And he's hardly the greatest correspondent. But then I tried to reach him through Comms. That failed, too. So I made an official request to Personnel for a status report. That's what they sent," she said, pointing to the second sheet of paper.

"Andrew Carr, Cottman IV. Mapping and Exploration. Missing, presumed dead following plane crash," Phil read. "I'm sorry, love," he said. "So he's dead. But there's nothing you can do about it now. I know you've always fancied yourself in love with him, but perhaps now you can get on with your life. The time

for hero worship is over." He tried to put an arm around Jenny, but she shrugged it off.

"But he's not dead. I'm sure of it. And I could always tell if anything was wrong with him. No one else seems to be doing anything about it, so I'm going to do my best. And if you don't like it, Phil, that is your problem." Jenny stormed out of his quarters, banging the door behind her.

There was plenty of time for thinking on the journey between the Finorra Space Station and Cottman IV. Jenny, surprised at how upset Phil had been on her departure, had buried herself in her studies. She meant to be fully prepared for Darkover as she had soon learned to call her destination. But Phil's parting words had a habit of creeping in, disturbing her work, spinning round her brain in those quiet moments. "I hope you find this Carr," he had said, his voice harsh to hide the pain. "Dead or alive, I hope you find him. Perhaps then you can bury the myth you've created. For until the Carr you carry around in your mind is dead, there will be no chance for any of us mere mortals." Then he'd kissed her and fled from the departure lounge.

Had she really created a myth around Andy Carr? He'd been her best friend throughout her schooldays. Together they had ridden, swam, studied, talked. They had even dated once or twice, though that had not worked out. He had eventually admitted that although he liked her, she was too much like a sister to him. But she could not remember a time when she had not loved him. She'd followed him into the Space Service, unable to bear their home town once he had left.

Darkover, on a winter's night, seemed cold and forbidding. Jenny shivered violently as she walked the short distance to the spaceport. She'd been in Thendara almost two weeks, and could not help wondering if moving there had been the biggest mistake of her life. She missed Phil more than she thought possible. No one seemed to know anything about Carr. He'd been here such a short time; had made no friends. After casual enquiries had drawn a blank, she moved on to more official channels.

The head of Mapping and Exploration had been kind but definite. No one could have survived the crash. He'd shown her aerial views of the area they'd gone down in, stats on climate and terrain. Life expectancy? Nil. The Missing status, he'd explained, was just a formality, due to no formal sighting of a body or return of name tags. Just a formality.

Just a formality. Jenny found that hard to accept. Somehow, she felt very close to Andy; his rare smile haunted her dreams. She tried to shut her mind and concentrate on work. Although she was very good at her job, there never seemed to be quite enough going on in the Communication Department to keep her busy. She spent more and more time in Mapping and Exploration, getting to know the staff, getting to know Darkover. When a new expedition was being set up, she was an obvious choice as Comms expert.

The Head called her into his office. "I want you to understand, Jenny, the extreme sensitivity of this operation. For the first time we are venturing out into Darkover, without using native guides. We mean to use our own maps and set up a series of beacons to aid in aerial navigation. It's not going to be a picnic, so speak up if you don't feel up to the job."

Jenny would have done anything to get out of Headquarters, and she was soon packing for the expedition. She barely looked back at the bright lights of the Trade City when, in the dead of night, their helicopter lifted off and headed toward the distant mountains.

She was kept busy, maintaining contact between the various bases and setting up the comms beacons. One evening they pitched camp on a plateau high in the mountains. Dozing in front of the campfire, she tried to imagine how Andy would look. Hardly the tall, skinny teenager she had last seen! As she thought of him, the picture in her mind seemed to change, as if he aged there and then, hair longer, face more worn, but with such a look of contentment. As she lay there, almost breathless, the picture seemed to widen, and shadowy figures took their places around him. Two women, alike yet different, red hair billowing out around their lovely faces. And a man, short, almost frail looking, but with such a caring, loving, all-embracing smile. Half scared, half reluctant to break the image, Jenny sat up and shook her head violently. "The air must be getting thin," she remarked to one of her companions. "I'm having the strangest dreams. . . ."

She woke first in the morning, and, in spite of orders, slipped out of the camp, determined to spend some time alone with the spectacular scenery. The weather was good, relatively speaking. She knew, from what she had been able to glean from Records, that Andrew's plane had last reported in from near these coordinates. If she said good-bye to him, alone, in this lonely spot, perhaps she could get on with her life. Yet . . . she could not rid her mind of the strange vision she had seen.

About half a mile from the camp, she sat and stared, lost in thoughts and memories. She was roused from her dreams by shouts, screams, dreadful sounds of panic and pain. Fear rising, she headed back toward the camp, her feelings in turmoil. Twice she nearly lost her footing on the rocky mountain track. As she turned the corner, a scene of total devastation met her. Bodies sprawled on the ground, equipment smashed and broken; there was nothing left. Biting her lip to prevent herself from screaming, she tiptoed into the ruins of the camp and surveyed the damage. Trying hard not to look at the mutilated remains of her colleagues, she checked out the comms equipment. Dead. The food was gone, and so was the weapons box.

"Think, Jennifer," she said to herself, over and over, "What should you do now? What do Instructions say?" Pacing round and round, hoping to find some vestige of civilization, some item left untouched, she finally sat down by the cliff edge and put her head in her hands.

"Some friend you are, Andrew Carr," she said out loud. "A girl comes halfway across the galaxy to help you, and this is what happens." The anger made her feel slightly better. "This is the last time I ever copy you, Andy," she called out across the ravine. "From now on, I lead my own life. Understand?"

I understand.

Jenny thought she was hearing things. Andrew's voice, loud and clear. She turned round, fully expecting to see him there. Nothing. And yet . . .

"Am I dead, too?" she asked, of no one in particular. "Is this heaven or hell I've wandered into?" In reply, she heard a faint laugh.

Jenny, keep calm. We'll be with you soon. You'll be safe.

"Andy? Is that really you?"

Shh. Don't talk now. The bandits might still be around. Keep calm, we'll be with you soon.

Keep calm. It was the hardest thing she had ever had to do. She could not decide if she had really heard the voices, or if she was hallucinating. Torn between her heart telling her to stay put and her head demanding she pack up what belongings she could and make her way back to the chopper, she finally gave way to the tears she had refused to shed.

"Jenny? It really is you!"

"Andy?" Jenny ran, and buried herself in his broad chest. When she emerged, she looked up at her friend. "They said you were dead. I knew you weren't. But how did you hear me?"

"I'll explain later," he said, motioning her toward where another man stood, holding the reins of two horses. "This is Damon Ridenow."

"Yes," Jenny said. "I mean, I saw you in my dreams. With Andy. This is all so confusing."

"Ann'dra," Damon said, touching his friend on the shoulder, "I think we should get back to Armida. There is nothing more we can do here. But the authorities should be told."

"There's something else," Jenny blurted. "The weapons box is missing, too." She found herself blushing, suddenly ashamed. "There were two blasters in it."

Damon Ridenow's face turned pale. "That is indeed a serious matter. The Terrans have agreed to uphold the Compact; such a breach will not easily be forgiven."

Andrew, however, was thinking along different lines. "Usual issue safety box?" he asked. "Tamper-proof? Two keys?" Jenny nodded, pointing to the bodies of the joint leaders of the expedition. Andrew hurriedly examined them, then returned, holding two keys. "They'll have fun trying to open that box," he said, dropping the keys in his pocket as he helped Jenny onto his horse.

"Perhaps," remarked Damon. "But that doesn't excuse the flaunting of our rules."

Jenny, her mind still awhirl, found she was shaking so much that she could barely hang on to the reins. Only Andrew's strong arms around her seemed to offer any comfort. He had changed so! He seemed so rugged, so confident, totally adapted to his surroundings. She found herself envying him; he had obviously found a place for himself.

Suddenly the sky lit up with a massive explosion. Andrew's horse shied, and for a moment Jenny thought she would fall off. Then, following Damon's lead, they galloped off in the direction of the blast.

For the second time that day, Jenny shut her eyes as a horrible scene met her eyes. Turning away, she buried her face in the horse's flank, breathing in the hot, sweaty smell. Eventually, Andrew came up behind her.

"Shouldn't have tried to open the box, should they?

Still, they got what they deserved for the murder of your friends."

Jenny looked up at Damon's stern face. "Will you still report me for breaking the Compact?" she asked, voice shaking.

Damon did not answer.

"I still can't believe I was quite so stupid," Jenny said, when, dressed in warm clothing and well fed, she sat by the fire with Callista and Ellemir. "Andy never needed me. I just always tagged along. But this time he went without telling me."

"I think it is touching," Callistra said in her quiet voice. "To have friends that will give up everything for you."

"You gave up everything for me," Andrew said, his voice gentle as he looked into his wife's eyes.

Callista lowered her eyes. "But I gained so much, too. Jenny has gained nothing."

"But I have," refuted Jenny, staring into the fire. "I set out to find Andy, and I did. Or rather," she grimaced, "he found me. But seriously. I think I've finally learned to stand on my own two feet. I've got to do what I want to do, instead of trying to follow in Andy's footsteps."

Ellemir shook her head. "You could still follow him, you know. You have some *laran*; that was how we could hear your cries. And most probably why you were so close to Ann'dra. You could join us here, in the Forbidden Tower. There is much to be done."

Looking around, at the friendly, cozy room where they sat, Jenny was sorely tempted. But finally, she shook her head. "I've got to discover *my* special place in life," she said. "And to start with, I owe an apology to someone back at Fionarra Station." She turned to Andrew, and raised her glass. "Andy Carr is dead. Long live *Dom* Ann'dra Lanart!"

Reunion

by Lawrence Schimel

Male readers never get tired of trying to tell me I am prejudiced against male writers—maybe that is because, quite erroneously, I have been tagged as "feminist" and so every male who appears in one of my anthologies takes on the character of a "token male."

I can only say that, considering everything, including the years when women were believed never to have a fair shake in fantasy, it's only right men should feel some prejudice, too, perhaps. But let's remember that our dear Don Wollheim, who started this whole thing, was himself a male, and didn't mind being a token male.

Lawrence Schimel is a sophomore at Yale University, who writes, draws, and edits for publications on campus.

He says of this story, "It was a viewpoint on Amazon life that I felt was missing in what Darkover literature I had read. Therefore, I felt obligated to supply it."

Stelen and his son walked toward the Guild House, the boy clinging to him as he grew more tired. As he looked about them in the fading light, Stelen remembered the last time he had seen these streets, painfully bright on the morning of his fifth birthday when he was forced to go to live with his father. Stelen smiled, remembering the tantrum he had thrown when they made him leave. The Amazon who was taking him to his father's domains had tied him to the saddle to insure he'd make the entire trip with her and not slip off and return to the Guild House.

Stelen blinked as his eyes became full. *I hated her so much for sending me away. I didn't want to leave.*

Praise Avarra Copal will never go through that. Stelen looked down at his son Copal. Although Alamena had decided to live in the Guild House Stelen saw both her and his son every day. For Copal, turning five just meant a change in which house he slept in rather than a nightmare. He still saw his mother every day, excepting times like this trip to visit his grandmother. *In twenty-two years I have not seen my mother.*

Seeing his own son turn five and painlessly leave his mother made Stelen decide to try and make peace with his own mother. *If she's still alive.* Stelen was ashamed that he didn't even know.

Alamena had wanted to come along with them, but their daughter Elena was too young to make the trip. Elena would grow up in the Guild House with her mother, but would always be free to live with her father whenever she wished. Alamena would not pressure her daughter into joining, and would be just as happy if her daughter never experienced the things which forced her to join the Renunciates.

Stelen had not forgiven his mother for choosing the Renunciates over him until he met Alamena. Hearing what she had suffered, he realized that he knew nothing about his mother save her name. Why she had chosen the Free Amazons he could only guess, and the speculation was never pleasant.

All too soon they were at the Guild House, standing together before the door but making no move toward it. *This is it. Now I find out everything.* He tried to compose himself, until Copal's silent fidgeting made him knock on the door which opened at his touch.

"I was beginning to wonder if you were going to knock or were just admiring the new coat of paint Kyella put on the door yesterday." The Renunciate, with dark eyes and close-shorn black hair, holding the door open for them came only to Stelen's shoulder.

While the woman was being friendly, Stelen realized that what she had said was all the opening he was going to get. *No one said this was going to be easy.* Still, Stelen admired what she was doing, for she made him draw the strength from within himself to ask, "I'd like to see Magen n'ha Ramilys." *It is started.*

"Who shall I say is asking for her?"

Shall I go by name? And as her son or his? "Her son and her grandson. Tell her that it is her son."

The woman stared at them for a moment. "I'll let her know you've come. I was beginning to doubt you. Especially when she took ill." She considered him again, their gazes locked. "I'm glad you proved me wrong."

She disappeared while he considered what she had said, returning soon with an older woman, wrapped against the night chill. She was much older now, but still the same woman he remembered. Stelen stood in the doorframe unable to move.

"Come," she whispered to him. "Come meet your mother."

And he came to her, bringing his son with him.

A Way Through the Fog

by Patricia Cirone

Patricia Cirone says "I always love reading your intros. Funny, before I started writing I never bothered with that 'stuff.' Now it's the first thing I read."

Well, perspective is everything in life. I was once asked whether I was editing for readers or writers. (WHY should that be mutually exclusive?) I can't help saying "both." Because without writers, readers would have nothing to read; but without readers, we writers would be talking to ourselves—like the minister who is preaching to the choir.

We're both important.

Pat Cirone has appeared in these anthologies before, and she says that her biography is mostly the same as last time. "If that's not enough, go ahead and make something up." Which is why I always tell my writers to update their biographies; otherwise I will *go ahead and make something up, and it might not be to your taste.*

As all experts do, but they often aren't so honest about it—they call it research.

The rain lashed against the solid walls of the hall. Irina cupped her hand around the flame of the lighting candle as she walked forward, to prevent stray gusts of air from blowing it out. In the chamber behind her, the large outer doors of the hall thudded open and swiftly shut again. The entire clan was gathering.

Not really clan, Irina thought. In the five generations since the first families had settled here on the shore, nestled against the protecting walls of the surrounding cliffs, they had grown into more village than large family.

Still, all would come tonight to honor the passing of her father.

Irina paused in her lighting of the candles and blinked back tears as she stared at the bier in the center of the room. It was so hard to realize he was dead; he had always been so large, so strong, so . . . *alive*. Yet two days ago, when heaving the heavy nets over the side of the boat, he had clutched his chest and fallen to the deck beneath him.

The men had carried him in. For a day, he had lain there in his bed, white and unmoving. Then, with little more than a sigh, he was gone.

Irina moved to the next candle. Tonight, they would all gather here to honor the man who'd been their headman, their *dai*.

"You'd better open the doors, now, dear," Anna said softly, from behind her.

Irina sighed. It had been peaceful here, alone with her father, completing yet another of the tasks that had kept her too busy to think.

Now the families would come in, the men large and awkward at being confined within walls, the women bustling and sympathetic, the children rain-washed, hushed and uncomfortable, straining to break free. And she would have to talk to them all, and let at least some of her numbed feelings show, lest she be thought heartless. She hoped desperately that the tears she hadn't once let fall would stay hidden, for her pride was all that stood between her and desolation.

"Is Mardic ready?" she asked Anna in a voice that was firm and steady.

"Yes, all dressed in his black goodstuff. . . . Don't you think it would be better if the boy just slipped in later?" Anna asked anxiously of her one remaining nurseling.

"No. His place is here," Irina said firmly.

"It's just so hard on him," Anna murmured.

"He's nearly ten," Irina replied. "He'll have to grow up fast."

"Yes," Anna sighed, and went off to send Mardic down.

Yes, Mardic would have to grow up fast now. As she would herself. No more carefree days at her father's side hauling up sails and heaving nets into the spray while letting all the women's duties fall to Anna. Without an older male relative, the presence of a young unmarried girl on the boats would be looked askance. Besides, once Mardic started going out on the boats, Anna would go, seeking a home with lots of the small children she loved so much. She had made that clear enough over the past year, but Irina had been pushing the day far off in her mind.

Now it was upon her. With Father dead, Mardic would have to take his place, even though he was just nine. And she would have to assume the heavy responsibility of running the house, of the gathering,

ing, the canning and the cooking. It didn't matter that she hated most of the chores. Someone had to do them. And at least she knew *how;* her mother and Anna had made sure of that.

But she would miss the sea.

Mardic arrived, putting a quick end to her moment of respite. Irina opened the double doors to the hall's inner chamber, and the fishermen and their wives and children began to flow in.

The evening was as long as she had dreaded, and the smell of damp wool and wet hair became nearly overpowering. Everyone was uncomfortable: feet cramped into "best" shoes, bodies stuck to rain-soaked clothes. And the men were as clumsy around words as they were graceful with nets and sails.

Irina was glad to notice when the fat white candles had burned halfway, and the women with children began to slip out of the hall to go home.

Irina glanced at her young brother and noticed his eyes starting to droop. Like her, Mardic had been up since dawn, helping with the many tasks to ready the hall and themselves for tonight. But even though her own eyes wanted to do the same, neither of them could afford to, tonight.

"Stay awake!" she hissed fiercely. "And stand tall."

He did, firming his chin and squaring his shoulders. Irina felt a pang of pride in him.

Hard as this was for her, at eighteen, how much harder this was for him, at only nine. She knew: she had been just nine when she had stood in Mardic's place and received condolences on their mother, lost in Mardic's birth.

Now Mardic had no one but her. She'd see he didn't lack, she vowed. She'd see them both through any awkwardnesses of him succeeding to their father's post so young, and willingly bear the responsibilities she had hoped to avoid for at least another year.

Paolo, her father's right hand and the second most important man in the village, approached her.

"We'll take him out at first light tomorrow," he said in his deep voice. "Weather providing, of course."

"Thank you," Irina murmured. "Mardic and I will ship on . . ." her voice choked, thinking of the brief finality of seeing her father's body given to the sea.

"Afterward . . ." Paolo twisted his damp woolen cap. "Well, you don't have to worry, Mistress. Whoever the men elect dai will make sure you and the boy are taken care of."

"Elect! What do you mean?! Mardic is dai now," Irina protested, her eyes snapping wide awake with shock and confusion.

"Mardic! He's only a boy!"

"He's Father's son. He's dai, now, as Father, Grandfather, Great-grandfather—as five generations were before him."

"Mistress, I know. But we're not one of those Domains, as they're calling them now, with *vai dom's* this and *vai dom's* that. We're a working village, and we need a leader, not a nine-year-old boy as dai. He's not even old enough to ride the boats!"

"He nearly is. He'll be ten in a few months. And he has the weather sense."

"He shows the weather sense already?" Paolo asked, astonished.

"Well, no. But he will. The men of my family have always had the weather sense; that's why they're dai."

"I know that, Mistress. And I don't know *how* we'll do without your father. But we can't not fish for five years while we wait for Mardic to grow up and go through threshold sickness and see if he really *has* got the sense. We need someone to lead now. Someone who knows the boats, knows the fish, and knows the men."

"I know the boats. I've been going out with my father for eight years. I know every one of you, too. And I know fish," Irina declared desperately.

Paolo spluttered, while the growing circle of fishermen and women looked from one to the other.

"You! You're saying you're going to be dai, now? It's not just that you're female. Mhari here has run her own boat for fifteen years, with nary a life lost, since her husband Teo was taken. But you're only eighteen! I've been working the seas for forty years. Raoul for thirty. And you want to set yourself up as leader over us? It's not as if you have the weather sense, that I *do* know."

Irina bit her lip in vexation. It gnawed at her that she didn't have the weather sense, that she had failed her father in that one important respect. Especially since she *had* gone through threshold sickness. All for nothing, apparently. It could be foggy, or sunny, or masses of thunderclouds outside, and she'd never know the difference until she stuck her nose outside the hall, let alone be able to tell what the weather would be like one, two, or three days ahead.

"But only Dygardis, of the whole village, has even a smattering of the weather sense, and his is so erratic it's practically useless. So why *not* me? Not as dai, I don't want that, but as sort of leader, to hold it for Mardic. You owe my father, my family that much."

"And what if the boy doesn't get the weather sense?

Or dies in the getting? Your family doesn't grow too many sons and daughters to adulthood, you know."

The swift hurt of remembering the beloved older brother, and the three children between her and Mardic stabbed through Irina, making her stand even straighter. "Then you've lost nothing," Irina said. "You can have your electing then."

Paolo shook his head. "I don't know, lass. I'd do a lot for your father, but this. . . ."

"You owe it to him," Irina pleaded, tears in her eyes. "You owe it to Grandfather. You owe it to Mardic! It's not his fault he's only nine. You'd keep a boat for him, if it was father's *boat* we were talking about."

Paolo looked upset, for it was true, a boat was kept—fished, but kept—for the young sons or daughters of a fisherman. Family was very important in a community that lost so many so young and so sudden.

"Try it," Irina pleaded. "At least try it. Until Mardic's sixteen. Until we *know*."

"Aye. Until we know. Until we can get one of those magic-sniffers. Those, what-d'you call them—*laranzus*. Aye, until we get one of 'em to come look at the boy and say whether he'll get the sense or no. Not a day longer." Paolo glanced around the circle, and the others nodded agreement with him.

Irina swallowed, tasting both victory and defeat. "Very well."

The men shook their heads, still muttering over the turn of events, and shuffled out. Mhari paused to brush her hand on Irina's shoulder, then followed the rest.

Irina stared at her father's bier, wondering what she had done. *She* couldn't be leader. *She,* who didn't even want a household, couldn't bear the weight of the entire *village* on her shoulders.

But what else could she have done? She couldn't let them whisk Mardic's heritage away from him. Why, if they had named someone else, it could be twenty, twenty-five years before Mardic could win back his rightful position. And whoever they named was sure to have sons who felt *they* should succeed their father, not Mardic, even if he did develop the weather sense. Which, Irina knew, wasn't as sure as she had declared it, here in the hall.

No, she had had to do it. But she shuddered at what lay before her.

It would be up to her to lead the boats out into the sunshine and the waves and bring them back safely. The fathers and the husbands and the sons, and a few of the mothers and the daughters—their lives would in her hands. And she didn't even have the *laran* that would keep them safe; she didn't have the weather sense.

"Oh, Da," she cried, and, for the first time since he'd died, Irina knelt by her father's body and wept.

Dawn came swiftly.

Irina greeted it with red eyes and a sense of impending doom, too young to know that what she was feeling was more truly a mixture of fear and grief. She and Mardic walked hand-in-hand to the boat where their father's body had been carried.

It was gloomy out, sullen and overcast. If it had been a regular day, the boats would have stayed in the harbor, and fingers and toes would have stayed busy mending nets and sails. But today's would not be a long journey, only out to the mouth of the harbor and back. Even if the storm of last night returned, the boats would make it back safely.

Silently they cast off. It seemed but moments later and her father's body was being slipped into the sea that had nurtured him. Once back on the shore, Irina walked home and removed her heavy, brown, woolen dress. The next time she went out on the boats she would be wearing the loose breeches the few women who fished wore. And she would be working in the boats as she never had in her carefree days under her father's tutelage, when the wind on her face had been fun and the spray of salt water exciting. Irina's hands shook and her heart felt leaden at the thought of what she had undertaken to do.

But the next morning the rains had returned, beating upon the shore with a sullen persistence. Sighing, Irina decided to use her reprieve to collect lumen roots from the caves.

She remembered the first time her mother had taken her, and how vast and dark the tunnels that snaked through the cliffs had seemed. She still cherished the feeling of awe the caverns generated in her, but she never felt afraid of them as many of the others did. Somehow, she always knew her way, even when going down a side tunnel she had never explored before. This time was no different, and she returned with two heavily laden baskets for the root cellar.

She spent the rest of the afternoon helping Anna sort through her father's clothes, laying some aside for Mardic, consigning some to the sewing basket for scraps, and bundling up the rest to pass on to the other men. It wasn't as if her father had had that much. When they were through, his room was swept clean. Irina closed the door behind her with a sound of finality.

The next morning, Irina knew before she got up that the boats would be going out that day. Not because of any magical arrival of the weather sense, but because the morning star and the last of the four moons shone clear through her high bedroom window.

She rolled out of the bed and put her feet on the cold stone floor. Shivering, she pulled the heavy, unbleached nightgown off her head and donned her workmanlike breeches. A heavy white shirt and a thick woolen sweater soon followed. She hurried downstairs for some herb tea, cupping its warmth to her body as the sky faded into the pearly gray of dawn.

Briskly she walked down to the shore, swinging her arms to warm herself, missing the vital presence of her Da.

Most of the men were already down by the boats; the rest were trickling in. Irina saw Paolo step over to Dygardis, talking to him. She saw Dygardis shrug. Paolo pressed harder. Dygardis shook his head, then waved toward the glowing sun and lack of clouds as if to say the whole day would be like this. Irina felt one small knot in the tangle of anxiety within her dissolve.

She clambered onto Paolo's boat, the lead boat, and rubbed her hands together to limber up her cold, stiff muscles. Soon the work of raising the sails and readying the nets warmed her. After the first few anxious hours, Irina relaxed and settled into the familiar routine. She missed the familiar teasing of some of the young men almost as much as she missed the steady, laughing presence of her father, but that was the only difference caused by her new, unaccustomed status.

After all, the dai was only looked to if something happened and a decision needed to be made. Otherwise, he was just another much-needed hand. Irina pulled nets and balanced herself as the boat rode the familiar waves. Maybe all the days of her "headmanship" would be like this, full of sun and lots of fish.

Irina stretched, and smiled to herself at the fancy. She was enough a daughter of the sea to know even a double handful of such days would be an unusual blessing, let alone five years' worth!

As she turned to bend her back to the nets again, her eyes glanced back to the distant mouth of the harbor.

She froze.

A thick, gray haze obscured it.

Rapidly, the bank of fog rolled closer.

"Ware!" she cried, her voice rising above the waves.

Backs straightened around her. Heads bobbed up on the nearest boats.

"Sail!" Paolo shouted. The cry was taken up on the other boats.

Backs heaved to bring the nets in on time. Calloused feet ran to raise the heavy beige sails.

But outrunning the fog proved futile. Within minutes they were enveloped by a blanket of wet, sound-deadening grey.

"This never would have happened if we had a dai with the weather sense," Paolo declared.

"Well, we don't," Irina snapped back, anxious and worried herself.

"It won't do, lass. We'll have to elect Dygardis."

"What good would that do? Dygardis obviously didn't sense this coming. I saw you talking with him."

Paolo's shoulders slumped. "True. But what are we to do? This fog could stay down for three days. We could drift against the rocks. Or be pushed so far out to sea we'll never find our way back. Look," he said, waving at the surrounding fog, "we don't even know which way is back to the harbor *now!*"

But I do, Irina realized with surprise. It was as if one particular direction was an invisible beacon; she could point to it as unerringly as she found her way out of the caves.

"Have the other boats light the lanterns," she commanded. "So we don't drift apart."

Paolo nodded. Several of the fishing vessels had already lit theirs. Soon all had followed suit.

"The harbor is that way," Irina said, pointing.

"Lass, no one can know which way the harbor is, now, no matter how good a sighting you got before the fog came down. The waves are constantly pushing us this way and that. We could be completely turned around by now!"

"*I* know," Irina said. "And it isn't by sighting. I *know.*" She said it with that particular inflection the common people used when referring to *laran,* when referring to matters they'd rather accept without thinking about too much.

"I see," Paolo said. "Well, if you're sure . . ." He looked at her anxiously.

"I'm sure," Irina said.

Paolo shouted instructions across to the next boat, and so they were passed on, until all the boats in the small fleet had heard.

Slowly the boats turned, and the men broke out the

oars. Carefully, staying close enough together to see each other's lanterns, they headed toward home.

Several times Irina had to order slight turns. *There* was the shoal of rocks, she *knew,* and *now* they had to work their way back up the dogleg.

When the cliff walls loomed out of the mist, towering shapes of darker gray, Irina breathed a sigh of relief. They tied the ships up in near silence.

"It isn't the weather sense," Paolo said.

"No," Irina agreed. "But maybe it will see us through the next few years."

"The goddess willing," Paolo agreed.

Irina walked home through the damp, heavy gray, her mind busy with ways to use her *laran* better. Maybe she could train herself to "find" storms the way she had found the harbor, and the rocks by just seeking. Maybe she and Dygardis could work together; between his ability to sometimes sense "wrongness," and her direction finding, maybe they could develop a way of finding the weather before it found them.

Of course, she would have to persuade Anna to stay with them. Or, better perhaps, find someone else to manage the hall for her while she was busy with the fleet. Perhaps one of Giselle's young daughters; she wouldn't have to sleep at the hall, and it would give her plenty of practice for when she married and kept a home of her own.

She would find a way. She laughed slightly at the thought; after all, finding a way was her *laran*, wasn't it?

"Anna, we're back safe," she called as she entered the house, not fully realizing, as she shed her damp sweater, that she had already donned a future quite different from the one she had seen stretching ahead just days before.

The Gods' Gift

by Mary K. Frey

Mary Frey has appeared in two previous anthologies, DOMAINS OF DARKOVER and SWORD & SORCERESS VII, and is still a teacher of high school French whose students "think I ought to change the curriculum so they can read my stories instead of learning irregular French verbs." We'd all like to do that.

They also want to know if any of them show up as characters in her stories, to which she says "Of course not."

Someone asked Bob Silverberg once if his characters were based on any real person. He replied that everyone in his stories was based on a real person: "His name is Robert Silverberg."

This is a true statement, with that truth which makes fantasy always truer, in essence, than fact. Writing is an endless exercise in telling lies . . . and also in telling inner truths about one's self. And if you're not prepared to Reveal All*—well, nobody told you not to be a plumber. Because, even when you're writing "pure" fantasy about dragons and elves, you can't help revealing everything—yes,* everything*—about what kind of* *person you are. So if you don't want to do that—well, if you can't stand the heat, what are you doing in the kitchen?*

I can remember when I as a boy of nine or ten hearing the men in the stableyard of Snowcloud Forest or coming from the nearby village's single tavern as they described Rafe as the greatest swordsman in the Hellers. I was pleased that *I* knew the man who merited such praise, but even better than that, he was my mother's kinsman. It was the same year when I had suddenly become all knees and elbows; I was willing to seize any available glory, even the reflected sort.

My more immediate experience with any skill Rafe had, however, came from the tales he told us of his adventures in the lowlands where he had passed the summer soldiering for Lord MacAran. There were many long, dark winter evenings when the winds howled around the eaves and the snow piled up above the doors when we all gathered around the hearth to listen to my mother's kinsman.

In some lonelier moments, I imagined how my life would be if it were revealed Rafe and I were actually half brothers, and I recall deciding upon an elaborate series of implausible events which would have explained how this came to be. The truth was less romantic: my mother was his mother's younger sister, and after his parents died of summer fever before Rafe was a year old, he had nowhere to go but to his mother's people. I think my grandmother must have been too old by then for the effort of raising another child and was content to let my mother do it, though she was still a child herself.

Like many mountain folk who made no claim of Comyn blood, Rafe was dark haired. The village men often let their beards grow in the winter, but since Rafe was one of *Dom* Valentine's officers, he remained clean-shaven. In the unsteady light of the hearth fire, his eyes often looked more black than gray. I have a vague recollection of women speaking to each other about his good looks when they thought no men were listening. I do not believe I ever paused to consider whether he was strong and brave; it would have been impossible for Rafe to have been otherwise. Much later, I would realize that he could not have been more than twenty in those days.

Meanwhile, my friends and I were convinced that the most marvelous future to which any of us could aspire was to become an officer in *Dom* Valentine MacAran's guard as my mother's kinsman Rafe had done. What we heard from him on those darkened, snowy nights was much more exciting than the cobbling, or forging, or whatever craft we were being trained to by our own fathers. Our dreams were filled with wonders.

My name is Alaric.

My father—and by this I mean the man I called by that name for the first twelve years of my life—was Hayat, *Dom* Valentine's blacksmith. After my grandparents were dead and before she was married to the smith, my mother had been a seamstress for the lord's first wife, the one who was the mother of the heir who drowned when—

But that tragic event is a part of Rafe's story as well, although I never heard it from *him* when I was a child. Until I left home, the winter of *Dom* Coryn's death was the standard by which the ages of an entire generation in the village were measured. I was born at the end of the next summer following the MacAran heir's demise.

At the end of our valley, just before the road to Neskaya disappears into the mountains, there is a lake. The grandfather of the grandfather of *Dom* Valentine's father was the one who ordered his *leroni* to build a dam across the path of the river to create the lake. It often froze over completely in the winter. Some years when the winter was particularly cold, the ice grew thick enough to hold many men's weight. More often, however, the appearance of the ice was deceptive, and the villagers repeatedly warned their children not to try to walk on it until adults had declared it safe.

Rafe was ten that year, old enough to be learning a trade except that he had no kinsman to teach him. When Midwinter Festival neared and the MacAran kin and sword men began to arrive at the forest with their families and retainers, there was work to be found helping in the stables with the extra mounts. This meant a place out of the cold for most of the day and a hot meal at midday in the yard with the rest of the stable help.

One day fifteen-year-old *Dom* Coryn, the MacAran heir, and his cousins decided to go hawking, and Rafe was one of the dozen boys they picked out of the crowd in the yard to help hold the horses and beat them some game out of the woods if need be. The nobly-born youths, strutting around with their wind-tossed coppery hair and elegantly embroidered vests, were determined to have their fun and bring whatever bloody trophies they could in order to set their younger sisters squealing.

All of that, as well as the things that were said and how many successful flights the birds made, were what Rafe heard others like the cobbler's son tell afterward. When he first heard the stories, they were as unfamiliar to him as if they had taken place in El Haleine or one of the Dry Towns with people centuries dead. When he told me of this years later, he also admitted he could no longer distinguish between others' tales and what memories of the day he had regained as the *laranzu* said he might with the passage of time.

The delicate hawk who settled on the frozen lake with her prey was one of *Dom* Coryn's favorites; she was the first he'd trained with his own hand. That day she seemed to have decided to declare independence. Whistles, calls, the swinging lures all failed to bring her back to *Dom* Coryn's wrist.

According to the village boys, *Dom* Coryn ordered Rafe out onto the ice to drive the hawk back to the shore. According to the MacAran cousins, the smallest of the stable boys had volunteered for the task. Everyone did, however, describe the same terrible cracking sound, like lightning striking a tree in a summer storm, as the ice gave way and he slid from their view into the frigid water.

All of our village knew some version of the story of how *Dom* Valentine's heir had leapt into the icy water and perished while attempting a heroic rescue of the stable boy. By the time I first heard it from Rafe himself, though, we were far away from the place, and I was no longer a child. The two of us were taking our turn at standing the mid-night watch at a border outpost in Lord Delleray's lands, Rafe with his sword hilt not far from his hand and I likewise with my starstone, in case the lowlanders were fool enough to attempt an attack of any kind in the dark.

When he was done relating how his unconscious body had been pulled from the lake more than an hour later, and how everyone had assumed he was as dead as *Dom* Valentine's heir until the *laranzu* discovered a trace of a pulse, Rafe picked up a snarled branch and held it out toward our fire as if in a trance.

"It was the worst thing that has ever befallen me," he concluded. I was certain he meant either the close brush with death or that length of time of which he had no memory at all, until a moment later when he added, "I would have been better off if I had died that day as the Gods intended."

I did not know how to reply to his statement. Rafe dropped the branch into the fire, and a shower of sparks flew out, pulled away from us on a rising spiral of wind until I felt dizzy trying to follow their path with my eyes.

"*Dom* Valentine says that what had happened since is the will of the Gods, but I know better. All this—" Rafe indicated the intricate sword belt and the officer's badges on the MacAran tartan sash of his uniform tunic. "—is not *their* wish, but his. He is too stubborn to accept the idea that his first-born son might have died for no good reason—"

I was quick to protest. "Saving a life is no small thing."

He made a snorting noise. "I could expect something the like from you, Alaric. You of all people have reason to be glad my life was saved."

"What do you mean?"

"Didn't your mother tell you how you came to be—"

"I know that *Dom* Valentine is my father," I interrupted. "How else could I have come by this coppery hair and enough *laran* to be given this starstone and an education at Neskaya Tower?"

"And did she tell you how Lord MacAran came to be your father?"

I could not help grinning. "I was nearly twelve when I learned who my father really was, more than old enough to know about men and women together. I did not think it necessary to ask *how* I was got." From the season of my birth, I always assumed that the traditional Midwinter Festival celebrations had played some role in it.

Rafe poked at the end of the stick he'd put into the fire, pushing it more firmly into the center of the flames. "*He* decided that my being saved when his own son died was a sign from the gods that I was meant for some special destiny. I was taken away from my mother's sister, the only family I knew, so that I could receive the same training as *Dom* Valentine's foster sons. He wanted me to be properly prepared to meet my great fate, he said. What he meant was that he wanted control of me to assure the rest of my life was proof his son had not died in vain. *She* even went to beg to have her sister's son back, since I was all she had in the world then. He laughed at her and said that if she was meant to have a child, the Gods would see to it she got another. And then he made certain of it."

I learned at that moment the matter of foster sons could still rankle. During my training in telepathic skills at Neskaya Tower, I'd had to struggle to overcome the anger I felt toward the boys in his household on whom my father had lavished all his care and attention while I, his own flesh and blood, was beneath his notice. I'd never minded my childhood until I became aware of how different it could have been.

I was so absorbed in my own thoughts, I almost did not hear the question Rafe asked. "Would it not be odd if the Gods' purpose in Coryn's death was not to save *my* life, but to get *you* born?"

I did not know if Rafe was correct when he said that *Dom* Valentine had insisted on having his way with my mother simply to provide a means for the Gods to send her a child. My mother was said to have been quite a beauty in her youth. What I did know was that by the time I was born, my father had no need to think of a *nedestro* heir. He had taken *Dom* Roualt Delleray's sister as his second wife and ensured the succession quickly enough that the new heir was only a few months younger than I.

As part of the marriage settlement, *Dom* Roualt and *Dom* Valentine had sworn a pact of mutual defense. Seventeen years after the oaths had been sworn, Lord MacAran and his soldiers and *leroni* were still fighting Delleray's war with the lowlanders for control of the lands between Neskaya and the river.

And seventeen years after Coryn had died, *Dom* Valentine was still watching Rafe with a keen eye, hoping to learn what great destiny the Gods had settled upon the boy for whose sake his own first-born son had died. The more I saw of this for myself now that I was old enough to understand, the more I wondered just what sort of proof my father needed from Rafe.

As I stated at the beginning of this tale, Rafe was known as a skilled swordsman. He may not have been the greatest living at the time—we had all heard of *Dom* Raimond Aillard—since he had no *laran,* and thus no ability to sense his opponent's next move. No *gifted* swordsman could have dueled with him legally nor in good conscience. No normal swordsman wanted to, for they knew they would lose. Yet, I never heard one word of praise for Rafe from my father for his skill.

He had a way with horses as well, and that says much, for all around him every day were men with the MacAran gift of rapport with animals. It seemed to me that he must have a way with people, too. The common soldiers in the troop who came from the vicinity of Snowcloud Forst all treated Rafe as if he were the next thing to the Lord of Light himself.

As the army moved toward Neskaya in an effort to draw Lord Lanart and his allies into a pitched battle, the cavalry sent out scouting parties which occasionally fought skirmishes with the lowlanders. After one of these, I happened to be present when my father spoke with the officers who'd been involved. One of Lord Delleray's cousins was praised for having gotten away from the enemy although he'd lost his horse and half a dozen men under his command. In an excess of zeal, Lord Storn's younger son had ordered a local farmer's barn put to the torch although the man's family had been loyal to Delleray for generations. He was praised for having thought to remove it as a source of supplies for the enemy—despite the fact that the structure was several hundred paces behind our own lines in the brief light.

And then *Dom* Valentine started with Rafe, who

had given up his horse to the hapless Delleray cousin and walked back to our camp. I struggled to comprehend what was wrong with that, but apparently it was nothing more than my father's conviction, expressed aloud to Rafe, that "my son did not die to save your life so you could be struck down by some miserable lowlander's arrow!" I wondered how my father could use Rafe as a soldier at all if that was the way he felt.

On the other hand, I realized later, *Dom* Valentine felt obligated to put Rafe into situations which carried great potential for heroic action.

As the army moved south, the birds we *leroni* sent out to reconnoiter revealed that we would come upon Lord Lanart and his men in a valley known for generations as the Plains of Zabal. It was as good a place as any for a fight. We camped on the heights at the western end where the two Comyn lords could have a clear view of the battlefield. The campfires of the enemy showed like hundreds of fireflies from the other end of the valley, and all the officers were ordered to an evening meeting to discuss the order of battle for the morning. A diagram of the deployment of soldiers into a center line, flanks, and reserves was drawn out on a width of pale leather. The likely sequence of the fighting was discussed. Lord Delleray and his allies had not made sporadic war on the lowlanders for more than a dozen years without learning something of their enemy's ways.

My stomach had been in turmoil for hours since this was to be my first battle. Somewhere inside the nervous anxiety, there was the persistent little hope that by the next setting of the sun, my name would be on all lips as the one who had made the critical difference and acted to assure our side's victory at just the right moment. I wondered how Rafe could have spoken so indifferently about the prospect of heroism.

The battle arrived more slowly and ended more suddenly than I could have ever predicted. In between the beginning and the ending was naught but confusion, or so it seemed to me—and I was one of the *leroni* who remained on the heights with the commanders and their squires in order to have a view over the whole at once: the noise, the tumult, the stink of fear sweat—and I could not separate myself from any of it so long as Lord MacAran needed me to communicate telepathically with his Tower-trained officers on the battlefield.

The two full moons which rose after midnight had enabled us to move some of our troops into position. Lord Lanart had done the same with his lowland soldiers, of course. When the sun rose, though, its warmth turned the night's dew to mist, and so all sat with varying degrees of impatience until the fog should burn off and the men might see more than an arm's length in any direction. We had about as many birds as we could manage. So did they, although without the MacAran gift of rapport with animals, the lowlander's information had to be less consistent than ours was.

"Some of their men are trying to sneak across the creek," I reported to *Dom* Valentine and pointed in the direction which I meant, "at a shallow place to the east of that bushy area." A moment later the breeze brought dulled shouting up to our ears.

By midday it seemed we were fighting to a standoff. I did not like the look of the number of wounded finding their way back to our camp, but neither *Dom* Roualt nor *Dom* Valentine seemed overly concerned.

My clothes were clammy with sweat, and I forced myself to drink the honey-sweetened fruit juice which the boy who held my horse carried. Although I did not feel the exertion of it yet, I had been using my starstone continuously. If the fighting did not go in our favor and we were forced to flee, I did not want to be too weak to sit the horse at all.

"This is it!" *Dom* Roualt exclaimed at the same moment his own *laranzu* and I became aware of a fresh enemy attack. No skirmish this; it ranged the full length of our lines. And we were having difficulty holding them off. The distinctively different feel of several individual officers' mental voices came at me all at once, each asking for assistance from anyone nearby who was not under attack. "The flank, Val!" Delleray shouted to my father. "Order the reserves on the right flank to charge now, or we're lost!"

All eyes on the hill turned to the right flank where the reserve troops from Stormcloud Forst waited. At *Dom* Valentine's express wish, they had been placed under Rafe's command.

"What is the name of Zandru's coldest hell is he waiting for?" Lord Delleray demanded. "Can't he hear your *laranzu*, oath brother?" I felt his agitated eye rest on me, as if Rafe's failure to move could be *my* fault.

The foster son has no laran. I recognized the flash of thought from the matrix worker on the far side of *Dom* Roualt. It was as hushed as a whisper would have been had he used his vocal chords. *He cannot hear any of us.*

Lord Delleray set his jaw, and I saw the veins begin to stand out on his neck as his face grew redder than normal.

"Rafe doesn't need to hear us," *Dom* Valentine explained. "He has been gifted by the Gods, and they, not we, will guide him."

Dom Roualt sputtered the sort of words I dared not say aloud. He turned to one of his young squires—*Dom* Valentine's second oldest son by Roualt's sister, as it happened—and ordered the boy to get himself over to the flank somehow and give their commanding officer the order to attack.

A moment after Doni and his pony vanished into a stand of trees, we saw one of a lowlander's banners in the same place. But there was no time to think on it, for at that instant, the reserve flank moved to attack. They fell upon the exposed rear of the enemy's main force and proceeded to rout them quite thoroughly. Victory was ours.

"Praise the Lord of Light!" *Dom* Valentine exclaimed. "Did I not tell you the Gods speak directly to my foster son?"

Victory or not, there was still the business to be faced of caring for the wounded and disposing of the corpses. I did not even notice when the torches were lit, but the moons had risen high in the night sky when I was finally able to make my way back to my pallet. I'd long since ceased to notice the stains and stench which soaked my Tower worker's robes.

Danvan, my father's oldest son by his second marriage and his recognized heir, was waiting for me at my tent. Dani was younger than I by only a few months. His smooth, freckled face could have been a fifty-year-old's that night, and I did not need to ask to know that his expression meant that Doni, the twelve-year-old who had ridden to alert the reserve flank, was dead.

"I killed a man today," Dani reported. "With this." I saw he had yet to clean his sword and wondered how our father or Lord Delleray could be so remiss with military discipline even under these circumstances. I made Dani sit on the single stool in my small tent. "What are we going to do about Father, Alaric?"

"What do you mean?" I asked. Someday Dani would be Lord MacAran, and since I was his half brother and had received more Tower training than anyone else so closely related, it would probably fall to me to be his chief *laranzu.* It behooved me to get along well with him. I put the thought that he was not yet the man Rafe was quickly out of my mind before Dani could pick up on it.

"He doesn't care that I killed a man with my own hand, or that I had to watch while I felt the man's thoughts as he died. He even looked at Doni's body, or what Lanart's men left of it, and I know he did not feel any grief at all—"

"He is accustomed to shielding his emotions from—" It was the correct thing to say. Inside, I was more in agreement with Dani than he could guess. Avarra knows, my father had never felt much about me.

"I know when he does that, Alaric. The only thing that matters to him tonight is that the Gods spoke to Rafe. He says this is the proof that my foster brother is favored by the Gods. He says this is the day he has been waiting for. He cares about nothing else! What are we going to do?"

"You understand, don't you, why it matters so much to him?" I asked.

Dani exploded off his seat. "Blessed Aldones!

Coryn may have been his first-born son, but he's been dead more than seventeen years now. You would think Doni and I don't matter any more than some bastard he'd got on a—" Dani shut his mouth as it dawned on him what he'd said and to whom. He had just enough naive grace to blush.

"Don't apologize. I know what I am," I replied and suggested he find a squire who could help him wash up and clean his gear. He looked about as weary as I felt. "If our father has finally got what he has wanted all these years, he may be willing to let the past go at last."

I did not tell Dani what had really happened to get the reserves moving: I had swooped one of my spy birds down onto Rafe, goading it to make such a flutter all around his horse, he would have had to be an idiot not to realize he was being signaled to send his troops into battle.

I also fully expected that by morning, Rafe would have found a chance to reveal the truth of the matter to Lord MacAran.

He did not. He gloried in the attention of his heroic moment, never once contradicting *Dom* Valentine's repeated description of how the Gods had spoken to Rafe in order to save the day for the mountain armies. The bird I'd sent to him was never mentioned at all.

It might have made sense in a backward sort of way if Lord McAran had been a rational man. Almost anyone else would have interpreted the events on the day of the battle as *the* great moment for which Rafe had been destined. Certainly, without the timely appearance of the reserves he commanded, the battle could have gone the other way and the mountain forces would have then been totally destroyed.

For my father, however, the day had only been a sign of greater things yet to happen.

Two days after the battle on the Plains of Zabal, we rode into Neskaya to sign the peace treaties with Lord Lanart and the other lowland lords who'd been his allies. We also buried Doni in the plot of ground which had received the bodies of Comyn-kin ever since men first settled this part of the world.

Rafe continued to be the hero of our victory. Dani should have sat beside his father at the treaty negotiations, as *Dom* Roualt's elder son sat beside him, but *Dom* Valentine had decided the place of honor at his left was for his foster son. I thought for sure Lord Delleray would have had something to say to that, since it was his own sister's son who was being slighted. But if that conversation between the two lords ever took place, I never knew of it.

What I did hear was a rumor that Lord MacAran had sent messengers to Lord Hastur of El Haleine, the most powerful of the lowland Comyn lords, in an effort to secure one of Hastur's daughters as a bride—not for Dani his heir, but for Rafe his foster son. The entire notion was preposterous since Rafe had no *laran* and Hastur had no daughters without it, and yet the stories would not die.

Mutterings reached my ears, as I am certain they were meant to since I was the only kinsman he had, from various Comyn-kin who thought Rafe was trying to acquire more than that to which he was entitled by birth or deed. I tended to agree, but I also knew that it was my father's stubborn doing, not Rafe's ambition, which had brought matters to this point. And what was Rafe supposed to do? He'd sworn oaths as a foster son and as an officer to honor and obey Lord MacAran, and in the Hellers, such oaths are taken very seriously.

I must admit Rafe tried to escape my father's plans, and at the time I admired his cleverness. On the day the messengers were expected to return from El Haleine, Rafe took a young woman whose father was a tavernkeeper in the city to an audience with *Dom* Valentine, asking for permission to marry the woman who bore his child. The story was just on the edge of plausible, since we'd been in Neskaya for a little over a month at that point. Rafe figured that a married man could not be asked to contract a second marriage no matter how exalted a position the second bride's father might hold.

Rafe's scheme might have worked if the girl he chose to be his wife had not had a greedy father. The man went to Lord MacAran separately in order to haggle over the bride price and ended up with a tidy little sum for making certain there were several witnesses to swear that his daughter had been handfasted to someone else last Midwinter Festival. To still the gossips, *Dom* Valentine circulated the excuse that Rafe had in all innocence been taken advantage of by a girl and her tearful story of abandonment by a lover. He'd only been trying to act gallantly to save her from her father's rage, or so the tale went.

The messengers returned with Lord Hastur's reply: he might be willing to talk about a marriage between *Dom* Valentine's heir and one of his own *nedestro* daughters if Lord MacAran would come south to El Haleine to discuss the details *next* summer.

Not long after that we received the order to pack for the return journey to Snowcloud Forst.

* * *

That last day began no differently from the dozen which had proceeded it as we traveled back through the mountains toward our home. It was now high summer in the Hellers; only in the remotest, shadiest parts of the passes had the snow not fully melted. From the height of the latest of these, we could see a farm spread out below us at the near end of the valley. *Dom* Valentine ordered me and Rafe to ride ahead and announce his imminent arrival to the farmer. I do not know why he happened to choose the two of us that day.

Rafe and I chatted about nothing in particular as we rode down the verdant mountainside until the talk finally made its way around to Lord Hastur of El Haleine.

"I'm certain I would make a perfectly terrible son-in-law for a man like that," Rafe commented. "But I might not make him such a bad army captain. If I thought it would do any good, I would try to persuade *Dom* Valentine to let me become a lowland mercenary for a season or two. Just think of the adventures, Alaric! I could see the ocean with my own eyes—do you think the seawives might take a fancy to me and leave me a pearl on the sands?" He grinned, looking more like the man I remembered from my childhood than he had since before the battle with Lanart.

"From what I've heard of Hastur's military ambitions, if you fight for him, the only sands you're likely to see in his service are the ones around Carthon." We all knew one reason we'd been able to defeat Lord Lanart was that Hastur had not been able to spare any troops from his own wars with the Dry Towns to bolster Lanart's.

I cannot say for certain when it struck me there was something not quite right about the farm. We'd passed an orchard where a few small pigs had been turned loose to fatten themselves up on windfall, and I'd noticed there was no child tending them. But perhaps he or she had fallen asleep on the far side of an apple tree. Later, when I strained to recall, I thought it might have been the absence of birdsong that alarmed me.

I do remember taking one hand from the reins as we rode into the deserted farmyard proper in order to get hold of my matrix stone. Where we had stopped for the night the previous day, there had been rumors of a bandit troop terrorizing the countryside a few days from here. It sounded as if they'd been emboldened in their activities by the absence of Lord MacAran and his guardsman. I glanced at Rafe and started to say, "Doesn't it seem a little too quiet in this place for a sunny, summer's day?"

And then we were attacked.

I was told later that there were more than twenty of them, and that they had been in the process of murdering the farmer and his sons when Rafe and I rode up. It was some consolation to know that our arrival, while disastrous for us, had distracted the villains long enough for the farmer's wife and her daughters to escape out the back of their barn and take refuge unharmed in the woods nearest the house.

I remember being thrown from my horse's back when he reared as I struggled to manage reins, starstone, and sword all at once. I must have hit my head when I landed, since everything went black. I can only guess that while I was unconscious, the bandits mistook me for dead already and left me to lie where I had fallen.

The first of MacAran's mounted troops were not far behind us, and they arrived in time to kill half a dozen of the bandits even though the rest of them managed to flee into the mountains.

There was no sign of Rafe or his horse.

Lord MacAran did not want to believe that the bandits could have killed Rafe. At first he was certain Rafe had ridden off to lure the bandits away from the farm and expected him to return as soon as it was clear we were in possession of it. When nothing of that nature happened, he insisted that Rafe had been captured and was being held for some kind of ransom. We waited four days at that farmstead for some kind of letter or message to be delivered naming the terms of Rafe's safe return. Of course, it never came.

If the bandits had indeed killed Rafe and carried the body off, previous similar experiences with their kind indicated that my kinsman's horse, sword, spurs, maybe even parts of his uniform and other gear were likely to show up among the trade goods in market towns just outside MacAran lands. Although *Dom* Valentine sent word to all the neighboring lords to be watchful, nothing of Rafe's ever reappeared in somebody else's possession. Neither did anyone report hearing even third-hand reports of any man claiming to have killed a dark-haired officer of Lord MacAran's guard.

I knew that Rafe must still be alive. I thought of what my kinsman said that last day about seeking out mercenary work in the lowlands, and it seemed to me that must be where he had gone. There was no way for him to escape the onus of *Dom* Valentine's expectations except by allowing those who wished to do so to think him dead. I doubt that he planned to run off and leave me to the bandits in the farmyard, until the moment when his chance for freedom arrived.

For Lord MacAran, the suggestion that Rafe had simply run away would have been completely intolerable—Coryn could not have died to save a man of so little fortitude. Therefore, the only possible conclusion *Dom* Valentine could reach was that Rafe had died once he finally accomplished what the Gods had kept him alive to do—

My father's keen eye came to rest on me at last.

I do not begrudge Rafe his escape nor his freedom, if he indeed survived to enjoy it. But I wish he had not left me to carry the weight of my father's fondest dreams.

The Speaking Touch

by Margaret Carter

Once again we have an unusual use of laran, *one of the things I am always looking for in these anthologies. Margaret Carter, who appeared in four of my previous anthologies, updated her* curriculum vitae *with a whole sheet of credits, mostly about Vampires. One would imagine from that that this story would be a horror story, but Ms. Carter knows me better than that. Although I admit I wondered, when I read the first line, which said "The doorknob gibbered at her." She says "Two of our four sons have been kicked out of the nest" which is par for the course among all of us. I keep feeling astonishment that my "baby" is now a young woman of twenty-five with a very fine soprano voice. Well, it happens to us all; that little pink thing will some day be six foot four . . . a lot sooner than you think. And that is, like everything else that happens to anybody, both good news and bad. As I always say about getting old, "it beats hell out of the alternative."*

Margaret Carter is looking forward to moving to San Diego, California; her husband is a Naval Commander. Her agent is currently submitting a vampire novel (I could have guessed that) to various publishers.

Judging by what's on the stands, everybody and his brother—or sister—has written a vampire novel. Why should Ms. Carter be different?

The doorknob gibbered at her.

It sprayed a scattershot of images into her brain—men and women of widely varied ages and complexions, swirls of color from Terran uniforms and Darkovan native costume, a babble of voices in several different accents.

I must be more tired than I realized, Fiona thought. Ordinarily she could shut out the silent messages from the inanimate objects she touched, or at least mute the communication to background noise. She clamped down her barrier as she hesitantly stepped into the front office of Alien Anthropology. It looked like the interior of any Terran base on any planet. Her eyes absorbed the familiar yellow-sun spectrum, though outside—as she'd noted in a fleeting glimpse upon disembarking from the ship—a ruddy glow suffused the sky.

A brown-skinned young man at the desk glanced at her ID, then buzzed the intercom. Seconds later, a solidly-built, dark-haired man emerged from one of the inner offices. "I'm Jason Allison. Welcome to Project Telepath, Dr. McGraw." He briefly pressed her hand in greeting.

That contact imposed no intrusive visions upon her. Her aberration didn't extend to living creatures. "I appreciate your taking the time for me, Dr. Allison."

His courteous smile widened to a genuine grin as he ushered her into the adjoining office. "Jason. We tend to use first names here, especially with the high density of advanced degrees per square meter. I'm not sure how much we can help you, though. Our staff doesn't specialize in folklore."

Shifting her harp case from her left arm to her lap, Fiona settled into the contoured chair he offered. "I was told your department was the best place to meet native Darkovans without spending a lot of time in Thendara proper—and my fellowship grant doesn't allow me that much time on any one planet."

"Bureaucrats and budgets," Jason chuckled. "We're all too familiar with those." After speaking into the intercom for a moment, he drew her into conversation about her trip and other polite banalities.

Minutes later, a slim young man with golden-red hair walked in. Jason introduced the two of them. "Fiona, Rafe will give you the basic tour and show you to your quarters. Looks like you're ready to plunge right into your work."

"Oh, you mean this?" She glanced down at the harp case she'd tucked back under her arm when she stood up. "I just feel uncomfortable about anyone else carrying it."

"I understand," said Rafe in passable Terran Standard. "My friends who are musicians feel the same way." He didn't offer to shake hands.

Facing him, Fiona saw her first Darkovan, a man about her own age with curly hair and an aquiline nose. He wore the embroidered leather jerkin, wool trousers, and soft indoor boots she'd seen in holograms illustrating Darkovan men's clothing. He saw a petite woman with deep auburn hair sleeked back into a tight bun. Close-reined excitement hummed within her; among all the cultures she'd studied, she felt a special affinity for this one since the planet had been settled largely by people of her own ethnic background.

"What is your *laran*?" her guide offhandedly asked as he escorted her along the corridor.

"My what?" She knew the word, of course; she was just shocked to hear it apply to herself.

He paused to give her a sidelong smile, his eyebrows quizzically arched. "Your *donas*—I believe your commonest Terran phrase is 'wild talent.' "

She waited until two men walking down the hall in the opposite direction passed out of earshot. "I don't have one."

"Forgive me—I assumed you were here as part of Jason's Project. My *laran* is—I suppose you'd call me an identifier." He fingered a small pouch suspended from his neck by a leather cord. "I sense a power in you. It seemed more courteous to ask than to probe without your permission."

Fiona's pulse hammered in her throat. *Don't be silly. This is the last place anybody will call you weird or crazy.* Nevertheless, the habit of concealment was too ingrained for her to toss aside lightly. "I don't have anything to do with Project Telepath. I'm a cultural anthropologist studying Darkovan folklore."

His gray eyes seemed to recognize her retreat into half-truth, but he didn't challenge her. She never discussed the way inanimate objects "talked" to her, as she thought of it, or the way she could sometimes talk back with her music, make things move through a force inexplicable by conventional physics. Nor did she want to confide her parents' fear and repugnance when she'd chattered about the messages she picked up, or the months of torment she'd endured, as a child, from well-meaning therapists, until she had learned to conceal her strangeness well enough to be pronounced "cured." She viewed her psychometry as a curse, one she would happily excise like a tumor if she knew how.

Politely ignoring her ill-suppressed tension, Rafe showed her devices used to measure various psi talents, then the roomful of computer terminals where she would be allotted a cubicle for her research, and introduced her to passersby, both Terran and Darkovan, whose names mostly slipped out of her mind at once. "Does it bother you," she asked when she'd had her fill of labs and offices, "to spend so much time inside the spaceport? The environment must be uncomfortably alien for you. Not only the culture, but even the lighting."

Rafe gave her a wry smile, apparently pleased by her perceptiveness. "You're right. And we finally persuaded Jason's 'bureaucrats' to do something about that. Come along, I'll show you."

He led her to an elevator that carried them two levels up. "We're not far from the dormitories. Lighting in the private quarters can be adjusted for either Terran or Darkovan eyes." A short walk brought them to a room so large that Fiona couldn't see the walls for the trees rooted in the layer of soil that covered the floor. Real dirt, not synthetic, as the moist scent assured her. The roof, entirely transparent, let in the dim red glow of the "bloody sun."

Rafe sank onto a stone bench with an audible sigh. "We can come here to rest when we don't have time to go outside. Some of my Terran friends enjoy the occasional change, too." The space replicated a forest, not a garden. Fiona recognized native trees and foliage from her studies. In the background she heard the buzz of insects and the ripple of a stream, which fed into a pond near the bench.

"Restful," she said. While the illumination would probably give her a headache in time, for the moment she found it soothing.

"May I ask about your work? What is it you're here to study?" Rafe spoke hesitantly, as if he expected her to tell him the topic was confidential.

"Sure, just stop me when you start to fall asleep from boredom," she said. "I collect folk songs, specifically on the subject of liaisons between human beings and mythical nonhuman creatures. On Terra they might have been elves—supernatural beings of extended lifespan and unearthly beauty. Those stories seem to travel with humanity to every world we've settled. The characters change, but the outline of the tale remains constant." She paused, embarrassed by her gush of words. Rafe didn't look bored, though.

"Here, then, you seek tales of the *chieri*."

She nodded. "And alternative versions of songs like the legend of Hastur and Cassilda. Do you realize that Darkover is one of the few known worlds on which the old legends have come true? The inhabitants of Faerie were mythical; my predecessors have long since explained the origins of the myths to death. The *chieri* seem to be real."

"They are," said Rafe. "And the ancient songs do hold some truth. The People of the Forest have—on rare occasions—mated with humankind." A faint blush tinged his cheeks. "A custom being revived, to a limited extent, because they are now so often infertile among themselves."

Fiona leaned forward excitedly, her hands clasped

around her drawn-up knees. "If, while I'm here, I could meet one— What are my chances?"

Rafe said, "The *chieri* have always been shy of outsiders, meaning anyone not of their race. Now that they're near extinction, they have even more cause to be wary. We consider ourselves lucky to have two working with us on the Project. Many people believe that the Comyn received their *laran* powers from crossbreeding with the *chieri*."

"I know." Fiona bit back the pleas that rose to her lips. Begging him to introduce her to one of these quasi-mythical beings would be rude and doubtless counterproductive.

His half-smile acknowledged the eagerness he could probably sense; of course, thought Fiona, he was, after all, a member of the legendary Darkovan telepath caste. "One of the two *chieri* in residence here is a close—friend—of mine. Perhaps you may meet, later."

As he showed her to her room, he said, "I'll be delighted to help you as far as I can in your study of our legends and ballads, though I confess the whole process is somewhat—alien—to me. The idea of amassing knowledge purely for the abstract accumulation of it, for no practical purpose—"

Stung, Fiona leapt to defend her work. She'd heard plenty of that "ivory tower" talk from her own people. "But it does have practical application. What happens when human beings meet other intelligent species and see them through the lens of myth? Do we treat aliens inappropriately because we see the creatures of our own imagination instead of what they really are? That's what I ultimately hope to find out."

"Then I wish you success," Rafe said gravely.

* * *

Thoughts of Rafe's cordiality sustained her the following day, through the necessary preparation for the interviews she planned. She spent a long morning at a terminal, accessing multiple versions of Darkovan ballads and epic fragments about human-*chieri* liaisons. Psychic residue from previous users clung to the keyboard like dust, cool and dry. Surrounded by stacks of printouts, Fiona looked up from the screen about noon, station time, to massage the back of her neck. No matter how far technology improved, nobody seemed to have learned to design a computer console that didn't give the operator aching muscles.

Fiona decided to spend a few minutes in the station's "forest" before lunch. Besides the room's tranquillity, it lured her because it represented contact with the world she'd encountered in the legends.

First she detoured to her room to collect her harp case. In the artificial forest, seated on the stone bench under overhanging branches heavy with yellow blossoms, she soothed herself with the familiar, mechanical task of tuning the temperamental strings. She gazed into the clear pool, where tiny, rainbow-hued fish darted, and stroked the harp.

Satisfied with the sound, she plucked chords as a background to her singing of an ancient ballad:

I am a man upon the land,
I am a silkie on the sea,
And when I'm far and far from land
My home, it is in Skule Skerry.

As she sang one of her favorite legends of supernatural love, she fixed her eyes on the pebbles that rimmed the pond. Her song, thrumming in her veins, became a chant that pulsed from her vocal cords and fingertips into the surrounding air to weave a net that gathered in the pebbles and made them dance. Pleasantly entranced, she watched the stones whirl in tight spirals over the still water. As always, this exercise melted her tensions and restored the energy spent in hours of close work.

At such moments she thought the pleasure of telekinetic play was almost worth the ordeals her psychometric talent imposed on her.

The back of her neck prickled with a sense of presence. With a smothered gasp, she turned to face the newcomer. The pebbles splashed into the pond.

A voice said in *casta*, which Fiona had learned during her study of the classic Darkovan songs, "Forgive me, I did not mean to intrude." The speaker was taller than the human average—the conventional adjective "willowy" seemed to fit, for he (or she?) displayed the suppleness of a young tree. Silver eyes and hair set off pearly skin.

A *chieri*. Behind—him—Rafe entered. "Fiona, my freemate, Merrak."

Dazed, Fiona murmured a greeting.

A *chieri* glided closer, his silken tunic shimmering with each movement. "Your playing was a pleasure. Why were you afraid?"

She gingerly set the harp down on its folded wrappings. "Where I come from, performances like that aren't—normal." She spoke slowly, choosing her words with care, for her knowledge of the aristocratic tongue was a scholar's, not a fluent speaker's. "When I was a child, and told my parents I could hear objects speak, and make them move, I was considered—ill.

In time I learned to conceal my abilities." The self-revelation spilled over without thought. From this shining creature, she sensed, it would be futile to try concealing her inner self.

She felt a quiver of revulsion from the *chieri*. "They tried to *cure* you of your gifts?"

Ashamed of her kind—though, with a flash of anger, she wondered why *she* should feel shame—she dropped the subject. "I have come here to learn the ancient songs and legends of contact between your people and mine."

With fluid grace Merrak sank onto the mossy ground near the bench, while Rafe sat down next to Fiona. "Yes, Rafe has told me. Fiona, what is an elf?"

She stammered, taken aback that he could read the exact words in her mind.

"I would not enter your thoughts without permission. You projected the image so strongly."

"On my home world, that is what people would call you." She tried to explain the myth of Faerie. Unsure of whether she was making the concept clear, she said, "We have songs about the Queen of Elfland and her mortal lovers." Picking up the harp again, she crooned the ballad of Thomas the Rhymer, who vanished into Faerie and was not seen on earth for seven years. Fiona tried to project a vision of the poem as she sang, knowing she could not adequately translate it from English into *casta*.

When she'd finished, Merrak's long, tapered fingers—six to a hand—reached toward the harp. "May I?" He tentatively strummed the strings, eliciting a tuneless ripple of chords. The discovery that he couldn't produce a ravishing melody with no prior training made the experience seem more real to Fiona.

Rafe said, "We'd like to hear you play again, but not here. Do you have time to come with us and meet someone else?"

Curious, Fiona quickly wrapped the harp and followed her two guides into the corridor. She was puzzled when Rafe led the way through the dormitory wing to a complex of rooms marked "Nursery." A pair of guards, wearing what she recognized as Hastur livery, flanked the main door, a precaution that struck her as ominous. Inside, two nurses on duty at the monitors, one Terran, one Darkovan, greeted Rafe and Merrak, accepting Fiona on Rafe's word.

From the quick scan she made as they passed through the central room, Fiona noticed that few of the crib-furnished alcoves on its perimeter were occupied. With Rafe and Merrak, she stepped into one, the three of them crowded close together in the small chamber. A mobile of spherical stained glass bubbles hung from the ceiling, bathed in rosy light that mimicked the planet's sun. The baby in the crib, no more than two or three months old, opened silver-gray eyes as they entered.

"Our daughter, Kyra," said Rafe. Merrak extended one slender finger for the baby to grip.

Glancing sideways at Merrak, Fiona abruptly felt her vision of "him" blur and refocus. Instead of a tall, slim boy, Merrak looked like a delicate young woman with soft though not abundant curves. *So the tales are true, the* chieri *are hermaphrodites!*

The baby girl had translucent white skin and a thick crop of red hair. She gurgled and smiled fleetingly, her eyes fixed on Fiona.

"I thought Kyra might enjoy your music, too," said

Rafe. He nodded to Merrak, who extracted a reed flute from a pocket of his—no, her—tunic.

Sitting in the chamber's single, padded chair, Fiona unwrapped the harp. When Merrak trilled the opening notes of a native tune, she struck the first chords of the accompaniment. At first she felt the awkwardness of any unrehearsed duet. Little by little, though, the music flowed together into a single stream. Liquid sound, almost tangible and visible, spun out of the flute to twine around Fiona like spider-silk. Their blended melody wove filaments that feathered around and among the glass bubbles, which twirled as if in a woodland breeze. Kyra kicked her legs and rotated her arms in an enigmatic semaphore.

Fiona lost touch with the chair beneath her, floating on the sound like a leaf on a river. She felt—opened up—like a leaf once curled tight against chill winds, now unfurling in the sun. After the music stopped, it took her several minutes to sink back into consciousness of the solid objects around her.

Dizziness swept over her when she stood. She grasped the crib rail. A bitter tide surged into her mind. She saw, blurred by searing emotion, a red-headed man in Terran costume. His malevolence blinded her—she snatched her hand back as from burning metal—

When her vision cleared, she saw and felt Rafe's hand supporting her by the elbow. His free hand fingered the leather pouch at his throat. "You'll be better in a moment. It is not unusual for contact with other telepaths to awaken and expand dormant *laran*."

Fiona answered with a shaky nod, "That must be it. I felt it so—vividly—more than ever before." She didn't mention the content of her vision, for she couldn't tell how far in the past it lay, or even, perhaps, if it anticipated a future event. If contact with Rafe and Merrak had "expanded" her talent, she needed time to relearn the interpretation of her visions.

In the corridor, she glanced again at the two sentries. Once out of their sight, she said, "Why the precautions? Why does a nursery need armed guards?"

Rafe's expression turned cold. "Unexplained deaths of Comyn children have occurred, in recent years, more often than chance allows."

"Someone has been murdering babies?" Her stomach knotted at the thought.

"Less than three months ago, after two years of tranquillity—the nurses as well as a newborn infant inexplicably dead, with no clue to the assassin. Some Darkovan groups believe that the survival of the telepath caste is less important than its 'purity.' They consider the Project—offering *laran* instructions to commoners and outworlders—an abomination. For fanatics who think that way, the children born here are a logical target."

Sensing a shudder from Merrak, who walked at her other side, Fiona shivered, too.

I've met a chieri*!* As Fiona lay in bed that night, the wonder of that meeting and the joy of merging with Merrak, Rafe, and Kyra in music warred with the acid memory of the images that had assaulted her immediately afterward. Only when conflicting emotions had exhausted her could she fall asleep.

She dreamed of the nursery. Subdued, indirect night-lighting replicated the spectra of two of Darkover's four moons. From shadow to shadow slinked a black-robed shape, recognizable only as upright and humanoid. It exuded hate like mist rising from the surface of a lake.

A baby's wail screamed inside Fiona's head.

Kyra!

She sprang up, awake before she fully realized the dream had broken off. Freshly roused instinct told her that was no ordinary dream. She grabbed a robe and shuffled into it even as she rushed from her room.

She was gasping from her run when she reached the nursery. Outside the door two guards lay unconscious or dead. From inside she heard a baby crying—an audible cry, not the inner call her dreaming mind had overheard. When she hurried inside, she saw Merrak beside Kyra's crib, holding the baby.

"Thank Heaven—is she all right?"

Merrak didn't question how Fiona had been alerted. "Yes—I heard her terror—found a man in black robes at the nurses' station. He knocked me down as he fled."

Glancing back into the main room, Fiona noticed the two nurses lying on the floor. Hurrying footsteps reached her ears. Rafe and Jason stepped into the room, followed by another man she recognized, from her introductory tour, as Dr. David Hamilton. Hamilton knelt beside the nurses' bodies. "Dead, like the guards outside—not a mark on them."

Rafe shouldered his way to Merrak's side and embraced his mate and child. Though no audible words were spoken, Fiona sensed that Merrak was telling Rafe the details of the attack.

Rafe briefly relayed the facts to Jason and Hamilton. "A man robed and hooded to hide his face—not much hope of identifying him."

At that moment a Terran security officer entered, carrying a bundle of black cloth. "Sir, we found this thrown into a corner in the next corridor." He handed it to Jason.

"That makes sense," said Jason. "Without his disguise, he could be anybody. Anybody who belongs in the station—an outsider couldn't get this far in at this time of night."

"Short of testing every man in the complex under truthspell," said Hamilton with a heavy sigh, "I don't see much hope of catching him."

Frustration boiled up within Fiona. "You mean you're just giving up—?" She checked her outburst. As an outsider herself, what did she know of their limitations?

Rafe and Merrak exchanged a silent look. Inside Fiona's head, Merrak's melodious voice whispered: *You can see what happened here, who invaded this place. You must help.*

Rafe took the robe from Jason and held it out to Fiona. She shook her head. "What are you talking about?"

She felt all eyes fixed on her. She yearned to run away, but she was surrounded. *Speak*, came Merrak's silent plea.

Disgust at her own fears overpowered the fear itself. "All right, I'll try." Fiona gathered the black cloth into her arms.

Rage hit her like a blow to the pit of the stomach. She almost dropped the robe. Clutching it to her chest, she drew long breaths to drive out the storm of hate. Behind her closed eyelids, the emotional maelstrom cleared, and images began to form.

"A man draped all in black walks up to the door.

Can't see his face. The guards challenge him. He stares at the one on his left. Pain—clutching, squeezing pain in the chest—the guard falls unconscious. The other one starts to call out. The man stares at him—his voice is choked off—he claws at his neck—he can't breathe. He collapses, too."

Fiona's own breath came short and labored. She relaxed her clenched fingers and breathed deeply to ease the tightness in her chest. "He uses the guard's key strip to get inside. The nurses jump up—they're frightened—one of them reaches for an alarm button. He looks at her—his eyes seem to glow—she convulses like from an electric shock. Then he does the same to the other nurse.

"Someone's coming—silver and white—it's Merrak. Anger, frustration, fear—Kyra starts crying. The man charges the door, knocks down Merrak, and runs into the hall. He dashes around the corner and rips off his robe. He's about forty—short, stocky—red hair—Darkovan, but he's wearing Terran-style clothes. Not a uniform." The vision faded. Gratefully she dropped the robe. "That's all."

She staggered. Rafe wheeled a chair over and helped her into it. "To kill with a look—a thought—" he said, his mouth twisting with revulsion. "Who can do such a thing?"

Tight-lipped with cold anger, Jason said, "I've heard about it from the *leroni* who've worked with us. A perversion of the Alton Gift. They thought that variant had practically died out."

Dr. Hamilton said, "Then identifying the criminal should be no problem. How many Darkovans on our staff, matching that description, could there be—and with Alton genes in their ancestry?"

Rafe's expression lightened. He gave Merrak's hand a gentle touch of reassurance. "Yes, we *will* find him. And perhaps by the use of truthspell, the *leroni* will uncover any accomplices he may have."

Fiona began to shiver with bone-deep chill. Jason's hand briefly touched her shoulder. "You're worn out. Better come to the infirmary for a checkup and a hot drink. Soon you'll be hungry, too."

She felt too sick from what she'd seen to consider food, but she didn't have the strength to argue.

"The Darkovans have a proverb," Jason said, "that an untrained telepath is a danger to herself and others. Would you consider joining us for a while? Learning to control that talent, instead of letting it control you?"

Fiona had to clamp her jaws shut to stop her teeth from chattering before she could answer. "Thank you. I'll consider it."

The Bargain

by Chel Avery

Chel Avery—who is female and her name is short for Michel—which is not an unambiguously female version of the name—in French the female version is Michelle—says of herself, "I don't know what to tell you about myself other than what I wrote you last year. I'm still a woman, still living in Philadelphia, still working as a mediator/conflict specialist, still a Quaker." She adds that "this is the year I turn 40"—well, it happens to all of us if we live that long—"and I am cooking up plans to throw my whole life up in the air and reassemble whatever pieces fall back to Earth."

She follows up by saying, "We won't talk about the novel that came back from the editor not with the classic rejection slip, but with a steaming diatribe about how much he hated it!" In case you don't know it, Chel, that's good news; the enemy of the good is not the bad, but the mediocre. Even after fifty years I remember a manuscript I read when I was seventeen years old, for a fanzine; it starred a pair of Siamese twins, one boy and one girl. (For those who don't know, Siamese twins are, by scientific necessity, always *of the same sex. Suspending disbelief does not mean hanging it by the neck till dead.) This at least insures he will* remember *your story—and read the next one with interest. I say this, as Abraham Lincoln said about politicians, with the more freedom being an editor myself.*

My father has wed me to a man with the character of a banshee and the wits of a rabbit-horn. Suppressing a groan, Caillen said out loud, "You were right to check with me, Eduin. It was, indeed, a misunderstanding. My husband did not intend to order the bola nut seedlings planted on the west slope of the back hill, where they would be shaded half the day by Brunner's Peak. *Dom* Raul means for you to plant them on the east slope."

The steward thanked her awkwardly, avoiding her eyes, and fumbled out of the room. Caillen finally let herself groan and collapse to a seat by the fire.

Only two seasons a bride, and already the steward and coridom slipped behind their Lord's back to seek the advice of his Lady, always under the pretext of asking Raul's "true wishes" in the matter.

Father, why did you give me to that self-important fool? I always believed you loved me well, that you raised me for something better than a marriage that drags at me like the shackles of a Dry Towner's wife. Did you think so little of me, after all, that you would trade my happiness for your own pride, to boast about the fine match you made with the heir to a Domain? Were you trying to recover our family's former prominence that we lost in the old wars, and which you always appeared content to forget about?

Fighting back a moment of dizziness, she tried to

look at her situation objectively. Perhaps she expected too much from marriage. After all, she was no child bride. Village tongues were wagging about her long spinsterhood by the time *Dom* Aldric Di Asturien had let his daughter, at twenty, leave for the bed of the young Lord Elhalyn. She should be more realistic. Marriages were arranged for the preservation of family lines and the stewardship of property—not for the wedded bliss of the bride. Had she let too many ballads turn her head?

No, she was no fool, nor ever was. Her standards of marriage and family life were learned at her mother's knee. *Domna* Alicia had been well content as wife of *Dom* Aldric and mistress of the Asturias estates. Her father's devotion to his wife and family was widely spoken of, at times with respect, at times in ridicule, depending on the speaker. Which made it all the more strange and upsetting that her father would make such an impossible match for his only daughter.

Caillen had not yet seen her twelfth summer when the last of the many small brothers that followed her into this world had, like all the others, died a few hours after birth, blue and gasping. The midwife said to *Dom* Aldric, "Enough! She will be ruined by this hopeless bearing. Be content with your daughter, and get her no more with child."

Dom Aldric waited a half-moon, until Alicia was on her feet and strong again, then he kissed her warmly in the open courtyard and rode away, attended by two men and three horses. When he returned two tendays later, the extra horse bore not the lovely young *barragana* that everyone expected and none would have blamed him for, but a stout, elderly nurse holding before her a small boy, perhaps four summers old.

The boy was the younger son of Lord Geom of Elhalyn. Aldric placed the child in Alicia's arms. "I have adopted him for my heir. Take him, my wife, and foster him for me." And gladly Alicia, whose arms had craved another child to hold, received him.

Young Corys, as he was called, was a beautiful, engaging child. "How bonny he is," exclaimed one of her mother's women. "I cannot understand how the Lady Elhalyn could part with him."

"The Lady of Elhalyn is dead," said *Dom* Aldric, "and Lord Geom loves both his sons enough to be glad that there will be estates for each, and that the younger will never threaten the rights of the one that is heir."

But the women scoffed. "How could such a babe be a threat to anyone?"

A few days later, *Dom* Aldric called Caillen to his study and bade her to sit and attend well. "Daughter, there was a second part of my arrangement with Elhalyn, a part that pertains to you." Caillen's eyes widened, for at first she could not imagine what he was speaking of. "I have betrothed you to Raul of Elhalyn, *Dom* Geom's elder son and heir." *Dom* Aldric grasped his daughter's two hands. "Now you must understand, my child. It is a good match, to be promised to the heir of a Domain, a better match than we had reason to expect for you. But I like not this practice of arranging our children's lives when they are too young to know what it is about. If you tell me now that you have no mind for marriage, if you wish to spend your life in a Tower, for example, it is not too late for me to make some excuse to Elhalyn and release you from this promise."

Caillen shook her head. "I had no idea about marriage, Father, but I see it pleases my mother well enough, and so I will do as you have promised."

Dom Aldric ruffled Caillen's hair, which she still wore loose as a young girl. "Well, you are young yet, so give it no more thought. The time will come soon enough. Now, I have another matter to speak of. Tell me, child, has your mother brought you up to manage a household? Do you already know about kitchen things and linens and maidservants and all that sort of business?"

"Yes, Father." Caillen spoke proudly, for Alicia had taught her well enough that she had been trusted to manage the household herself the last two times her mother lay in childbed.

"Good," said Dom Aldric. "Then it will do no harm for me to take you away from your mother's care. I have waited too long for a son to ride beside me in the fields and hills. It will be a few years yet before young Corys is grown to sit a pony saddle. So, while your mother is busy with him, I will claim my daughter's company."

It was those years she spent as her father's daily companion, more than any of the others, that had left Caillen with the certainty of her father's love for her. As they rode side by side, he spoke to her confidingly of all the things that concerned him, of crop rotations and the breeding of chervines and when to be stern and when to be lenient with the peasants that worked the land. When he met to do business with traders, she sat beside him in his study, and when agreements were made or messages sent, he permitted her to fix his mark in wax on the parchment with the great iron ring that bore his personal seal. One summer, against her mother's protests, he took her to the fire lines where she carried messages between fire-fighting teams. In time, he came more and more not just to tell her his opinions, but to ask hers, to discuss estate management with her as he might with his own steward.

At age fifteen, she was sent to Dalereuth Tower to learn control of her awakening psychic gifts. And although her *laran* was only of moderate strength, she remained in the Tower for three years, watching other young women with *laran* stronger than her own stay only a season or two before returning home, often to their weddings. Each midsummer her Keeper, gentle Ballart of Dalereuth, called her aside and said, "Your father has agreed that we may keep you in the relays another year." So, obediently, she served, helping to transmit messages from Tower to Tower, until she knew the business of all the Domains, the relationships and arrangements of the Comyn families and their squabbling sects, the intrigues of Thendara. When the wife of Lord Alton died in childbirth, she accurately guessed, before any outward indications, that the youngest daughter of Serrais, the Domain which had most recently contended with Alton in Council, would soon be riding eastward.

It was her mother's death that called her home. Her father and Corys, now grown to be a tall, lively boy, welcomed her to share their mourning, which was deep and heartfelt. "You are already eighteen summers," her father muttered, clasping her to him. "By all rights, I should have let you wed two summers ago.

But I cannot part with you and Alicia so close together. Stay with me a time."

When the spring snows melted, *Dom* Aldric said to Caillen, "I have engaged a tutor for Corys. I think it may be a good thing for a man to know a little of letters so that he might write and read his own messages and not be cheated. But I've no mind to send the lad to Nevarsin, so I have sent for a monk to come here, a stern-looking fellow. No doubt a strict teacher will do Corys good, but the boy still grieves for his foster mother, and it may be well to have a loving elder sister at his side. Work with Corys and the tutor, Caillen, and I will be sure to get my money's worth in this man's wages."

So, under the tutelage of Brother Domenic, who was indeed a stern taskmaster, brother and sister grew to know and love one another as they also acquired the rudiments of spelling and ciphering.

Eight years passed from the time Caillen was told of her betrothal until the day her marriage was consummated. In all those years, she never met her promised husband, though Lord Elhalyn visited several times. She liked the aging *Dom* Geom, a hearty man who liked to tease, but who was unbending in his arguments for the things he believed in. He made a special effort to acquaint himself with Caillen, and that gesture charmed her. *If his son has half his warmth and spirit, I have much to look forward to,* Caillen told herself. The last summer before her marriage, as *Dom* Geom took leave of her family at the end of a visit, he kissed Caillen's two cheeks and held her hands. "I am counting on you, my daughter," he said obliquely before he rode away.

Nine moons later, the old Lord was dead. Twelve

moons later, Caillen, her heart heavy for the loss of the one member of her new household whom she already knew and loved, rode from Asturias a bride at the side of *Dom* Raul, new Lord of Elhalyn.

In a short time, it became plain to her that Raul was not lordship material. He was, as her mother's fowl woman would have said, "half hatched." He blundered along, managing the estate with the finesse of a verrin hawk mothering a kitten. If he did not destroy it entirely, and make enemies of every neighbor to boot, it would be through the combined efforts of his steward, his coridom, and Caillen cleaning up behind him, covering his tracks with self-effacing subtlety, for Raul was proud and quick to take offense if he imagined his authority was being challenged.

Oh, my father, why? Why have you sent me to such a fate? He was seventeen when you pledged me to him. Could you not see his faults, or did you not care? I cannot love or honor such a man. I dare *not obey such a one. Didn't my feelings matter to you, Father?*

She rose from her seat with a mind to visit the stables and find comfort, or at least distraction from her woes, checking on the care of the dumb beasts. When she stood, the room went black around her.

She awoke in her own bed. Seated beside her was the estate midwife, beaming as if she herself had just carved the four moons out of colored beeswax.

Caillen was back on her feet in a matter of hours, but the following days were more of a trial than all her married life up to that point. Raul swaggered about as if he were the first bridegroom ever to get his consort with an heir. He treated Caillen as if pregnancy had suddenly made her feeble of body and wits, constantly ordering her to her rooms to rest, scoffing at her protests as a "breeding woman's excitements."

Just as Caillen was reaching the point of intolerance, a message arrived that offered some relief in the form of distraction. A party from Aillard was traveling to Hali, and wished to stop at Elhalyn. To Caillen, the visit promised a chance of conversation with some interesting people, perhaps with a woman her own age. To Raul, however, the visit was a chance to show off.

"Order a banquet for them, Caillen," he commanded. "Wear my mother's copper filigree tiara—I'm sure the Aillard women have nothing like it, for all their pearls. And have the cook make pastries and fresh roast chervine."

Caillen laughed. "I will wear your mother's baubles, if it pleases you, husband, but we would do better to serve fowl or rabbit-horn. All the plump, tender chervine are nursing their calves at this time of year, and we don't want to serve up a gristly old one, or a bitter bull."

The laughter was a mistake. Raul bristled. "You will do as I say. I won't have the Aillard thinking we are stingy, or worse, poor. Order a chervine slaughtered, and make sure it will be a tasty one."

"I assure you, my Lord," this time Caillen lowered her eyes in a display of deference, "the Aillard will not think us stingy or poor if we don't kill a chervine. Rather, they will think us foolish and wasteful if we do. No one slaughters chervine in the spring, before the young are weaned. If we did, it would make a story for jeering at us behind our backs."

Raul changed the subject. He would never openly

capitulate, but nonetheless, he exacted revenge for losing the argument. "I'm going to send that ugly black dog home with one of my men. It sheds all over the rooms. Perhaps Eduin can make a herder of it."

The dog was Caillen's pet, a going-away gift from Corys, and one of the few comforts she had found at Elhalyn. But she knew better than to argue or beg. She had already learned that once Raul began acting mean, resistance only made him progressively meaner. She spent much of the afternoon weeping across her bed, and presented herself at the banquet that night wearing the previous Lady Elhalyn's copper tiara and red, swollen eyes.

Meloria Aillard and her husband Morgan, who had been a Lindir, were making a visiting tour out of the occasion of escorting Meloria's young sister, Genavie, to Hali Tower. Caillen remembered Meloria, who had been one of the young women that had passed through Dalereuth Tower for a season during her own tenure there. Although Meloria was a year younger than Caillen, she seemed older. She had filled out and adopted a warm, matronly manner that made her seem almost like an aunt to her younger sister.

Caillen blushed as she felt, through the old telepathic touch of the Tower-trained, Meloria's careful scrutiny of her swollen eyes and Raul's pompous bluster. She knew Meloria had a good assessment of how things were for her at Elhalyn.

Meloria said nothing, but as they parted in the morning, she squeezed Caillen's hand. "We will pass by again in two tendays. Let us take you back with us for a time. You can comfort me over the loss of my sister, and it is said that our sea air at Aillard is good for women in your condition."

Caillen's heart brightened, but Raul quickly intervened. "You mean well, I'm sure, and I thank you, but no wife of mine travels unnecessarily while she is breeding. I want her here, near her own midwife."

Caillen contained her rage. Even this temporary reprieve was to be denied her. She was sure Raul knew nothing about the needs of pregnant women, and cared less. He just had to show that he was in charge.

When she was safely in her room, she gave vent to her frustration, throwing pillows against the walls. *I cannot tolerate this marriage any longer.*

Could she run away? It would be disgraceful, but could any shame be worse than what she now endured? There had been a time when she would not have done a thing that could so embarrass her own family. But when she felt herself quail, she remembered it was her father who had put her in this situation. *All these years, he acted as if he loved me, as if he was proud of me, and then he threw away my happiness for an advantageous match. I will not think of him. I am on my own now. I must think only of myself, and of my child.*

She began to plan her escape. Meloria's party would return. She could not openly go away with them, but if she followed, Meloria would hide and protect her. She could shelter at Aillard until the child was born, and then. . . ?

On the fire lines there had been women from the old Sisterhood of the Sword. It was said they had gotten a charter from Comyn Council permitting them to live together and work for their living as an order of women. She would go to them, if they would have her and the baby.

What if the baby was a boy? Would they accept her then? *No.* She pushed down her doubt. *I will fly that hawk when its feathers are grown. First, I must get away. Any child, boy or girl, will be better off away from such a father, even if it must grow up in poverty and shame.*

She began to sort through the things she would need to take, and the things she could leave behind.

Which is why, when the word came from Asturias three days later, she was prepared to ride.

The rider who brought the message was a man in her father's service whom she remembered from days past. The tears in his eyes told her, before he found the words, that *Dom* Aldric was gone.

"He fell from his horse, Caillen child, I mean *Domna.* But he never would have lost his seat on old Groby unless it had been his time, anyway. We think perhaps he had a stroke. At any rate, it was swift and painless.

"Thank Avarra for that," Caillen whispered. But even as sorrow swept over her and threatened to make her insensible to all else, in another region of her heart she raged. How could her father abandon her so completely, first by casting her into this hated marriage, then by leaving life before she could call him to account?

Before, she had told herself she would run away from all the misery of Elhalyn and face the world alone, but now she recognized that in the back of her mind, the home of her father had still existed as a refuge, if not for herself, at least for her child.

Now I am completely alone. Corys loves me, of course, but he is a mere boy of twelve, and will be under the hand of a guardian for several years. She prayed that her father had made provision for some regent other than Raul, or the home of her childhood would be ruined.

"I must go to my brother," she declared, and for such a purpose, even Raul could find no reason to detain her.

Corys met her in the courtyard of Asturias Castle. He had grown. The seasons apart, or sorrow, or new responsibility, had made him more adult than he had been when she last saw him at her nuptials. "I sensed you coming, sister." He hugged her. "Is it the beginning of *laran*, or just that I wanted you here so much?"

They sat in the chapel and talked at random of great matters and small. "So, you are with child, so soon. In this one year, your father-in-law and our father—I really do think of Aldric as my true father—are gone, and a new generation begins. Tell me, Caillen, are you happy at Elhalyn? No, don't answer. I take back the question. I know you cannot speak of happiness now."

After a silence, she asked, "Shall we carry our father to Hali?"

"No, he wanted his remains to stay on Di Asturien soil."

"He spoke to you of such things, little brother?"

"Yes. After Geom died and you went away, our father began to prepare for his own turn to go. He asked me to put his wishes in writing. Later, we will go to his study and I will show you his legacies."

After she had rested from her travels, she wandered about the grounds. She went to the stables and petted

Groby, whose neck hung low in dejection. If her brother appeared older and stronger, her father's horse seemed older and weaker. "It wasn't your fault, old friend. If he had to go, he would have wanted it to be from your back."

She felt restless, and she could sense the restlessness of the tiny life within her. For her brother, her father's men, even her father's horse, grieving for *Dom* Aldric was straightforward and uncomplicated. A beloved friend was gone.

Her own sorrow was mixed with confusion, and with an anger that would not die with the man. Had he loved her, or not? If he were alive today, would he accept and shelter her if she fled home to him, or did he think so little of her that her present unhappiness would count less than the pride of the Di Asturiens? Now, she would never know.

Now, whatever happened, Asturias would never again be her home. She wanted to wander alone in its paths and fields, where once she had belonged, but wherever she showed her face, her father's men, their wives and children, approached her to express their grief, and to remind her that everything had changed forever.

Some of the wives, with sharp eyes for subtle changes in another woman, or perhaps with a little more intuition than is considered natural, expressed along with their grief congratulations for the joy to come.

Would there ever be joy again?

After dinner, she went to her father's study and paced aimlessly, touching the leather-bound stud books that went back ten generations, the heavy ring with her father's personal seal, the tankard from which he'd always had his ale. After a time, Corys joined her.

"I want to tell you what he wished. He made some small gifts, and tomorrow we should distribute them. He wanted his own steward, Varzil, to act as advisor and unofficial guardian to me. Ballart of Dalereuth will be official regent and overseer, until I am fifteen, so Council should make no objections."

"I think no arrangement could be better," Caillen replied. Her relief was mixed with resentment. Could he have not thought so well about his own daughter's welfare?

Corys went on. "Varzil is to be given the cottage at Craghorn, once I am of age, and the land as far as the river."

"Varzil has been faithful. I am glad Father was so generous."

"There are three mares for the horsemaster, plus stud services. There is a pension for the housekeeper when she reaches an age to retire, or sooner if I marry and my bride wishes to bring a new housekeeper." He went on, listing various arrangements.

"Finally, there were a couple of things for you."

"I can hardly think so, Corys. I was given all such gifts at the time of my marriage."

"So it may be, but there were other things our father designated for you. First, you are to have our mother's jewelry."

"That is not right. I have Raul's mother's jewelry to wear. Alicia's should be for your wife."

"No, there is an amount set aside for the crafting of new ornaments when I marry, so my wife need not be disgraced, but Father did not want Alicia's jewels to go to a stranger. He wanted them for you. He wished you to have something of value that was entirely your own, something you could sell or trade if you were ever in great need."

Caillen did not know what to make of these words. Any way she thought about them, they troubled her, even as they opened new possibilities.

"And another gift, a sentimental one. He wanted you to have his seal ring to remember him by."

"No, that cannot be." This, she protested strongly. "The seal is for the Lord of the estate. It is a treasure of Asturias. I am sure it must be for you."

"Trust me, sister. It is for you. He explained it to me fully, because he wanted me to understand that it was not a slight to me, not that he loved me less for being adopted. He told me that the seal was to comfort you and to remind you that he was as proud of you as if you were his heir. And he told me that if the responsibility fell on me when I was too young, I could always turn to you for counsel, because you had had the full training of a Di Asturien heir."

Caillen took the ring in her two hands and burst into tears. Corys, in consternation, awkwardly tried to pat her shoulder. "No, don't worry. I am all right. Please, leave me alone for a little while."

After the tears stopped, she sat quietly with the new understanding that was suddenly obvious, after so many years. *Those two conniving old men, Aldric and Geom. Now I see what bargain they struck.*

The full import of that bargain was evident to her for the first time. Aldric got a fine heir for Asturias, one he could raise himself with no shame to his wife, and a valuable alliance for his clan. Geom got an estate for his younger son, but even more, he got for his heir a wife that could save Elhalyn from that heir's incompetence. *Now I know what my dowry was. I never thought to ask. It was my education, all the preparation a wife would need to rescue a Domain from Raul's bungling and to preserve it for the next generation.*

That next generation was growing inside her now. Caillen placed her hand over her abdomen, sensing the tiny life impulses, and knew, with certainty, what she had already begun to suspect. The child within her was a girl.

Well, then, Father, I accept my part in your bargain . . . for now. It would be easier, knowing that her fate resulted not from her low worth in her father's eyes, but from the very great worth in the eyes of the two dead men she had loved. She would go back to Elhalyn and do her best. If it became intolerable, her father had left her a way out, in the form of her mother's jewels.

But hear this, Aldric and Geom, wherever you are. I add my own clause to this bargain. This is my price. If the child I carry is worthy, if she is her mother's daughter rather than her father's, I will see her have the opportunity to rule Elhalyn in her own name, and not her husband's. I dedicate myself to it.

The Witch of the Kilghard Hills

by Aimee Kratts

Aimee Kratts says "I am shocked, pleased, amazed and excited beyond belief that you have chosen to put my story in your anthology! I have read and admired your work the last few years and only recently have I mustered the courage to submit something to you. I never dreamed it would be published. You see, it is my first work of fiction submitted for publication. Whew! Who would have thought?"

However, as I could have guessed, she says she has been writing all kinds of things for years. (Me, too; I started writing before I could physically hold a pencil, dictating poems to my mother. I live in terror someone in search of an obscure subject for a doctoral thesis will someday unearth them.) She grew up in a small town in upstate New York called Saranac Lake and she adds "Believe me, it's colder than the Hellers up there."

I well know; I, too, grew up in upstate New York. (And I didn't invent the Hellers from living in Texas.) Like me, she is a "towering" 5'3", and "for those people interested in physical descriptions, I have brown hair, hazel eyes, and freckles. I am 75% German, but look Irish enough to get frisked at Heathrow." Her interests include sports, sewing, old movies, craft fairs, traveling, chocolate, and Drambuie. Well, you can have my share of the chocolate and the sports. Differences of opinion, says an old proverb, are what make horseraces interesting. That, of course, assumes that horseraces are *interesting; the wise Chinese says "it has long been established that one horse can run faster than another." But Dick Francis and his mystery novels about horseracing—and other things—are still favorites of mine.*

Amilha peered furtively past the mist-shrouded trees to the road straining to hear sounds of pursuit. And she heard them, distantly, but unmistakably coming her way.

Choking back her fright and tears, she murmured calming noises into the stolen pony's ear. "Shh–shh, little one. You must keep silent. Please. There, there, eat some grass. Yes, that's right. You'll need a full belly for our . . . travels. Shh, now. Shh."

The pony bent its head to the green grass and started to graze silently.

The sounds of galloping horses drew near. And nearer. Amilha gulped and held her breath, fear shaking her violently. As the four riders passed by, the pony raised its head to look at the road in curiosity. Amilha's heart sunk. She waited for the pony's salutatory nicker to the horses, but it never came. The pony merely looked at the riders, looked at Amilha, and resumed grazing.

The young girl let out her breath slowly as she sunk to the ground weak with nervous relief. *I must rest for a while,* she thought. Sitting there, unable to move her aching muscles, she let her mind race back to the events of the previous night.

Bard. Bard Di Asturien, she thought with vehemence. Anger began to replace fear. *If only I hadn't walked by his room last night! If only I hadn't looked back when he called my name. He took my will from me with his* laran *and he made me* do *things! Things I had never done before. I hate him!*

Oh, why did my parents send me to Lady Jerana to be one of her maidens? They knew Bard's reputation and they sent me anyway. Why? I know I was never my father's favorite and it's bad enough that he wouldn't let me go to the Towers, but how could he have put me in such danger!

Sobs escaped from her clenched teeth. She rocked back and forth on the grass with her arms wrapped around her knees. Her mother would never believe it was Bard's doing. "Why would Bard choose you?" she would ask. "Certainly you're nothing to look at with all that wild curly hair you never take care of properly. Besides, you're all skin and bones with no womanly flesh on you," she'd conclude in that matter of fact way she had whenever she took stock of Amilha's marriage potential. She would tell Amilha that she'd always known something like this would happen. If she only had the proper decorum befitting young maidens like her sisters.

But Amilha knew why Bard had taken her. He loved taking innocent-looking virgins and shaming them with his manly vulgarity. New tears of anguish poured down her face as she thought of last night's pain and humiliation. *I'm never going back to that castle! Never! They can search for me until the Hellers thaw. They'll never find me.*

The pony gently nickered and nudged Amilha back to the present. She took a slow deep breath and stood up, her knees wobbling. "What are we going to do tonight, little one?" she asked the pony. "Where are we going to stay?" With dusk turning to darkness, she knew she needed to make a decision soon. She'd been riding all day, thinking only about putting as much distance as possible between her and Castle Asturias. Now she was beginning to realize the importance of planning.

"At least I visited the kitchen before I left, little one. Or else I would be eating grass with you." She took a handful of dried fruits out of her pouch to appease her complaining belly as she tried to think of possible destinations. "Neskaya Tower isn't that far south. But no, they won't take me for training now. Bard has seen to that. Besides, what little *laran* I seem to have the house *leronis* couldn't identify. She thought I'd only be useful as a monitor." She sighed. "Besides, Father would look for me there first. He knows how badly I wanted to go."

"Edelweiss isn't that far south, either." Amilha looked down at her soiled dress. "But the townspeople would know I should not be riding around unescorted like this. The first man who sees me will take it into his head to bring me back to the castle for my own good. And for my father's reward money."

"There are hunters' shacks throughout the hills. I could hide there, little one." A hunter's horn blew. Amilha shivered and knew what if felt like to be the prey. "Hunters' shacks mean hunters."

Then another thought crept into her mind. It was unheard of, but she was out of options. "What about the Sisterhood of the Sword?" she asked the pony excitedly. "Maybe they need a cook or maybe there's something else I can do." Amilha was pleased with her idea. Taking the pony's reins up in her hands she took one look around and realized it was now full dark. She stopped short. The times that she'd been outside alone at night were very few, and fear froze her reflexes for just a moment.

"Oh, little one! What am I going to do?" she pleaded as she leaned back against a tree.

An unbidden thought flowed slowly into her mind, *Get farther from the road. It's not safe here.* It was so gentle, Amilha thought she must be remembering some advice from an old aunt.

The pony nickered softly, walked over to the girl, and nuzzled her gently. Amilha yawned, exhausted by the past hours. The gnarled old tree she leaned up against was oddly comforting in its hugeness. "Little one, I am so tired I feel drunk," she said softly. "But we must not stay here. We must get farther away from the road.

She turned and peered apprehensively into the dark, forbidding forest behind her. *Maybe it wouldn't be so bad if I went back to the castle,* she thought fleetingly.

Chiding herself immediately she spoke aloud, "You fool! You silly girl! Certain punishment waits for you at the castle and worse—Bard. Push on, you silly girl. There's nothing but trees here and they won't harm you."

She took a deep breath and headed into the forest. In her mind soft, sibilant voices sang to her, *Stay here,* chiya. *We offer you comfort,* chiya. But the bushes and branches caught at her long skirts and unbound hair, causing her to stumble and sometimes stop altogether to untangle herself. Her heart was racing by the time she had covered 200 yards. "Someone is watching us, little one. I wonder if it's the Witch of the Kilghard Hills." Giggling nervously from exhaustion, she began to relate a childhood fairy story to the pony.

"You know of the Kilghard Witch, don't you *chia*?" She patted the pony's neck, comforting herself with the motion more than the pony. "She is an ugly old hag that kills little children and eats them in a stew. She offers up young maidens to her demons to appease them. She causes hunters to lose their way and their weapons to break and trees to fall upon them. Her cruelty is without boundaries, she is evil incarnate. Why, I personally know an old woman who has seen the witch. . . ." At that she stopped and remembered that she was only talking to a pony. A pony who neither cared for nor was frightened by fairy stories.

Rubbing her temples, Amilha sat on the chilled ground. "The truth is, my friend, I don't know a single person who has really seen the witch. I've only heard tales." Upon more reflection, Amilha realized that she could not come up with one incident that was caused by or related to the witch.

Fairy stories, the whole lot of them, she decided.

Night sounds all around were lulling her to sleep, buzzing, humming, hooting, and the wind rustling in the leaves. The giant roots of a tall old tree made a bed for her. She crawled up into a nook to feel safe and immediately fell asleep. The last thing she remembered was looking up at Darkover's four moons and thinking how magical they seemed.

In her dreams she met Bard. He was approaching her slowly in the castle. She wanted to run, but her feet had turned to clay. Fear became a monster crushing her will and mind. Amilha struggled helplessly and hopelessly. Bard reached out to grab her arm and suddenly they were in a glen. An oak tree stood between Amilha and Bard. He tried to move around the barrier, but Amilha caused a lower branch to shoot out and catch Bard's neck to choke the life from him. He turned purple and his eyes rolled back into his head.

An old woman appeared and looked slowly from Bard to Amilha. She smiled a toothless smile. "You have the power to do this," croaked the old witch. "And this . . ." Amilha saw herself healing a hart wounded by a hunter's poorly placed kill shot. "Which will you choose?"

"Ah ha ha ha ha ha ha . . ." echoed the witch's laughter like switches waving in a storm.

Amilha woke with a start. She'd always thought that if she ever had the power to kill Bard, she would do so. Watching herself actually killing made it clear to her that she would never abuse power the way Bard did. She sighed. A darker spot of her mind was not completely pleased with her or that decision.

The red sun had been in the sky for several hours. The dew on the grass had long since evaporated. Amilha groaned. "Little one, did you trample on my body while I slept? I feel like a dance floor feels after a Midwinter Festival." She rose slowly, sore but rested.

The pony was silently cropping grass a few feet away. That reminded Amilha of her own empty stomach. Chewing a handful of dried fruit from her pouch to ease the grumbling, she contemplated the journey she was about to undertake.

I must go east to find the Sisterhood of the Sword. I have heard that sometimes they go to the Isle of

Silence for healing. Perhaps a healer on the island can teach me how to use my laran *in the same way.* She smiled grimly, thinking of Bard. Then, shaking her head to clear her thoughts, she began again. *Maybe if I go east to Marenji and the Isle of Silence, I will meet a warrior sister to travel with.* She shuddered slightly at the thought of traveling with lawless women. At least she'd always heard they were lawless. Thinking aloud, "They have no shame. They cut their hair and wear breeches."

"What do you think they'll say when they see me, little one?" She smiled a sad, lopsided smile at herself. The hopelessness of her self-imposed adventure hung heavy on her young shoulders. Trying to shrug the hopelessness off, she took the pony by the reins, looked up at the red sun to get rough bearings and turned to walk east deeper into the Kilghard Hills.

Toward nightfall, Amilha began to feel uneasy. All the versions of the fairy tale she'd heard about the Kilghard Hills witch held that she lived in the eastern part of the forest where the magical waters ran deep and strange creatures lurked. Would she run across the witch? She tried to put the thought from her mind.

How far she had traveled the first day, she didn't know. She only knew that it seemed slow going, especially when she had to walk in her long skirts. Bugs had made nests in her hair, too, even though she tried to keep it tied up out of the way. She scratched at her scalp until it bled.

Three days she traveled. Three nights she dreamed of Bard, the trees, the witch and the hart.

On the fourth day, filthy and exhausted, she heard a large stream running in the distance. She also heard men's voices. "I wish I could bathe, little one," she whispered. "And we need water, too." Desperation made her more brave than she would have normally been. Leaving the pony behind, she walked closer to the sound of running water. As she got closer she could hear the singing more clearly.

We are bredin till the day we die!
Bredin are we, everyone shall cry!
We live for the brotherhood of men today!
Together we shall live and never part ways!

Amilha shrunk back farther behind a thicker bush. Boys. They were splashing around in the water, making an awful racket reveling in their newfound brotherhood. Amilha peered through the bushes again. They were naked and obviously enjoying it. *A few days ago I would have watched in innocent wonder.* Her eyes narrowed and she moved back. *But I know you for what you are now, you pigs.*

Suddenly a horse snorted. She jumped. Not ten feet from her there were two geldings tied to a tree. Both had saddle bags over their backs. *What luck!*

Quietly and slowly she approached the horses. One reached out to sniff her hand and once having done so, resumed grazing. The other saw that its partner ignored the small stranger and decided to ignore her, too.

Opening the closest bag, Amilha pulled out a pair of old brown breeches, a rough homespun shirt, and a heavy woolen tunic. From the other bag she took a pair of boots. Beneath them she spied a heavy woolen blanket. "Oh!" she gasped involuntarily. There was warmth looking her in the eyes and she dared not take it. *I never knew that a simple woolen blanket would be such a luxury to me.* Amilha ran her hand lovingly over the rough surface. Before she was tempted further, she closed and strapped the bags. The blanket would be missed immediately because of the weight difference and she didn't want any chance of pursuit. She had stayed too long already.

Grasping the precious stolen clothing, Amilha headed back to the pony as quickly as she dared. She didn't want to trip and fall, crashing into the dry underbrush, alerting the boys in the stream. The pony was waiting for her, patient as ever.

Amilha secured the clothing to the pony's neck with a piece of her torn underskirt. Then, she took the reins and led the pony northeast, away from the stream, but not backtracking. Because Amilha feared pursuit, she walked through the forest until dark. When they finally stopped, Amilha was too exhausted to do anything but sleep. She curled up against the nearest large tree and fell to sleep immediately.

In the morning, she unfolded the clothes and discovered that a short dagger had been hidden in the woolen tunic. "What luck! Now I can . . . well . . . I can use it for something I suppose. Although what, I'm not sure." She tried on the breeches and boots first. Both were just a little too big. The shirt was loose and comfortable, as was the tunic. Amilha danced around the trees in her new found freedom. "Look, little one! No skirts to bind my legs!" She danced and twirled until a branch caught her hair and stopped her short. "Ouch!" She tried to gently untangle herself from the bush but this time was left with tresses full of burrs.

"I wish I was a boy. Then I wouldn't have to worry about long hair." She spotted the dagger lying on the ground near her dress. The blade gleamed in the morning light. Its presence suggested a solution.

"Oh, no. I can't cut my hair," she said in a small voice. "It wouldn't be right. No man will ever marry . . ." She didn't finish the thought. Swiftly she plucked up the knife and within moments her beautiful copper tresses were on the forest floor like red-brown leaves in autumn. She shook her head in angry defiance at what she had done, but when she knelt to the ground to hide the locks under a bush, she started to sob. "I am truly no longer a maiden."

A sympathetic breeze blew through the trees. It felt warm and comforting on her bare neck.

On the seventh day, she reached a high ridge that looked over the lower hills. A young tree bent by the wind offered a natural seat for her tired body. The trees were fully green now that it was high summer. In the distance she could see naught but leaves carpeting the hills and valleys. Turning to look behind her she could no longer see the Great North Road.

Amilha sighed. "Will we ever make it to the Isle of Silence, little one? And if we do, what can I possibly offer to the Sisterhood of the Sword, if I find any of them there? I have nothing of value to offer them."

Except yourself.

Amilha whirled around to look behind her but there was no one there. At the end of her patience and control, she demanded, "Who are you? Why do you follow me and scare me so?"

No reply. Only the wind in the leaves.

"That's not the first time I've heard you!" she cried, angrier than ever.

No reply. Only the buzzing of a bee in the flowers.

Then, curiosity getting the better of her, she sat on

the bent tree again and remarked conversationally, "Why can't I see you?"

You can, I am all around you.

"But I can't see any beast, four-legged or two."

See me not with your eyes, but your mind.

Amilha closed her eyes and concentrated. She tried to picture the witch that she saw in her dreams, but nothing appeared to her except the veins in her eyelids illuminated by the red sun.

"I cannot see you. Please tell me who you are?"

There was a faint echo of a chuckle. Or was there? She couldn't tell.

Weary of the game, she stood up to scout a destination in the hills. She could discern no feature in particular to head for until the clouds parted over a small patch of forest and let the sun shine down on a white structure. "What is that over there, little one? Is it someone's home? It looks like it's made out of gray wood, or stone. Is that a steeple on the roof? Maybe it's a chapel!" she cried. "That means there's a holy woman there! And I could rest there for a few days and gather more food before journeying on. Or maybe she could tell me what to do." Excited by her discovery, she turned and ran back down the hill, completely forgetting about the pony, who trotted along after her.

It took her two hours to find the chapel in the forest. It was set in a small glen. She didn't see it until she was almost upon it. *Maybe I had better not run right up there. What if there's someone living there who doesn't like people. Or what if it's (gulp) the witch.* Shrinking back behind the bushes she realized her mistake. It was too late. A witch with laran would already *know* she was there and there was no getting away from someone who wanted you. Bard taught her that. But this time, she had a dagger.

The leather-wrapped handle still felt strange in her hand, but it was reassuring. She approached the house slowly. The stone steps looked wildly overgrown with beautiful forest flowers in pinks and yellows and oranges. She shook her head defiantly. She would not be lulled and then captured again.

"Is anyone here?" she asked in a small voice. Then, remembering she had a small amount of *laran* training, she sent out a thought. *Is anyone here?*

No answer except a welcoming—thought?

Her heart pounded as she tried to slink slowly up the steps. She felt sick. Surely this was the end of her life. The rusty hinges screamed as she pushed the oak door open in front of her. Feeling as though she was jumping off a cliff, she threw her body against the aged door to force it the rest of the way.

"Ah-ha!" she screamed in a shrill voice flinging herself inside the room, immediately tripping and landing facedown on the stone floor. Twisting her body around, she scrabbled for the knife that she had dropped in her fall. Surely the witch would strike now while she was unarmed. She knew she must lash out immediately, for she couldn't dodge *laran*.

Jumping to her feet, she spied a terrified mouse running squeaking out the door behind her. Beyond that, the chapel was empty. "Empty? How can this chapel be empty? Where are you?" she screamed. "My heart's pounding, I have a bloody nose and scraped fingers and all because of a mouse?" she stated to no one in particular. The humor of the situation struck her as hard as the stone floor had and she collapsed to the floor, alternately laughing and crying hysterically.

After what seemed an eternity, Amilha stopped. Still hiccuping, she started to explore the chapel to see what she could find. It was a small building, only as large as Lady Jerana's sewing room. The stone floor was covered with dust and debris that the wind had blown in through the open windows. There was no furniture except a moldy pallet which Amilha carefully pushed out the door with her foot. The small altar at the front of the room was bare and the alcove that once housed a statuette of some god or goddess now housed the absent mouse. There was a window on each wall of the chapel and a small fireplace in one of the back corners near the door.

"Maybe I'll rest here for a few days anyway," she sighed. "And if I'm going to do that, I guess I'd better clean this place out." She placed her hands on her hips in a determined fashion and said, "The first thing that goes is that mouse's house!"

She carefully picked up the nest of leaves, grass and downy things, brought it outside, and placed it neatly in a half-rotten log near the edge of the glen. Just as she was getting back up, she heard the rustle and scamper of a small creature in the underbrush. Smiling to herself, she turned to catch a glimpse of the creature. Instead, she saw something flash for a brief moment in the setting sun.

She walked to the outer corner of the building. "What was that, little one?" The pony looked up at the question but didn't answer. "There's something on the ground over here that's shiny. Maybe it's another knife or a cooking pot." Kneeling once more, she picked through the large pile of dead leaves and twigs that the wind had blown against the side of building.

"There doesn't seem to be anything here. Wait. What's this? Cloth? Under a pile of leaves?"

She picked up the edge of what looked like a rotten cape or cloak and tried to dislodge it from the pile. Something stuck. She yanked at it. Bones rolled out. "Aaahhhh!" Amilha screeched. They were human bones, almost completely rotted. In her shock, she nearly missed the little green stone that rolled free. Snatching it up, she fled toward the forest.

She stopped when she could no longer see the chapel spying at her through the trees. Gasping for breath, she tried to gather her wits and soon realized the foolishness of running. *I'm in no danger from an old pile of bones,* she rationalized. But she couldn't come up with anything that sounded better than that small assurance. It was dark now and the sounds of the night hummed and chirped and howled at her to go back to the safety of the stone chapel. Turning around slowly, she walked back to the chapel as if she were walking toward death herself. She skirted the moldy, rotted bones as widely as possible and entered the chapel. The wooden door made an ear-shattering whine as Amilha pulled it shut behind her.

Slumping against the wall, she asked herself, "What am I doing here?" Then, pleading to no one in particular, "Where can I go?" She sat down and cried. "My parents will not welcome me back, I am no longer useful to them for a political marriage. The Tower will not take me in, I am no longer a virgin. I have no trade to ply in any town. The Sisterhood would think me too frail to train. Oh, Avarra! Help me, what can I do?"

The memory of the stone in her hand returned when she wiped her runny nose and scratched her face.

"Ouch!" Since there was no light to examine it by, she put the stone in her food pouch for safe keeping.

She curled up against the wall farthest from the entrance and waited for dawn. Sleep claimed her shortly, aided by her exhaustion. She was dreamless for hours.

Then, a voice woke her. It was still full dark except for Idriel casting her moonbeams down into the room where she lay. "Who's there?" she whispered.

No one answered.

After a few moments of waiting, she decided that her weak *laran* was once again playing her false. Determined not to hope for more, she tried to take stock of her situation, but all she could think about was the green stone at her waist. It felt like it was pulsing through the pouch. Gingerly she opened the bag and took the stone out. It felt neither hot nor cold, but it glowed green in the moonlight unlike any green she had ever seen. "It is beautiful," she said to herself.

She turned it around and around trying to make the moonlight glint off the edges, but she never could. It seemed to take the moonbeams into it and not let them out again. Then she realized what it was. A starstone.

But a green one? She had only seen blue, but that didn't matter; starstones were not toys and she should put this back in her pouch immediately. She tried to yet couldn't. It was so beautiful and there seemed to be someone beckoning her to look in. "No! I won't look! You can't make me! I will smash you first!" she cried. She felt around on the floor for her dagger, but as soon as she found it, her hand snatched itself away. Now both her hands cupped the stone. "You can't make me look into you!" she screamed.

But it did.

She felt herself drawn down and down into the emerald green depths of the stone. Green starbursts blinded her eyes and numbed her mind. Down and down she sunk into the welcoming, waving ribbons of green, the greenness that was life in the forest, and leaves on the trees and grass on the ground. The green of nature itself.

Hello, Amilha, said a soft voice.

She was still swallowed by green, but there was no fear anymore. "Hello?" she answered.

Can you see me now? the voice asked.

It was daylight!

"No, who are you? Are you the spirit of the bones I disturbed?"

She heard sweet laughter like the patter of summer rain. *No, I am not the owner of those bones, but I knew her. She was once a young girl like you.*

"Then who are you? Where are you?"

A voice with the sweetness of springtime and the ripeness of fall answered. *In the forest,* chiya. *And in your mind. Your* laran *lets us speak.*

"My *laran*? But the *leronis* said I have no *laran* to speak of."

Oh, but you do. It's a very special kind of laran, chia. *Only one in ten thousand has it. It's the special gift that lets you talk to—*

Amilha interrupted, "But you still haven't told me what you look like or who you are!"

The soft whiteness of the snows colored the response. *Look outside the windows and you will see me in every tree, every blade of grass, every flower, stream, raindrop and sunbeam. I am who you've been searching for. I am Nature. The Witch of the Kilghard Hills.*

The Gift

by Lynne Armstrong-Jones

There are two things about reading slush that I have to refute—with fifty years of experience—every time I do it. There seems to be a common misconception that a would-be writer has to "know somebody." That's not true; when I started out I was a drab little housewife in the wilds of Texas and I didn't know a soul—certainly not any editors. My first husband told me I shouldn't send in my early clunkers; editors, he felt, would get to where they would think of me as an unusable writer and groan every time they saw my name in the slush pile.

Well, he was wrong, and now I am old enough to articulate why. *I see a familiar name in the piles of unread manuscripts; and regardless of whether I can use this particular story or not, I am interested in the work of somebody who now seems like an old friend; somebody whose work—whether I can use that particular story or not—will, I know, from experience, be worth the time and trouble of reading it. When I am dealing with floods of stuff which reads as if it might as well have been sent to PLAYBOY or AMERICAN GIRL, it's nice to read something by someone who knows what I want and even more what I* don't *want. I am fairly sure Lynne won't send me any more stories about vampires with AIDS—don't laugh, I get some—or any spaceship stories where the spaceship is more interesting than the people. And if she did, I'd trust her enough to* read *it before rejecting it.*

Lynne sent me four stories for this anthology. I am almost sorry that policy dictates only one story per anthology per writer.

There's only one thing I like better than meeting an old friend in the slush pile—and that's making a new one.

Lynne Armstrong-Jones is in her thirties, married with a young son, and lives in Canada.

Garren stared out the window at the colorful leaves drifting lazily to the ground. He sighed, enjoying the feeling of—at last!—being able to drop his guard and simply relax. He moved his head and neck about in an effort to chase the aching tension from his shoulders.

After so long . . . after such a long time of serving as little more than his brother's paxman, all was his. His brother, Piers, had been missing now for several weeks—leaving Garren as lord of the area. It was only logical, after all, for Garren and Piers looked as alike as two peas in a pod—

Twins. Virtually identical. And yet . . .

And yet there was a secret which only the family knew—

For Garren had not inherited the family gift.

Garren had no *laran*. But Piers' skills were strong . . .

Which had made Garren's position all the more difficult.

Garren passed a hand through his auburn hair and sighed again. But he wasn't to have much time for musings.

"Yes," he said, more loudly than he'd intended. He straightened, his frown giving his face the stern look which he felt it needed.

They must think me as strong as Piers—even if it isn't so!

"*Dom* Garren." The door opened and a swordsman appeared, bowing slightly. "A messenger has arrived from *Dom* Win. It is urgent, *via dom.*"

Garren swallowed, hoping that his anxiety didn't show. He carried himself erectly, silently cursing the fact that it had been his brother—his elder by only fifteen minutes—who'd inherited all of the talents necessary for being a leader.

His eyes seeking those of the messenger, he led the way into the hall. Silently he pleaded with Avarra to please let the news be good—

But it was not. Of course.

The messenger finished, his face relaxing once more. Being a trained messenger, he'd of course sounded and even looked somewhat like *Dom* Win while relaying the *dom's* words. But now he was himself.

Garren muttered his thanks, hating the way his hand trembled when he gestured.

"*Dom* Garren," began the swordsman. "What shall we do if these men attack? We must protect our lands! *Dom* Piers would have used his great *laran*—"

"I am *not Dom* Piers!" Garren's eyes flashed as he

masked his indecision, biting the inside of his lip. "I know what needs to be done, Ronnado. Leave me."

Ronnado studied Garren a moment, then bowed and turned to go. Garren did not give in to his trembling until he saw the door begin to close behind the man.

"Yes! What is it!" He scowled in the direction of the household *leronis* who now peered at him from the still-open doorway.

She blinked, not yet accustomed to the new lord's foul humor. "*Dom* Garren, have you seen anything of *Dom* Piers in the overworld? I can monitor for you if you wish to search further. You're his twin; surely—"

"No!" Damn the woman! Garren took a moment to collect himself. "No, Rafa. I have not."

He did not return the woman's gaze. He knew this was difficult for her. She'd been quite fond of Piers.

Of course! Hadn't everyone been? And now *he,* Garren, was saddled with the impossible task of trying to fill his brother's shoes—

Without the *laran* which had brought his brother such respect. His neck was beginning to feel as stiff as a corpse again.

Suddenly a marmalade cat leapt into his lap. It seemed almost as though she'd sensed her master's distress. She pushed her head against his hand, murmuring reassurances.

Garren sighed, finally allowing himself a small smile. Yes, while his brother had been busy developing his *laran*, Garren had usually been in the stable or the yard, seeking the unquestioning acceptance of the animals.

* * *

It was in the dead of night that Ronnado roused him. *Dom* Win had been only too correct—

In their quest for the land and power which had once belonged to their forefathers, the men of Rafe MacEwan were claiming Garren's territory. Despite the coolness of the night, sweat was trickling down Garren's neck as he hurried down the stairs after Ronnado. His eyes were wide with terror as he thought of the inadequacy of the defenses he'd prepared.

Blessed Avarra help us all!

"Vai dom," Ronnado was shouting over the confusion of men rushing about. "We must ride out and head them off! We cannot allow them any closer!"

Garren nodded, knowing the words made sense, yet at the same time knowing that they had little chance against the dozens of men which MacEwan was reputed to have. He mounted, casting a glance at the *leronis* who had clambered onto the back of her small pony.

She locked eyes with him—

She knew. He could feel it.

And the despair inside reminded him how very different he and his brother truly were . . . how much *less* he was than Piers—

"*Dom* Garren!" Ronnado's stare was intense.

"Yes," Garren managed to breathe. "Onward, then!"

Outward they rode. Above, the black sky was lit by two moons while the men's torches broke the dark monotony of the shadows.

The sun was stretching tendrils of ruby over the horizon when Garren and his men saw the advancing attackers . . .

Too many, too many—

Garren touched a hand to the stallion's neck, calming him—

Or was he seeking to calm himself?

The *leronis* was suddenly by his side. He gazed downward at the woman on her pony, noting how fatigued both appeared.

"I—I have done what I can to slow them down—but I fear there are simply too many for my skills alone! And, though their *laran* may not be strong, their determination may make up for this. If only *Dom* Piers were here—"

Use *your laran*, her eyes seemed to plead.

I wish I could, thought Garren.

A scream tore him from his musings. He watched as one of his men went down, his mount crippled by an arrow.

*No! I cannot let this happen! If only I could—if only I could do something—*any*thing—*

In his mind he saw a strange fantasy. A brief flash of horseflesh suddenly taking control—

"Wait! What—" He pulled on the reins, gazing down at his stallion and turning him back around toward the front once more.

Realization hit him like a blow!

He stared straight ahead at the steadily advancing enemy. He cleared his mind of that image and concentrated instead on sending his own message.

As he had to the cat when he'd been lonely as a boy; as he had to the chervine when he'd wanted her to follow him through the woods; as he had to . . . had to . . . yes!

The concentration was making his head throb.

Sweat filled his eyes so that he could see nothing clearly—

"Via dom," Rafa said quietly, "what strange talent is this of yours which can tell a dozen horses at once to suddenly turn in their tracks and head in another direction?"

Garren opened his mouth to speak, although he was not certain what to say. But the *leronis* continued, "How fascinating! *Dom* Garren, if you would, I'd be very much interested in learning something of this skill of yours with the beasts. I know not whether I could master it, although I'd be willing to try. I am not confident, however; I have only *laran* of the usual sort, I'm afraid."

Garren blinked, then returned the woman's gaze.

She was smiling.

He returned *that*, too, feeling his neck and shoulder muscles relax once more.

Invitation to Chaos

by Joan Marie Verba

Joan Verba lives in Minnesota which—at least in the winter—has much in common with Darkover. I understand the Eskimos have eleven words—or forty-seven or something—for snow; if Minnesota doesn't, it's not for want of experience. Joan has been a friend of Darkover and one of my writers for these anthologies from the beginning, and the only thing new in her updated biography that I can see is that she is writing a book of nonfiction astronomy about the Voyager spacecraft.

For other details, see the introduction to her stories in four of the previous Darkover anthologies.

I felt as if I had just fought a battle. Comyn Council meetings were generally easy; Council Season was seen as more of a social occasion than a political one. No one expected any opposition to the proposal that the Keepers and workers in the Towers be allowed to sit and vote in council, but I was delighted to surprise them by objecting. It was an even bigger shock to them when the Domain of Alton split on the issue: me, the heir apparent to the Domain, in opposition, and my father, Lord Rafael Alton, just as strongly in favor. We argued to an impasse. The vote was delayed, which was a victory for me and a defeat for my father. I could almost hear the echoes in the now-empty Crystal Chamber. I sat back, put my feet up, and stared idly at the ceiling, savoring the moment.

"Admiring your handiwork?"

King Stefan Hastur reentered the chamber. Quickly, I put my feet down, but he motioned me to stay seated. With a smile, he walked to the Alton section and sat beside me.

I smiled back. Stefan and I were contemporaries. We were playmates as boys. I was fostered out for a year to Castle Hastur; he had been fostered out later to Armida.

"Quite a place you built," said Stefan. "If I had erected Thendara Castle, I think I might find a hill and gaze at it until I fainted from thirst."

I laughed. "*That* vain, I'm not. It just seemed to me that since all the Domain heads met here every year at the Thendara marketplace, we might as well make ourselves comfortable rather than camping out in the muck. Besides, it gave me something to do when I was penned up in that damned Tower."

"Ah," said Stefan, laying a finger to the side of his face. "So that's why you opposed the seating of the Tower Keepers in council—revenge."

"Revenge be damned," I said. "The telepath workers are getting too large for their clothes. I don't mind that they're organized so that they can do together what no telepath can do alone. But put them in Council and they'll begin to run Darkover, mark my words. They already want *another* Tower here at Thendara Castle, when I generously built them one as is. When my bones are moldering on the shores of Hali, that's when they'll add another Tower to this castle. I didn't build it for them; I built it so that they could serve *us*."

"You designed it, Gwynn. But they built it."

"They built it to my plan, and my specifications. I was in the Tower circle that erected it. They needed the power of my damned Alton Gift." I sat back. "That's all they're getting from me."

"Far be it from me to challenge the Alton Gift."

We both smiled. Stefan had the Hastur gift, awakened in him by his father before Stefan became king. As a child, Stefan had had white hair; it darkened into red as he grew older. He stood, tall and slender as a *chieri*, but, of course, he already had an infant son; he was no *emmasca*. I matched him in height, but I was the meatier one. Especially after leaving the Tower, I devoted myself to supervising the guards under Father's direction, and to other, more honest, physical work.

As we walked out of the chamber, Stefan said, "I wonder if you'd check out the mint for me. The city is growing so quickly, we'll need the coinage. Neskaya and Arilinn can't keep up."

"I'd be happy to, your highness." I executed a bow that was both properly respectful and a little playful. He turned a corner to the Hastur apartments.

I knew, of course, that Father was annoyed. Ever since he had imposed his damned Gift on my adolescent brain, I was aware of his every mood. Distance softened it to a low background murmur, but he was always there, as if he had scuffed my brain and left his scent on my mind forever.

He turned from his chair as soon as I walked in the door to the Alton apartments. His large, thick, red mustache would have looked ridiculous on any other man. On Father, it made him seem even larger and more powerful. The dark eyes in the huge face tried to pin me down, but I was almost oblivious to his physical appearance. It was the state of his *laran* that caught my attention.

He rose in a smooth motion. In a voice gentler than his mood, he said, "I don't blame you, son, not at all. I know what's really wrong."

"What?" I refrained from reading his mind which would have been easy under these circumstances.

"Damnit, son, do I have to spell it out? Get yourself a wife! It's about time!"

I turned away from him, stripping off my gloves and throwing them on a nearby table.

"All of your younger brothers and sisters have children already. . . ."

"Good for them!" I tried to walk away; he followed me.

"What's wrong with you? You're not an *ombredin;* I would know if you were! You're 34 years old, and long past due! Now get yourself a woman before you make yourself sick! You don't have to marry one, though it would be nice if you would. Just get it over with! I don't think you've ever been with a woman, have you?"

I turned on him. "There are some things in my life that are out of your control, Father."

"I'm not going to stand by and let you ruin yourself. You're not an ordinary man; you're heir to Alton! Commander of the Guards! Builder of Thendara Castle! That disgraceful speech you gave today. . . ."

"I meant every word!"

He thrust his finger in my face. "You wouldn't have proposed such an idiotic idea if you'd been married!"

"The reason why I've never bedded a woman is that I don't want you in there with me!"

"What do you mean, you. . . ."

"You know what I mean! Ever since you gave me that damned Alton Gift, you've never been out of my mind!"

He put his finger in my face again. "I saved your life!"

I slapped his hand away. "You needn't have bothered. I was in no pain whatever. I was peacefully slipping into the arms of Avarra, when all of a sudden there was this excruciating pain in my head—you, Father!—tearing my mind into pieces. You left a little of yourself in there, and it's been there ever since, making my life a living hell. I would have been better off, dying of threshold sickness. I had younger brothers—you didn't need me for an heir. But no, you used the full force of your Alton Gift to bring me back, which, as an Alton heir, gave me the same damned thing, for which I had to leave home and live in that damned Tower with strangers, away from Mother and my brothers and sisters. Despite all the claptrap I hear about all the wonderful caring and sharing"—here I waxed sarcastic—"that comes from *laran*, all I felt was power. Raw power, and the stench of it made me want to vomit on my boots."

This was the first time in my life I had seen Father shocked speechless. He wasn't at a loss for long, however. "I loved you."

"You *loved* me? You ripped my mind apart, and

then sent me away from home, from everything I loved. . . ."

"An untrained telepath is a danger to himself and everyone around him."

"Oh, *spare* me! Stefan told me how his father had awakened his Hastur Gift, and taught him how to use it. Far different from my experience with you! Stefan's father *loved* him. What you did to me, you did for yourself!" I stomped past him, retrieved my gloves, and left, without going to my apartments and eating first, as I had planned. Father always had that effect on me, making me so mad I forgot everything except how much I wanted to get away from him.

"Gwynn?"

I stopped and turned. It was Michela, standing in the open doorway to the Aldaran apartments.

"Do you have a moment?" she asked.

In answer, I walked to the door. Michela was smaller than I was, in her early twenties. She was quite fetching; Stefan and I thought it probable that old Aldaran would arrange a marriage for her this council session.

"Would you come in?"

I smiled. "Certainly, *damisela*."

She led me to a parlor where a table was set for a meal. There were three plates, three chairs. Looking over to the hearth, I saw her father, Donal, Lord Aldaran, standing there.

He gestured to the table. "Will you join us, Lord Gwynn?"

"I was ready for a meal, thank you."

When we had been served, Aldaran said, "That was a good point you made in Council today. My daughter here, who has the Aldaran Gift in full measure, has warned me that she has seen far into the future, and that if the Towers gain in power, there could be wars fought with terrible weapons."

"There is much more that can be done with *laran* than to simply communicate, or to build things, or to mine for metals," said Michela.

"I know," I said. "I have heard some say that they think they can breed for certain gifts, beyond the *donas* that lie within each Domain."

"If they try that," said Aldaran, "there will be many supporting you, and not just me. No one wishes to be bred like chervines." He took a sip of his drink. "I will back your position for as long as I am in council. Beyond the horrors that my daughter foresees, I will not let the Towers usurp my authority. *I* rule my Domain, and I will not be ruled by the *laranzu'in*."

"Are you planning to leave Council, sir?" I asked.

"No, not in the foreseeable future." Aldaran smiled at his unintentional joke, turning to his daughter. "But the journey is long from my home to Thendara. It has been useful and pleasant, gathering here every summer, to buy from the market and to exchange news and ideas with the other Domain lords. With your new addition, Gwynn," he looked around at the walls, "I find it even more comfortable, almost like a holiday. But the Towers have given us a faster way to run messages, and although I'm willing to acknowledge the Hastur king, I'm not going to put up with the Council very long if they're going to try to run my affairs." He gave me a knowing look. "Besides, my son is coming of age, and I intend to gradually hand the burden over to him. I look forward to an old age where my only care is how long I can bounce grandchildren on my knee." He smiled again at Michela.

By the gods, I wished the man was *my* father. He was firm without being tyrannical, kind without being patronizing. Most of all, there was nothing but a normal telepathic awareness of him, which I could overlook if I wished. My own father, on the other hand, was impossible to ignore.

We had a pleasant conversation over a pleasant meal. When we were finished, Aldaran retired. I lingered over my farewell to Michela—she was pleasant, like her father, had an unobstrusive telepathic presence, and was good looking, on top of that—and excused myself to run the king's errand.

Naturally, any excuse to go out in the city would do. Was there any man in the history of Darkover who could claim to have built such a city? The cobblestones of the street, the gutters below the walkways, the houses of both great and small, all carefully planned by me. Of course, it was not all matrix-built. Some of it was the result of good, honest labor. But the overall effect was just as beautiful as I had anticipated. In addition, I had left plenty of room for new buildings, taking thought for the future. In sum, Thendara was a thriving city, grown twice the size it was when I was a boy, and which would probably be twice the size it was now when I was old.

The most difficult task, of course, was the drainage system. There was no river of any size within easy walking distance. Standing puddles of rain, or worse, standing puddles of sewage, would invite plagues of insects and plagues of disease. At last, I created an underground conduit of stone and slate which brought everything to a large cave in the surrounding hills, where it would separate and filter into the silt and finally reach the streams that fed the River Valeron, and eventually go to the sea.

My destination that day, though, was the mint, newly created by King Stefan in deference to Thendara's growing importance as a trade and market center. With the almost unlimited potential of the Towers to mine metal, there was more wealth to go around—distributed carefully, of course. And that was another thing I had against the Towers: they could sit on that wealth like a dragon guarding its hoard. So far, they had obeyed the will of the king in these matters, but with them in Council, they could just as well try to reserve all such decisions for themselves.

For now, the mint was working well. All the mint workers were nonhuman *kyrri,* to whom the value of the metal meant nothing. Metal was so scarce, so frugally distributed, that it was too much of a temptation to anyone else. I saw that the metal was correctly mixed, with copper and silver in their proper proportions, that the ingots were all of standard size, and stamped according to size and composition; the *sekals* and *reis* coins were stamped correctly with King Stefan's visage. I tested the weights for the scales, which merchants bought from the mint in order to confirm that the ingots their customers used had not been shaved or adulterated. Everything was as it should be; the Thendara mint was the equal of the ones in Neskaya or Arilinn.

I went to a potter's shop next. I didn't really want to buy anything; I just visited every once in a while to see what they were using for slips and glazes, what sort of clay they were making pots out of, what designs they were using. I often got ideas for materials and shapes to use in my building projects. Little had changed since my last visit to this shop. However, a blue stone embedded in a pot caught my eye. I took it over to the proprietress, an older woman with a few missing front teeth.

"You really shouldn't be using matrix stones in your pots anymore, *mestra.* By the king's command, matrix stones must only be handled now by licensed matrix mechanics, Tower-trained. I know they're pretty, and you've used them for a long time, but they can be dangerous." The woman looked abashed. I felt awkward, too, but this new law was one I agreed with, whatever other differences I had with the Towers. I pulled out my purse. "Here. I'll buy this from you, and any other pots you might have with matrix stones in them. And then please don't use them anymore. Do you understand?"

"As you say, *vai dom,*" she said, avoiding my gaze.

"Will you please check in your back storage for others? And please give me all the matrix stones you have, too." I touched my own matrix, which was in a pouch at my throat. "Don't worry about getting them all; I can check to see if you have missed or misplaced any."

Her face fell even more. "Yes, *vai dom.*" She went into the back.

As usual for a Domain lord or a Domain heir going into the city on official business, I had a couple of retainers following at a discreet distance. I called them into the shop to take the pots back to the castle; I took the matrixes in hand. After checking to see I had all the matrixes in the shop, I paid the woman generously and left, thinking that I ought to ask King Stefan to have the Towers send some people into the city to collect more of the loose matrixes, especially among potters and jewelers. It would give the Tower workers something useful to do for a change.

We left the shop, but outside the door one of my men slipped, and almost dropped the pots. As I helped him rearrange the burden, I heard the old woman's low complaint, probably to the younger woman who had been helping her. Doubtless the woman thought I had walked well out of earshot by now, but I caught every word.

"Those Comyn, they take the best of everything! It isn't enough that they sit in their nice houses with their metal forks and spoons while us plain folk have to make them out of wood and clay! Now they want our pretty blue stones, which are hard enough to come by as is, without them taking those, too! And those were my quickest-selling pots, my prettiest!" The woman wept softly.

As we walked away, I felt sorry for the old woman, but took comfort in the fact that I had paid her far more than the pots were worth. Besides, there were jewels other than matrix stones she could use, and other ways to make pots attractive. If she was as clever a potter as her pots showed that she was, she would not be going out of business over the loss of the matrix stones.

I reported the condition of the mint and the incident at the pottery shop to Stefan. Unexpectedly, the king showed more interest in the matrixes at the pottery shop. Seated in his overstuffed chair, he waved a hand at me from across the rug. "Of course, now that we have Towers to deal with them, the matrixes have to be kept out of the hands of those who do not know how to use them. But it wasn't all that long ago that there were no Towers, and to nontelepaths, matrixes were just jewelry." He shifted from a leisurely sag to a straighter, more kingly posture. "My great-grandsire, for instance, had a special sword made for him by the forge-folk in the Hellers. In the hilt is a rather large matrix. He had it made for ceremonial occasions, but the matrix made it feel so . . . alive . . . that he kept it in a vault in Castle Hastur nearly all the time. It hasn't seen the light of day in years, except in the passing on of the Hastur Gift."

"Have the Towers seen it?" I asked, interested. "I mean, when you were tested for the Hastur Gift."

He had a conspiratorial look on his face. "No. They tested me later, at Hali. When my father awakened the Hastur Gift in me, it was a ceremony only between the two of us."

"Don't tell them," I urged. "They'll take it from you for certain."

"I have no intention of telling them. The only reason I'm telling you is that you are the one person it *is* safe for me to tell." He smiled.

The rest of the summer went better than I expected. The debate on whether to allow the Tower workers a voice in Council went on without a consensus being reached, though more and more were being won to my way of thinking every day. Most of the Council session dealt with the usual: mountain bandits, road repair and transportation, harvest expectations, and so forth.

Outside the Council, I spent most of my time in the Aldaran apartments. I had become more and more attached to Aldaran and Michela, and they seemed equally fond of me. My engagement to Michela became official at midsummer. Lady Aldaran and

Michela's younger brother came for the occasion, as did my mother, from Armida. Mother seldom came to the Council sessions because of the inevitability of Father and me arguing when at close quarters. Mother always felt caught in the middle, and found it easier to avoid us both. In fact, when at home, Father and I were seldom in the same room at the same time; things were more civil that way.

Watching Father talk to Aldaran as if the two were pledged *bredin* almost made me sick. I shut down my *laran*, for courtesy's sake. Michela could tell something was wrong, but didn't ask right then. She left with her father at the end of the reception. Mother could also see storm clouds above my head; she excused herself, leaving Father and me alone.

Before I could say anything, Father swung around to face me, "Damnit, son, can't you contain your anger for your own betrothal party? It's supposed to be a happy occasion. I can't understand what you're upset about."

"That's the problem—you don't understand," I snapped. "And I controlled my *laran* just fine. The only reason you picked up on it is because we're linked, mind to mind."

"Then why can't I tell what's bothering you?"

"Because I'm blocking my *laran*, that's why. But if you weren't so deliberately blind to my feelings, you could tell what's wrong. What's wrong is that you treat total strangers with more courtesy than you do me, your own son," I thumped my chest for emphasis. "You don't speak with Aldaran except once a year, and you treat him as if he was your long lost beloved brother. Me, on the other hand, you treat like property!"

"And how about the way you treat me . . . the way you're speaking to me right now?"

"If you'd shown me half the courtesy you showed Aldaran, we wouldn't be having this discussion. But no, you act as if the world is centered around you. You imposed your Alton Gift on me because that is what *you* wanted. You sent me to a Tower because that is what *you* wanted. I only got out of the Tower because *you* thought it was time to learn how to command the Guards. You tell me that I'm to run the Domain someday, but *you* do all the running of it. King Stefan gives me more responsibility than you do. If you were to drop dead tomorrow, I would only know how to run the Domain because *Stefan* has taught me how to do it. The only thing you do is give orders and expect me to carry them out. You pull me around like a *cralmac* on a chain, and then you wonder why I'm angry when you show Aldaran more courtesy than you do me?"

He looked genuinely puzzled. I could tell, with my *laran,* that he *was* genuinely confused, which irked me even more. "I let you choose your future wife, didn't I? Some Domain lords would introduce you to your bride on your wedding day."

I executed a mock bow. "Thank you, thank you very much," I said sarcastically. "And let me tell you, one of the reasons I'm marrying her is that Aldaran has been more of a father to me than you have, even in the short time I've known him. Since you think he's such a wonderful man, why don't you ask him how to do it?" Without waiting for an answer, I turned my back on him and went to my own room.

He did not pursue the matter.

* * *

I really did not know what I was going to do when my wedding night came. Ever since I acquired the Alton Gift, I was always aware, on some level, of my parents' lovemaking. I learned to block it out, but the fact that such knowledge was available to me, unbidden, bothered me. I presumed that the reverse would be true as well: that if I ever made love, my father would know about it. That's why I was still a virgin at my age.

To prepare, I tried to get physically intimate with Michela at levels just short of lovemaking. We would sit for hours, side by side on a couch in a parlor in the Aldaran apartments, with Michela's deaf maid, Ariel, doing embroidery across the room under the light of a lamp. Ariel was a *nedestro* daughter of the Ardais domain, and had *laran*, which greatly helped her to communicate with her Aldaran employers, though she could use gestures to speak, as well.

One night, as Michela and I were enjoying each other's company, my head on her shoulder, I suddenly gasped and straightened. Ariel had lowered her embroidery, and cocked her head as if actually listening to something.

"What was *that?*" asked Michela.

I stood. "I don't know, but I'm going to find out."

Before I could take a step, there was a knock at the door. Aldaran stuck in his head. "It's the Tower, son; let's go. Michela, you stay here."

We stepped into the corridor and found ourselves in a procession with King Stefan at the head, flanked by his bodyguards. Every person with *laran* in Thendara must have sensed the same thing. I knew something they didn't: that my father was also a part of whatever we had felt.

I was in the front with Stefan by the time we got to the Tower. The king went right into the Tower's public rooms. My father and the Keeper of the first circle, a man named Edric, met us.

"There is no cause for worry, your highness," said Edric. "Our experiment just got out of hand, that's all. We'll shield it better the next time."

"What sort of experiment?" asked Stefan.

"Weather control," said Edric. "It would serve us well in fire season if we could move rain clouds to the affected areas."

"We had just not anticipated the amount of shielding needed, your highness," said my father, "and there was a certain amount of leakage. It won't happen again."

"Were you successful?" asked Stefan.

"A little," said Edric. "It was our first try. Perhaps we used more power than we needed. We weren't able to direct it as we had hoped; that caused the discomfort you felt. Again, I apologize."

The king's expression was stern. His voice, when he spoke, was softer. "I think it would be best if you halted your experiments for the next tenday. You also might take more time to plan your projects before you begin them."

"But we do, highness," protested Edric. "And we can't stop our experiments. Mining, at first, was an experiment. So was matrix healing. So was building at an architect's direction." He gestured toward me.

"Leave me out of this," I said.

"I'm not asking that you stop trying things out," said Stefan. "I'm commanding that you cease your experiments for a tenday. I also insist that you plan your operations more carefully. You should try out things gradually: do things on a small scale before proceeding to more powerful uses of *laran*."

"But we do this already," said Edric.

"If so, what went wrong tonight?" asked Stefan.

Edric was silent. He looked to my father, but he said nothing either.

"If you can't control your experiments or be consistent in what you do, be assured that the crown will step in," said Stefan. "My order stands: no more experiments from this Tower for the next tenday."

"Yes, highness," said Edric.

Stefan turned to the assemblage of Domain heads and Domain heirs who had accompanied us to the Tower. "I will be retiring to Castle Hastur for a short time; Lord Gywnn will preside over the Council in my absence." Stefan touched my shoulder."That will be all for now."

The others turned to go. Stefan held my elbow to keep me with him.

"Tell Michela I'll be along shortly, Father," I said to Aldaran. Aldaran nodded and left. I sensed, rather than saw, my own father gape when I called Aldaran that. His mouth was closed by the time I had turned around, with Stefan.

"Good evening, then," said the king, nodding at my father and Edric.

Stefan and I walked back to the Hastur apartments alone. "Yes, the Towers do need a tight rein on them. I think the debate will turn to your favor now. Gwynn."

"I noted that they deemed it necessary to have my father helping them," I said.

". . . the Alton Gift, yes, the most powerful *laran* among us," said Stefan. "That was my thought, too."

"May I ask why you're returning to Castle Hastur?"

He rubbed his fingertips with a thumb. "Something I need . . ." he said, but he elaborated no further.

Stefan came back with a wooden case the size of a coffin. He put it in a storage room under a personal matrix lock and stationed two guards in front of it at all times. He lifted his ban on the matrix experiments. Meanwhile, the Council debate got hotter. Although no Keepers were allowed a voice in council, there were Domain lords and Domain heirs and others allowed to speak in council who were former or current Tower workers. My father was their chief spokesman. They maintained that the Towers already had a code of conduct, which was being changed and improved as their knowledge and experience grew. Matrix work was a science, they claimed, and could not be fully understood by people not familiar with that science, and should not be regulated by those who did not understand those principles. Ultimately, they said, Keepers should not be responsible to anyone or anything but their own consciences.

The opposition, which I led with vigor, countered that as long as what the Towers did affected the people and lands of Darkover, then the Domain heads, and the king, who were responsible for the people and lands of Darkover, had the right to lay down the rules for what the Towers could and could not do. To allow the Towers to do anything they wished, we believed, would be an invitation to chaos. Self-regulation with the Towers was the same as no regulation, we argued, because then the Towers would simply do as they pleased, answering to no one, and bearing no responsibility to anyone outside the Towers for their actions.

While this discussion went on, day after day, my father and I grew more estranged, which I had not thought possible until it happened. My mother, fed up with the situation, returned to Armida. Aldaran arranged to quietly move my things from the Alton apartments and into the guest quarters of the Aldaran apartments. While my father and I still sat in the same section in the Crystal Chamber, it was as if we were in different domains. I addressed him as "Lord Alton," and he addressed me as "Lord Gwynn."

Stefan and I had anticipated that the Towers, especially Thendara Tower, would try some outlandish experiments, in the fear that their activities would soon be tightly restricted by the Council. Whatever they were doing, however, they appeared to be doing it carefully. There was no more leakage. I was suspicious of the quiet, but Stefan reasoned that if they were careful enough to prevent leakage, they were probably using caution in other areas as well, and left them alone for the moment.

Late summer was the height of the fire season. Thendara itself was in little danger. The city walls would keep fire from the town, and the surface mining that had been done in the Venza hills before the Towers started mining had left areas of barren ground, acting as natural firebreaks. Therefore, whenever a fire was sparked in the country surrounding Thendara, no alarm was sounded.

That was why, when smoke was spotted on one of the hills, I took Michela to an observation post on the roof of the castle to watch it burn. Stefan joined us.

"No clouds in the sky," I said. "It must have been a careless hunter, whose fire had not been covered properly. It could have smoldered for days before igniting the brush."

Suddenly, a gust of wind lifted us up and threw us against a parapet. Stefan and I each grabbed one of Michela's arms and struggled to the doorway. Inside, out of reach of the gale, Stefan said, "What in Zandru's seven hells was that?"

My unending link with my father told me. "The Tower circle is in operation. I think they're trying to blow it out."

"They're . . ."

Stefan did not complete his sentence. A hideous sound stilled his voice. I had heard the banshees cry in the Hellers; that was a lullabye compared to this. Michela stopped her ears with her hands. Stefan bounded down the stairs.

Using my matrix, I got a clearer contact with my father. Indeed, they had been trying to blow out the fire, but it had gotten out of control. My father had not just put the Alton Gift into the wind, but also his resentment and anguish at my rejection of him into the circle. There was not just wind out there—it was a wind demon, composed of Alton anger, driven by Alton power. Realizing what he had done, my father was now trying desperately to reverse it, with the help of the others in the circle.

I knew it was dangerous to break into a circle, but my father and I were already deeply in rapport, and my telepathic eavesdropping had not affected the circle thus far. I lent my strength to theirs. But my father thrust me away, with such force that I was dimly aware of my feet buckling under me. My shoulder hit the inside wall of the parapet and I slid to the floor.

I was not going to let him push me away so easily. With a renewed grip on my matrix, I tried to reestablish contact, but was blocked. Trying another approach, I thrust into the overworld, the psychic plain mirroring physical events in the real world. There I saw that my father had thrust not just me, but all in the circle away, while he battled alone with the demon's surrogate in the overworld. We all tried to get to him, but it was as if there was an impregnable wall between us. Father matched the demon, strength for strength, height for height. They grappled.

I was no longer looking at the embodiment of my cursed gift tackling a monster of his own creation. Instead, I saw Darkover, personified, fighting against a Tower-made weapon for domination of the world. If the demon won, all of Darkover would be in chaos.

Linked together with the other Tower workers, I broke the barrier that Father created to protect us. Immediately, the demon grew, drawing from our combined strength. Realizing that we were only making the demon stronger, Edric dissolved the Tower circle. I remained, reaching out to snatch Father from the demon's grip, but the beast—now doubled in size—hurled Father to the floor of the psychic plain, smashing the astral form.

The shock of my father's death threw me out of the overworld. Back in my own body, I gradually became aware that I was staring at a stone ceiling. I could hear the howl of triumph of the wind demon outside.

Stefan bent down and touched my shoulder. "Come, Gwynn, before it gets to the castle gate."

My castle. My city. They were still in danger. I stood. For the first time, I noticed that Michela was still there.

Stefan unwrapped a package. The matrix at his throat glowed so brightly I could see it clearly through its spider-silk wrappings. "Have you ever worked with other telepaths?" he asked Michela.

She nodded and touched the matrix at her own throat.

"Good." Stefan lifted the sword in his hand, as if testing its balance before a fight. He nodded at me, then Michela. "Let's go."

I opened my mouth to tell him that standing outside in the demon wind was impossible, but he was already out the door, Michela at his elbow. I sprinted out behind him. He waved the sword as he stepped out. Around us, the wind crashed against the parapet like a mighty wave, but the air where we were was calm. Stefan glowed. A nimbus surrounded him. He laughed as a man laughs when he goes into a fight, confident of victory. Before my eyes he was transformed: he took the shape of the legendary Hastur, son of light, so *real* that the images I had seen in Castle Hastur looked like childish scrawls in comparison. I almost knelt. Without touching me, the champion took me in hand, and, together with Michela, we faced the demon as it strode toward Thendara Castle and the city gates. Stefan matched the demon, strength for strength, height for height, power for power. The wind-demon roared angrily. Stefan stepped forward and extended the sword.

In words that rose over the demon howl and echoed among the castle rocks, Stefan ordered, "Begone! Go back to the hell that spawned you!"

Immediately, there was calm. If it had not been for the leaves and debris scattered around, ripped from the trees and bushes, I would not have believed that there had been any wind. Then I saw that we were not on the roof of Thendara Castle, but on the plain in front of the city gates. I turned to Michela. She looked fine, though bewildered. I swung around in the other direction to find Stefan. He was there, in his normal shape, with a smile on his face. It took me a few moments to tell what had changed—Stefan's hair had turned back to the white color it had been when he was a young boy.

"I think the Council will approve your proposal now, don't you think?" said the King.

Mother returned for Father's funeral, as did my scattered brothers and sisters. We buried him in an unmarked grave by the shores of Lake Hali, beside the newly-erected vault of my design in which we placed Stefan's sword—behind double-barriers to keep it from the hands of the Towers. I finally cried at Father's funeral, but not for the man who invaded my mind and lived there afterwards. I wept for the man who read to me as a boy, soothed my fears, tucked me into bed, and for the man, who, at the last, saw the horror that he had created and had tried to stop it. But most of all, Father's death left me with a great sense of relief, as if I had been bound in irons all my adult life, and had been newly freed.

I was installed as Lord Alton in Council, and won my fight to bar the Tower Keepers from a voice or vote there. My triumph was further sweetened by my marriage to Michela. Stefan locked the *catenas* on our wrists himself. This, however, felt not like a binding, but as a seal of our affection.

That night, when all others had gone, I made love with my whole heart. Afterward, we lay in each other's arms, and talked.

"I hope that I don't offend you by saying this, husband," Michela said, "but I do believe that in spite of everything, your father loved you."

I sighed. "Yes. He did love me. I can see that now, but not when my mind was chained to his. We were so—damnably—close, I think it was impossible for us not to strike sparks when we were together. And Father's attitude didn't help—he thought that as long as *he* knew he loved me, he didn't have to do anything to show it." I took a breath. "If we are ever in danger of losing children to threshold sickness, I will do anything—but I will *not* force the Alton Gift on them. No child of mine will suffer that kind of hell."

Michela caressed my forehead. "Gwynn . . . that wind-demon we fought . . . that is not what I saw in my foresight. I saw more hideous weapons than these, created by the Towers for war."

I caught her hand and kissed her fingertips. "Be at peace, my love. None of that will happen while Stefan and I live. All we can do is to be sure that none of us call up such horrors, and teach our children not to create them. What our children or children's children do when our bones are dust is not ours to command."

"I know. But the images are no less disturbing."

For that, I had no answer.

The Keeper's Peace

by Patricia Duffy Novak

Pat Novak has sold to the last two Darkover anthologies, and also to Marion Zimmer Bradley's Fantasy Magazine. *She has been, since the last anthology promoted from Assistant to Associate Professor of Agricultural Economics and has also received tenure.*

Hooray for our side! When I started writing, professors who just happened to be women—except at women's colleges—were almost as rare as full-time science fiction writers who happened to be women. Naturally we're all delighted.

Like her story "Clingfire" in DOMAINS OF DARKOVER, this story uses characters from STORMQUEEN. And it's very much worth reading.

As the last rays of the bloody sun cast long red shadows across the snow-covered yard, Renata leaned her brow against the cold window pane and struggled to accept the grim truth: her friend was dying; there was nothing she could do.

"Lady Renata."

Renata turned around. "What is it, Doria?"

"I think you should come. The child will not wait much longer."

Renata nodded and followed the midwife to the room where Arielle, pale and exhausted, labored to bring forth her baby. While Doria busied herself preparing hot water and warm blankets, Renata placed a hand on Arielle's hot forehead. "How is it with you, my friend?"

Arielle shook her head softly and damp strands of blonde hair tumbled about her face. "Not so well, I'm afraid." She tried to smile, but could not, as a new contraction gripped her. She took Renata's hand and squeezed it so hard that Renata herself nearly cried out in pain. Finally, after a full minute had passed, Arielle exhaled loudly and released Renata's hand. "Oh, Renata," she said in a soft lifeless voice, "I am so afraid."

"Do not be afraid, little one. This will soon be over and you will have a fine son to hold."

Arielle turned tear-washed eyes toward Renata. "I will not survive the birth of this child. We have both known that for some time."

Renata felt hot tears forming in her own eyes. Unbidden, the memories of their years together in Hali Tower flooded Renata's thoughts: Arielle, bright and gay, a golden girl with a wide smile dancing at the Midsummer festivities; Arielle, calm and capable, the circle technician, efficiently testing batteries; and Renata herself, serene and untroubled, knowing nothing of love and loss.

The woman on the bed seemed only distantly related to that other Arielle, as she herself seemed so different from the carefree Renata of the Tower days. Could it have been only two years? Renata's own tragedy had been unavoidable, as inevitable as a storm in the Hellers, but this, this—she wiped the tears from her eyes and studied Arielle's gaunt face—this was inexcusable. *Oh, Coryn, Coryn,* Renata raged, trying mightily to shield her thoughts from Arielle, *how could you have let her come to this?*

Arielle grimaced as another contraction began. When it was over, she spoke again. "You will look after my child as you promised? And when the time is right, you will send him to his father?"

"I will," Renata promised. "But I wish you had let me tell him."

Arielle did not answer. Nor did she say another word. As her child reached forward to embrace life, her own essence ebbed away, overpowered by the baby's lethal *laran*, the psi power that destroyed, all unknowing, the mother who had loved him enough to give him life—even though she knew her own would be the forfeit.

Doria, the midwife, gently suctioned the mucus from the newborn's tiny nose and the infant let out a squall. "See how strong and lusty he is. A fine boy, my lady." She started to place the baby on Arielle's chest, then stopped. "Oh, my lady, my lady," she cried.

Renata took the infant from Doria's arms. "He is my child now, as I promised Lady Arielle. He shall be reared as a younger brother to my own son, until such time as I must send him forth to take his own place."

She handed the baby back to Doria. Then the tears in Renata's eyes became rivers of grief as she took Arielle's limp hand in her own and kissed it one last time.

* * *

Miles away, in Hali Tower, the youngest Keeper, traveling in the overworld on business of his own, saw Arielle's spirit slip quietly past the border which the living can not cross, and the psychic storm of his anger and grief shook the Tower to the very foundation stones.

* * *

Outside, the first rays of the rising sun striped the surface of the lake with blood-red rays. From his window perch, Ari Ridenow watched the oncoming dawn with a mixture of impatience and resignation. He had arrived at Hali Tower over an hour before, after riding all night, and was both hungry and tired. He was more than ready for someone, anyone, to come and escort him from the visitors' room into the Tower itself.

But, he almost laughed at himself, what was his hurry? He stood up and stretched. He did not want to be here. He had all but begged the Lady Renata not to send him away, but she had been unyielding on this one thing.

It was not that he did not want to study in a Tower; he would have been perfectly content to pass a year or so in Tramontana, close to home and his foster-brother, Brenton Aldaran. Ari had no other home, no other family. His own mother, Arielle Di Asturien-Ridenow, had died in birthing him, and he had nothing from his father, Regis Ridenow, save a name. He had never even met the man.

And now the Lady Renata had also cast him out. He wondered if he was too low, too humble, in her eyes, to be *bredu* to her own son. That Ari's mother had once worked at Hali would offer a convenient excuse to send him away. As his thoughts turned to his foster-mother, he felt a curious awareness, as if she were near, somehow linked to him, instead of far away in Aldaran. He shook his head. Hunger and fatigue were giving him strange fantasies; the Lady Renata was nowhere near Hali Tower.

Hali Tower. He repeated the name in his thoughts and sighed. Gods, he did not want to be here. Even in the far Hellers, Ari had heard stories about the First Keeper of Hali Tower: a man who lived only for his work, a monster of *laran*; cold, almost inhuman in the discipline he set upon himself and his matrix workers. It was said that Coryn Hastur would not allow so much as a single human touch to deflect his intense concentration.

And that was not the worst of it. The Hali Keeper was a man obsessed by weapons: *clingfire* missiles, matrix traps, and the new and terrible scourge of *bonewater dust*, which he alone knew how to make. If Allart Hastur of Elhalyn, the King in Thendara, were not a just and reasonable man, the whole world would now kneel as vassals to the throne at Thendara. But the king had forbidden the use of the dreadful new weapon. For the first time in generations, a universal peace stilled the constant bickering of the Domains. And those of the lowlands called it, with grim irony, the Keeper's Peace.

Ari shivered slightly, knowing that no weapon, once discovered, would remain long unused. He did not need *laran* to foresee a time when the Domains lay ravaged by the fearsome new weapon. Even now, there were rumors that the *leronyn* of Ardais were close to discovering the secret of its manufacture.

Nothing, Ari feared, would put that genie back in the bottle. And still, undoubtedly knowing all this, the Lady Renata, his foster-mother, had sent him to Hali Tower. He could not begin to understand why.

Mira Lanart, the oldest matrix worker in Hali, felt the growing impatience of the boy in the visitors' room and gently signaled Coryn that it was past time that he released his hold of the circle. The night's work was well done, and the others needed rest.

The Keeper's irritated reply rippled along the link, *Are we to bend ourselves to the will of this upstart Ridenow brat?* But he let his hold of the circle slip slightly, acknowledging, at the same time, that her second concern had merit: his matrix workers were tiring.

He is Arielle's son, too, Mira replied, not caring who else besides Coryn picked up her thoughts. *We who were her friends should be kind to him for her sake.* Coryn said nothing. She had not expected him to answer.

She watched Coryn wave a strong but slender hand, breaking the link. His face, despite the hash of long-healed scars, the legacy of a matrix accident, was a mask of perfect Hastur arrogance beneath flame-colored hair; hair that was only just beginning to be touched by silver. It was a face Mira knew well; she had been a veteran matrix worker when Coryn first appeared on the doorstep of Hali.

Still without speaking, Coryn left the room. He no longer dined with his circle, but took his nourishment alone. With sadness, Mira watched him go. Just once could he not be one of them, could he not be the laughing boy she remembered from so long ago? She looked away from Coryn's retreating form. She supposed that dream was impossible.

With little enthusiasm or appetite, she forced herself to take some of the sticky fruit and nut candy and swallowed it dutifully. Even monitoring required energy, and at her age, she must be careful to replenish what she used.

When she had finished eating, she stepped out of the room and traveled down the stairs and through the long halls, finally reaching the visitors' room. She stepped through the force-field and saw, for the first time, Arielle's son.

What she saw nearly froze her heart. There was nothing at all of Arielle about the boy, and certainly he was no Ridenow. She would know that face anywhere. Eyes, hair, the arrogant tilt of chin. So very like! Renata should have warned them, should not have sent him here like this. Then she felt the boy's awareness of her own shock and she quickly barricaded her thoughts. "I am Mira Lanart," she said. "I knew your mother when she was here."

The boy stepped forward, a shy smile on his lips. "The Lady Renata told me of you. She said you were kind."

Mira smiled back. *Perhaps not so very like,* she thought. *The boy lacks the arrogance and careless charm. There is something of Arielle in him after all.* Aloud she said, "We welcome you to Hali, little brother. We have heard well of you from your foster-mother. She is certain you will make a Keeper."

Ari sighed. "Pardon me, Lady Mira. But I have no desire to remain in the Tower. Perhaps in a year or two the Lady Renata will rethink her position and recall me to Aldaran."

Mira tilted her head. "Ah, then. Perhaps she will." Quietly, beneath tight barriers, she came close to cursing Renata, who had sent the boy to Hali without telling him his true bloodlines. She forced herself to smile. "But come. You have traveled long and must be weary."

"A little."

Again the shyness, the hesitation. *No, not like Coryn at all. Not in any way that matters.* Mira gently took his arm and led him through the barrier, toward the apartments they had prepared for him.

Later that day, Dyan Syrtis, the young man in the apartment next door to Ari's, poked his head into Ari's room. "Hello. Done with the unpacking, I see."

Ari grinned. "Come in, cousin." Any blood link between Ari and Dyan, if it existed at all, was weak and distant; he used the familial term as a friendly courtesy. Dyan had come in once already that morning, and Ari had taken an instant liking to the open-faced young man from Syrtis.

Dyan came fully into the room and looked around slowly. "Not bad. Homey, if a trifle plain." Dyan plopped down in one of the two stuffed chairs. "Have you been told when you will be tested?"

Ari shook his head. "No, Lady Mira says I should rest first. Then she will send for me, tomorrow, perhaps, or the next day. Tell me, is the test very difficult?"

"Not at all. One of the Keepers will look at you, that is all." Dyan waved a sturdy hand. "I had hoped to make a Keeper, but they say I am better as technician."

"You mean you want to stay here?"

Dyan laughed. "Well, why not? I am the youngest son and will get no land. In the Tower I am free of my kinsmen's constant quarreling. The life is not so bad."

"But I have heard the First Keeper is a demon, who drives his workers beyond endurance."

"Oh, Coryn Hastur, yes." Dyan made a face. "He is something of a demon. But I have little enough to do with him. Leander Aillard is the Keeper of my circle, and he is a most pleasant fellow. You are destined for our circle, I think." Dyan smiled. "And speaking of my circle, I had better go and rest. We are mining metal tonight. That is the worst job. You will see." His grin broadened as he stood up to go.

The crimson-robed Leander Aillard, Third Keeper of Hali, held a blue starstone in a six-fingered hand. Behind Leander, Mira Lanart and Barak MacAran readied a row of unlit candles. Ari had met Barak, an aging bear of a man, at dinner the night before and had liked the big man almost on sight. Of Coryn Hastur, Ari had as yet caught not so much as a glimpse, but that, he had been told, was not unusual. The First Keeper stayed much to himself when not working in the circles.

Leander raised the stone slowly, attracting Ari's attention. "Look into the stone," Leander said, "and think of flame."

Ari did as he was asked. When he looked up, he saw that all the candles were lit. Behind Leander's head, Mira and Barak exchanged glances.

"Now," said Leander, "gaze into the stone and let your mind go blank. Can you do that?"

Ari nodded. He had done this before, for Lady

Renata, when the threshold sickness first hit him. It was easy.

He hung suspended in time and space, only vaguely aware of Leander's mental touch. After some time had passed—Ari had no idea how much—Leander dropped the contact and Ari fell out of the link. Leander was smiling. "You will make a Keeper, young man. A good one, I think. That talent is in all too short a supply now."

Ari felt his heart sink. This was not the fate he had chosen for himself, but all things seemed to be pushing him into a role he did not desire. "I will discuss it with my foster-mother. I have little desire to be a Keeper, but I must bow to her will in this." He excused himself politely.

When he had gone, Leander turned to Mira and Barak and said, "He has the Hastur *laran.* Strongly. There is nothing of Ridenow in him and very little of Di Asturien." Leander raised an eyebrow, making a question of the last point.

Mira sighed. "He is much like his father." Leander's eyes remained full of questions.

"Coryn's son," said Barak softly.

The Keeper spread his long six-fingered hands in a gesture of astonishment. "Gods!" He swallowed audibly. "Does Coryn know?"

Mira shook her head. "No, he has not seen the boy. You did not know Coryn as a young man, but Ari is the very image of him as once he was. And the *laran* gift runs true as well. I suppose Coryn will have to know. Even if he is so self-occupied as to fail to see his own features in the child, he would realize that the Hastur *laran* could only have come from himself." She sighed heavily. "A pity, but it cannot be helped."

Again Leander's brows knotted in puzzlement. "Why should you want to hide the boy's parentage? Given his devotion to the Towers, Coryn will probably be pleased to find a potential Keeper, no matter how fathered." His tone, as he uttered this last, held a dry sarcasm. There was little love between Coryn and the two under-Keepers.

Barak slowly shook his bearlike head. "It is not as simple as that. A bad business this. Renata should have warned us." He folded his heavy arms across his chest. "You were not here when Arielle died," he said to Leander. "That was fifteen years ago. When Coryn learned of Arielle's death, he went nearly insane with rage and grief and shook this Tower to the very foundation stone. It took the combined strength of an entire circle of us, with an Alton Keeper, to restrain him. You remember, Mira?"

Mira sank down onto one of the chairs. "I have not forgotten," she said, and then her voice dropped for a moment. "I would to all the Gods I could forget." She rubbed her face with a hand. "You, Leander, see Coryn as nothing save a harsh over-Keeper with a terrible temper, but as a young man he could be—" She hesitated, searching for a word, then smiled slightly as she found it. "—charming. Oh, he was always a bit obsessed with the work, but he was human enough. After that night, he changed, became as you see him now, not allowing so much as a single human touch to disrupt his concentration. In fifteen years, he has neither laughed nor wept. He has barricaded himself behind the walls of his *laran,* driving himself relentlessly to become the perfect vessel for his gifts."

Mira paused for a moment and took a breath. "It

was his choice, you see. He could have married Arielle, but he would not give up his work in the Towers. And so she left, and her father married her to Regis Ridenow. Coryn thought she died giving a son to the Ridenows. And he was filled with both anger and guilt. Anger that Arielle should give up her own life for the Ridenow child—Arielle had *laran* enough to monitor the unborn child for lethal genes. And guilt because he had driven her away, into the marriage that killed her, or so he thought."

She sighed again, lightly this time. "You know him now. Perhaps you think he was always so." She shook her head. "Sometimes I could weep for what he lost when he lost Arielle."

Barak crossed the room and looked out the narrow window, down to the yard below. "He was dangerous before," he said, "but this time, should he desire it, he could crack the planet at the core."

Mira turned toward Barak and studied his outline against the stone walls. Then she shrugged. "But perhaps wc arc worrying for nothing. Coryn is not so much swayed by emotion anymore. He might not even care that Arielle died giving birth to his son, not Regis Ridenow's as he thought. Or perhaps the knowledge would do him good, make him human again"—she shuddered—"instead of the monster of *laran* he has become."

Barak turned around, his heavy face grim. "I would not take that chance. For all the Gods, I would not take that chance."

"There is no other choice," said Leander. "He must be told that the boy has the Hastur Gift. After that, he can draw his own conclusions." Leander rose.

"Wait, Leander," Mira said. "Let us tell him. We were his friends once."

Leander shrugged. "As you will." His crimson robe swayed behind him as he glided out of the room.

"Why so glum?" Dyan clapped Ari on the back and settled into a chair beside him. The common room was nearly empty at this hour of the evening, as the matrix workers prepared for the night's work, and Ari had thought he would be left alone. But he wasn't unhappy to see Dyan. The other boy's cheerful presence almost made Ari smile. Almost. He was still far too wrapped in his own misery to feel much amusement.

"It seems that all the fates are conspiring to make me a Keeper. I am to be trained."

Dyan gave a low, light whistle. "Congratulations. You shall be Ari of Hali in time. That's as good as heir to a Domain. Better, perhaps, for your sons won't be fighting over your corpse before you are even dead!"

This time Ari did smile. "I would I had your taste for it. I still pray the Lady Renata will allow me to go home." Again, when he thought of Renata there was that curious awareness, as if she were present. Fatigue and homesickness, he told himself, as he sank down farther into the sitting chair in the opulently decorated room.

Dyan stood up and went to look out the window. "I think you will come to like it here. Life in the Tower has its compensations." He pointed to the yard some two stories below, "Hey, look, there goes Coryn Hastur. Have you seen him yet?"

Ari shook his head and then joined Dyan at the

window. Through the gently swirling mist, he could make out a red-robed figure walking along the lake shore. Ari shrugged. "He seems ordinary enough."

Dyan grinned. "Oh, he is nothing much to look at. Built along small lines, like you. In fact—" Dyan studied Ari's face, as if seeing it clearly for the first time. "You look like him." Dyan laughed. "Although Hastur's face is scarred from some matrix accident, there is quite a strong resemblance otherwise. How odd!" Dyan continued to study Ari's face, obviously puzzled.

"The Di Asturiens are kin to Hastur," said Ari, growing uncomfortable under Dyan's scrutiny and turning his face somewhat to the side. "Perhaps the resemblance comes through my mother's people."

Dyan nodded, then laughed. "With the breeding program, we are becoming so inbred that in another generation it would not surprise me if we all wore the same face."

Ari looked at Dyan's heavy features, so unlike his own fine-boned face. In spite of himself, he grinned. "I think there is little danger of that, my friend."

Dyan, picking up the direction of his thoughts, laughed again. "No, we are not much alike. But you really do look like old Hastur. I wonder I had not noticed before."

Ari shrugged. "It is not important, I am sure." But something inside him, which he tried to ignore, warned him that the resemblance might prove very important indeed.

At dusk, the next evening, Mira came to Ari's room. The boy glanced up at her and gave a tremulous smile. "I thought I was to work in Leander's circle," he said, with just a hint of surprise in his voice. "Or is this a social visit? If so, you lend me grace." The thin smile broadened.

Mira shook her head. "We would have you tested again. You have a rare and unexpected *laran* gift, and it was thought that the First Keeper should test you before you are assigned to a circle."

She saw the boy's face pale as he stood up and prepared to follow her. "He is not an ogre," she said with more acerbity in her voice than she wanted.

"No, *vai leronis,*" Ari said. "I know he is not. He was a friend of my foster-mother once, and of my mother, too. Or so I understand."

"Yes," said Mira softly, as she closed the door behind the boy. "He was indeed. Now come."

She led him down the corridor to the small room where Coryn and Barak waited. They had all come dressed in their matrix robes: Coryn in the Keeper's crimson, Barak in technician's blue, herself in a white monitor's robe. Only the boy looked out of place, lost and bewildered. *Oh, Renata*, Mira thought, carefully shielding herself so that none could overhear, *how could you have sent him here like this, so vulnerable and alone?*

Then Mira's attention turned to Coryn. She almost held her breath as the Keeper's gaze swept over the boy, but there was no sign of the reaction she half dreaded, half prayed for. "You do not look much like your mother," was all Coryn said.

She had hoped it would be enough simply to bring the boy to Coryn's attention. She eyed Barak, but the big man shrugged. They had spent hours trying to devise a way to tell Coryn about Ari's true parentage, but had finally come to realize that direct confrontation would be needed. Coryn would be too stubborn and proud to believe what he did not experience. Now, they would have to let Coryn link with the boy.

She nodded at Barak, and he came up behind her. "Will you begin?" he said to Coryn.

The Keeper nodded his head. "In my own good time, Barak. And I do not see why you insisted on being here. A monitor would suffice."

"I am here for my own reasons," Barak said firmly, folding his arms across his chest. In spite of the tension, Mira almost smiled. Even Coryn had never been able to deter Barak from a course of action.

"Very well," Coryn said, taking an unkeyed starstone from the pocket of his robe and turning to Ari. "Let me see you match resonances with me."

"Yes, *vai tenerezu,*" Ari said, and Mira was pleased to hear the strength in the boy's voice. She knew he was afraid of Coryn, as was most of the world beyond the Tower gates, but the boy betrayed no fear.

As Coryn and Ari let their consciousness slip into the stone, Mira followed them, but she also linked with Barak, her friend and anchor. As the terrible moment of realization shattered the link between the Keeper and the boy, she and Barak held Coryn in a firm mental grip.

Coryn stood up abruptly, his face gone white, the lines of his scars glowing purple against the skin. He pushed aside the link that tied him to Barak and Mira. "Gods, no! Arielle!" he screamed. "Why did you not let me know?"

Ari crumpled forward, almost in a faint as the backlash hit him, but Barak and Mira managed to shield him from the worst. *See to Coryn,* Mira directed Barak as she put her arms around the stricken boy.

Coryn was already halfway out of the room. "Coryn,

wait," Barak called, as he followed him. Mira was vaguely aware of Barak's mind seeking Coryn's, finding it, soothing it, as she turned her attention more fully to Ari.

"My father," Ari whispered. "Oh, Gods. It is no wonder the Lady Renata sent me away. Am I to become a monster, too?"

Mira lifted his chin with her hand and stared deeply into his gray-green eyes. "No monster," she said. "He has many fine qualities. As do you."

"Why did not my foster-mother tell me?" Ari asked. "All these years I did not understand why the Ridenows would not have me." He shook his head and a solitary tear coursed down his cheek. He wiped it away with a quick angry stroke. "All these years!"

Mira, holding him in light rapport, saw that the hurt was not fatal. The boy was as resilient as she had believed. Then, as her mental touch met his, she felt another presence in the link. "Renata?" she said aloud. No, she was not mistaken. There sharing the link with her foster-son was the Lady of Aldaran.

"It is I," said the voice of Renata, and the air in front of Mira began to shimmer and take on a form Mira remembered well: a slim, unimposing woman with an upturned nose sprinkled with freckles, wide mouth, luminous dark eyes, hair the color of copper, with no hint of gray.

"Foster-mother," Ari said staring at the image. "How came you here?"

"I am not here," said Renata's voice. "But rather in Aldaran. What you see is only a sending. Before you left, I keyed my starstone to yours, so that I could be in touch with you. Do not think I have deserted you, my son. I love you well."

"Renata," Mira said, "what have you done? For the sake of old friendships, yours and mine among others, you should have warned us."

"I could not, *breda,*" Renata replied. "Although I wanted to do so. When Arielle came to me, outcast from Ridenow because of the child she bore, she made me promise to tell no one, but to send him to his true father when the time arose. I could not break that vow. I have watched all the while. I would have let no harm come to Ari."

And Renata had the Alton Gift, Mira reminded herself. She could hold even Coryn for a while.

Ari turned blank eyes to the ceiling. "And so my mother was outcast because of me. I am doubly cursed."

"Do not think so of yourself," Renata answered. "Let me tell you of your mother and your father and how it was."

"I will leave you now," said Mira to the boy, "so that you may speak with your foster-mother in peace."

She went to find Coryn, whom she suspected had more need of her presence than had the boy. She found him, in his apartments, sitting silently with Barak at his side. As she entered the room, Barak glanced at her in silent understanding, and then left her alone with Coryn.

"Coryn, I—" Mira began, but Coryn did not let her finish.

"How long have you known of this?" he demanded, not meeting her eyes.

Mira shook her head. "Not until the boy came. His face, your face. So very like."

Coryn turned toward her, and she flinched, as if from a blow, when she saw the unhidden pain in his eyes. "Why, Mira, why? Why did she not tell me? Why did she let herself die for my child? Gods, how she must have hated me."

"She loved you, Coryn," Mira said softly. "Never doubt that." She reached forward, to touch him lightly on the hand, but he drew back and shook his head.

"No, Mira," he said with a soft sadness in his voice. "Do not touch me. It will take some effort for me to undo what I have done to myself."

"Do you want me to stay with you?"

He shook his head. "No, I will be all right."

She bowed her head, and in her heart she felt that he had spoken the truth. For all the pain, for all the memories that haunted him, he would, in the end, be all right, the kind of man he was meant to be. "You lend us grace, *vai tenerezu,*" she said as she left him.

Back in his own room again, exhausted by the night's events, Ari sat slumped on the bed, his mind too numb for full understanding of what had been revealed to him. One thing, though, he clung to. Renata had promised that if, at the end of a year, he did not wish to remain at Hali, he could return to Aldaran and have an honorable position there. She loved him. Brenton loved him. He would always have a home.

But was that what he wanted? He no longer knew. He almost laughed at his own perversity. *Deny me something and I will want it all the more,* he thought. *Give it freely and I cannot choose!* In any event, he told himself, he need not decide tonight.

He stretched and gave serious thought to getting ready for bed when a knock sounded on his door.

"I'm sleepy, Dyan!" he called. "Can it wait until later?"

"It is not Dyan," replied a voice, which was muffled by the door. "May I see you for just a moment?"

Ari's heart beat hard in his chest, as with his *laran* sense he recognized the unseen visitor. But still he rose and opened the door.

The First Keeper of Hali Tower came into the room. Without the crimson robe, he appeared very much an ordinary man, small in stature and wiry, like Ari himself. And Ari saw that the Keeper's eyes were no longer filled with a cold arrogance, but were open and vulnerable, truly windows of a soul.

"There are some things I would tell you," said the Keeper in a soft, low tone.

Ari motioned politely for Coryn to take a chair. He himself sat down across from him, on the bed.

"I would tell you of your mother," Coryn began. Then he reached forward, letting his fingers rest above Ari's hand. "Would you like to hear?"

Ari nodded, and Coryn let his hand descend. Ari felt a mild but not unpleasant tingling, like a small electric shock, as, for the first time in fifteen years, Coryn Hastur, Keeper of Hali Tower, touched another human being.

Food for the Worms

by Roxana Pierson

This welcomes back an old friend of Darkover. Roxana Pierson, whose "Swarm Song" in FOUR MOONS OF DARKOVER showed us a really *unusual use of* laran, *tells us that in her childhood books were "the only friends I had except for the animals and insects." Her father kept bees as a hobby, and she says, "I will never forget seeing him remove the dripping honeycomb, wiping the bees off with his bare hands." She adds that in those innocent days, "even though we didn't use bee-suits," they never got stung. "It was only years later, when I discovered I was allergic to bee-stings, did I realize how fearless and foolish we were." She adds that she might have become an entomologist, but her father didn't believe in educating girls, and she only went to college after a disastrous marriage. (Me, too.)*

This is a new and clever twist on the usual Dry Town story.

In the Great House of Shandar, shimmering in the red heat of the noonday sun, all was silent. Servants spoke in hushed voices and the physicians conferred in whispers. The Lord of the House, Zhalara, was dying.

The senior physicians pulled their beards and shook their heads dolefully while their younger assistants diligently examined Zhalara, poking and prodding the wasted flesh that hung in a flabby dewlap across his abdomen. Only months ago, the old man had been hale and hardy, so heavy, in fact, that he had difficulty finding a horse that could carry him. And now. . . . A wasting disease of some sort accompanied by odd hallucinations. It was nothing they had ever seen before, but then, Zhalara was old and no one lived forever.

"My lady." The eldest physician, Valeron, bowed deeply to Zhalara's wife, Julana, who sat stiffly on a small gilt stool next to Zhalara's bed, her chained hands clasped about her swollen belly.

"You may speak," she replied tonelessly without lifting her eyes from the jeweled manacles that bound her wrists.

"I . . . we have done all there is to be done," Valeron said, clearing his throat nervously. Silently, he condemned the old man for taking to wife a girl who looked to be barely of marriagable age, but he had to give the old fellow his due—she was already heavily pregnant. "My fellow physicians agree, we have never seen the like of this illness."

"He does not eat, you say?" asked Falyn. As second eldest of the attending physicians, it was his right to assist Valeron in questioning the patient and his family. The younger physicians, who dared not speak face-to-face with a female member of the household, had to make do with examining the patient himself. Unless the patient was a female, of course, in which case a servant would be sent to tell the physicians where she hurt.

"He says his food has . . . bugs in it," Julana said softly. Her hands fluttered to the veils concealing her face as though she wiped away tears. "I have urged him to eat, but he has only a bite or two and throws the plate. You see how he is—those sores all over—he picks at his skin. Says he has lice, but there are no lice. There's nothing."

"It's true," the serving woman standing behind her nodded. "When I served him dinner last week, he said it looked like worms."

"What did you serve him?" Falyn asked.

"Why, noodles, of course! We always have noodles on the Fourth Day of the New Moons, the same as everyone else."

Valeron exchanged a look of exasperation with Falyn. "What else have you served him?"

"Rice," Julana said faintly. "It was always his favorite."

"And did he eat it?"

"No," the servant answered. "He said it looked like maggots. Maggots, mind you! I told him, right off, that if he didn't eat he would be food for the worms himself—much good that it did! And just yesterday I saw him scratching and scratching, but there was nothing there. He sits for hours staring at the wall, just like you see him now."

"It's too bad," Valeron said with a tired sigh.

"Yes, a shame," Julana agreed.

"It is a disease of the mind, I think," Falyn said with studied seriousness. "This happens in old age, sometimes, you know."

"Nothing much to be done, I'm afraid," Valeron said.

"Nothing," Falyn concurred. "Just try to feed him things that don't resemble worms."

Julana leaned on the carved balustrade overlooking the gardens. The suns were just fading into the lingering violet of twilight, and with the coolness, things were coming back to life. The nighthawks were exchanging their squawks of "pea-soup!" "pea-soup!" and the insects were taking flight. She held her hand out to a dragonfly that alighted ever so delicately on her outstretched fingertips.

This was her favorite time of the day. Here, in the garden, she found her only moments of peace, a few precious seconds stolen away from the household and Zhalara. He usually slept the afternoon away until she called him in for the evening meal. What would happen if he died, she wondered? She hoped she would be free, at least as free as any woman in the Dry Towns could be said to be, until her son came of age—she was sure she carried a son. Long before that, she hoped, she would find a way to escape to her mother's relatives in the Domains. It was that hope that had sustained her sanity through the long, miserable months of her marriage.

Julana had begged her father not to force her to marry Zhalara. She had hated the fat old man from the first time she saw him. Just thinking of their wedding day made her heart harden with anger. What had she ever done to be so ill-used? When he had locked the golden chains on her wrists that signified their bonds of matrimony, she had wanted to scream and bite at him like a trapped animal. And the night that followed—even now it made her ill to think of it. She had not even fully understood what was expected of her, and Zhalara's piggish rooting had been both painful and frightening. The thought that she would have to endure a lifetime of such treatment had been beyond bearing. Worse yet, she soon discovered that Zhalara was not only old and ugly, but cruel. Julana remembered overhearing her mother say to her father once that, "The only thing hard about a man that age is his head!" At the time, she had not understood; now she knew all too well what Allira had meant. And Zhalara never hesitated to take his frustration out on her with his fists. The first night he beat her, Julana had crawled away and wept. The second time, fearing for the child she already knew she carried, she had vowed revenge.

"My Mistress?" A serving woman approached hesitantly, quickly knelt, and touched her head to Julana's sandals as was the custom.

"Yes?"

"Forgive me for disturbing your peace, but your parents have arrived."

"Where are they?"

"In the Lord's apartments."

"You have offered them food and drink?"

"The Lord Jharek accepted our hospitality, but your mother wanted to see you first."

"I will go to them, then." Julana gathered up her robes and hurried away, followed by the servant.

"He doesn't look so good, does he?" Jharek observed, leaning over Zhalara curiously. The old man continued to snore, seemingly oblivious of his visitors.

"He doesn't, does he?" Allira echoed from behind him.

"How long has he been like this?" Jharek asked.

"Months," Julana answered with a shrug.

"He looked well enough at your wedding," Allira said. "Have you called the physicians?"

"Of course. They don't know what it is. Some kind of wasting disease."

Allira sighed heavily. "You're too young to be a wife, let alone a widow, but at least you'll be well off."

"I wouldn't count on that," Jharek said. "He comes from a large family."

"Are they *all* 300 pounds, then?" Allira asked.

"You know what I mean," Jharek shot back. "That brother of his—the one who stood with him at the wedding—he'll get everything. Including Julana. She's part of his possessions, you know."

"No, I don't know! Widows can't remarry in the Dry Towns. You told me so yourself."

"Not outside the family. It's perfectly legal for Zhalara's brother to marry her and keep the estate in the family."

"You . . . you can't mean that!" Julana exclaimed with dismay.

"What did you think would happen?"

"I . . . I thought the child is a male . . . everything would be his." She sat down heavily on the nearest chair.

"You mean you *hope* it's male," Jharek said, hard-voiced. "Even if it is, you would still be a ward of Zhalara's family until the boy's of age. It's about time you grew up and learned your place, girl. If you don't answer to me, you'll answer to a husband, his relatives, or your son. It's about time you got that through your head."

"I understand you perfectly, Father." Julana's resolve hardened. She might never be able to hope for true freedom, but that did not mean she had to be helpless. Her mind reached out to touch the thousand-legger that was busily investigating a crack in the ceiling. Without warning, the creature lost its hold and landed directly on Jharek's head.

He struck at it with a surprised shout and roared as it curled to deliver a vicious sting to his hand. He threw it hard, smashing the hapless centipede against the far wall. Rubbing his throbbing hand, he exclaimed, "Why do there always seem to be bugs wherever you are!"

"Don't be silly," Allira replied. "There are bugs everywhere."

"Yes, Father," Julana said quietly. "That's true, you know—there are more bugs than people. In fact, there are probably even more bugs than Zhalara has relatives!"

Behind her veils, she smiled grimly.

Childish Pranks

by Diann Partridge

Diann Partridge lives in Wyoming. She has "one husband, three kids, one old dog and two cats." She is a veteran of the Armed Forces, and says she has been writing for as long as she can remember. "Childish Pranks" came about from "something I remember from an earlier Darkover story—something about Thendara Castle being very old and having rooms and suites built on as necessary and no one really knew what or where all the rooms were. The word Castle always gives me a thrill, I think of secret rooms and ghosts and things that go bump in the night. I combined that with all the childish pranks we played on each other during basic training. Finding shaving cream in your shoes was not an uncommon occurrence."

Alizia Aillard gripped her young cousin by the arm, expecting her to try and pull away. But Luz Valeron didn't struggle. She stood stock still in the Tower courtyard, her muddy skirts hitched up with both hands to leave her bare legs free. Alizia brought the switch down sharply. She struck the dirty little legs five times. Not once did Luz cry out. Hatred sat on the thin, pointed face with its gritted teeth and near mirror-image to Alizia's own.

Luz's two cohorts weren't quite so stoic. Korin Ardais was younger; he had to be dragged up, then he screamed and yelped with each blow. Dainty little Callina Alton begged piteously, streams of tears spilling from her large blue eyes. Alizia shortened her sentence to three. Luz's face darkened in further outrage.

"Now, I want you three to know that in the history of Thendara Tower we have never had such a terrible thing happen to its Keeper. Furthermore . . ."

"But, Aunt, we didn't mean for it to happen to Lady Alaynna. It was supposed to fall on Caleb. And we did . . ."

"Luz!" barked Alizia sharply, "don't interrupt me. You are in enough trouble without being impolite. What you did was wrong, I don't care who it hit. *Dom* Caleb is a fine teacher and you will never learn to work in a Tower unless you start to obey him. Now, I am ordering the three of you to your rooms until the morning. You will not attend the Midsummer Festival tonight and there will be no supper. I expect you to remain in your rooms quietly, until your parents are notified. I am quite sure that your mothers will be mortified to find out what you three have done."

"She isn't my mother," muttered Luz.

"Be quiet! Now go to your rooms."

The three turned and left the courtyard, Korin snuffling and Callina weeping into her hands. Luz stomped off unrepentant.

Alizia leaned her head against the stone wall of the

Tower and her shoulders shook. Izak Ardais, the Tower monitor, came over and touched her shoulder gently.

"You shouldn't let these punishments bother you so much, Liz. The little brats deserved it, especially Luz. We both know she's the ringleader of those three, though how she can rope Callina into her plots each time is beyond me. That child's such a pretty timid little thing. Come on now, let's go have a drink before we start for the Festival."

Alizia pushed herself away from the wall and Izak was amazed to see that she was shaking with laughter instead of tears. He still didn't understand these Aillard women.

"Oh, Izak, if you could have seen Lady Alaynna's face when the contents of that chamber pot fell on her. I have to laugh now or else I will laugh right in her face. I know it was meant for Caleb, but stars above 'Zak, she just stood there like she was in another world. Then she began screeching like she was being stung by scorpion ants."

"It was a terrible trick to play on anyone, Alizia, and you know it. And it's not the first trick that Luz had tried. We both know who put the numbweed salve in the jam pot and who short sheeted all the beds. If it wasn't for the fact that she has the highest *laran* potential of any of the new group she'd be sent home straight away."

"Oh, don't get so stuffy, 'Zak. I trained with Alaynna and, believe me, we pulled our share of pranks. Besides that, I happen to know that Luz hasn't had much of a home life since her mother died. Her father remarried straight away and she has a whole batch of little brothers and sisters. It may take her a while to realize that coming to the Tower was the best thing that ever happened to her, but one day she will be glad of it."

"Well, that day can't come too soon for me. Just yesterday I found that someone had filled all my boots with sand. Now I wonder who did that?"

"I wonder?" chuckled Alizia. "Now, did you say something about a drink?"

Luz slammed the door to her room with a bang and then pounded both fists against it.

It wasn't fair, she raged silently, it just wasn't fair. She kicked off her indoor boots as hard as she could, sending them flying into the wall. Missing the Festival hurt worse than the switching. She'd waited and waited for this. Her clean Festival dress lay on a chair. Wadding it angrily into a ball, she shoved it under the bed. It just wasn't fair!

The more she thought about it, the angrier she became. She threw herself on the bed and wailed her anger and frustration into the pillow. If her mother were still alive, she wouldn't be stuck here in this place. She'd still be at home where everyone loved her.

Thinking of her mother immediately reminded her of her father. Damn him to Zandru's coldest hell, she thought. He deserves it. He didn't even wait six months after Momma died before he married that stupid Alton woman. And the first thing she did was make him send me off to this place. And now I can't go to the Festival!

She looked around for something to throw and her hand fell on the smooth round rock her father had given her on leaving the Valeron hills. "This way," he'd said gently, "you will always have a piece of home with you." Her fist closed tightly around it and she hurled it with all her might toward the fireplace.

It hit with a satisfying crash. Then there was a creaking screech and Luz watched in surprise as the left-hand side of the fireplace slid back, leaving a square of darkness.

Her room and those of the other trainees were in the coldest, oldest part of Thendara Castle. It had taken Luz several tendays to grow accustomed to the snow and cold of Thendara City after the dry heat of Valeron. And this damp, tiny room was nothing like the large airy one she had had at home. It was just another mark against everyone who had sent her here. But the room did have a fireplace large enough to occupy one entire wall. The mantle was white translucent stone with deep intricate carvings of flowers and animals.

She slid off the bed and padded silently over to the fireplace. Her rock had struck a funny carving of a round-backed little animal she didn't recognize. She had never really looked at the carvings closely before. Reaching out, she pushed the same animal. It didn't move. She pushed harder and this time it slid inward. The fireplace wall slid closed. Luz pushed again and it slid open.

She squatted down flat-footed and wrapped both arms around her legs, resting her sharp little chin on her knees. A secret panel. That could lead to a secret room. A place where she could hide and no one could find her. That would serve them right. They would really be upset if they couldn't find her. Her father would probably make them let her come home if they couldn't take better care of her. Just wait, she'd show them.

She stuck her head inside and called up a glow light. Calling up light had been one of the easiest tricks she had learned in this place. In the orange glow she could see that the opening was some kind of a tunnel between the walls. There was another knob inside and she pushed it when she stood up. It opened and closed the panel from the inside. She ducked and scooted back out, grinning from ear to ear.

No supper wasn't much of a punishment. All the potential Tower students were kept supplied with fruits and nuts and sticky sweet candy made from *kireseth* honey. Luz gathered it up and tied it securely in a work apron. Then she pulled on several heavy sweaters and a clean skirt, along with woolen drawers and stockings. Slipping the soft suede boots back on, she decided to take a thick woven shawl. She draped it around her shoulders and tied the ends in a knot. Picking up the apron, she ducked into the opening. Calling up the light, she pushed the inside knob and listened with growing satisfaction as the panel slid shut. This would teach them!

The tunnel wound down and around for over two hundred strides. Luz counted them. The air was dank and musty smelling. Then there was nothing but a blank metal wall. It set flat and smooth against the rock of the tunnel walls. Cold radiated up from the floor, she could feel it through her boots, but the wall was warm. She ran both hands over it, but there was nothing in the way of a handle or a knob. Remembering what *Dom* Caleb had said about using one's *laran,* Luz took a deep breath and calmed her thoughts.

Everyone said she had talent. She forced herself to

concentrate on the wall, willing it to open. She ran her hands over the smooth warm metal, thinking that it felt as if it were alive. There was one spot, waist high and to the right. She was normally left-handed and using her right was awkward. Channeling all her thoughts, all her *laran* into that one spot, she willed it to open. Luz felt a number of clickings under her fingertips and the wall slid upward into the ceiling.

She stepped through. Her glow light fluttered, dimmed, and went out completely. She shrank back against the wall, then watched in amazement as strips along the top of the walls began to brighten. A bell chimed softly, once, twice, three times.

Luz stood at the edge of large circular room. It was a Tower workroom, of that she was certain, but oddly different. There was more metal in this room than she had seen in her life. Chairs, tables, lattice screens, stools and benches; literally a Keeper's ransom in metal. She clapped her hands and laughed delightedly.

And it was warm. Blessedly warm. After two seasons of Thendara's cold and snow, the warmth was wonderful. She pulled off both sweaters and the drawers and stockings and even her underslip. Clad only in her thin chemise and skirt she danced barefoot around the room. The chairs, she found out, all rolled. She shoved them every which way. They also twirled around and around. Luz spun around in one until she was dizzy.

The lattice screens were enormous. And empty. Luz could not imagine a starstone big enough to fit one of them. The power they could generate would be incredible. She found a flat slick pad embedded on each desk with a pen attached by a tiny flexible chain. She twined the chain around her wrist, thinking it would make a very attractive bracelet. Touching the pen to the pad, she discovered it left marks. She sat down and spelled out her name in careful stilted letters. At least she remembered that much from *Dom* Caleb's classes.

A sharp, loud ringing began and Luz jumped. A section of the wall to her left lit up and a voice began repeating over and over: **"INTRUDER ALERT! NO SUCH TOWER WORKER AT THIS STATION. INTRUDER ALERT!"** Letters appeared in the lighted strip, running from left to right, over and over.

Being afraid was nothing new for Luz. She had cried herself to sleep many nights since her mother had died. But outwardly, to most adults, she seemed a brash, "I don't care" type of child. This type of breath-snatching fear was new even to her. She fought down the urge to scream and nothing came out but a small whimper. Hiding in the knee-hole of one of the desks, she wrapped both arms around her head. That voice, whatever it was, seemed to shoot right through her brain.

It went on and on until Luz thought she *would* scream. She forced herself to crawl out from under the desk and ran back toward the door. It was closed now and no amount of thinking at it would make it open. Who could think calmly with that banshee wailing all around?

The words changed. Now the voice shouted out **"AFFIRMATIVE ACTION REQUIRED IMMEDIATELY. LEVEL FOUR HAS BEEN REACHED."**

It was repeated again and again. Luz backed up against the closed door. The room was growing colder, sucking the heat from her body. Why didn't someone come and save her? She screamed, beating at the door with her fists. There was a hollow popping sound and she whipped back around to stare in frozen fright as a ghostly matrix stone began to form inside the lattice screen. With each ragged breath it grew more solid, swirling golden streams inside the azure facets. She rubbed her cold arms with even colder hands, but her clothing was on the other side of the room. She was too afraid to move.

The screen tilted up and slowly turned to face her. For a second, inside the swirling blueness, Luz could have sworn she saw a face. It wore an avid, hungry smile. Light flared and stabbed toward her, answered in a small way by the starstone she wore in a little silk pouch around her neck. She felt the cold hunger envelop her and had time for only one sharp mental scream for **HELP!** before the matrix power pulled her inside the stone.

The screaming wail died and the voice spoke new words: **"AFFIRMATIVE ACTION COMPLETE. RETURN TO LEVEL ONE."** The lighted strip along the wall dimmed and went out completely. The cold dissipated and the warmth returned. All that remained of the intruder was a pile of dirty clothes beside one desk.

Aching heads prevailed the morning after the Midsummer Festival. Only servants, who had to get up, did so. It took the Tower workers several days to realize that Luz Valeron was really missing. A search of the entire castle was made and while the remains of old Lord Fergus' favorite dog was found in an unused storage room, no one found one small red-haired girl. The search widened to include the City and then the outlying areas, but they still had no luck. Her father came immediately to Thendara, upset and outraged that his eldest child had been allowed to come to harm. She wasn't dead, they knew that for certain. Her starstone still showed up alive and well on the Tower monitor. In fact, that also told them that she was someplace inside the Castle. But no one could find her.

Everyone knew it was a trick, a prank that Luz had thought up. Her usual co-conspirators were questioned until they were in tears, but they had no idea where Luz could be. Finally, everyone gave up. Her father went home. They knew she would return when she was good and ready and not a moment before.

Several months after her disappearance, a massive early winter storm began building north of Thendara. From the screens, the Tower workers could tell it would paralyze the city and surrounding area with blizzard cold and snow. Alizia's group gathered in the northern Tower. Under the Keeper Alaynna, they would divert the storm so that it slid to the east into the bare Alton hills.

They began working with one of the smaller matrix screens, a device of woven wood and a small palm-sized starstone. As monitor, Izak Ardais was the first to notice the cold. He realized that the blue stone was slowly sucking all the warmth out of the room, draining everyone. His breath misted in front of his face as he tried to reach the stone. His group was deep in rapport with the stone, their overworld selves far to the north with the storm. Cold lashed through him. He watched helplessly as the starstone froze, then cracked and exploded. Jagged pieces burst across the room, one thin sliver slicing his cheek.

The cold faded. But before it was completely gone,

he could have sworn he heard a young girl laugh. It was a pleased, delighted laugh and sounded absurdly like Luz Valeron. But that just couldn't be. There was no way she could be inside the matrix stone.

He lost this train of thought as he began helping his friends recover. The loss of the starstone was immense. The backlash of power wasn't as bad as he expected. At least there hadn't been a fire. Everyone was thrown out of rapport at the moment the stone cracked. They all were suffering from varying degrees of hypothermia and frostbite. Workers came running from all over the Tower to help.

Alizia sat next to him, wrapped in blankets and holding a cup of hot *jaco* in her hands. Her fingertips were covered with numbweed. She wore a puzzled look on her face as one of the workers cleaned the cut on Izak's face.

"Thanks to Avarra it wasn't an inch higher or it would have been your eye. And it isn't deep enough to need stitches. If you don't make any faces for a couple of days, it won't even leave a scar."

He nodded his thanks and the worker walked away.

"I just don't know how it happened, Liz. I was watching the same way I always do. It was just that the cold was suddenly *there*, inside the room. Like we were in the middle of the storm."

Outside the snow began to fall. Wind whipped and shrieked around corners and under windowsills.

"I haven't told anyone else this, 'Zak, but just before the rapport broke as the stone shattered, I could have sworn I heard Luz laugh."

His eyes widened and he looked at her in shock.

"You heard it, too, didn't you," she said. He nodded.

"Alizia, if she has found some way to get inside a matrix stone, there will be no end to the tricks she can play. We will never be safe."

Alaynna di Asturien limped regally into the room on frostbitten feet, her heavy red robes swishing softly.

"I can't believe what I am hearing. You two of all people believing that child could have caused this accident. You should know better. No one but The Hastur herself has the power to enter a matrix stone and work from within it. Not even the most powerful Keeper in history could do that; certainly not an untrained child. I don't want you to repeat this nonsense to any of the others, do you understand me? What happened was merely an accident. We underestimated the strength of the storm. We must just be glad that no one was killed."

Alizia and Izak nodded, speechless.

"Now I am going to my quarters to lie down. Before either of you retire, I want you to question the other trainees about who put sand in all my shoes this morning. These childish pranks have got to stop."

With that she turned and walked from the room. As she went through the door, faint childish laughter echoed from nowhere. Alizia and Izak looked at each other and Alizia shook her head.

"I didn't hear a thing. Did you?"

Cherilly's Law

by Janni Lee Simner

Janni Simner starts off by saying that "unlike many contributors to these pages, I'm not raising any children and I'm not married to any computer programmers. I do, however," she adds, "have the requisite two cats (one of which my sister lent me for the occasion)." That's what I'd call going to extraordinary lengths to fit in.

She works as an assistant editor for Washington University Publications. Anticipating my question "Is that in Washington D.C. or Seattle?" she said, "Actually, it's in St. Louis. Really." Her job involves editing other people's copy, along with quite a bit of project management. She also occasionally writes feature or news articles for the newsletters her office produces."

She adds, "On the off chance that my name doesn't make my gender unmistakably clear, I am female and will be 23 in November" of 1990. She started out as a chemistry major, but somewhere along the way got the idea that she could major in English and not live on the streets after graduation. Yes, skill at writing a literate English sentence may now be the rarest skill education has to give. It's all those computers out there.

Darian and Ryll walked through the fields, not speaking, not even allowing their minds to touch. They moved with the same gait though, the same slight slouch, and their feet hit the soft earth together.

As the sun edged over the distant mountains, Darian broke the silence. "I am sorry, my brother," he said.

Ryll did not look up. "It is not your fault. Besides, I should be glad to leave."

"But you're not."

"No. I suppose I still hoped Father could learn to love me."

"He'd send me away, too, if he could."

"I know," Ryll said, and looked resentfully at the copper chain encircling Darian's wrist.

"According to Cherilly's law, only a starstone is unique," the nurse Maura had explained to King Ridenow twelve years earlier. Everything else—whether it's a tree, a horse, or a human being—has an exact duplicate somewhere. Rarely is this duplicate one's twin, however. Even between twins, there are usually small differences."

The king looked at her impatiently. "Yes, I understand all that. But which one was born first?"

"This one entered the world first," Maura said, lifting an infant. A thin copper chain hung loosely about his wrist. "I've no doubt, though, that they came to consciousness at the same moment."

The king looked at the wet, red baby in Maura's arms, at its brother lying nearby. Most men would be pleased; his wife had given him not one, but two sons. She'd also given her life, however, and unlike most men, King Ridenow had not been willing to pay such a price.

"This chain—it's how I'm to tell them apart?"

"Well, that and—" Maura stopped herself. Ridenow was head-blind. The thoughts of the infants would mean nothing to him.

"And what?"

"Nothing," Maura said softly. "The bracelet will suffice."

"Good. Keep the children out of my way, and see that they aren't any trouble." Without looking at the infants again, King Ridenow turned and left the room.

From the start, the similarity between the boys was eerie. They would laugh at the same jokes, reach for the same piece of bread at the same moment, give the same answer to the same question at the same time.

Only King Ridenow saw a difference. When a glass of wine was spilled, he looked for the copper bracelet before reacting. Darian would get only a few harsh words, but Ryll would be sent from the table, and probably beaten as well. Ridenow didn't love Darian any more than Ryll, but he had to be patient with the older twin, to teach him how to manage the domain.

If possible, Ridenow would have fostered Ryll somewhere as soon as he was walking. But the king didn't make friends easily, and not until the twins' twelfth year did tensions ease, just slightly, with Syrtis. Ridenow wasted no time, and made plans to send Ryll away.

"Stop looking so gloomy," King Ridenow snapped at Ryll when the boys returned from their walk. If

Darian's sad, thoughtful look echoed Ryll's own, he didn't notice.

Ryll scowled and ran down the hall. *I wish I had been born first,* he thought. *I wish I had a copper chain around my wrist. I wish—* A sudden, awful thought. Ryll slowed his pace and walked, very deliberately, toward the kitchen.

Darian stared at his twin across the lunch table. Ryll's mind was closed to him, as it had been all day. *I can't really blame him. It isn't fair. We're so much alike, Ryll and I. Actually, he's taking this better than I would. If I were in his place, I would—horrible as it is, I would see to it that I wasn't sent away. Even—yes, even at Ryll's expense.*

Darian reached for another glass of wine. Only then did he realize that the walls were not quite solid, and not at all perpendicular to the floor. He tried to stand, but the floor betrayed him, sliding out from beneath his feet. Ryll stood above him, his face as unreadable as his barriered mind. The room began to spin, and faded away.

Ridenow knew Ryll was unhappy about being fostered, but he was still surprised when the child resorted to lying.

"I'm not Ryll; I'm Darian. Can't you tell?"

Is Ryll really so foolish as to think I'd believe him without Darian's bracelet? No doubt he is trying to take advantage of the fact that his brother chose this afternoon to go riding in the hills. Well, I may be head-blind, but I'm not a fool.

With the help of several servants, Ridenow forced his son from the house.

* * *

I will not stay there, Darian decided on the road to Syrtis. *I will run away, become outlaw, reclaim my birthright by force.* Such plans were not unreasonable; legends told of sons who had done similarly before. Yet Darian's resolution lasted only halfway through his first day at Syrtis, when the king called Darian to his private quarters. King Ridenow had often pulled Darian aside in such a manner, usually to school him in some aspect of defending or managing the lands he would one day inherit.

Syrtis looked at Darian, and smiled. "Did you have a good journey?" he asked.

Darian began to scowl, but realized that if he planned to run away, acting rude and unhappy would only make his escape more difficult. "Yes, thank you. The weather was fair, and the winds were light."

"I am glad you will be staying with me," Syrtis said. "I suppose you know that I have no sons."

And my father has one son too many, Darian thought bitterly, but stopped the thought abruptly. King Syrtis was not head-blind; unlike Darian's father, he probably could read thoughts.

But the king only said, "If you need anything, let me know. You are welcome in my home."

The kindness in Syrtis' voice startled Darian. His father, if never as cruel to him as to Ryll, was never more than cold, efficient. *Maybe I will stay here a while after all. There will be time enough, later, to reclaim my birthright.*

He resolved, however, to keep his identity hidden. His father had been patient with him knowing he was Darian. If this man was kind thinking him Ryll, so be it.

* * *

To his surprise, Darian was happy at Syrtis. The king treated him as if he belonged there. Around his father he always felt he was in the way, even in the remotest corners of Castle Ridenow.

Darian was allowed to explore Castle Syrtis and the surrounding lands freely. He found a ledge, in the foothills of the Kilghards, where he could sit and look toward Ridenow lands. Here, away from King Syrtis' gentle tone and understanding smile, Darian sometimes let his anger resurface. Looking toward Ridenow, he wondered whether his father was now training Ryll in farming techniques and household management, oblivious to the change.

He decided to find out. Leaning back against the stones, he closed his eyes, pulled his mind free of his body, and flew toward home.

Ryll was sitting on the edge of the bed—Darian's bed—polishing a sword. He looked up, surprised at Darian's presence, and for a moment it seemed he would stand and embrace his brother. But then he drew back, and his face hardened.

"Why are you here?" he asked.

"It is my room," Darian replied. "Or have you already forgotten?"

"Haunting it won't enable you to return," Ryll said.

"Doesn't taking my place bother you? Even a little?"

"No," Ryll answered calmly, "for I know you would have done the same."

Darian moved to slap his brother, but stopped with his hand in midair, remembering that he was present in mind only. Ryll rose from the bed.

"Get out of my room," he said, the color in his

cheeks belying his quiet words. Darian looked back at Ryll defiantly, anger boiling within him. If his judgment hadn't been clouded by that anger, he later thought, he might not have taken Ryll's blow; he might have realized that Ryll could only hurt him if he believed he could be hurt. But as it was, Ryll pushed Darian roughly out the bedroom door, and forgetting the shove was not real, Darian felt himself fall out the door, fall toward his body, physically fall from the ledge. He felt his body crash into the rocks, and then the world went black.

Darian wasn't sure how long he was unconscious, or how long he moved deliriously in and out of troubled dreams—dreams of falling, of bones cracking, of someone sliding the bones around and sewing his leg back together. He knew only that when he awoke, King Syrtis was looking down at him with concern.

"How do you feel?" the king asked.

"My leg hurts."

"I know." Syrtis looked at Darian sadly. "The *laranzu* said the bone was shattered into so many pieces that he may not have been able to join them back together properly. You will be able to walk again, but you'll probably limp, and you'll never run."

Darian forced a smile. "I guess you're wondering how this happened," he said.

"I know how it happened," Syrtis replied. Darian bolted up, and winced as he felt weight on his leg. Syrtis eased him back into bed. "Your barriers were down while you were delirious," the king explained.

"Then you also know that—"

"Yes."

"Are you very angry?"

"Angry? About what?"

"About the deception which has been played on you. I am not who you thought I was."

Syrtis began laughing, but stopped when he saw real anguish in Darian's eyes.

"Child, it is you that I care about, not your name. Don't you realize that I love you as a son?"

Darian blinked in surprise.

"Or are you too set on reclaiming your birthright to hear such things?"

Darian's eyes now reflected confusion, rather than anguish.

"I wasn't going to say this until you'd been here a while, until you'd had time to come to love me as I love you."

"But I do love you, Foster Father."

"Call me Father. Please."

"Father."

"Darian Ridenow, will you be my son, and inherit my lands after me?"

"Heir? Heir to Syrtis?" King Ridenow screamed. Ryll limped to his father's side—he'd been hurt in a knife fight with a servant boy several weeks before, and the wound had never healed quite right—and examined the message. He nodded sympathetically, agreed it was an outrage. But he was oddly relieved. *So I haven't cheated my brother, after all.*

Ridenow, head-blind as ever, continued raving. "He's my son. If Syrtis is to be his, it shall be mine, first."

What is he yelling about? He doesn't have to call his other son back home at the end of his fostering. Isn't that what he wanted?

"This is an insult," Ridenow yelled, "and I'll not stand for it. I declare war on the Syrtis lands." He stopped to catch his breath, and turned, suddenly calm, to his son. "Well," he said, "next tenday, you ride beside your father into battle."

Ryll nodded, grateful that his father couldn't read his thoughts.

"Men," Darian announced, looking down from a castle tower, "bearing Ridenow colors."

"We shall give them the welcome due your kinsmen, of course." Despite Syrtis' friendly tone, Darian suspected from the icy look in his foster father's gray eyes that the king offered a kinsman's hospitality grudgingly. "What else do you see?" Syrtis asked.

Darian reached down to the approaching men with his laran. "There are many of them, and they carry swords and arrows. I doubt my father plans to join us for dinner or visit a son he doesn't love." Closer to the castle, Darian could see a man approaching rapidly on horseback; presumably a border guard, delivering news of the army.

"Well, then, your father forces us to fight him," Syrtis said. Darian could tell that, despite his foster father's grave tone, he was not unwilling to enter into such a battle. After a moment, Syrtis asked, "Are you still very angry with your brother?"

Darian scowled. "Yes."

Syrtis laid an arm lightly about Darian's shoulders. "How would you like to avenge yourself at last?"

Ridenow knew that his lands were larger, his armies stronger, then those of Syrtis. What he didn't count on was the strength of Syrtis *laran*. The Syrtis arrows, though few, were all ablaze with *clingfire;* the Syrtis *leroni* caused Ridenow's men to run from phantoms which the head-blind king could not see. "Is my son lending them his strength?" Ridenow wondered aloud. "Is he being used against me?"

"Darian," Ridenow called, and Ryll came obediently to his side.

"Darian, is your brother fighting against us?"

"I don't know, Father."

"You have *laran.* Don't tell me you can't read your brother's thoughts."

Ryll shifted uneasily from one foot to the other.

"He's been barriered to me ever since you sent him to Syrtis." Actually, until a few days ago, Ryll had thought the barrier entirely his own. But after Darian was named heir to Syrtis, Ryll tried to reach him, thinking there was no more reason for anger between them. He couldn't find Darian, though, and finally a throbbing headache forced him to stop trying.

"Well, then, you'll have to break the barrier down," Ridenow said, as if this were the most obvious thing in the world.

Ryll spoke slowly. Ridenow didn't notice that he was shaking. "I can't do that."

"I'm not asking whether you *can* do it. I'm telling you to do it. Or are you going to defy me? Perhaps you do not want to inherit my lands after all."

Ryll backed down under that threat. "All right," he sighed. "I'll do it."

Ridenow smiled. "Of course you will."

Ryll and his father found a spot away from the fighting, under a tree. "I can't look for him if you stand right over me like that," Ryll snapped. When Ridenow stepped back and sat down nearby, Ryll reached out toward the castle. To his surprise, his mind swept easily up the steps, toward the balcony where his brother stood alone, watching the battle.

Contact was easy to make. Darian's mind was familiar—just like his own mind, after all.

"Darian?" Ryll reached out tentatively, expecting to be rebuffed, to be sent spiraling back down to an angry father. But Darian spoke without resentment.

"I'm glad you've come," he said. "I would have looked for you if you hadn't."

"Then—then you aren't angry anymore? But your mind was barriered."

"Only because I feared you; you threw me from my room with such force. But I'm happy here."

"Really?"

"How could I not forgive you for what I myself would have done? We are so much alike, after all."

Darian's easy acceptance startled Ryll. *If it were I, I would not forget my anger so quickly. I would have been plotting against Darian these past months.*

Someone stood behind Darian. Ryll hadn't seen him step onto the balcony. Or was it only in thought that someone looked down at the two boys?

"Who is that, brother?"

"Only my foster father, Ryll."

"Oh." Some instinct made Ryll back away.

"He has been good to me."

"I'd better get back to Father," Ryll decided suddenly. "Shall I tell him anything for you?"

"No. No, I don't think that will be necessary."

Ryll turned and began to run.

"Leaving so soon?" Darian asked. "When we've been apart so long?"

King Syrtis' arm, grown suddenly long, reached for Ryll's fleeing figure, grabbing his throat and squeezing it tightly. Darian threw his head back and laughed. "Tell me now that you were justified in stealing my place, in throwing me from the cliff."

Ryll tried to speak, but managed only a hoarse cough. He reached for his throat; then both his head and hands went limp. Darian laughed again. *This time Ryll is the one who believes the illusion and takes the pain. Thank you, Father, for vindicating me.*

Syrtis did not respond to the thought; with both hands, he was reaching for Ryll's heart. Darian ran to his foster father's side. "Father, what are you doing?"

"Just what I promised; avenging you at last. And avenging myself on the presumptuous king who covets my lands."

"You were only supposed to scare him. You never said anything about killing him!"

Syrtis squeezed Ryll's heart, forcing blood to spurt onto the balcony. The blood wasn't real, Darian knew, but still he flinched and turned away, running to the balcony's edge.

And a stray arrow arched up from the battlefield, piercing his heart. Darian, or Ryll, or maybe both, screamed.

If Syrtis heard the cry, he did not react. He continued squeezing Ryll's heart until all the blood had gone out of it, until the boy's form slipped from his firm grasp and back down to a lifeless body, where Ridenow waited in vain for color to return to his son's pale cheeks. Much later, Ridenow would charge at the balcony, demanding that Syrtis return his other son, his only remaining heir.

He couldn't know that while he waited for Ryll,

Syrtis stared in horror at Darian, lying still on the cold stones. Against all reason Syrtis knelt by the boy's side, hoping for some sign of life. But no breath came from the lips which, slightly parted, left Darian's final thought unspoken.

We're so very much alike, after all.

Avarra's Children

by Dorothy J. Heydt

I write a little note on every story when I accept it, in order to tell in my introduction what it's about; all I wrote on this one was "the kind of story I would have written if I could." I'm getting used to running short of superlatives for Dorothy Heydt's prose. We both started in Berkeley; but while we were raising children our lives branched very far apart. I spent my time in childrearing and writing; she preferred to work and let someone else raise her kids and yet her kids have turned out as well, by and large, as mine; which only goes to prove what Kipling said:

> "There are forty thousand ways
> Of constructing tribal lays
> And every single one of them is right."

Which is especially hard for me to admit, because like all opinionated people I tend to think the way I do things is the one and only way to do it. It must be worth something to do things about as differently as they can be done and write, by and large, Darkover stories about as well.

As for what Dorothy is like personally, well, she's had stories in four previous Darkover anthologies, four volumes of SWORD & SORCERESS, and SPELLS OF WONDER. You can look her biography up as easily as I can. I don't want to repeat myself.

For any Darkovan cutpurse worthy of the name, a Terran spaceman was a Goddess-given target of opportunity. Not only did he carry money to burn—literally, in the form of that flimsy Terran paper that was worth more than copper in Thendara these days—but he carried it in a fabric pack nestled against his backside, easier to cut than a proper leather beltpouch and much easier of access than those tight flat pocket things the Terran merchants wore. It was singularly unfair of this particular spaceman to have pulled his pack around and slung it over his belly like a sporran, but since he was standing there in the marketplace, staring up at Comyn Castle on its high hill and paying no attention to what was going on around him, he looked worth a shot.

It was especially unfair that he had such quick reflexes and such strong hands. The boy tugged and twisted, but Donald Stewart kept his grip on the skinny wrist and looked him up and down with the deceptive mildness of a prize bull in his own meadow.

"That wasn't a very good idea," he said. "Take it easy, kid. You don't have to make a living picking pockets. What's your name?"

But the boy said something crude, and twisted again and kicked Donald hard in the shin, and broke free. The Terran ran after him, kindness forgotten, leaping over the carpenter's horse the boy had ducked under and weaving through a platoon of space marines with scarcely an "excuse me."

Thendara's market square was beginning to show signs of life again, after months of planetwide depression and the days of near-anarchy that had culminated in the strange coup of Festival Night. The cloth merchants had brought out their bulky wares into the public view, and bread was being baked daily and would probably come off rationing within the week. Even a goldsmith had risked the clement air of spring and brought out a trayful of rings that glowed like coals under the ruddy sun. There were no customers at his booth as yet, and he snatched up his tray and backed up against the wall as the child skidded by with the angry man close on his heels. They took a sharp turn at the onion-seller's and disappeared into an alleyway.

Here it was darker, and the pavement uncertain, and Donald thought he had lost his quarry till he turned another sharp corner and nearly collided with him. A man in nondescript Darkovan gray woolens had wrapped the child up in his arms and pinioned the feet between his own. Donald looked the man over while he caught his breath.

A Terran, in spite of the clothes: tall and thin, with smooth golden skin. "Picked your pocket?" he asked.

"Tried to. You know this kid?"

"I've seen him about. There are a lot of these homeless children in the city. Now, I'll tell you what." He took the boy by the shoulders and held him out of kicking range. "I'm going to take you to my house, and we'll talk. My name's Peter Yoshida. What's yours?"

The child looked him up and down. "How much?" But the tall man only laughed.

"Silver and gold have I none, but I can give you lunch. Care to come along, sir?"

"Sure," Donald said. He supposed the man's motives were nothing but good, but there was no harm in making sure. He thought he'd caught a glimpse of something familiar and disturbing under the shabby gray cloak. He fell into step beside them.

Yoshida lived in a shabby small house not far from the market square, a timber building that over the years had leaned against a taller house till they almost touched. A single room inside served as living space and kitchen, and a ladder against the back wall led to a sleeping loft above. Yoshida closed the door firmly, and hung his cloak and Donald's jacket on hooks in the wall, and Donald's suspicions were confirmed. Under a woolen tunic the man was wearing a clerical collar and a cross.

There'd been rumors that missionaries were coming in to Darkover. Donald, who had had no use for religion since he was not much bigger than this kid, went through the mental motions of washing his hands and concentrated on being polite.

Yoshida brought out a Terran foil-packed meat roll and Darkovan bread, and a better small beer than Donald had tasted in weeks; the breweries must be getting back online. The boy, after a first suspicious taste, chewed his way steadily through everything that was offered him. He could have used a few more kilos of flesh on his small bones—the child could be no more than seven or eight—but he hadn't the look of one who is really starving, such as Donald had seen in the hills. Someone had been taking care of him, at least until recently.

"I still don't know your name," Yoshida said after a few minutes.

"Anndra."

"Anndra what?"

"Just Anndra. Did you think I was one of those dumb girl Renunciates who go by their mothers' names?"

"Well, no," Yoshida said. He and Donald exchanged glances. Unusual for a little boy to use the proper word "Renunciate" instead of the commoner "Free Amazon," but the kid had clearly been brushing up his language skills; his fluent Thendara trade-talk was already spiced with *cahuenga* obscenities and a few choice words of Terran.

"Where did you live?"

The child's mouth was full; he only shrugged. So did Yoshida.

"I'd like to start a shelter for these street children," he said. "Traditionally, on this planet, the poor and abandoned move in with their kinfolk and they cope somehow. But with the famines and the riots, these kids haven't got any kin left—or none that are willing to claim them. Some of them are half-Terran, like this one. Some are Renunciates' sons, who have to leave the House at the age of five—the worst age I can think of for a boy to have to leave his mother. That's why—" and he gestured toward a picture hung on the far wall, a woman in a long blue cloak, sitting on a bank of turf starred with flowers. She had a baby in her lap, and a dozen or more children of all ages clustered around her.

"I want to start a halfway house where they can eat without having to steal, and learn how to be civilized again. I've got the funds, the trouble is finding a large enough house."

"The city's full of empty buildings."

"Whose owners are escaped into the country, or dead, and nobody knows who the heirs are. There's no red tape like a family-based society whose records are kept in the memories of people who aren't here any more."

"Well," Donald said, "I'm in the service of someone who has Lord Regis Hastur's ear. I'll ask her if there's anything he can do. There ought to be."

Anndra, licking his fingers, had got up from the table and wandered over to the nearest wall, to look at the picture the priest had hung there. "Who's that?" the boy said now. "Is it the Lady Evanda?"

"No," said Yoshida. "Her name is Mary, and once she was a poor man's daughter, but now she is the Queen of Heaven and the mother by adoption of all mankind."

"Not mine," the boy said, and spat. "I belong to Mother Avarra." And seeing them glance at each other, he made a dash for the door and was gone before they could catch him.

"I am not going to make you do anything you don't want to do," Marguerida said. "I couldn't if I want to. This is your house—" they were sitting in the entrance hall of Thendara House, and the traffic in and out was fairly brisk—"and any time you cared to you could go inside and get a dozen of your sisters to throw me out."

"My sisters are not such fools as to lay hands on a Keeper," Raquel n'ha Mhari said; but she smiled with one side of her mouth and seemed to relax a little. "I think all the fools have moved into the Castle. Do they really expect to find *laran* in a hillwoman whose grandmothers *and* grandfathers have all been nut-farmers since the memory of mankind runneth not to the contrary?"

"That's a long time," Marguerida said. "Gifts don't go with bloodlines any more, I thank the Gods. I am an Elhalyn, and the Elhalyn Gift was the multiple foreseeing that drove its owner mad as often as not. I'll settle for the small skills I've got.

"You, they tell me, are a tracker, and you can trace and find things the Gods themselves would have given up on. Everyone tells me so, from the beggarwoman whose child you found in the forest, to the Terran Commissioner whose escaped murderer you found in the scullery of the Officers' Club. Did you never wonder how it happened that you could do those things? Have you no idle curiosity? Come, it'll take an hour of your time, and if they don't find anything you can come home, and if they do find anything you can come home anyway. Lord Regis isn't forcing anyone into anything. If he did I should have to speak to him, and so would the Lady Desideria."

Raquel had been glancing at Marguerida from under her eyelids and digging her toes into the cracks between the flagstones—if she had been a horse she would have dug her hooves into the earth—but now she laughed.

The front door opened again, and a crowd of children came in, nominally under the charge of two sisters who seemed very glad to be home. Most of them were carrying bundles and all were talking at the top of their lungs, girls of all ages and boys of no more than five. Raquel put her hands over her ears and got to her feet. "Getting crowded in here. I'll go with you."

"According to what I've read," Father Yoshida said as they came out of the alley, "there used to be an order of priestesses of Avarra, before the Compact; they were healers and contemplatives. Under Varzil the Good they became an active Order and merged with the Swordsisters."

"The Renunciates still swear by the Goddess, I'm told," Donald said, "but the oath doesn't call her by name."

"And in any case," Yoshida went on, neatly sidestepping a dung-cart that limped on one wheel, "I don't believe those devout ladies would have sponsored pickpockets. Not unless they've fallen on very hard times. Now over there—see the tiled roof, over behind the cobbler's shop? That's the house I'd like to get my hands on. It belonged to a merchant prince called Bran mac Adhil who died of plague last year, and nobody can find the heirs. . . . What's the matter?"

"Nothing's the matter," said Donald. "Look there." A path was opening, right in the thickest part of the crowd; people stepping hastily aside, dragging their sacks and goats and servants aside lest they brush against the hem of the Keeper's gown. A small dark woman with the short hair of a Renunciate followed in her wake, glancing from side to side and concealing her amusement as best she could.

They met in the center of the market, and introductions were made. "I'm fortunate in meeting you, *mestra,*" Donald said. "Perhaps you know the answer to the question we've been puzzling over. Do you know anything of a cult of Avarra surviving into the present day? People who say 'I belong to Mother Avarra' and don't scruple at cutting purses?" (Sudden image of the boy, eyes glowing, face grubby.)

"No, I haven't," said Raquel, the color draining out of her face, "and now I hear of it I don't like it. If I learn anything, perhaps I can let you know. We should be getting on, *vai domna.*" And Marguerida led her away, clearing her path through the crowd like Moses parting the Red Sea (the mythic image bubbled up into Donald's mind out of a quarter-century of oblivion. It must be the company he was keeping).

"There's not that much of a hurry," Marguerida said. "They'll be ready for us whenever we get there."

"I want to get there," Raquel said. "There's a bad smell about this place. Haven't you noticed it?"

"No," said Marguerida.

"Yes, I know about them," Security Commissioner Grey said. His prefabricated Terran-style office was almost unnaturally neat, a place for everything and everything in its place, with no ornament but a long mural behind his head of a lunar landscape and a crescent Earth rising. The room felt cold, and the Commissioner looked tired. (Donald had been lucky to find him in. He had been doing three men's work ever since the troubles had started, and unlike most Terran officials he lived outside the Terran Zone.)

"Not the part about Avarra, but the kids. They're running in packs all over Thendara; no parents, or none that will admit to them; thieving and begging and living on I don't know what. One of them was caught in the act on Monday and his throat cut on the spot. About nine years old, we think." Grey's voice was level, but his jaw was tight. He was a tall man, with a long face and a long neck and long fingers that turned a stylus over and over along the desktop.

"Just one more pixel in the picture. Fire, plague, erosion, homeless children—and the woman who's responsible for it all is up at Comyn Castle under Lord Regis' protection. I don't know what he thinks he's doing."

"As I understand it, she's helping to undo what she did," Donald said. "We'd all have a harder time of it without what she knows. I shouldn't have thought she was the type to play Fagin to a gang of street kids, but I'll ask her if she knows anything about them. I'm living up at the Castle now; God knows there's room. There'd be room for Yoshida to set up his shelter in a wing of it; only I don't suppose the kids would come there."

"Thanks for reminding me," Grey said. "I need to send Father Yoshida mail and tell him he's got my support."

"I don't think he's on the network," Donald said. "He's living in that little shack just off the market."

Grey shrugged. "I'll send him hardcopy. We've got messengers. Thanks, Stewart." He half-rose as Donald went to the door, and sank back into his chair as if he were tired. As Donald went out he thought he heard Grey whisper, "Oh, God—!" which was so unlike the reticent, efficient Commissioner that he thought he must have imagined it.

"So I asked Andrea—" Donald said, and broke off as the door opened and the chambermaid came in with the hot water. Servants were invisible, and never heard what was said in their hearing, that was the convention; but Donald couldn't bring himself to subscribe to it. He had grown up on Terra, where there was a machine for every task, and up in the mountains he had learned to do all for himself with natural materials; but Comyn Castle was a blend of primitive luxury and unexamined hardship that kept taking him by surprise. The maid was a woman of thirty-five or so, thin and hard-faced and frail-looking, but she hefted the heavy stoneware water jugs without apparent effort. Donald found it embarrassing. He could have carried the water up himself, and would rather have, if it couldn't come out of a faucet the way normal water ought to do! But the woman needed the work, and seemed glad to have it. "Dinner in half an hour, *vai domyn,*" she said, and closed the door behind her.

"You asked Andrea, yes?" Marguerida prompted.

"I asked her if she knew anything about these kids. She said she hadn't had anything to do with these particular ones, but she had dealt with street gangs in the past and might have some ideas. She said she'd do up a précis for Grey, and be available for his questions. And she doesn't know anything about a cult of Avarra."

They were silent for a moment. "Maybe I'm overreacting," Donald said finally. "What do you think? How serious is this?"

"Very serious, I think," Marguerida said, "from the way Raquel is taking it. She is one whose Gift is to sniff things out, if you follow me, and she smells something very bad somewhere in this business, and she won't discuss where it is. The Gods know," she said, rising to her feet and clenching her small hands into fists, "that it is a very bad thing for little children to be followers of Avarra. They should belong to Evanda and Aldones, growing up in the sun without fear. It's the old and sick who call on merciful Avarra, and mothers worn out with childbearing and the deaths of their children, who pray for sterility. The mercy of Avarra is that you die and are released from pain. And whenever little children come to know about this, it is a sign that times are very bad. Which they are," she sighed.

"If you weren't a Keeper you could cry on my shoulder," Donald said, and because this was an old joke between them she sighed again and smiled. "Where has she gone? Raquel, I mean."

"Home to Thendara House, with her test results," Marguerida said, "to think them over and decide what she wants to do with them. She'll come to us, I think; by the day at any rate. She'd be happier going home at night than living here."

"I didn't know Renunciates could live in—" he gestured at the wall, to indicate Comyn Castle's echoing halls and its current population of about two hundred (males, females, and several *chieri* to whom the question did not apply)—"mixed company."

"Oh, they can live wherever they want, once their half-year's novitiate is over," Marguerida said. "They prefer their own Houses where men are not allowed. Most Renunciates I have met are willing to acknowledge there are some decent men among all the bullies and brutes; just the same, they don't trust them on the premises. Put a man into a group of women, they seem to think, and by very nature he'll take over. I wish they had more confidence in themselves. It's time we washed and went down to the Hall."

* * *

Over the next few days, they began clearing fire debris away and bread went off the ration and a fleet of airtrucks came in from Regulus Base to ferry supplies into the hills, and Commissioner Grey set his men to rounding up the young pickpockets. They caught three, and brought them in to shelter inside the Base, with the other homeless children who had been trickling in ever since the troubles began. The three boys, the oldest perhaps twelve, cried nonstop and said they wanted to go home. Asked where home was, they shrugged. Their faces appeared with the others on posters in the marketplace, but no one identified them; and one night they tore out the screening over an airduct and escaped. Commissioner Grey began to look very grim, and it took the luck of the Gods to find him at his desk any more. People would see him, stalking through the narrow streets with one or two of his men, searching, searching.

The next day there was a heavy rainstorm that washed filth from the gutters into the wells, so that Terran water trucks had to be set up in the city again. The day after that, one of the city police tried to catch a pickpocket, and was brought in on a stretcher.

"Not a mark on him," Commissioner Grey said to Lord Regis when he reported to him in the mid-afternoon, "except the bruise on the back of the skull that he got from falling over. The doctors say 'catatonia'—"

"I don't know the word," Regis said.

"No reason why you should. It's Greek for 'he's pulled himself back into his skull and thrown away the key.' He lies in bed, doesn't speak, doesn't move. Frequently brought on by shock. And I thought some of your people might like to take a look at him—at the least they might find out what it was that delivered the shock."

The Commissioner looked uncomfortable. Long used to giving orders, he had almost lost the knack of asking favors. Regis smiled. "We'll be right down."

Lord Regis came to the Base Infirmary himself, and brought with him his promised wife and her grandmother. They stood together, fingers just touching, alongside the bed where the unconscious man lay, curled up like a small bud among a great many papery leaves.

"He's very deep," said Desideria after a long while, more to herself than to the Commissioner. "I don't—" she glanced at Linnea and at Regis. "I don't think there's anything we can do here. This room is too small, and many of our people wouldn't like the idea of coming here. Could you bring him up to the Castle? Say, tomorrow?"

"Whenever you like," Grey said. They left him standing by the bedside, drumming an irregular rhythm against the wall with two fingertips; and on the way back to the Castle they spoke of the Commissioner and his virtues, and how he had aided them so many times during the recent troubles, and how they might contrive to take some of the load off his shoulders. Of his fallen guardsman they did not speak at all; they'd shear that sheep when they got him home from market.

"I'm sorry, Donald," Lord Regis said. "A shelter for homeless children is a splendid idea, and I want to help Father Peter any way I can. And you're right, if there are no heirs the property comes to me in default of a surviving King. But even if we knew for certain that Bran mac Adhil left no heirs, I'm not going to bestow any more Darkovan land on Terrans, not at this time with feelings running so high. I could grant it to your Lady Marguerida, if you think she'd be willing to sponsor a project run by Terran priests, or to some other Darkovan. Not to Father Peter; not just now. I'm sorry."

Marguerida woke to a presence in her room, a whisper by her bedside: Raquel n'ha Mhari, crouching on her rug and murmuring, "*Vai leronis,* please wake up. I have to show you something."

"I'm awake. Show me what? What's the hour?"

"It's the middle of the third watch. I have to take you down into the town, before the bakers and flower-sellers begin to get up. Please, *domna,* there's no one I can trust but you."

"Why such secrecy? How did you get into the Castle at this hour?" But as she spoke she was dressing, not in her Keeper's finery but in a tunic and trews she'd hidden in her wardrobe against need. She knotted her bright hair up under a dark cap, and took down the warmest cloak she had.

"You mean, past the guards?" Raquel said. "They don't know how to listen." That was all she said, but she led Marguerida down the stairs and out the gate under the guards' noses without even interrupting their conversation.

Raquel led the way through the town to the market square, and skirted its edge, slipping from the shelter of one building to the next, till they reached the western side. Even in their fleece-lined boots, their feet left prints on the frosty stone. Liriel, now visibly past the full, was high overhead and turned all the square to cold silver. Raquel stopped in front of a heavily boarded-up stall with the boot-shaped sign of a cobbler swinging overhead. "You can feel it here," she whispered. "I didn't want to track it farther without help. Listen."

The square was utterly silent, not even a breath of wind or the crack of a stone in the frost breaking the stillness. They waited; and after a time Marguerida began to sense a light somewhere behind her eyes, a dim warm reddish light that the violet frost of the moon could not reach, and a sensation of drawing inward, of contracting into a place that was very deep. It was beating like a heart. Form and texture melted in the warmth. She was slipping into the overworld without intending to, an overworld soft and red with blood and hidden things. She was walking among planes of warmth, no, crawling hands-and-knees, drifting down into darkness. There was nowhere to breathe.

(She lay in state upon the couch of darkness, arms outspread. Her head was crowned with shining shapes, a thousand little moons. Her dark hair flowed into the shadows.) Come to me and rest. The whole world came out of my womb, and shall return there. Come to my embrace, and I shall never let go. (A womb that—) *Wherever you go, I shall be with you. Drink peace* (A womb that refuses to give up its fruit) *drink peace and forgetfulness from my breasts.* (—is diseased, and will die.) *(The crown upon the shining head was made of little skulls.)*

Marguerida brought her head up with a jerk. She was back in the square, and Raquel was saying, "*Domna,* come back, come back."

"I'm back," she said. The sweat was icy on her face. "Aldones! What was that?"

"Ai! I was hoping you'd tell me." They looked bleakly at one another. Across the square, a door slammed, and a man ran briskly from one building to another, slapping his arms against his chest to ward off the cold.

"It's like a parody of the Goddess," Marguerida said. "All of Avarra's traits amplified and extended to a conclusion that is logical and insane."

"Was it She?"

"I don't know."

"Can the Goddess Herself go mad?"

"I don't *know,*" Marguerida said firmly. "But I know whom to ask. There's only one who's dealt with the gods in our day, mad or sane, and that's Lord Regis Hastur."

Lord Regis sat in the back row of seats, under the wall that once had borne the Alton banner. Not that such things mattered any more; all the banners had been torn down by hands unknown on Festival Night, and the Crystal Chamber had been converted into what Jay Allison called an operating theater. For the purposes of today's work, the telepathic dampers had all been turned off; they sat idle in their niches like so many worn-out shoes. On the central dais, where once the Comyn had debated the future of Darkover, the unconscious Terran guardsman lay on a low cot. By his side sat a circle of ten. Two of the circle were *chieri,* and a third sat in the second circle that surrounded the first—learners and observers, these, and what the Terrans called "backup" and "redundancy check."

Marguerida sat in this second circle, Raquel n'ha Mhari at her elbow. If anyone could have proved the man's illness had nothing to do with what the women had sniffed out this morning, Regis would have filled his mouth with gold. He shifted uneasily in his chair. Behind Marguerida sat her paxman, his cold blue eyes glancing this way and that under his dark brows, on watch against anything that might threaten his sworn lady and would have to chew its way through him first. And far back on the opposite side, where the Aldaran banner had not hung for generations (but such things didn't matter now), Commissioner Grey sat like a kyorebni perched above the earth, waiting to see what he could find.

Deep, Desideria had said. (She was sitting halfway back, not far from Commissioner Grey, and appeared to be paying more heed to the observers than to the circle: so it seemed. She caught his eye and smiled briefly.) The circle went into the upper chambers of the man's mind like one who walks down a mountain path, around and around, and finds it empty. Regis had not their training, and they left him behind. He stretched again, and caught sight of a man sitting by the door. Heavy cloak tossed aside onto the chair next to him, he sat there in his formal Terran clerical black—*so as not to deceive us by false appearances,* Regis thought. It was unnecessary effort, perhaps, since many in the room knew the priest by sight, but one could appreciate his good will. Regis would have to make an effort to speak to him—

Someone in the circle drew breath noisily: less a gasp of surprise than a desperate gulp for sustaining air. A silent rustle of unease went through the room.

One moment, please, the Keeper said, and Desideria got up to relay her words to Grey. *We've found something: a memory, or a command; it's pinning him down. Chained down in the dark. If we cut him loose from it we'll lose it; if not, we'll lose him.* Regis shifted again. Back in a dark room in his mind where he had hidden her, dead Sharra leered at him suddenly, and sank again into darkness.

Desideria spoke softly, and Grey stared at her as though she had grown an extra head. "You're *asking* me? Of course I— Sorry. Yes, please, cut him loose. Bring him back."

Everyone, make ready to observe, please, and the circle joined its severed ends and there was a moment when nothing moved, and then instantly it had been over for some time and the Terran thrashed convulsively on his cot and opened his eyes. Grey let out a long sigh of breath, and so did many others in the room. They were exchanging glances—*You saw it, too? Buried alive. Buried unborn.* Regis had felt no more than an instant of claustrophobic warmth that had spread through the hall and vanished, leaving a foul taste in the mind. He caught Marguerida's eye, and she nodded.

The circle was dissolving, humans and *chieri* helping one another to rise and stretching out their cramped limbs. The Terran was sitting up, grimacing, reaching backward to dig his knuckles into the muscles of his back. "What happened? Geez, my back is stiff. Commissioner, what am I doing here?"

Commissioner Grey had well-nigh teleported over the railings and slipped through the circle to reach his guardsman's side. Two Terran medical staff followed him, chilly in their lightweight coveralls. They got the man to his feet and led him away.

* * *

They met later in Regis' own rooms: Raquel and Marguerida, and Commissioner Grey, and Donald (who as usual had come in unrequested, trailing Marguerida) and Father Yoshida (who had come in with Grey).

"I can understand your not wanting to alienate any more Darkovan land," the priest said. "Perhaps we could arrange a long-term lease, with yourself as trustee? What I'd really like is to get a roof over the children's heads now and do the paperwork later. I have two in my house now and there's not room for more.

"Names? ages?" Grey asked, and Raquel, "Where did you find them?"

"Anjali is three, I think, and has no idea who her parents were. Mikhail is ten. I found them in the streets, begging because they hadn't the skill to steal. Mikhail came originally from your House," he nodded toward Raquel, "but had to leave at five, because of your rule, and his foster-mother abandoned him when things got tight."

His tone was carefully nonjudgmental, but Raquel flushed. "That rule is a halfway mark," she said, "between those of us who would like to be more lenient, and those who complain about having 'baby men' in the house at all, and would prefer to toss them out at birth." (The Terrans winced.) "There's one woman in Thendara House, the staunchest friend the Terrans have there; not because of the way they keep going on about equality, but because with their technology males could be diagnosed and flushed at conception."

"In any case," Grey said, his voice level, "I brought

Father Yoshida today because he shares my opinion that we have one problem here, and not two."

"Homeless children picking pockets," Father Peter clarified, "and something nasty in the telepathic woodshed, somewhere near the marketplace. Now, I have no psionic talents at all, and what people like me do is to extrapolate what other people are thinking from how they move. Body language, they call it. It's below the verbal level, and I find it hard to explain what I see in these children. But if I stand like this, the feeling it brings into my mind—" He stood up, his arms curled against his body, his head slightly to one side—and through every telepath in the room there went a quick shudder, as they sensed his thought, a dim echo of what had been touched in the Crystal Chamber.

"Retreat-to-the-womb, I'd call it, if I had to call it something," Father Peter said, sitting down again. "The two things have something in common, and I think it's centered near the market—"

"West of the cobbler's shop," Marguerida said. "And someone has to go and find it. That's really all this meeting is about, isn't it, Lord Hastur? Raquel has to go, to track it to its source; and yourself, to deal with it when you find it; and whomever else you choose to go with you."

"I won't go without *Domna* Marguerida," Raquel said. "Saving your presence, Lord Hastur, she's the only person here I can trust."

"Very well," Regis said. "I'll chose a few of the Guard—we don't want too large a force—Commissioner, can you lend a couple of your men?"

"As few or as many as you like," Grey said. "But I'm going, too."

"Commissioner, I hardly think—"

"I have a right to go," Grey insisted. "One of my people was attacked; I have the right to avenge him."

("Old Darkover hand," Donald murmured behind his hand to Father Peter.)

"Very well," Regis said again. "I want to do this at night, when the markets are closed and the square is empty. We'll meet there at midnight, will that suit everyone? Thank you, then; I'll see you tonight."

"And are you going to let your lady go on this mission, and not insist on going with her?" Father Yoshida asked as he and Donald made their way out of the Castle.

"Of course I'm going," Donald said calmly. "*Domna* Marguerida knows it and Lord Regis probably knows it, too; I saw no point in prolonging the discussion by mentioning it."

Father Peter chuckled. "Sam Gamgee," he said. Still talking, they went out the great door and down the ramp into the city.

Liriel, rising a little later each night, was high overhead when they met in the square. They were ten all told, booted and trousered and wrapped in short bulky cloaks and muffling hoods. The Regent and the Commissioner each thought the other had brought more troops than he had, so that they were deep into the streets behind the cobbler's shop before anyone had a chance to notice either Donald or Father Peter. The priest kept his face well back in his hood. Donald had a leather bag slung over his shoulder.

The night was bitter with the cold of a Darkovan spring, but the close-set houses cut the wind and made it warmer in the narrow alleys. Raquel walked slowly down the alley to a wider cross-street where a whitewashed wall shone in the moonlight, frost glittering on the nails that fastened a dozen planks across the heavy door.

"Can we get in without making a racket?" Grey murmured. But Raquel led the way around the house into another alley, to another door criss-crossed with planks, and when she nudged the door with the toe of her boot it swung silently open inside the barricade. One by one, cautiously stepping over and under the planks, they filed into the house of Bran mac Adhil.

Inside, it was at least ten degrees warmer; the house had been securely built. The door had let them into the Great Hall where once the merchant Bran had kept a princely state in his high seat. The tapestries were torn from the plastered walls, the high windows shuttered, the fires in the fireplaces long burnt out. "And from here, I'm not entirely sure," Raquel said. "The stink is all around us. Does anyone have any preferences?"

A warm draft was coming down the main staircase, so they went that way. Donald lengthened his stride and came up behind Marguerida's elbow. When had she changed back into her red Keeper's robe? The light swirled around her face like a fine veil. It was warmer here, but not that warm. Donald checked that he still had his bag, and drew his plaid closer around his shoulders.

The torches in the hands of Grey and his men were smoking and going out, and presently they let them fall to the ground and crushed them out underfoot. The walls were giving them enough light to see by, the deep red light of the hidden sun. In the shadows before their feet something moved, a figure like a little man with the face of a mouse; it ran ahead of them, tittering, for several yards before ducking aside and vanishing into the dimness.

One of Regis' men half-drew his sword, and put it back again. Raquel looked at him with disdain, and took her bow from her back and an arrow from her quiver. She did not put the nock to the string, not yet, but her eyes kept glancing about for targets. Regis kept his sword in his sheath; his skin glowed faintly from the Hastur blood within. His feet left prints that shone for a while after he had gone past.

Grey's men carried their crossbows casually under their arms. Their mailshirts chimed faintly as they walked. Grey's steel breastplate shone like copper in the rich light, but the torn place over his heart showed blackened edges. The tears trickling from his eyes had worn long furrows in his cheeks, and the sword in his hand flickered like flame along its edges. Donald glanced again at Marguerida, still safe at his side; strands of her coppery hair drifted through the light like plant tendrils through water. His bag was still strapped over his shoulder, snug under his arm, and he could feel the comforting hard lumpy shape inside.

There was a light up ahead, a silvery light that stood out against the general red dimness of the place, and a dark figure stood outlined against it. A manlike shape, bigger than the little mouse-man, and it had an arm raised in greeting. "Welcome," it called, the high fluting voice of a child.

Grey took a step ahead of the party, toward the figure. "Who are you?"

"Me?" the child said. The light was brighter now, almost revealing the child's face. A shaft of it seemed to come through his throat, as if it were hollow. His brown hair fell in tangles to his shoulders, and he had a long face like a fox. "You don't know me—"

"Dammit, I do know you!" Grey cried. "You're dead!"

"In my Mother's house we're all alive," the child sang. "Come and live in Mother's house where we're all alive, all dead. It's all the same."

But Grey bellowed "NO!" and fell back a pace as the shaft from the child's throat touched the fissure in his armor. He recovered and raised his sword, but the child had vanished.

The attack came without warning, a long streak of darkness that swung like a whip. It knocked Grey off his feet, casting him back against his own men and the Darkovan guards. Donald scrambled to put Marguerida behind him, and from her other side Raquel was doing the same, but she put them both impatiently aside and raised her hands. From the light in her hair she drew a handful of fire, shaped it like a snowball, and threw it into the heart of the darkness. The tentacle drew back. Grey and the others scrambled to their feet. Both crossbows shot at once, but the darts found no target. Marguerida shaped another fireball and threw it.

It was answered by a shower of darts, dark and cold as ice. One of the Earthmen was down. Lord Regis was on one knee, raising over the fallen man like a fold of his cloak a shield of light that seemed to repel everything that hit it. One of the second volley of darts got Donald in the shoulder, and his arm and his side went cold and numb. He couldn't tell any longer if he had the bag on his shoulder, and he tried to twist his head round to look for the strap. His feet were uncertain under him.

A light was growing behind him, a golden light like the sun of Earth, and Father Peter stepped forward. Naked, or nearly naked, his skin glowed like Regis', but he had no shield. The cold darts struck him, and struck again, but through every rent in the bright skin, as through rifts in the clouds, poured streams of sunlight that seemed to melt the rest of the darts in midflight. Deep in the darkness something groaned. Donald was beginning to feel his arm again, and he fumbled with the fastenings of his bag.

Regis, Grey, and Father Peter stood together: shield and sword, and armor and sword, and those glowing wounds that admitted no martial metaphor. Marguerida stood behind them, her fingers twisting light into a net of many strands where little sparks pulsed like stars.

Another tentacle swept out, low over the ground, and caught Grey's feet out from under him and began to drag him away. Gently Marguerida cast her net, and it hovered over the cursing man as he bumped along the ground, hacking with his sword at a tentacle that seemed not to feel it. But Raquel cried, "You bitch, let go of him!" and shot her arrow into the shadows.

The net of light was growing overhead, and shapes were becoming visible. She lay upon her couch of darkness, arms curved round the children huddled around her. Some of them were still alive, and some shone with the silvery light of death, but they slept together in her arms. Grey lay unmoving at her feet. Raquel drew her belt knife and stepped over the fallen guardsman, throat-cutting plain on her face. And Donald finally had his bag open and drew out what had been inside.

It was a shape that made no sense, a thing with neither light nor color. The eye could hardly see his hand as he held it, let alone the thing itself, and the Goddess raised one arm to shield her eyes. And one of the children looked up and said, "My God! *Mama!*" and ran to clasp his arms round Raquel's waist. And Donald raised the thing he held, and turned it on.

Most of the light was gone. A shaft of violet moonlight poured through a crack in the window screen, and Donald stepped carefully around the couch and pulled the screen open all the way. Then he laid the damper on the windowsill, safely out of reach.

The woman lay on the couch, her arms over her face, the children beginning to stir around her. A vast shape, white-haired, white-eyed, doubly blind now with her *laran* disabled by the damper. She moaned and wailed, the incoherent sounds of one who has never heard human speech, and the children wept and began to pull away. (The silvery dead had vanished, with no one to make them real in their minds.) One of them stood beside her, his back rigid, his face turned away. "Anndra," Grey said.

The child started and looked up. "Oh. Hi, Dad. How'd you get here?" he said in good colloquial Terran and with seeming nonchalance. "Cold, isn't it?"

"Come on." He laid his hand on the boy's shoulder and led him away. As they passed Raquel, standing alone in a puddle of moonlight, Grey caught her eye. "Come on," he repeated. "We have *got* to talk."

"Who was she?" Donald asked. "Did she live here?"

"Oh, I think so," Marguerida said. "Hidden away, so the neighbors wouldn't talk. Bran died of plague and the servants ran off and left her—if they knew she was here at all. She reached out with her Gift for people to tend her and feed her—and to love."

"Most of these kids are boys," Donald remarked. "Terran anthropologists have known for centuries that the most fervent worshipers of the Mother Goddess are men—in cultures where boys are taken young from their mothers to learn men's work."

One of the Terran guards had retreated down the corridor and brought back the flashlights, which luckily still worked. He returned Grey's to him without quite meeting his chief's eyes. Lord Regis, one hand to his head as if it ached, sent his two men looking for materials to make a litter—"so we can get her into isolation as quickly as possible and take this misbegotten damper off us."

"Clever Donald," Marguerida said, "to think of a damper." She sat on the end of the couch, stroking the wretched woman's matted hair, giving her the only kind of communication she could feel. Father Peter had taken away the bewildered children and was sitting with them in a corner, talking about Mary.

Donald smiled, and shrugged. "Those dampers were the second piece of Darkovan technology I'd ever seen," he said. "Once I found out what they did and what they were for, it seemed logical to pick one up. Put us all on an equal footing." He looked down at the pallid, blind face. "So to speak. Is there anything that can be done for her?"

"Maybe. Those up at the Castle may be able to reach her mind. Your Terran doctors might give her her sight and hearing back, make her less dependent on her *laran*."

"The Alton Gift: the forced rapport," Regis said. "I wonder where she got it."

"Where did the Altons get it in the beginning?" Marguerida said. "I'm not going to worry about it. Look there."

Commissioner Grey and Raquel n'ha Mhari stood halfway down the corridor, leaning against opposite walls, speaking by fits and starts. Between them Anndra sat on the floor; he had found a bent spoon and was blasting imaginary monsters with it. Even Regis could not make out what they were saying, which was just as well.

"Grey is one of these old-fashioned Terrans," Donald remarked, "who wants to support and protect the people he loves. This is not the same as the other old-fashioned type who wants to isolate the people he loves for his exclusive possession. Trouble is, from where she stands they look like the same thing. They need to meet each other halfway."

"That's what I was thinking," Marguerida said. "Lord Regis, how would you like to give this building to the Thendara Guild House, for them to lease to Father Peter? A 'halfway house,' he called it. I am thinking of a house where Renunciates could live, when they chose, under a slightly modified Rule, in the company of other people such as their sons and—others of their choice."

"I'm sure I've no objection," Regis said. He looked down the hall where Grey and Raquel still stood, backed up against their walls, grim-faced, but at least speaking to each other. "Who's feeling very brave and wants to volunteer to tell them?"

The Tower at New Skye

by Priscilla W. Armstrong

I met Priscilla Armstrong in Baltimore at Darkovercon this last year; and recognized the name; she was one of "my writers." Her memory is better than mine, though; she says she remembers getting rejection slips from me on blue paper with my "inimitable typing." She said in her letter that she treasured them because they gave her "hope and the energy to keep trying."

She is a pastor's wife; an unenviable job; among other things one of her duties will be to start a prayer group focusing on healing. She says, "I also teach laying on of hands; surprising to think it can be taught." Not too surprising; any form of human knowledge can probably be taught, or at least learned.

Sarah Lovat-McAran looked into the starstone held in her cupped six-fingered hands, and focused her thoughts on her husband. Through the stone, around the stone, beyond the stone, she saw him, where she had expected, in the hills, tending sheep. She called silently. *Duncan, Duncan.* She saw his head move as he looked toward home. *Duncan, Duncan.*

He smiled. *I hear you, Sarah. I'll be home tonight when Gavin relieves me.*

It works, she smiled. *Just as we thought it would. Now all we have to do is see how far it works.*

She got clumsily to her feet, wishing she could dance with the joy that was in her. Soon, when the child was born, when their daughter put in her appearance, then she would dance again. She tucked her starstone back into its wrappings and let it rest again on its thong around her neck.

We'll show them, Duncan and I, that these talismans have more to them than a little fire-starting and children's tricks. They do more than enhance the Lovat-McAran Gift, too. And if they are small, they are safe. When we are ready, we will demonstrate their uses. When we are ready. When.

She sighed. When. When indeed. The opposition of their parents had lessened now that she and Duncan were married and expecting their first child. "Marriage will settle them both," she'd heard her mother thinking. She wondered if they would let her baby have a starstone for her naming. Both her mother and Duncan's were beginning to campaign actively against the talismans. For all of Judy's arguments for tradition, this was one she wanted to change.

When Duncan returned, she greeted him enthusiastically, and he gave her a sideways kiss, patting her belly. "I'll be glad when she puts in her appearance," he said. "I can't get close enough to you with her in the way all the time."

"Don't talk so, Duncan! She'll hear and feel rejected before she is born, poor little thing!"

Duncan patted her again. "Sorry, daughter, I do want you for your own sweet self, truly I do," he laughed. "Now, Sarah, about today. Tell me what you saw and heard."

Sarah reported. Duncan nodded. "I was not expecting the call just then, it interrupted my thoughts. I could see you, too, very clearly."

"How far can a person send? We need some others who can help us. Without a faraway person how can we check distance?"

"Oh, I forgot to tell you. Gavin will help. He is with the sheep tonight and we can try together to reach him. He will expect us."

"That's one more. Who else can we get? Mother Judy does not approve of testing anything. She says we should be grateful for what our ancestresses gave us, and ask no questions."

"I know," he said wearily.

"Come husband, they are calling us to the night meal," and Sarah pulled him to his feet and they entered the hall where the tables were already laid for the meal.

With more than a dozen at table, of all ages from the parents to the littlest who were boosted on tall chairs, the tumult of the meal precluded any further conversation between them.

As they finished their sweets, Dougal and Rafael together banged on the table for attention. "Children, be still and listen to us," said Rafe. "You, our eldest children, Duncan and Sarah. Yes, you two, soon to be made three. It is time for you to establish your own household."

Sarah's jaw dropped. She looked uncertainly at Duncan, who was as startled as she. *What shields they must have used so we didn't even guess.*

The two older men laughed at their startled faces.

"Oh, yes, we have planned this for months, even before you started your daughter, Sarah," said Dougal. "The younger children will soon want to marry, and will need space here for a time. And you have grown into maturity and are well able to establish your own home, with your own children, and your own fosterlings when the time comes."

"We have found land for you, it is there for the taking, and less than a half-day's journey from New Skye. By the time your little one is walking, all will be ready. We will go tomorrow to look at it and choose your house-site. No, Sarah, you will not come with us. Your time is too close now. Duncan can report when he gets back."

Talk burst out then from the whole table. Judy and Duncan's mother Laura were talking about supplies of herbs already prepared, to give them a start, and about planting crops before the house was ready; Dougal and Rafael were talking about moving their share of the flock, and the kind of land and crops they could expect, and Sarah's nearest sister Mhari was asking how soon she could have their private apartments for herself so that she and Ian could marry.

"The sooner you go the better," Mhari said. "We know you and Duncan have been practicing with your stones in your apartments. You are departing from tradition. Mother and Laura say so." Her voice dripped triumphant scorn.

"Mhari! How *can* you!" Sarah was appalled. *I haven't been as tuned in as I thought, or their shields have improved.*

"Our shields have improved, silly. How else could we make this plan to get rid of the two of you without?" Mhari answered Sarah's unspoken thought.

"We've only been communicating with each other at a distance. What is wrong with that? I've seen you light a fire many times with your stone, Mother, too, and even the little ones can do that. And we all listen and talk to each other without words. What is wrong with increasing the distance?"

"It's not tradition. Judy and Lori gave us the stones and the tradition. Lighting candles and fire was part of the tradition. So is mind-reading. But not talking over miles. That's not natural or right. If they had talked over miles, or wanted us to, they would have left word how to do it. Anything out of tradition is evil." Mhari was triumphant.

Without another word, Sarah turned away from Mhari and walked toward her rooms, but not before she heard her mother's thought, *So now she knows.*

Heartsick, she entered their apartments and found Duncan white and angry. "Shield, Sarah, shield." She fell clumsily into his arms with tears streaming down her cheeks. "What did I ever do to her for her to hate me so? What did either of us do to make them all want to get rid of us?"

"Never mind, *chiya,* it will be our own home and we can do as we like. Our daughter will grow up to be gifted with the Lovat-McAran. And all our other daughters and sons. They can test and experiment, as you and I will have done before them, only they will do it with our help. You won't have to see any of them again if you don't want to."

"But I love them. So do you. How can they do this to us? I thought they just thought we were silly, not that we are evil and a bad influence. It makes me feel contaminated, as if I am contagious."

* * *

Sarah followed Duncan with her starstone when he went to view the land selected by their fathers. She saw through his eyes the green and fertile land, the hills, the rocky outcroppings and the forest, some of which would have to be cleared. He felt her touch and her agreement with his choice of location for the house, the view down the little valley and up again into forested hills. There was space for the traditional firebreak around the house and buildings they would construct. In his mind she saw the great house he was planning: a central building to start, outbuildings, and above, a tower, square and stern with windows high in the walls.

New Skye will follow us there. The town will grow in that direction. Eventually, our home will be surrounded by the city, for it will be a city. She shook her head to clear her mind. The Sight, again. That was not in Duncan's mind, it was in the future. Far ahead in the future. Maybe the completion of the tower would be in the future also. She sighed. There was no way of being sure when the Sight came whether it was a now or a future, or how far in the future. This she was sure, was future. A long way in the future.

Their daughter was born a few days after Duncan returned. Red-haired, blue-eyed, she was the most beautiful human being either of them had seen. They named her Judella, a combination of Sarah's mother's name and Duncan's father, thus honoring both strains from which she had come. Sarah carefully recorded Judella in the book in which records of the gene pool were carefully kept.

"We are doing less marrying according to the gene pool now," said Duncan. "But I hope we can marry our daughter to a man with red hair at least. We will need to preserve and strengthen the Gift now." *Especially now when some want to crush it out of existence.*

Sarah nodded her agreement to his unspoken statement.

"We can think about that later. In about fourteen years, husband. Right now, Judella is hungry, and I must feed her."

"How do you know she is hungry? She is not crying."

"Can't you hear her, Duncan? I hear her feeling hungry."

"Oh. Yes. I had not tuned to her. She will cry soon if you don't feed her. I didn't realize we could hear her so young. Let's ask our mothers—could they hear us this young, or was the Gift manifest at a later age?"

Sarah looked at him in disgust. "Oh. Right. You think they'd admit it if they did?"

Life was very busy for the next few weeks. The harvest was being brought in, the sheep moved to winter quarters closer to the town, and Duncan was trying to get the foundation for their house laid before the winter storms were upon them. Sarah and the baby rode out with him to their new homesite and they camped in a rough tent while they began the foundation. It was a brief idyll for them: the hard work digging the cellar hole, lining it with the rocks, fitting the foundation wall together, cooking their meals over a small open fire, and watching little Judella swing in the hammock they hung between two resin trees. The foundation was well begun, but not completed when the first snows came and they returned to New Skye for the long months of the harsh winter.

Their personal shields had become impeccable.

They had seen to that after Sarah's encounter with Mhari.

There were visits in the winter, among the households, and Gavin was often with them with his sister Fiona. Sarah had been fostered for a time by Gavin's family and loved them as dearly as she did her own parents, and Duncan's. She'd done her first sewing with Fiona and the two little girls had tried to use their starstones to unpick stitches out of cloth. She smiled now at the memory of the giggles turning to wails when they were caught. *My daughter won't be treated so.*

One evening Duncan took Gavin to their rooms and built up the fire, on the pretext of going over the plans for the house he would continue building in the spring.

The house plans took only a few moments. "Sarah and I are convinced that there is a lot more to be done with the starstones than we know. You have already helped with the communications. We think that some of the tricks everyone does as children can be enhanced for useful work."

"Don't tell your parents, Duncan. They are beginning to say we should get rid of the stones. Have they given one to your baby yet?"

"No, and she has had her naming, too. Our mothers are really afraid of them. Judy is old-fashioned, she would go along with the idea of a talisman as has always been done, but Laura was so frightened by the story of her long ago cousin who died that she would like to get rid of all starstones. She tried to take the stones away from the younger children, but they have had them so long, they cried and got sick. That scared her even more. She talks about witchcraft and evil, and Judy quotes the followers of Valentine about the evils of fortunetelling. We don't talk about any of this with them and Sarah and I have to be very discreet."

"I have found a cave full of the stones. Big ones, too. We can find one for Judella there."

"Thank you, friend. Sarah will appreciate that, too. That is one of the things I brought you here for, Gavin. Sarah and I want to really work on this, but we have to do it in secret. We want to ask if you and Fiona will come and live with us and share our life and work together. With four of us, we should be able to test our ideas and care for the land and the animals as well."

"I will have to talk with Fiona. She makes up her own mind. Can we call them here and talk all four together?"

"Sarah and I thought not tonight. We don't want the parents to suspect what we are planning. It will be more natural later, when everyone can see that it will be a good way to farm, to do what they and others have done, to have more than one family together."

"They'll never permit Fiona—she is my sister, and unmarried, and not pledged to anyone. Nor am I. They will let me, I don't know about Fiona."

"Leave that to Sarah. She is already talking about how lonely it will be, how hard to be a woman alone on the land with her husband out with the animals and the farming all day.

Gavin grinned. "I see. I suppose in time, I will marry with Camilla Delleray. She is pleasing to me, and is gifted. She can move tables and chairs with her stone. She has the children awed with her powers, and has been teaching some of them how to lift small objects."

"Isn't she getting into trouble? What do they say

about that, the adults, I mean, and don't our parents know? They haven't said a word."

"Camilla keeps it quiet and has sworn the children to secrecy. Besides, everyone knows how conservative Judy and Dougal and Laura and Rafe are. Haven't you noticed some people are avoiding them? I had trouble persuading my family to come tonight—except Fiona, of course."

"Then what makes you think they'll let either of you come live with us? If people think we are involved in evil?"

"Nun-no, you mistake me. They aren't concerned about you and Sarah, but about your parents, especially Rafe and Laura. They are the ones who are trying to get rid of starstones. They have the only starstone supply and they won't give them for talismans any more. Hadn't you heard *any* of this?"

"Not a word. But then, we have not been out and about. Dougal and Rafe haven't wanted to attend any of the festivals this year."

"That's what I mean, old boy. They stand for the conservative side, and not too many people want to be with them any more. Don't you see, if they won't release the starstones, what it means?"

"Yes, I guess I do. But about Camilla. How soon can you marry? She would be a good addition to our group. What we could do with five of us! And one who can already move tables and chairs!"

"Now mind, Duncan, I will not marry her just to please you and your plans for the Lovat-McAran. Besides, she won't be of marriagable age until next summer. Maybe then . . ."

"Work on it, Gavin."

* * *

By summer's end, the main body of the house was finished, and Duncan, Sarah, and baby Judella moved in permanently. The sheep had been moved and garden space fenced. Crops were growing and the harvest would be good, enough to see them through the winter and more if need be. Gavin and Camilla, his promised bride, were building a small cottage for themselves, and Fiona was Sarah's companion. Sarah was pregnant again, this time with a boy, who would be born in the spring.

By working together they were able to begin their work with the starstones in earnest. Each evening after the meal, they gathered with their stones, and learned. Sarah suggested that they use not only their own single stones, but other stones gathered together, in order to enhance the power. Instead of four or five individuals, the power would be gathered together into one strand, and put forth to the object of the exercise; they were moving larger and larger things and would soon be able to lift stones into place in the building of their homes. Sarah became skilled at keeping all the strands together and directing the energy.

One evening, they were yanked out of rapport by Sarah's cry of pain, which they all felt. Sarah doubled over, clutching her belly, and collapsed in a pool of blood on the floor.

"I will ride for the midwife," shouted Gavin.

Fiona and Duncan bent over the now moaning Sarah. "What is it, my love?" asked Duncan. "Is it the baby?"

"He is dead, Duncan, dead, and he is being born right now. The starstones killed him."

Fiona touched her gently, running her fingers delicately over her waist and belly. "I can see it, Duncan, broken blood vessels. She will bleed to death long before Melora can get here. Help me stop the bleeding!"

"How can we do that?"

"If we can move heavy objects we should be able to move a few cells to close the breaks in the blood vessels. Try to see, concentrate."

They went back into rapport, the two of them, putting cells back into place. Slowly, the bleeding stopped. The contractions went on, tearing more blood vessels. Again, they stopped the blood-flow. At last, they were able to lift Sarah onto the bed. By the time the hours had gone by for Gavin to bring the midwife, the child was born, almost unidentifiable as a child, so unformed it was. Sarah had roused only briefly during the ordeal, and now lay whiter than the linen sheets. Fiona went to make a thin porridge for her, and meat tea. "She must have something to restore her," she said. "Duncan, clean up the mess. Get cold water for the stained sheets and clothing." As he looked at her with dazed eyes, "Just *do* it Duncan. Do it!"

Blindly, he wrapped the unformed fetus in a piece of cloth, and carried it to the hearth and laid it down. He then got the cold water and put sheets and garments to soak, and warmed more water to wash the silent unconscious Sarah. Fiona brought the meat broth and began to drip it on Sarah's lips. Automatically, she opened her mouth and licked tiny sips of the broth. Her eyes fluttered open.

"My baby?"

"No, Sarah." Fiona shook her head. "Drink the broth. You lost a lot of blood, you need the broth, and porridge for strength." Sarah let Fiona prop her on pillows so that she could drink, and obediently ate the broth and the porridge, and then began to eat nut bread.

Judy was right, the starstones are dangerous. I have killed our baby, Duncan's son it would have been. Where is Judella?

Duncan held her hand to his face. "Judella is asleep in her cradle, Sarah. Don't blame yourself. We could not have foreseen this. We have lost our son, but don't let me lose you as well. Take my strength until you have your own, but live, Sarah, my own, my dear one, live for me and for Judella."

Melora and Gavin arrived, out of breath from their journey. "If she had been at her mother's house, I could have done something," Melora said for the dozenth time. "She must have known she was breeding, why didn't she move home right away?"

"She lost the baby, Melora," said Fiona. "I don't think you could have stopped it happening."

Melora bent over the silent, staring Sarah. "Let me examine you, *chiya,*" she said. Her hands were gentle, soothing. Sarah drifted again. Melora stood up. "Has she had anything to eat?"

"Yes, some broth and some porridge. She ate some nut bread as well," reported Fiona.

"Keep feeding her. Anything she will eat. She lost a lot of blood. I don't know how you stopped the bleeding, but she will mend now. It will take time and rest and care, but she will mend."

Fiona looked at Duncan and raised an eyebrow in query. He shook his head. They did not tell Melora what they had done. Fiona moved quietly to the kitchen to get more food. Duncan took Melora to show her the fetus. She looked at it long and hard, and shook her head. "It would have happened anyhow, Duncan," she said. "The fastenings were not strong. Any time it could have happened. Better sooner than later." She shook her gray head, and turned to Gavin. "I could use something to eat myself, Gavin, after that wild ride you gave me."

Gavin went to the kitchen with his sister, and brought beer and nut bread to the midwife. Sarah watched it all through dazed eyes. *Not my fault after all, it would have happened anyway. But I felt the power and then a tearing. It must have been the power of the starstone. Perhaps it could have happened later if I lifted something too heavy. It must have been the stone that made it happen now.*

For days Sarah lay, resting, sleeping, and eating. She roused only for little Judella who was walking now and trying to talk. "Mama, Mama," she would say, and pat Sarah's cheek. Duncan and Fiona tried to rouse her to speak, to say anything to them. Sarah's shields were firmly in place and she refused to respond. Behind the shields, she was in turmoil. *Should they continue their testing? There was no baby now to risk. Would there be damage so she could not have other children if she continued working with the stones? Melora had not been told what happened. If she knew, if she knew, gods if she ever told Judy, where is Judy? She is my mother, why doesn't she come to see me at least, it is only a few hours' ride, and winter will be on us soon and travel will be hard, was it really my fault after all?*

* * *

Gavin and Duncan continued the work on Gavin's cottage, getting in the harvest and tending the sheep. There was no time to sit with Sarah and coax her. Fiona took Judella with her while she helped the two men, and came home early to prepare meals, care for Judella and Sarah, and try to keep the house in order. Sarah at least had the grace to begin to feel guilty about leaving the work to the others. One day, she tried to get out of bed alone without help. She was surprised to find that she could do it and that except for being wobbly in the knees, she felt almost strong again. After that she began to carry more of her own responsibilities about the household.

She began to eat her meals with the others, and even to make a little conversation about daily activities. She wouldn't talk about the death of the baby, and refused Duncan's offer to take her to the little grave he had made. Judella continued to babble cheerfully, but Duncan and Fiona who were easily in rapport with the child knew that somehow her baby mind knew her mother was in trouble and she was trying to cheer her.

One evening, the three of them pounced on Sarah. "We are not going to let you do this to yourself or to us, Sarah," said Duncan firmly. "We are going to go ahead with our testing. You may watch, or you may help us, or you may stay behind those shields. We are going to go ahead."

His words fell like stones on Sarah. Her eyes filled with tears. "Don't you understand? I daren't use the stones again. I will lose the Lovat-McAran, but I can't use my stone again, never."

"Lah-ran! Lah-ran!" chirped Judella.

"Lovat-McAran, baby" corrected Duncan automatically.

"Lah-ran, lah-ran," said Judella, laughing.

"Oh, all right then, laran," chuckled Duncan. "It's easier than Lovat-McAran Gift."

"See lah-ran, Da, see it!" demanded Judella.

"She wants a demonstration, Duncan," said Gavin.

"Then she shall have one," said her father. He pushed his bench back from the table and took out his starstone. He concentrated, and Judella's porridge-bowl rose from the table and floated to Gavin. Gavin grasped it and set it firmly on the table as Duncan released it. Fiona laughed as the baby clapped her small hands together.

"Give her back her bowl, Duncan," said Sarah.

For the first time in weeks she looked alive. "Oh, I don't know about that," he said, grinning.

"Don't worry, baby dear," said Sarah, and spun the bowl into the air above their heads, circled the table with it, and brought it down gently in front of the crowing, ecstatic baby.

"You did that without your stone!" said Fiona.

"Never was a short time, Sarah," laughed Duncan.

"Yes. I won't use the stone any more, but I can do some things without the stone. For now. I don't know how long."

Suddenly, everyone including Sarah realized that her shields were down. At that moment, they fell into rapport for the first time since Sarah's illness, and such love filled them that they almost missed the fact that there were five of them in the circle of rapport, and that one of them was very small and young and not strong at all.

"Judella!" Sarah looked at her daughter. "*Chiya,* you!"

Judella raised her chubby hands over her head, and laughing, brought them down onto the table with a thump. "Lah-ran!" she announced.

The testing began after that, and Judella became a small part of their circle when they moved small objects. Duncan, Gavin and Fiona took it in turn to gather the strands and keep the circle together as they practiced ever more difficult maneuvers.

The weather began to close in. The nightly rains turned from showers to storms, and began to be laced with sleet.

"It is time to go home," said Gavin. "I have left Camilla too long. We will be married at mid-winter, and I want you all there if you can make the journey. Yes, you, too, small Judella. Teach this child how to make shields before you come. Your mothers will have fits."

"Gavin, do you know why my mother didn't come when I was so ill? You have kept something from me this whole time."

Gavin ducked shamefacedly. "Yes, I do and I have. Your mother, and yours, too, Duncan, blamed themselves for sending you away where you could play with such dangerous things as starstones without them to stop you. They are embarrassed. They blame you and themselves and it has made them more angry and fanatic than ever. I don't know whether they will come to the wedding or not. The McAran is no longer chief of the village, only of his own clan. The new chief is my father, the MacLeod. I'm sorry. I didn't want to add to your distress."

"Thank you for telling me." Duncan put his arm around her and they shared their sadness silently.

The wedding was held at the MacLeod's house, and all the village attended, including the McArans and the Lovats. Judy and Laura stiffened when they saw Duncan and Sarah with Judella, but maintained good manners and greeted them as they joined them. Judella soon melted both her grandmothers and they vied for the honor of holding her during the ceremony. The feasting and dancing following the marriage was lavish with every table the MacLeod could borrow filled to capacity with food of all kinds. Sarah found herself sitting with the married women, holding Judella while Duncan did his duty by the bride, her sister-in-law, and the older ladies. She tried to talk with Judy, but they seemed only to be able to converse about small Judella. Sarah wondered that her mother had not answered any of her unspoken questions as she used to do, but a quick silent probe revealed that Judy had erected barriers as strong as those of the head-blind. She asked her directly: "Why didn't you come when I was so ill? Surely Melora told you about me?"

"Those two, your husband (she spat the word) and Gavin's sister used evil methods on you, to heal you. If God had wanted you to live, He would have healed you Himself. You used the means of the Evil One."

"Mother! How can you say that? Life is a gift of the gods, if my life was preserved it was their doing, by whatever means."

"Sarah, you must understand. You have been gone too long. Your father and I have joined the Christoferos. By their teaching, all contact with the Lovat-

McAran Gift is evil. Sorcery is forbidden by the sacred writings which blessed Saint Valentine brought from the sky when we came here. We are learning to barrier ourselves."

"But you always pitied the head-blind, Mother, because they could not have the kind of closeness . . . and what about Mhari, the other children?"

"They will be baptized into the faith with us. When spring comes, we will go to Nevarsin together, and be among the families who live there and support the brothers in their monastary."

"And Rafe and Laura? What about them?"

"They will leave here also. Even now the men may be talking with Duncan about the property."

"I don't understand any of this," said Sarah. "You are saying that the entire McAran and Lovat clans are leaving New Skye? That Duncan and I will be alone here, clanless?"

"New Skye is no place for any of us any more. Better you leave also before you are more contaminated with this evil than you already have been. Come with us to Nevarsin while you still have a hope of heaven."

Sarah's world again was reeling around her. She had thought that with the naming of Judella the breach would be closed eventually. Judella would grow up part of a large family, with grandparents and aunts and uncles to share feast days, maybe even to foster for a time. Through all the estrangement she had hoped. Her eyes swept the room looking for Duncan. Yes, he was talking with Rafe and Dougal. He was looking very serious. She tried to reach him and found confusion and anger. He stirred at her touch, looked toward her, shook his head, and went back to his absorption in what the men were saying. "Mother, I don't know what to say to you. I will have to talk to Duncan." She knew as she said it that she was simply using this as a way to avoid further unpleasantness. She knew she and Duncan would not go to Nevarsin, she knew they would not give up their exploration of the l'aran gift, she knew that if they ever left New Skye it would not be for this reason.

She and Duncan spent the night with Gavin's family. They were no longer welcome in their own home, even with Judella. They wanted the opportunity to talk with Lew MacLeod and his wife Jenny. "What should we do, Lew?" asked Duncan. "They say they are leaving in the spring. Rafe and Laura and my brothers and sisters will go to Dalereuth to find the others who went to the sea, and Dougal and Judy are going to Nevarsin to join the Cristoferos. They're going to leave the house and the land, and they expect me to take it over, me and Sarah, or to go to Nevarsin or Dalereuth with them. Sarah and I don't want to leave New Skye."

"Then don't leave, boy, don't leave. Gavin and Camilla will be at your place with you, and Fiona, and we will be right here, being The MacLeod and his Lady. Stay in New Skye if that's what you want to do."

"Can I say something?" Fiona leaned forward. "They aren't my family so I can't really know how you feel without intruding, but I am involved in our group. I feel that we are a family, the five of us, six counting you, Judella, don't look so sad, and that if we are together, that's the important thing. Maybe family is something you choose at some point, even more than being born into it. I don't know. But whatever you decide, I will go with you. I want to belong with you."

Suddenly all the barriers came down. Sarah and Duncan were weeping for their lost family, and everyone was sharing the love and grief together. Finally Jenny said, "Let's not solve it all tonight. Right now, everyone needs sleep before you all start out for home tomorrow. I know you will stay in New Skye, and we welcome you."

***

Sarah stood looking out of the tower window at the town which had grown up around their home. Ten-year-old Judella was on the little street, leading the two younger children with their heads of flame; they had just spent their gift money on sweetmeats. The brief vision of so long ago had come to pass. New Skye had, bit by bit, moved out to their tower, and now surrounded them. Sarah sighed. She cherished these few moments alone. The house—three stories high now, and with the great tower where she stood—was so filled with humanity, all with laran, that she sometimes ached for the quieter days, when neither human body nor human mind invaded her silent life. She shook herself impatiently. This was what they wanted, this is what they worked for all these years, this even surpassed the dream they had had about learning more of the Lovat-McAran Gift. Why should she feel discontent?

Above her in the tower, a circle was working, a training circle of beginning workers, below, people were going about the daily tasks of the house and farm, and half a day away, the tenants of the McAran estate were tending flocks and gardens, supervised by The MacLeod and his household. More and more people wanted their children tested for tower training, and other villages on the planet were asking for trained workers to come and live with them to provide weather working and midwife services. Even far Dalereuth had requested help. *How can I hold myself together with these demands? Yes, Duncan and Gavin head the real working circles, Fiona is my right arm in running the household, and Camilla is in charge of the education; instead of being grateful as I ought, I feel the weight of it on me, as if I held it all together.*

With a sigh, she got up and went down the stairs to the great hall, where she found Fiona and Duncan. "Just the person we want," greeted Duncan, kissing her. "Fiona and I are anticipating problems again. We are feeling too much the presence of so many minds pressing into ours, whether they mean to or not, until they have their training, they don't know how to barrier. The newest ones broadcast all over the place."

"Yes," said Sarah. "I was feeling troubled about that . . . perhaps we were inadvertently broadcasting ourselves. But what can we do about it? If I only had some time alone. . . ."

"Exactly! But we need the space to have time, don't you see. Here's what I propose." Fiona spread papers on the table, showing the plans of the house.

"You see, Sarah, this is a plan to provide private rooms for everyone, even the children. Small, but solitary. It will give everyone their own space. And out here," he pointed to the stable block, "out here, the dormitories for the newest students."

"Marvelous. Peaceful space. Now if we can use those power storage batteries to build something that will block laran, we won't have to depend on inadequate shields and barriers."

"Good. We're off on another project." Suddenly, Sarah and Fiona caught a vision from Duncan—a tower in another village, training the young, and another tower, and another, communicating with each other and flashing news and information from one city to another.

"Yes. That's in our future," said Sarah, "and like New Skye, it will come to pass in our lifetime." She was sure. The future was before them: towers in the cities, serving as relay stations for communications, doing the heavy work of building, raising buildings by laran power alone, locating and mining minerals, bringing prosperity to all of the planet, not just New Skye. Yes. The future was good.

Homecoming

by Lana Young

Among other things, Lana Young is a dog person; she has a pair of rottweilers and eight puppies. (Gasp. The mind boggles, fond as I am of dogs; hope you have a nice big country place, then.) She states that one of her ambitions is "to start a kennel." Better her than me.

This is her first published work, but she hopes to have more. So do we.

Just as night falls swiftly on Darkover, the sun rises slowly, as if reluctant to face a new day. It was in that time that was no longer night, but not yet day, that the ship landed at the Terran spaceport in Thendara. It was a small craft compared to the huge transport ships that normally came to Darkover, well maintained and privately chartered. In a forward cabin, the ship's sole passenger prepared to disembark.

She had discarded the thin clothing that was standard Terran dress in favor of low-topped boots, loose fitting trousers and tunic, and a heavily embroidered coat. On her belt she wore a knife, almost, but not quite, long enough to be called a sword. As she slung a bag over her shoulder, she thought back to the night she had left Darkover with nothing but the clothes she wore and a novice Renunciate from Thendara House in tow. Now the clothes she wore had a small fortune sewn into their linings, and the girl, a last minute addition to her escape from Darkover, was the head of a Guild House on another world.

As she stepped from her cabin, her thoughts were interrupted by a young crewman.

"Shall I carry your bag, Miss Lorne?"

Smiling, Magda Lorne replied, "I carried it on, I can carry it off. It's not our way to ask a man for help. No offense." Leaving him behind, she made her way to the exit hatch and stepped out into the chill air of home.

At the arrival gate, a bored-looking clerk asked her the standard questions, to which she gave well-rehearsed answers. She was, she said, a native of Darkover, had been traveling the Terran Empire for the past five years, and was now returning home. The answers, true but incomplete, satisfied the clerk, who promptly returned to his warm office and comfortable chair.

Leaving the bright lights of the spaceport behind, Magda disappeared into the pre-dawn darkness of the city. Once more, she was alone with her thoughts.

It seems like yesterday, that bloody night of horror. Friends and family murdered because they spoke truth and taught freedom. She paused for a moment to shift the weight of her bag.

It feels like a lifetime. Andrew, Callista, Damon and Ellemir, all dead; Cleindori and my darling Shaya, both their young lives cut short by butchers. Of all those I loved, only Camilla remains alive.

At the thought of Camilla, Magda's eyes filled. When the murderers had struck, Camilla was with the Sisterhood in the mountains, and couldn't be reached. During the next few days of hiding, there was no way to send word. Magda, and anyone in her company, had been marked for death. Her only choice was to vanish, or bring destruction to the Guild House and all who would give her aid.

Damn it, I couldn't even say good-bye.

As she neared her destination, her steps slowed.

It's been so long, with no word from me. Will I even be welcome? What if Camilla's gone, or with someone else . . . NO! I'll not invite trouble by worrying. Camilla WILL be there. She has to be, she has to be.

Her resolve strengthened, Magda dried her eyes and hurried down the gray street. At last, Thendara House stood before her. To dispel any doubt, Magda reached for the small silken pouch that hung by a cord around her neck. Removing the small blue starstone, she focused her mind.

Reaching out with her *laran,* she searched for, and found, the one she had crossed the universe to find. She felt Camilla, just beginning to wake as their minds touched. She felt the flicker of a question, followed by a start of recognition. Magda returned the stone to its pouch, as she knocked firmly on the door. After a moment, the door was opened by a sleepy-eyed young girl. Peering out at Magda, the girl opened the door wider and spoke in greeting.

"Welcome, sister. I don't recognize your face; what House are you from? Is there some trouble, that sends you traveling through the night?"

"I'm from this House." Magda replied. "I've been

long years traveling, not just one dark night. I've returned home to see Camilla."

"At this hour? I'm sure she's still asleep. No one is stirring about before sunrise, without reason."

"Trust me," Magda insisted, "she's up, and probably dressing right now." The doorkeeper looked doubtful, but before she could reply, there came the sound of running feet and a voice from behind her.

"Move over, *chiya,* let me through!"

Camilla, flushed with excitement, appeared at the doorkeeper's shoulder. Bodily moving the girl aside, she rushed out the door and stopped, staring, wide-eyed and breathless, at Magda.

"*Breda,* is it really you? I thought you were dead! All these years I've mourned your passing, now you've returned to me. Where have you been?"

"For these past years, I have been dead, inside," Magda replied. "Now, seeing you again, I live. Cara Mia, I'll never leave again." In a moment that needed no words, two pairs of eyes were wet with tears. As they embraced, their minds met in rapport, and as they swore one to another, the sun rose, at last, on Darkover.

A Meeting of Minds

by Elisabeth Waters

One of the things I like about having Elisabeth in the same house—not the only thing, of course—is that when I am about to finish up an anthology I can tell her what I most need and she can sit down and write it. That's probably the most useful talent there is; just to sit down and write something. What I most needed for this one was a short funny *piece of fiction; and she almost magically produced the story I would have written if I had the time. But then I'm beginning to take miracles for granted with Lisa. One does. She can even add up columns of figures—which I* can't *do—and won the Gryphon Award, given by Andre Norton for the best unpublished novel by a newcomer. When I first met her, she had never had any fiction published—but that didn't last long around me; after meeting me, people realize anybody can do it.*

My Dear Father,

Cassilda's marriage to Edric Ridenow took place yesterday, so she is now Lady Serrais, which seems strange to me—she still looks like my big sister. It is really a shame that you and Mother could not be here for the wedding, but Coryn deputized for you admirably, and Donal and I were here to support and encourage Cassilda. She was really nervous before the ceremony, but she seems happy enough this morning.

Coryn and I will be remaining here until spring because my *laran* has finally starting developing (I thought I'd *never* grow up, but it looks as though I will after all), and Auster, who came home from Arilinn for the wedding, says that I shouldn't try to travel while I'm still getting threshold sickness. Don't worry; I'm not sick enough for it to be dangerous; I just feel miserable.

I know that you and Mother have been concerned over what type of *laran* I'd develop, so I hasten to assure you that it won't be nearly as inconvenient as that of my brothers and sister. Even I remember how the hawks followed Cassilda around when her rapport with them developed. They made themselves terribly unpopular with Mother (to say nothing about how the servants felt about them) until Cassilda finally managed to break them of their quite natural impulse to perch on the edges of Mother's tapestry frame. And nobody is going to forget Donal's rapport with the wolves—especially how they all howled every time he got threshold sickness. At least Coryn's rapport with horses was comparatively quiet, and even useful, although you did have to add on to the stables that year.

I have developed rapport with animals, of course, but the animals in question are small, silent, and won't follow me around the house. As you no doubt know, Lerrys Ridenow has traveled around the Empire, and he brought back a considerable number of small fish from the tropical seas of Terra. I have developed a rapport with the fish, and Lerrys has given me 500 of them for a Midwinter gift, which was really awfully nice of him. Donal will bring you with this letter the plans for the tanks which will be needed to house them. Most of the fish can go in the 200 gallon tank, but the tetraodons should have a tank to themselves, the anastomus are definitely too aggressive to be put in with any of the other fish, and the cichlids will kill off even each other, but I believe that if we put them by themselves in the 75 gallon tank I can persuade them to leave each other alone.

Coryn and I will bring the gravel, filters, and heaters when we come home, and Auster has very kindly volunteered to borrow the aircar from Arilinn to bring the fish home as soon as the weather gets warm enough (the fish die if the water they're in gets much colder than tropical temperatures on Terra—that's why all the tanks have to have heaters). The tanks should all fit along the wall in my bedroom that doesn't have windows or doors, but the heaters will probably have to go under the bed.

I hope that you and Mother had a good Midwinter, and I shall see you in the spring.

Your loving daughter,
Arielle MacAran

A note concerning:

THE FRIENDS OF DARKOVER

So popular have been the novels of the planet Darkover that an organization of readers and fans has come into being, virtually spontaneously. Several meetings have been held at major science fiction conventions, and more recently specially organized around the various "councils" of the Friends of Darkover, as the organization is now known.

The Friends of Darkover is purely an amateur and voluntary group. It has no paid officers and has not established any formal membership dues. Although the members of the Thendara Council of the Friends no longer publish a newsletter or any other publications themselves, they serve as a central point for information on Darkover-oriented newsletters, fanzines, and councils and maintain a chronological list of Marion Zimmer Bradley's books.

Contact may be made by writing to the Friends of Darkover, Thendara Council, Box 72, Berkeley, CA 94701, and enclosing a SASE (Self-Addressed Stamped Envelope) for information.

MARION ZIMMER BRADLEY'S FANTASY MAGAZINE

Fans of Marion Zimmer Bradley will be pleased to hear that she is now publishing her own fantasy magazine. If you're interested in subscribing and/or would like to submit material to it, write her at:

P.O. Box 249
Berkeley, CA 94701

(If you're interested in writing for the magazine, please enclose a SASE for her free Writer's Guidelines.)

(*These notices are inserted gratis as a service to readers.* DAW Books *is in no way connected with these organizations professionally or commercially.*)